The Best American Mystery Stories 2013

GUEST EDITORS OF
THE BEST AMERICAN MYSTERY STORIES

The Best American Mystery Stories™ 2013

Edited and with an Introduction
by **Lisa Scottoline**

Otto Penzler, *Series Editor*

A Mariner Original

HOUGHTON MIFFLIN HARCOURT

BOSTON • NEW YORK   2013

www.hmhbooks.com

ISSN 1094-8384
ISBN 978-0-544-03460-0

Printed in the United States of America
DOC 10 9 8 7 6 5 4 3 2 1

"Smothered and Covered" by Tom Barlow. First published in *Needle*, Vol. 1, No. 3, Winter 2012. Copyright © 2012 by Thomas J. Barlow. Reprinted by permission of Thomas J. Barlow.

"A Fine Mist of Blood" by Michael Connelly. First published in *Vengeance*, April 3, 2012. Copyright © 2012 by Michael Connelly. Reprinted by permission of Michael Connelly.

"Misprision of Felony" by O'Neil De Noux. First published in *Ellery Queen's Mystery Magazine*, December 2012. Copyright © 2012 by O'Neil De Noux. Reprinted by permission of the rights holder.

"The Sailor in the Picture" by Eileen Dreyer. First published in *Crime Square*, May 1, 2012. Copyright © 2012 by Eileen Dreyer. Reprinted by permission of M. Eileen Dreyer.

"The Devil to Pay" by David Edgerley Gates. First published in *Alfred Hitchcock's Mystery Magazine*, April 2012. Copyright © 2012 by David Edgerley Gates. Reprinted by permission of the author.

"The Street Ends at the Cemetery" by Clark Howard. First published in *Ellery*

Contents

Foreword

As preparation for writing the foreword to each new book in this wonderful series, I reread those I wrote for previous volumes. This serves the purpose of reminding me of things I may already have said and therefore assists my efforts to eschew repetition in the off-chance that readers actually pay attention to these things instead of immediately diving into the stories on these pages (as I heartily recommend).

The second goal is for this rereading process to suggest something that may be of interest to readers, to provide a slim thread that might be followed to produce a few worthwhile thoughts. Or even a single one, for that matter, which usually exhausts me.

Although I'm not certain either goal was achieved when I read the sixteen earlier forewords produced for *The Best American Mystery Stories,* that stroll down memory lane did provide an interesting (to me) autobiographical view of my connection to the series that illuminated numerous changes in attitude and process.

Naively and foolishly, an early foreword somehow seemed to display my comfort, perhaps even pride, in the fact that I didn't have a computer and wouldn't have known how to turn one on if I did. As it happens, almost immediately after I wrote that I went to the London Book Fair and returned to find my much-loved IBM Selectric typewriter missing from my desk, replaced by a computer. I asked my assistant what the hell was going on and she said simply, "It's time. I used your credit card and ordered it." I told her she was fired. "I know," she said, "but first I'm going to teach you how to use it." It was a struggle for an old Luddite, but I recognize now that I couldn't function without it.

As evidence of the change in me, and the world, since those simpler days, I now run a publishing company, MysteriousPress .com, devoted entirely to e-books. Okay, I still may be technologically challenged, but I've accepted the inevitable.

My life has always been deeply involved with books, beginning when I read them at a very young age, followed by collecting them, then editing and publishing them, and finally selling them through my bookshop. I lament that the number and influence of independent bookstores has dramatically diminished over recent years, and that Nooks and Kindles are now seen more frequently during my travels than hardcover books are, or even paperbacks, for that matter.

On the other hand, I have embraced some of the valuable elements of this change. It is now possible to have access to hundreds of thousands of books that would have been difficult, if not impossible, to find less than a decade ago, for instance.

At a more pertinent level, perhaps, the *BAMS* volumes have (finally) just recently become available as e-books, and sales of these electronic versions just about match the sales of the physical books, giving them a much wider readership than ever, a turn of events that doesn't appear to have any downside that I can see.

The ubiquity of computers in most of our lives has also transformed the publishing landscape a great deal, as would-be authors can now self-publish and any number of websites publish original stories, many of which are in the mystery and crime fiction category. This, too, points out a major change from the beginning of this series to the present time. I thought that my wonderful reader, Michele Slung, and I had done a pretty good job by reading five hundred to six hundred stories to find the best for that 1997 edition of *BAMS;* the number of stories that Michele checks out to see what might be worthy of consideration now approaches five thousand. Many are not read all the way through, of course, as it is clear that some writers really ought to find a different outlet for their creative impulses, but still, it's a daunting challenge.

A challenge, I am pleased and proud to say, that yet again has been met with triumph, as the superb pieces of fiction in this collection will attest. One can only speculate, either with fear or with excitement, depending on one's personality, what changes will transpire over the next seventeen years. As technology not only changes but changes at an ever-faster rate, the person who will make the next great leap forward is now probably seven years old, ecstatically watching *Toy Story* for the fifty-fifth time, mouthing the dialogue while multitasking with a laptop on which he or she has created a stunning website to publish a collection of original illustrated stories.

After Michele has gathered the stories to be seriously considered, I read the harvested crop, passing along the best fifty (or at least those I liked best) to the guest editor, who selects the twenty that are then reprinted, the other thirty being listed in an honor roll as "Other Distinguished Mystery Stories."

Sincere thanks are due to this year's guest editor, Lisa Scottoline, the *New York Times* bestselling author of such novels as *Don't Go* and *Come Home* as well as the hugely popular mystery series featuring Rosato & Associates. She is a former president of the Mystery Writers of America and won an Edgar Award in 1995 for *Final Appeal*.

This is an appropriate time to thank the previous guest editors, who have done so much to make this prestigious series such a resounding success: Robert B. Parker, Sue Grafton, Ed McBain, Donald E. Westlake, Lawrence Block, James Ellroy, Michael Connelly, Nelson DeMille, Joyce Carol Oates, Scott Turow, Carl Hiaasen, George Pelecanos, Jeffery Deaver, Lee Child, Harlan Coben, and Robert Crais.

While I engage in a relentless quest to locate and read every mystery/crime/suspense story published, I live in terror that I will miss a worthy story, so if you are an author, editor, or publisher, or care about one, please feel free to send a book, magazine, or tearsheet to me c/o The Mysterious Bookshop, 58 Warren Street, New York, NY 10007. If it first appeared electronically, you must submit a hard copy. It is vital to include the author's contact information. No unpublished material will be considered, for what should be obvious reasons. No material will be returned. If you distrust the postal service, please enclose a self-addressed, stamped postcard, on which I will acknowledge receipt of your story.

To be eligible, a story must have been written by an American or a Canadian and first published in an American or Canadian publication in the calendar year 2013. The earlier in the year I receive the story, the more fondly I regard it. For reasons known only to the nitwits who wait until Christmas week to submit a story published the previous spring, holding eligible stories for months before submitting them occurs every year, causing much gnashing of teeth as I read a stack of stories while my wife and friends are trimming the Christmas tree or otherwise celebrating the holiday season. It had better be a damned good story if you do this. Because of the very tight production schedule for this book, the absolute firm deadline is December 31. If the story arrives one day later, it will not be read. This is neither whimsical nor arbitrary but utterly necessary in order to meet publishing schedules. Sorry.

O.P.

Introduction

ABRAHAM LINCOLN FAMOUSLY said, "I'm sorry I wrote such a long letter. I did not have the time to write a short one."

I understand exactly what Lincoln meant by that, and nothing illustrates his point better than a short story. I've written almost twenty-five novels in as many years, but I've written only three short stories for anthologies: one for breast cancer research, another to preserve open space, and the last for Otto Penzler.

Bottom line, I avoid the short form unless I'm saving the world or working for Otto Penzler.

Why?

Because I adore Otto, who knows more about crime fiction than anybody on the planet.

And also because it's too much work to write something short. I don't have the time.

Plus I'm Italian, and Italians need three thousand words just to say hello.

Hand gestures not included.

On top of that, I'm a woman, which means that at eight thousand words, I'm just warming up. A typical novel is ninety thousand words, but mine always run longer, and even my acknowledgments don't get to the point anytime soon.

By the way, I'm divorced twice, and these things may be related.

Anyway, you get the idea. It's harder to write something short than something long.

Why?

Because you have to know exactly what you're doing before you do it. You have to know where you're going before you get in the car. You have to think what to say before you open your mouth.

That's not me.

People ask if I know how my book ends when I begin to write, and I have to tell the truth. Not only do I not know how it ends, I don't even know how it middles.

I start with the idea and see where it takes me, then live by the motto "Great books aren't written, they're rewritten."

Come to think of it, probably anybody who's divorced twice isn't the type of person who looks before they leap. In fact, I bet that all of the wonderful authors herein are happily married, or at least have not made as stupendously bad decisions as mine.

Their stories prove as much. Because without exception, each of these stories is perfect, and told in just a few pages. Each one plunges the reader into the plot with the very first sentence, and there are no wasted words, no excessive descriptions to establish setting, time of year, or barometric pressure. We aren't told a lot of irrelevant backstory, all dialogue is pithy and pertinent, and, most important, once a point is established, it isn't reestablished. The writing is lean, lacking cellulite and stomach flab.

These are stories with abs.

And to my mind, the great value of having them all in one collection is that when you read through them all, you, as the reader, will begin to see the similarities that construct a great story, and, equally important, though perhaps paradoxically, you'll also see the great breadth of the stories and come to understand that though their settings, characters, plots, and voices are radically different, what makes them all great is exactly the same.

My point is illustrated by a comparison of two stories, Randall Silvis's "The Indian" and Eileen Dreyer's "The Sailor in the Picture." These stories could not be more different in almost every respect, except that they're both sensational stories, for exactly the same reasons.

Silvis's story begins with a man walking into a bar, which in itself is kinda brilliant, and Silvis tells us, without missing a beat, that the man, an angry truck driver named Harvey, wants to kill his brother-in-law in a dispute over a motorcycle, an Indian. Silvis's voice perfectly captures, if not epitomizes, a working-class taproom outside Pittsburgh, where the Pirates game is always on and the patrons drink Schlitz. The bar is tended by Harvey's mild younger brother, named Will, who admits that he's "nobody's genius," even in a world populated by handymen, ditch diggers, and trash haulers.

So the central conflict is established on page 1 of the story, and before we know it, Harvey will suck Will into a plot to ruin his brother-in-law, during the commission of which the story's plot will twist in such a completely shocking manner that the blood is flowing only a few pages later, the motorcycle forgotten.

The story is not only lean, it's positively muscular, and the prose so clean that it borders on poetry. Even as the plot charges toward its horrific conclusion, Will's sleep is disrupted by a dream in which he's hunting and comes upon a deer. The hunter confronts the hunted, "the two connected by the invisible thread of the bullet about to fly."

The dialogue is equally pithy, as well as doing double duty to inform character and advance plot. For example, Silvis tells you everything you need to know about Will when he writes that Will asks a group of golfers if they're ready for another pitcher "with the lift of his eyebrows." The golfers answer, as they would, "We're good." That's pitch-perfect dialogue, without a wasted word.

All this, plus two sex scenes in the first eleven pages!

What a story!

Now let's compare Silvis's story with "The Sailor in the Picture." I am a huge fan of Eileen Dreyer's mysteries, which feature strong and smart women, and the story is classic Dreyer, though it takes place in a different time period, during World War II. The story's jumping-off point is the iconic picture of a sailor kissing a nurse on VJ Day, and Dreyer takes us into the world of that picture through the eyes of a bystander, one Peg O'Toole, who was "facing her own sailor" that very day in Times Square. He was her husband, Jimmy, home from the war, and Dreyer tells us that Peg now carries his memory "like a sharp shard of glass," because that was the day he died.

Dreyer is skilled enough to make us feel instantly sympathetic for Peg's loss, then take us back to a time before Jimmy died, and we're happy at her upcoming reunion with him. In the process,

Dreyer deftly brings to life wartime America, where women on the home front wear hairnets, "sturdy shoes and work pants," and carry lunches, cigarettes, lipstick, and bus fare. They find a way to deal with the terrible grief when they lose a son or husband, and Dreyer describes the "quick stab of an envelope" when the dreaded Western Union telegrams are thrust into their shaking hands.

The war has taken Peg's dreams as well as her husband. She had dreamed of becoming a nurse, of wearing a white cap and a "gleaming white dress" and always looking "clean and bright," but instead she has to work in a butcher shop for the war's duration, to support herself and her children. But Peg learns to enjoy the work, slicing meat, filling the parts bucket, and grinding hamburger until her back and arms ache. She's a practical woman, not a complainer, and her self-esteem grows. In just a few sentences, Dreyer makes Peg instantly relatable to every working mother, transcending space and time.

Dreyer's story moves to the day when Peg is going to Times Square to meet her returning husband, and the reader goes along as Peg makes the trip into New York City, with its "hard energy," touching her savings-and-loan passbook as if it were a "talisman against temptation." Once she gets there, she's kissed, "standing there flat-footed," by the sailor in the iconic photo, then left behind when he moves on, kissing other women while the photographer snaps away. But as soon as Peg sees Jimmy in the crowd, she freezes, with "the instinctive reaction of all hunted animals," and in that moment Dreyer's plot turns about-face and the unthinkable happens.

Dreyer's prose is as heartfelt as Silvis's is spare, but the voice of her Peg O'Toole resonates with such truth and power that the heroine's plight, problem, and solution make absolute sense, and you'll find yourself cheering her on. Both stories, Silvis's and Dreyer's, pack a dramatic wallop, and both explore families, relationships, and the deep hatred that can come only from the deepest love — the weightiest of themes, in mere pages.

Both stories are page-turners, and I think you'll race through them and the other ones in the collection. Read them all in one sitting and your head will be spinning. Read them again, more slowly, to examine the skill, talent, and artistry it takes to write stories that fire with the speed of an automatic weapon and are over just as fast.

That's what's between these covers, pure explosive fiction.

Otto Penzler sure knows his stuff.

And so did Abe Lincoln.

LISA SCOTTOLINE

The Best American Mystery Stories 2013

TOM BARLOW

Smothered and Covered

FROM *Needle*

THE YOUNG GIRL WALKED into the Waffle House, alone, at 3
A.M. on a Thursday morning. We all looked up from our coffee
and cigarettes, waffles, sausage and hash browns. She stood on her
tiptoes to take a seat on a counter stool, picked up a menu and
held it close to her face, like one of the 6 A.M. retirees without his
bifocals.

Sandy, the night shift waitress, looked at me and raised her eyebrows. I knew the look; she gave it to me four or five times a week.
It meant, *Do you think I should call the cops?*

I considered the idea. The girl looked no more than twelve,
black, slim, but composed. Her hair was plaited so tight I wondered if they tugged at her eyebrows. Her perfume, spicy with a
hint of sandalwood, cut through the onion and batter odors of the
diner. She wore clean, well-fitted jeans, a pink fuzzy sweater over
a lime green top, and new-looking Nikes. Gold chain, oversized
plastic watch. Not enough clothes for February.

She displayed no fear or uncertainty, which struck me as odd.
Twelve-year-olds are always uncertain around adults.

I turned to look outside. The day manager had finally replaced
the broken lights in the lot, so our cars were brightly lit. There
were none I didn't recognize, and I would recognize a new one.
I'd been running into the same people at the same hour of the
night for almost three years, and had come to know them by their
cars, the sound of their nasal congestion, and their bathing habits.
We rarely spoke.

"What you doing here this time of morning?" Sandy asked the girl.

"I'm here for the atmosphere," the girl said, keeping her nose in the menu. The sarcasm in her voice sounded bitter as a fifty-year-old's.

Sandy looked at me again. This time she was asking me if it would be okay if she dumped a pot of hot coffee on the girl's head. Sandy's skin got pretty thin by 3 A.M.

I shook my head. "The lady's just trying to be friendly," I said to the girl. "No need to be rude."

The other regulars stared at their plates and cups, but I could tell their ears were locked in, the same way they had been a couple of weeks before when the place was held up.

"Mind your own business, old man." The girl pronounced it *bidness*.

Sandy laughed. She knew the "old man" would piss me off. "I like that, Tim. From now on I'm calling you 'old man.'"

"You suppose you could take my order?" the girl said to her. Not a hint of a smile to soften her words.

"What'cha want, honey?" Sandy said. "Lucky Charms? Count Chocula?"

"Two waffles, hash browns smothered and covered, coffee with cream, bacon, crisp." She folded the menu and stuck it back in the chrome holder next to the napkins.

Sandy didn't write it down. "You got money, honey?"

The girl shook her head in disgust, reached two fingers into her back pocket, pulled out a Visa card, and flashed it toward Sandy like she was trying to blind her with a hand mirror.

Sandy rolled her eyes toward me but turned to the grill. Otilio had gone outside for a cigarette ten minutes ago, but this time of night, it often took him forty-five minutes. His girl, who worked at the Wal-Mart next door, took her break about then as well, and they liked to pooch up in his old Chevy van.

The show apparently over, I returned to my book, the last one Ed McBain wrote before he passed. I read another ten pages and drank another half cup of coffee before I heard a car horn outside. I looked up to see a bright red Escalade parked as close to the front door as the curb would allow. Through the heavily tinted windshield I could make out the driver, a white man, bald, fortyish, tan coat with a thick white wool collar. His nose and right ear were pierced.

The girl seemed to expect the car. She made eye contact with the driver, smiled, pointed to her plate, and crammed a piece of bacon in her mouth. The rest of us stared at the car.

The guy opened the car door, slid off the seat and onto the curb. When he closed the door, I could see his beefy shoulders, leather pants, sharp-toed cowboy boots. He wore a Fu Manchu mustache that had overgrown his chin and hung loose like a couple of air roots.

When he first pulled up, I'd assumed daughter and grandfather, but she didn't appear to have any white blood, and he didn't show any black. Everyone but Sandy, the girl, and me stared down at their tabletops as the guy entered, probably sensing the same threat vibe I had. An old couple, Vernon and Viv, regulars—she the western omelet woman, whole wheat toast, dry, he the pecan waffle, sugar-free syrup, two link sausages, decaf—began buttoning up the layers of shirts and coats they wore until midsummer.

The man ignored us and walked to the girl's stool. She swiveled to face him, still chewing her toast. He leaned over until his mouth was at the level of her ear. I could hear him saying something, couldn't make out the words, but the tone sounded tense—not commanding, not pleading, something in between.

Sandy retreated behind the swinging door to the storage room and office and watched through the window in the door. When she saw me looking, she held up the cordless phone. She obviously sensed something wrong about the guy.

I shrugged my shoulders. I was slowly easing my way to the edge of my booth, my hand lightly holding the glass ketchup bottle.

As I shifted my weight, though, I could feel the stiffness in my knee. My shoulder, the one not completely fixed by surgery, creaked, and the roll of fat around my middle wedged me between the tabletop and the booth seat. And I had so much money tied up in my new bifocals that I couldn't afford to replace them.

Still, if the girl had appeared frightened rather than pissy, if she'd shrunk away from the man, if she'd looked around for help, I'd have stepped in. I'm sure I would have helped.

Instead, she stood up, not looking at any of us. He pulled out the wallet chained to his belt and threw a ten on the counter. As she walked out he followed so close behind her it looked like they were glued together, back to chest.

He kept his hand on her back as she climbed into the Escalade, shut the door behind her before getting in the driver's side. Before he drove off, he turned to me, winked, and gave me a two-finger salute from his temple, like a Boy Scout.

Sandy wrote down the license plate.

"Should we call the cops?" she said, refilling my coffee. I noticed her hand was shaking. Her hair, usually neatly pulled back and pinned with one of a variety of barrettes, had escaped and hung loosely on the shoulder of her yellow and black uniform.

"Tony'll be here in half an hour," I said. Tony and his partner usually took their breakfast break about 5 every morning. We all felt comfortable when their cruiser was in the lot.

Sandy nodded. "She wasn't much older than Iris would have been." The comment caught me by surprise. Our daughter would have been twelve, but I carried a picture from Iris's eighth birthday party, so I tended to remember her as that age.

Tony stopped by a short time later with a cadet on ride-along, a fish-faced woman who couldn't sit still. She kept swinging on the counter stool. At this hour of the night, we saw a lot of speed freaks at the Waffle House, and cops weren't immune. Especially ones new to night shift.

Tony listened to our story, took the license plate info, and handed it to the cadet. She returned to the cruiser to call it in.

Tony worked on his waffle and bacon, chatting quietly with Sandy. I figured they were working their way toward a half-assed affair. I'd seen it before, from both of them.

The cadet returned a moment later, her hand resting on the grip of her pistol in its holster. She stared at Sandy until she walked away from Tony, picking up the coffeepot to take a refill swing through the dining room. Fishface then whispered in Tony's ear.

He whispered back, finished his coffee in a single gulp, and pulled a tablet and pen out of his breast pocket.

"Nobody leaves till we talk to you, okay?" he said to the room in general.

The young guy in the corner who spent every night muttering and writing in a ratty spiral notebook muttered a little faster.

Tony told us the girl had been spotted jumping out of the Escalade at a light at the Hague Road exit to the freeway, on the other side of Columbus. The driver chased her on foot to the top of the overpass. Just as he was about to grab her, she jumped over the railing and landed on the freeway right in front of an eighteen-wheeler hauling corn syrup. From the timing, the whole thing, from the time they left, must have been a matter of half an hour.

After the cops finished questioning us, I stayed to help Sandy make some CLOSED signs. Since Waffle House never closes, they don't have any. The front door lock, seldom used, wouldn't work, so we wedged a ladder under the door handle to hold the door closed and left via the back door, the one that had a working lock.

I walked her to her car, a ratty old Escort. I gave her a half-assed hug, which she tolerated.

My roommate, a Mexican guy that had answered my local room-mate-wanted ad, worked days at the local brake replacement place, so he was still asleep when I arrived back at the house. He yipped and muttered in his sleep, one reason I spent my nights at the House. I turned up the television until I could hear Katie Couric over his snores.

I slept like shit, which I always do when I'm sober. It had been almost three years since my last sound night's sleep.

The girl was still on my mind when I woke later that afternoon. I surfed the television for news until my roomie arrived home from work. He went by the nickname Texaco, which fit since he wore ostentatious cowboy boots tooled with pictures of rattlesnakes and longhorn steers.

"Hey," he said, the extent of our usual conversation, since he didn't speak much English. He carried a plastic gallon jug of milk out the back door onto the landing, where I heard him light a cigarette. He spent hours leaning on the railing, watching dump-sters and alley cats, drinking milk from the jug.

I got nothing off the TV, so I dressed and walked next door to the library to use their computer and Internet access.

According to the web edition of the *Columbus Dispatch*, the girl's name was Nancilee Harper. Local girl, city school, basketball player. An angel, but aren't they all, when they're dead? No par-ents mentioned. Her grandmother's picture was up on the home page, a pencil-thin black woman with carrot-orange hair and a bombed-out look in her eyes; maybe they caught her on the way home from the clubs. She looked younger than me.

According to the lead story, Nancilee had no enemies. She attended the Baptist church on the east edge of downtown. Good grades. She'd been asleep upstairs when Grandma left that evening for work. Grandma, Phara Johnson, waited tables at Caddy's, a near eastside dive. Grandma returned home at 7 A.M. to find her front yard full of cops and reporters.

No mention of the white guy, the Escalade, no artist's sketch of a person of interest. I figured he was in the can already or two states away with his pedal to the floor. The license plate we'd written down was no doubt in a dumpster somewhere.

I signed off and drifted to the magazine room. I never knew what to do with myself late afternoon, early evening, the time when families would be regathering after school, work, errands, fighting for the remote, doing homework, arguing about dinner.

My disability check didn't cover entertainment, so the library was my second most frequented haunt. I was sitting by the picture window reading the latest *Popular Science* when Sandy called.

"You see the news?" she said.

"The girl? Nancilee?"

"Yeah." I knew she was leaning against the door frame in the hallway between her kitchen and dining room, probably twisting her index finger through the phone cord. She never sat down when she talked on the phone. I once asked her why. She told me her father used to sneak up behind her, take up some slack from the cord, and pull it around her neck like a garrote. All in fun, he'd said.

"We should've called."

"We couldn't have known," I said. An old man across the table, holding a copy of *Home and Garden* an inch from his face, pulled it down to glare at me.

I ignored him. "She went with that guy like she wasn't worried."

"I'm going to call on that girl's grandma. It's the least I can do."

"Don't. You don't have anything to tell her that would be a comfort to her."

"She'd want to know," Sandy said, her voice rushed, breathy. "I wanted to know."

"Talking to the EMTs only made it worse for you." One EMT had told Sandy he thought I had alcohol on my breath. That one off-the-cuff remark had driven a stake through our marriage. I never realized when I was a kid that every day of your life is a high-wire act. Twenty years you can say the right thing, and then *pow* —one casual comment, one inattentive moment, and you're in freefall. Ask Karl Wallenda.

"Would you go with me?" Sandy said. "In an hour or so?"

I saw Tex walk out of our apartment building toward his Civic. He was dressed to kill, clothes tight and shiny, the silver on his belt buckle sparkling under the streetlights.

I agreed to go with Sandy. Not because I wanted to, but because I couldn't think of anything else to do. I was also perversely drawn to pain, and I assumed there would be plenty there.

I looked through my closet for something more formal than blue jeans. I considered my black suit but decided it might suggest I was claiming grief I didn't deserve, as I'd only met the victim that one time. I settled on gray slacks, a dark green checked shirt, and a black sport coat, no tie.

Sandy picked me up twenty minutes later. The temperature had dropped back into the twenties, and the heater in her car was broken, but she wore only a thin overcoat. Her teeth were chattering.

"Where are your gloves?" I asked as I pulled the door shut and belted myself in. I had given her a nice pair of kid leather gloves for Christmas a couple of months before.

She pulled away from the curb right into the path of an old Volvo wagon. I could read the lips of the woman behind the wheel as she screeched to a stop to avoid hitting us.

"They're at work," Sandy said, oblivious to the close call. Her tone of voice was part of a package I recognized. It went with her head held high, and a way she has of drawing her upper lip down over her teeth, then curling it up, as though trying to dislodge something in her nose without touching it. That package says, *Don't talk, don't touch.* I regretted agreeing to accompany her.

We rode in silence for a few blocks. The address she had was on the other end of town. I waited until we were on the freeway before I said, "This is a mistake."

Another nose twitch. "You can't spend the rest of your life hiding. She needs us."

"The last thing she needs is us. She's probably suffering enough as it is."

That was enough chitchat for our car ride. A short while later,

she turned onto Bryden Road. We cruised slowly down the row of
huge old houses, now subdivided into apartments, until we spotted the address. Most of the houses were dark upstairs, with a few
lights on downstairs. We could see a group of people on Phara's
front porch. Or, more accurately, we could see cigarette glows,
moving in arcs from waist level to head level, growing in intensity,
then descending.

Sandy parallel-parked a few doors down the street, which took a
few minutes. We walked up the unshoveled sidewalk, snow squeak-
ing under our shoes. We could hear conversation, laughter, even
the clink of a glass from the porch. Sandy took my arm.

The concrete steps up to the front yard were broken, uneven,
without a guardrail. I took them one at a time, favoring the hip
and knee I'd had replaced. I could feel the eyes on us. The conversation on the porch stopped.

Sandy stopped at the foot of the stairs onto the porch. A small
black man separated himself from the circle, crossed to the top
of the stairs, and said, "May I help you?" He said it politely, usher
polite.

Sandy stood mute, so I said, "We came to express our condo-
lences to the girl's grandmother."

The man didn't move aside but looked at me. "Do we know you,
sir?" He had a subtle accent, not Western Hemisphere.

"No, I don't think so. We were in the restaurant where the
girl was kidnapped." As soon as I said it, I realized how pathetic I
sounded. Grasping.

One of the men farther back on the porch, deeper in shadow,
made a snort of derision. I could hear muttering. Sandy was studying the stairs, holding on to my arm as if it were a life preserver.

"You saw my daughter? Last night?" The man didn't come down
the steps, but he leaned forward at the waist, as if he were looking
into a fish tank.

I nodded. "This morning. About three. She came in the diner
for some breakfast."

The muttering grew louder. "And the police have talked to
you?"

"Sure. They were there this morning. They catch the guy yet?"

"What guy?" he said, placing his cigarette in the corner of his
mouth.

"The bald white guy," Sandy said. "That picked her up."

Another man emerged from the group. He was black as well, much larger, younger, beefy with the wide head, nose, round cheeks and chin I'd come to associate with Central Africa.

The bigger man said, "What did this guy look like?" He had no accent. He stood well apart from the first man.

I described the bald white guy. As I talked, I could see faintly someone deeper on the porch writing on a spiral pad. The large man turned toward the porch when I was finished, said something I couldn't hear, listened, and nodded.

"Mrs. Johnson's not here. Who shall we say came to call?" He said it perfunctorily, like the kiss-off from a good administrative assistant.

I gave him our names. He nodded, as did the smaller man. Neither seemed prone to continue our conversation or move aside to invite us in, so we nodded in return and headed back to the street. My heart was beating so loudly I could almost not make out the laughter as one voice said, "You tell 'em Phara's back at the club?"

"Well, that was a clusterfuck," I said as Sandy started the car. I was plenty warm now, although the heater still didn't work. I hadn't been exactly scared, but I was certainly on edge.

"How can they laugh with that poor girl dead?" Sandy said, nose twitching again. "With her father standing there? Have they no respect? And that grandmother? What a bitch."

"What I don't get is why they didn't know about the bald guy."

"Maybe the cops are afraid they'd go after him themselves."

"Maybe they should."

Sandy dropped me off at home after a silent ride across town. We didn't even say goodbye, just nodded, knowing we'd see one another again in a few hours at the Waffle House.

Tex had not returned yet so I had the apartment to myself. I filled the tub with hot water and soaked for a while, until my back and hip stopped aching. I usually shower, because the tub brings back memories of bathing my daughter, Iris, when she was two or so. I'd keep an old pair of swimming trunks on the rack on the back of the bathroom door to wear, because she loved to soak me with hand splashes of water, and I enjoyed it too much to convince her to stop.

I found the same old crowd seated in their same old places when I arrived at the Waffle House about 3 the next morning. Sandy was on break, her feet on the manager's desk and Art Bell on the radio. Otilio waved to me and slid a coffee cup down the counter, following with the coffeepot to fill it.

"How you doon?" he said, accent heavy. I knew he didn't expect, even want, a reply. He understood English fine but didn't have any confidence in his ability to speak it.

I shrugged and unfolded the *New York Times,* my daily indulgence, a buck from the box outside the door. I could, and usually did, spend hours working my way through each day's issue, even before I began the crossword.

I didn't get far this morning, though. About 3:30 A.M., just as Sandy came back on duty, a TV truck pulled up outside. An attractive young black woman, buried inside a thick down parka, got out. The parka fell lower on her thigh than her skirt did.

She came inside. The truck kept running, and I could see the silhouette of the driver, his head against the headrest. I recognized the woman as a reporter on the morning news, which I usually watched before going to bed. She did the weather reports, too.

She flagged down Sandy as she was carrying the coffeepot on a circuit of the counter. "Can I talk to you for a minute?"

Sandy put the pot back on the warmer and took a step back. "What you want?" She was beginning to do the nose thing again.

"I understand Nancilee Harper was in here last night before she was killed?"

I waited for the reporter's notebook to appear, but the woman kept her hands in her parka pockets. Sandy looked at the floor, shook her head, and walked into the back room.

The reporter glanced around the room, appraising the rest of us, before approaching Notebook Guy. I heard her repeat the question to him. Sandy peeked through the door just as the guy replied with a word salad, the way he does when he's been palming his medications. I winked at Sandy.

Unfortunately, the reporter persisted by moving down one table to the old couple. Vern and Viv knew who I was. They knew about Iris. The reporter sat down at his invitation, and the three of them talked for a long time.

Sandy finally had no choice but to come out of the office when a four-top of security guards came in. When I saw the old guy and the reporter looking at me, then at Sandy, I threw a few dollars on the counter and left. Sandy watched me go as she dealt a tray full of waffles to the guards.

Against my better judgment, I watched the early news later that morning. They led with the girl's report. She did a standup with Vern and Viv in front of the restaurant.

"This is Tayndra Stephens. Behind me is the Waffle House restaurant on Staley Road, where twenty-four hours ago young Nancilee Harper was abducted, in front of eight witnesses who did nothing to stop her kidnapper. An hour later, she was dead."

She skewered, skinned, and hung the old couple, who seemed oblivious to the callous impression they were making on the audience. All the time they talked, Sandy was visible in the background, moving back and forth in the same forty feet of behind-the-counter space that now circumscribed her life. The reporter made sure to work my name into the report.

"Among the witnesses was Tim Parker, ex-husband of the waitress you see behind me, Sandy Parker. Only three years ago, Parker was charged with drunken driving and negligent homicide in the death of their only daughter, Iris, who, ironically, was also twelve. The charges were later dropped. Neither Parker nor his ex-wife would comment for this report."

Jesus.

I was seriously mulling over the bars that I knew were open and quiet at 8 A.M. when Sandy called.

"You saw the news," she said.

"Yeah. Good decision, refusing that interview."

"Thanks. Tony got here a little bit ago." I could hear her twisting the cord again.

"The detectives say he's somebody she met online. They found a bunch of messages on her computer from a chatroom, going back a couple of months, from a boy named Torrey, who claimed to live on a horse farm near Springfield. The plan was his cousin would pick her up here and take her to his estate."

I smacked the table. "It was a scam, right? One of those trolls?"

I heard her strike a match, the sipping sound of a cigarette. "The bald guy has a record. He did time for molesting his own daughter. There was a court order prohibiting him from using the Internet. That did a fuck of a lot of good, huh?"

"They catch him?" Although Iris was only three years gone, I couldn't quite remember what it was like, worrying about your daughter in a world where there was a boogeyman behind every door.

"Yeah, in some strip club in Whitehall. Tony said he was throwing himself a going-away party. He'd been passing rocks of crack around like they were jelly beans, had himself quite a posse."

"Shit."

"Yeah, boy. You want to get some breakfast? I'm off at eight."

I begged off, claiming I'd taken a Vicodin and was ready to crash. In truth, I was in pain, but not the kind a painkiller would help with. I was afraid to leave the house, since the bars were calling to me again. Also, Texaco had left half a bottle of cheap merlot in the fridge, although I'd asked him when he moved in to keep any booze in his room, and I wanted to reserve my option to uncap it.

The knock on the door an hour later caught me standing at the fridge with the door open, staring at the wine. I slammed the door closed and limped over to the peephole. Sandy stood there, her cheap pile jacket wrapped around her black and yellow uniform. I let her in.

"Jesus," she said, "what a pigpen." She smelled faintly of grease and flour. The room looked messy in a way you only notice when someone you care about enters. Papers stacked against the wall, CDs in disorder, lint on the couch. The windows hadn't been washed for at least a decade.

She fixed a pot of coffee; out of habit, I suppose. "You know what I don't get?" she said as she filled the pot with water.

I played along. "What's that?"

"Where the hell are the girl's parents? How could you walk away from your own baby? What do they expect to find in their lives that they think is going to be better than sleeping next to your own baby?" She lit a cigarette, although she knew I didn't allow smoking in the apartment. "And the grandmother. What kind of cunt lets her kid go to a Waffle House in the middle of the night to meet some pervert?"

When Iris was killed, we were on our way to visit Sandy at work. On her break.

She walked to the back door, pulled the blind to one side, and looked across the backyard fence like Texaco did, watching a truck upend one dumpster after another. I pretended to resume the crossword I'd given up on twenty minutes before.

When the coffee was ready, she poured herself a cup and took a chair across from me at the kitchen table. She picked up the metro section of the paper and began to leaf through it, licking her finger before each page turn.

I took some relief from the page interposed between us. Then I heard the clunk of metal on the linoleum tabletop.

I reached over and lifted the paper a few inches, until I could see the revolver. I recognized it as the one Sandy had shown me one night, when the manager forgot to lock his bottom desk drawer. A .38, five-shot, cheap. I could see the shells in the cylinder.

"Have you lost your mind?" I said.

She picked up the gun by the end of the grip, letting it dangle in front of my face.

"So what—you're Jack Ruby all of a sudden?" I said.

"Who?" She slugged back the rest of the coffee in her cup.

"Never mind." I thought to myself I used to know what to do with her. I didn't anymore.

"You owe me," she said, swinging the gun like a hypnotist's watch. "You owe me this."

"You want me to walk into the police station and murder this guy? I owe that to you?"

She shook her head as though I'd made a bad joke. "No, asshole. I expect you to kill Grandma. Tony promised me the bald guy's going to get what's coming to him. She's the one that's going to walk away."

Sandy cocked the trigger. "She was supposed to look out for the girl. Instead, she went partying. The bald guy was the boogeyman. There's a boogeyman under every bed. Anybody knows that. But that's why we're on this earth, right? To stand between our kids and the bad guys?"

I didn't know what to say.

"Right?" she said again, challengingly. She stuck the barrel in my face. "Right?"

A Fine Mist of Blood

FROM *Vengeance*

THE DNA HITS came in the mail, in yellow envelopes from the regional crime lab's genetics unit. Fingerprint matches were less formal; notification usually came by e-mail. Case-to-case data hits were rare birds and were handled in yet a different manner — direct contact between the synthesizer and the submitting investigator.

Harry Bosch had a day off and was in the waiting area outside the school principal's office when he got the call. More like a half a day off. His plan was to head downtown to the PAB after dealing with the summons from the school's high command.

The buzzing of his phone brought an immediate response from the woman behind the gateway desk.

"There's no cell phones in here," she said.

"I'm not a student," Bosch said, stating the obvious as he pulled the offending instrument from his pocket.

"Doesn't matter. There's no cell phones in here."

"I'll take it outside."

"I won't come out to find you. If you miss your appointment, then you'll have to reschedule, and your daughter's situation won't be resolved."

"I'll risk it. I'll just be in the hallway, okay?"

He pushed through the door into the hallway as he connected to the call. The hallway was quiet, as it was the middle of the fourth period. The ID on the screen had said simply *LAPD data*, but that had been enough to give Bosch a stirring of excitement.

The call was from a tech named Malek Pran. Bosch had never

dealt with him and had to ask him to repeat his name twice. Pran was from Data Evaluation and Theory—known internally as the DEATH squad—which was part of a new effort by the Open-Unsolved Unit to clear cases through what was called data synthesizing.

For the past three years the DEATH squad had been digitizing archived murder books—the hard-copy investigative records—of unsolved cases, creating a massive database of easily accessible and comparable information on unsolved crimes. Suspects, witnesses, weapons, locations, word constructions—anything that an investigator thought important enough to note in an investigative record was now digitized and could be compared with other cases.

The project had actually been initiated simply to create space. The city's records archives were bursting at the seams with acres of files and file boxes. Shifting it all to digital would make room in the cramped department.

Pran said he had a case-to-case hit. A witness listed in a cold case Bosch had submitted for synthesizing had come up in another case, also a homicide, as a witness once again. Her name was Diane Gables. Bosch's case was from 1999 and the second case was from 2007, which was too recent to fall under the purview of the Open-Unsolved Unit.

"Who submitted the 2007 case?"

"Uh, it was out of Hollywood Division. Detective Jerry Edgar made the submission."

Bosch almost smiled in the hallway. He went a distance back with Jerry Edgar.

"Have you talked to Edgar yet about the hit?" Bosch asked.

"No. I started with you. Do you want his contact info?"

"I already have it. What's the vic's name on that case?"

"Raymond Randolph, DOB six, six, sixty-one—that's a lot of sixes. DOD July second, 2007."

"Okay, I'll get the rest from Edgar. You did good, Pran. This gives me something I can work with."

Bosch disconnected and went back into the principal's office. He had not missed his appointment. He checked his watch. He'd give it fifteen minutes, and then he'd have to start moving on the case. His daughter would have to go without her confiscated cell phone until he could get another appointment with the principal.

*

Before contacting Jerry Edgar at Hollywood Division, Bosch pulled up the files—both hard and digital—on his own case. It involved the murder of a precious-metals swindler named Roy Alan McIntyre. He had sold gold futures by phone and Internet. It was the oldest story in the book: there was no gold, or not enough of it. It was a Ponzi scheme through and through, and like all of them, it finally collapsed upon itself. The victims lost tens of millions. McIntyre was arrested as the mastermind, but the evidence was tenuous. A good lawyer came to his defense and was able to convince the media that McIntyre was a victim himself, a dupe for organized-crime elements that had pulled the strings on the scheme. The DA started floating a deal that would put McIntyre on probation—provided he cooperated and returned all the money he still had access to. But word leaked about the impending deal, and hundreds of the scam's victims organized to oppose it. Before the whole thing went to court, McIntyre was murdered in the garage under the Westwood condominium tower where he lived. Shot once between the eyes, his body found on the concrete next to the open door of his car.

The crime scene was clean; not even a shell casing from the nine-millimeter bullet that had killed him was recovered. The investigators had no physical evidence and a list of possible suspects that numbered in the hundreds. The killing looked like a hit. It could have been McIntyre's unsavory backers in the gold scam or it could have been any of the investors who'd gotten ripped off. The only bright spot was that there was a witness. She was Diane Gables, a twenty-nine-year-old stockbroker who happened to be driving by McIntyre's condo on her way home from work. She'd reported seeing a man wearing a ski mask and carrying a gun at his side run from the garage and jump into the passenger seat of a black SUV waiting in front. Panicked by the sight of the gun, she didn't get an exact make or model of the SUV or its license plate number. She'd pulled to the side of the road rather than following the vehicle as it sped off.

Bosch had not interviewed Gables when he had reevaluated the case in the Open-Unsolved Unit. He had simply reviewed the file and submitted it to the DEATH squad. Now, of course, he would be talking to her.

He picked the phone up and dialed a number from memory. Jerry Edgar was at his desk.

"It's me—Bosch. Looks like we're going to be working together again."

"Sounds good to me, Harry. What've you got?"

Diane Gables's current address, obtained through the DMV, was in Studio City. Edgar drove while Bosch looked through the file on the 2007 case. It involved the murder of a man who had been awaiting trial for raping a seventeen-year-old girl who had knocked on his door to sell him candy bars as part of a fundraiser for a school trip to Washington, D.C.

As Bosch read through the murder book, he remembered the case. It had been in the news because the circumstances suggested it had been a crime of vigilante justice by someone who was not willing to wait for Raymond Randolph to go on trial. Randolph was intending to mount a defense that would acknowledge that he'd had sexual intercourse with the girl but state that it was consensual. He planned to claim that the victim offered him sex in exchange for his buying her whole carton of candy bars.

The forty-six-year-old Randolph was found in the single-car garage behind his bungalow on Orange Grove, south of Sunset. He had been on his knees when he was shot twice in the back of the head.

The crime scene was clean, but it was a hot day in July and a neighbor who had her windows open because of a broken air conditioner heard the two shots, followed by the high revving and rapid departure of a vehicle in the street. She called 911, which brought a near-immediate response from the police at Hollywood Station, three blocks away, and also served to peg the time of the murder almost to the minute.

Jerry Edgar was the lead investigator on the case. While obvious suspicion focused on the family and friends of the rape victim, Edgar cast a wide net—Bosch took some pride in seeing that—and in doing so came across Diane Gables. Two blocks from the Randolph home was an intersection controlled by a traffic signal and equipped with a camera that photographed vehicles that ran the red light. The camera took a double photo—one shot of the vehicle's license plate, and one shot of the person behind the wheel. This was done so that when the traffic citation was sent to the vehicle's owner, he or she could determine who'd been behind the wheel when the infraction occurred.

Diane Gables was photographed in her Lexus driving through the red light in the same minute as the 911 call reporting the gunshots was made. The photograph and registration were obtained from the DMV the day after the murder, and Gables, now thirty-seven, was interviewed by Edgar and his partner, Detective Manuel Soto. She was then dismissed as both a possible suspect and a witness.

"So, how well do you remember this interview?" Bosch asked.

"I remember it because she was a real looker," Edgar said. "You always remember the lookers."

"According to the book, you interviewed her and dropped her. How come? Why so fast?"

"She and her story checked out. Keep going. It's in there."

Bosch found the interview summary and scanned it. Gables had told Edgar and Soto that she had been cruising through the neighborhood after filling out a crime report at the nearby Hollywood Station on Wilcox. Her Lexus had been damaged by a hit-and-run driver the night before while parked on the street outside a restaurant on Franklin. In order to apply for insurance coverage on the repairs, she had to file a police report. After stopping at the station, she was running late for work and went through the light on what she thought was a yellow signal. The camera said otherwise.

"So she had filed the report?" Bosch asked.

"She had indeed. She checked out. And that's what makes me think we're dealing with just a coincidence here, Harry."

Bosch nodded but continued to grind it down inside. He didn't like coincidences. He didn't believe in them.

"You checked her work too?"

"Soto did. Confirmed her position and that she was indeed late to work on the day of the killing. She had called ahead and said she was running late because she had been at the police station. She called her boss."

"What about the restaurant? I don't see it in here."

"Then I probably didn't have that information."

"So you never checked it."

"You mean did I check to see if she ate there the night before the murder? No, Harry, I didn't and that's a bullshit question. She was—"

"It's just that if she was setting up a cover story, she could've crunched her own car and—"

"Come on, Harry. You're kidding me, right?"

"I don't know. We're still going to talk to her."

"I know that, Harry. I've known that since you called. You're going to have to see for yourself. Just like always. So just tell me how you want to go in, rattlesnake or cobra?"

Bosch considered for a moment, remembering the code they'd used back when they were partners. A rattlesnake interview was when you shook your tail and hissed. It was confrontational and useful for getting immediate reactions. Going cobra was the quiet approach. You'd slowly move in, get close, and then strike.

"Let's go cobra."

"You got it."

Diane Gables wasn't home. They had timed their arrival for 5:30 P.M., figuring that with the stock market closing at 1 P.M., Gables would easily have finished work for the day.

"What do you want to do?" Edgar said as they stood at the door.

"Go back to the car. Wait a while."

Back in the car, they talked about old cases and detective bureau pranks. Edgar revealed that it had been he who had cut ads for penile-enhancement surgery out of the sports pages and slipped them into an officious lieutenant's jacket pocket while it had been hanging on a rack in his office. The lieutenant had subsequently mounted an investigation focused squarely on Bosch.

"Now you tell me," Bosch said. "Pounds tried to bust me to burglary for that one."

Edgar was a clapper. He backed his laughter with his own applause but cut the display short when Bosch pointed through the windshield.

"There she is."

A late-model Range Rover pulled into the driveway.

Bosch and Edgar got out and crossed the front lawn to meet Gables as she took the stone path from the driveway to her front door. Bosch saw her recognize Edgar, even after five years, and saw her eyes immediately start scanning, going from the front door of her house to the street and the houses of her neighbors. Her head didn't move, only her eyes, and Bosch recognized it as a tell. Fight or flight. It might have been a natural reaction for a woman with two strange men approaching her, but Bosch didn't think that was the situation. He had seen the recognition in her eyes when she looked at Edgar. A pulse of electricity began moving in his blood.

"Ms. Gables," Edgar said. "Jerry Edgar. You remember me?"

As planned, Edgar was taking the lead before passing it off to Bosch.

Gables paused on the path. She was carrying a stylish red leather briefcase. She acted as though she were trying to place Edgar's face, and then she smiled.

"Of course, Detective. How are you?"

"I'm fine. You must have a very good memory."

"Well, it's not every day that you meet a real live detective. Is this coincidence or . . ."

"Not a coincidence. I'm with Detective Bosch here and we would like to ask you a few questions about the Randolph case, if you don't mind."

"It was so long ago."

"Five years," Bosch said, asserting himself now. "But it's still an open case."

She registered the information and then nodded.

"Well, it's been a long day. I start at six in the morning, when the market opens. Could we—"

Bosch cut her off. "I start at six too, but not because of the stock market."

He wasn't backing down.

"Then fine, you're welcome to come in," she said. "But I don't know what help I can be after so long. I didn't really think I was much help five years ago. I didn't see anything. Didn't hear anything. I just happened to be in the neighborhood after I was at the police station."

"We're investigating the case again," Bosch said. "And we need to talk to everybody we talked to five years ago."

"Well, like I said, come on in."

She unlocked the front door and entered first, greeted by the beeping of an alarm warning. She quickly punched a four-digit combination into an alarm-control box on the wall. Bosch and Edgar stepped in behind her and she ushered them into the living room.

"Why don't you gentlemen have a seat? I'm going to put my things down and be right back out. Would either of you like something to drink?"

"I'll take a bottle of water if you got it," Edgar said.

"I'm fine," Bosch said.

"You know what?" Edgar said quickly. "I'm fine, too."

Gables glanced at Bosch and seemed to register that he was the power in the room. She said she'd be right back.

After she was gone Bosch looked around the room. It was a basic living room setup with a couch and two chairs surrounding a glass-topped coffee table. One wall was made up entirely of built-in bookshelves, all filled with what looked by their titles to be crime novels. He noticed there were no personal displays. No framed photographs anywhere.

They remained standing until Gables came back and pointed them to the couch. She took a chair directly across the table from them.

"Now, what can I tell you? Frankly, I forgot the whole incident."

"But you remembered Detective Edgar. I could tell."

"Yes, but seeing him out of context, I knew I recognized him but I could not remember from where."

According to the DMV, Gables was now forty-one years old. And Edgar had been right: she was a looker, attractive in a professional sort of way. A short, no-nonsense cut to her brown hair. Slim, athletic build. She sat straight and looked straight at one or the other of them, no longer scanning because she was inside her comfort zone. Still, there were tells: Bosch knew through his training in interview techniques that normal eye contact between individuals lasted an average of three seconds, yet each time Gables looked at Bosch, she held his eyes a good ten seconds. That was a sign of stress.

"I was rereading the reports," Bosch said. "They included your explanation for being in the area—you were at the police station filling out a report."

"That's right."

"It didn't say, though, where your car was when it got damaged the night before."

"I had been at a restaurant on Franklin. I told them that. And when I came out after, the back taillight was smashed and the paint scraped."

"You didn't call the police then?"

"No, I didn't. No one was there. It was a hit-and-run; they didn't even leave a note on the car. They just took off, and I thought I was out of luck."

"What was the name of the restaurant?"

"I can't remember—oh, it was Birds. I love the roasted chicken."

Bosch nodded. He knew the place and the roasted chicken.

"So what made you come back to Hollywood the next day and file the report on the hit-and-run?"

"I called my insurance company first thing in the morning and they said I needed it if I wanted to file a claim to cover the damages."

Bosch was covering ground that was already in the reports. He was looking for variations, changes. Stories told five years apart often had inconsistencies and contradictions. But Gables wasn't changing the narrative at all.

"When you drove by Orange Grove, you heard no shots or anything like that?"

"No, nothing. I had my windows up."

"And you were driving fast."

"Yes, I was going to be late for work."

"Now, when Detective Edgar came to see you, was that unsettling?"

"Unsettling? Well, yes, I guess so, until I realized what he was there for, and of course I knew I had nothing to do with it."

"Was it the first time you'd ever encountered a detective or the police like that? You know, on a murder case."

"Yes, it was very unusual. To say the least. Not a normal part of my life."

She shook her shoulders as if to intimate a shiver, imply that police and murder investigations were foreign to her. Bosch stared at her for a long moment. She had either forgotten about seeing the armed man with a ski mask coming out of the garage where Roy Alan McIntyre was murdered or she was lying.

Bosch thought the latter. He thought that Diane Gables was a killer.

"How do you pick them?" he asked.

She turned directly toward him, her eyes locking on his.

"Pick what?"

Bosch paused, squeezing the most out of her stare and the moment.

"The stocks you recommend to people," he said.

She broke her eyes away and looked at Edgar.

"Due diligence," she said. "Careful analysis and prognostication. Then, I have to say, I throw in my hunches. You gentlemen use hunches, don't you?"

"Every day," Bosch said.

They were silent for a while as they drove away. Bosch thought about the carefully worded answers Gables had given. He was feeling stronger about his hunch every minute.

"What do you think?" Edgar finally asked.

"I think it's her."

"How can you say that? She didn't make a single false move in there."

"Yes, she did. Her eyes gave her away."

"Oh, come on, Harry. You're saying you know she's a stone-cold killer because you can read it in her eyes?"

"Pretty much. She also lied. She didn't mention the case in 1999 because she thought we didn't know about it. She didn't want us going down that path, so she lied and said you were the only detective she'd ever met."

"At best, that's a lie by omission. Weak, Harry."

"A lie is a lie. Nothing weak about it. She was hiding it from us and there's only one reason to do that. I want to get inside her house. She's gotta have a place where she studies and plans these things."

"So you think she's a pro? A gun for hire?"

"Maybe; I don't know. Maybe she reads the paper and picks her targets, people she thinks need killing. Maybe she's on some kind of vigilante trip. Dark justice and all of that."

"A regular angel of vengeance. Sounds like a comic book, man."

"If we get inside that place, we'll know."

Edgar drove silently while he composed a response. Bosch knew what was coming before he said it.

"Harry, I'm just not seeing it. I respect your hunch, man, I have seen that come through more than once. But there ain't enough here. And if I don't see it, then there's no judge that's going to give you a warrant to go back in there."

Bosch took his time answering. He was grinding things down, coming up with a plan.

"Maybe, maybe not," he finally said.

*

Two days later at 9 A.M., Bosch pulled up to Diane Gables's house. The Range Rover was not in the driveway. He got out and went to the front door. After two loud knocks went unanswered he walked around the house to the back door.

He knocked again. When there was no reply, he removed a set of lock picks that he kept behind his badge in his leather wallet and went to work on the deadbolt. It took him six minutes to open the door. He was greeted by the beeping of the burglar alarm. He located the box on the wall to the left of the back door and punched in the four numbers he had seen Gables enter at the front door two evenings before. The beeping stopped. Bosch was in. He left the door open and started looking around the house.

It was a post–World War II ranch house. Bosch had been in a thousand of them over the years and all the investigations. After a quick survey of the entire house he started his search in a bedroom that had been converted to a home office. There was a desk and a row of file cabinets along the wall where a bed would have been. There was a line of windows over the cabinets.

There was also a metal locker with a padlock on it. Bosch opened the venetian blinds over the file cabinets, and light came into the room. He moved to the metal locker and started there, pulling his picks out once again.

He knelt on the floor so he could see the lock closely. It turned out to be a three-pin breeze, taking less than a minute for him to open. A moment after the hasp snapped free he heard a voice come from behind him.

"Detective, don't move."

Bosch froze for a moment. He recognized the voice. Diane Gables. She had known he would come back. He slowly started to raise his hands, holding his fingers close together so he could hide the picks between them.

"Easy," Gables commanded. "If you attempt to reach for your weapon I will put two bullets into your skull. Do you understand?"

"Yes. Can I stand up? My knees aren't what they once were."

"Slowly. Your hands always in my sightline."

"Absolutely."

Bosch started to get up slowly, turning toward her at the same time. She was pointing a handgun with a suppressor attached to the barrel.

"Easy," he said. "Just take it easy here."

"No, you take it easy. I could shoot you where you stand and be within my rights."

Bosch shook his head.

"No, that's not true. You know I'm a cop."

"Yeah, a rogue cop. What did you think you were going to find here?"

"Evidence."

"Of what?"

"Randolph and McIntyre. Maybe others. You killed them."

"And, what, you thought I'd just keep the evidence around? Hide it in a locker in my home?"

"Something like that. Can I sit down?"

"The chair behind the desk. Keep your hands where I can see them."

Bosch slowly sat down. She was still standing in the doorway. He now had 60 percent of his body shielded by the desk. He had his back to the file cabinets. The light was coming in from behind and above him. He noticed she had now lowered the muzzle to point at his chest. This was good, though from this range he doubted the Kevlar would completely stop a bullet from a nine-millimeter, even with the suppressor slowing it down. He kept his hands up and close to his face.

"So now what?" he asked.

"So now you tell me what you think you've got on me."

Bosch shook his head as if to say, *Not much.* "You lied. The other day. You didn't mention the McIntyre case. You didn't want us linking the cases through you. The trouble is we already had."

"And that's it? Are you kidding me?"

"That's it. Till now."

He nodded at her weapon. It seemed to confirm all hunches.

"So without a real case and the search warrant to go with it, of course you decided to break in here to see what you could find."

"Not exactly."

"We have a problem, Detective Bosch."

"No, you have the problem. You're a killer and I'm onto you. Put the weapon down. You're under arrest."

She laughed and waggled the gun in her hand.

"You forget one thing. I have the gun."

"But you won't use it. You don't kill people like me. You kill the abusers, the predators."

"I could make an exception. You've broken the law by breaking in here. There are no gray areas. Who knows, maybe you came to *plant* evidence here, not find it. Maybe you *are* like them."

Bosch started lowering his hands to the desktop.

"Be careful, Detective."

"I'm tired of holding them up. And I know you're not going to shoot me. It's not part of your program."

"I told you, programs change."

"How do you pick them?"

She stared at him a long time, then finally answered.

"They pick themselves. They deserve what they get."

"No judge, no jury. Just you."

"Don't tell me you haven't wished you could do the same thing."

"Sure, on occasion. But there are rules. We don't live by them, then where does it all go?"

"Right here, I guess. What am I going to do about you?"

"Nothing. You kill me and you know it's over. You'll be like one of them—the abusers and the predators. Put the gun down."

She took two steps into the room. The muzzle came up toward his face. Bosch saw that deadly black eye rising in slow motion.

"You're wearing a vest, aren't you?"

He nodded.

"I could see it in your eyes. The fear comes up when the gun comes up."

Bosch shook his head.

"I'm not afraid. You won't shoot me."

"I still see fear."

"Not for me. It's for you. How many have there been?"

She paused, maybe to decide what to tell him, or maybe just to decide what to do. Or maybe she was stuck on his answer about the fear.

"More than you'll ever know. More than anybody will ever know. Look, I'm sorry, you know?"

"About what?"

"About there being only one real way out of this. For me."

The muzzle steadied, its aim at his eyes.

"Before you pull that trigger, can I show you something?"

"It won't matter."

"I think it will. It's in my inside jacket pocket."

She frowned, then made a signal with the gun.

"Show me your wrists. Where's your watch?"

Bosch raised his hands and his jacket sleeves came down, showing his watch on his right wrist. He was left-handed.

"Okay, take out whatever it is you need to show me with your right hand. Slowly, Detective, slowly."

"You got it."

Bosch reached in and with great deliberation pulled out the folded document. He handed it across the desk to her.

"Just put it down and then lean away."

He followed her instructions. She waited for him to move back and then picked up the document. With one hand she unfolded it and took a glance, taking her eyes off Bosch for no more than a millisecond.

"I'm not going to be able to read it. What is it?"

"It's a no-knock search warrant. I have broken no law by being here. I'm not one of them."

She stared at him for a silent thirty seconds and then finally smirked.

"You have to be kidding me. What judge would sign such a search warrant? You had zero probable cause."

"I had your lies and your proximity to two murders. And I had Judge Oscar Ortiz—you remember him?"

"Who is he?"

"Back in 1999 he had the McIntyre case. But you took it away from him when you executed McIntyre. Getting him to sign this search warrant wasn't hard once I reminded him about the case."

Anger worked into her face. The muzzle started to come up again.

"All I have to say is one word," Bosch said. "A one-syllable word."

"And what?"

"And you're dead."

She froze, and slowly her eyes rose from Bosch's face to the windows over the file cabinets.

"You opened the blinds," she said.

"Yes."

Bosch studied the two red laser dots that had played on her face since she had entered the room, one high on her forehead, the other on her chin. Bosch knew that the lasers did not account for bullet drop, but the SWAT sharpshooters on the roof of the house across the street did. The chin dot was the heart shot.

Gables seemed frozen, unable to choose whether to live or die.

"There's a lot you could tell us," he said. "We could learn from you. Why don't you just put the gun down and we can get started."

He slowly started to lean forward, raising his left hand to take the gun.

"I don't think so," she said.

She brought the muzzle up but he didn't say the word. He didn't think she'd shoot.

There were three sounds in immediate succession. The breaking of glass as the bullet passed through the window. A sound like an ice cream cone dropping on the sidewalk as the bullet passed through her chest. And then the *thock* of the slug hitting the door frame behind her.

A fine mist of blood started to fill the room.

Gables took a step backward and looked down at her chest as her arms dropped to her sides. The gun made a dull sound when it hit the carpet.

She glanced up at Bosch with a confused look. In a strained voice she asked her last question.

"What was the word?"

She then dropped to the floor.

Staying below the level of the file cabinets, Bosch left the desk and came around to her on the floor. He slid the gun out of reach and looked down at her eyes. He knew there was nothing he could do. The bullet had exploded her heart.

"You bastards!" he yelled. "I didn't say it! I didn't say the word!"

Gables closed her eyes and Bosch thought she was gone.

"We're clear!" he said. "Suspect is ten-seven. Repeat, suspect is ten-seven. Weapons, stand down."

He started to get up but saw that Gables had opened her eyes.

"Nine," she whispered, blood coming up on her lips.

Bosch leaned down to her.

"What?"

"I killed nine."

She nodded and then closed her eyes again. He knew that this time she was gone, but he nodded anyway.

O'NEIL DE NOUX

Misprision of Felony

FROM *Ellery Queen's Mystery Magazine*

DETECTIVE JOSEPH SAVARY counted nineteen people on Felicity Street. Four older men sat on folding chairs outside Ojubi's Barbershop, two women swept the sidewalk beyond the shop, two others hosed off their stoops while chatting with each other, three boys rode around on bicycles, four girls hovered between a parked blue Chevy and a dark green Pontiac, two young men leaned against the outer wall of the laundromat, another two sat on the loading dock of the long-abandoned warehouse and pretended they weren't watching the plainclothesman. Savary tapped down his black sunglasses and gleeked the men on the loading dock. No reaction.

Savary had left his suit coat in his unmarked gray Chevy Impala. He was glad he wore a white shirt today, as the sweat wouldn't show. He loosened his sky-blue tie and rested a hand atop the grip of the nine-millimeter Glock 17 semiautomatic resting in its Kydex holster on his left hip, next to the gold star-and-crescent NOPD badge clipped to his belt. He stood stiffly in front of the boarded-up door of Jeanfreau's Grocery and glanced at his watch. Two P.M. exactly. Same time, same day—a Wednesday—as two months ago. On that Wednesday, a lone black male put a bullet into the forehead of Jack Hudson, the owner of Jeanfreau's. Grainy black-and-white video showed a young, thin African-American male in a white T-shirt and low-riding jeans, pulling out a forty-caliber semiautomatic, pointing it at the gray-haired old man. The weapon was tilted on its side, gangster-style, waving in the right hand of the shooter. Jack Hudson, a man who'd bragged he was part Zulu and once shook Martin Luther King's hand, exchanged words with the gunman, touched his chin, and the big pistol went off, snapping Hudson's head back. The shooter went around, had to kick Hudson out of the way to empty the cash register, stuffing cash in his pockets, snatching two candy bars on his way out. Looked like Milky Way bars, maybe Snickers.

Savary fitted his sunglasses back up and stepped over to Ojubi's Barbershop. The four men outside, all over fifty, stopped talking. The barber, in a white smock and black pants, stood and stretched.

"Afternoon," Savary said.

The barber nodded.

"Back again, huh?" The barber was Willie Ellzey, who lived on Terpsichore Street but stayed with his woman on Eurphrosine, as he'd explained. Savary looked at the only man he hadn't spoken to on his four previous canvasses, twice in the morning, twice in the evening.

"I'm Joe Savary," he told the skinny man with blue-black skin as dark as Savary's. "I'm working on—"

"Jeanfreau." The man didn't look up. "We know."

"What's your name?"

A pair of bloodshot eyes met his and the man said, "Joe Clay. You wanna see my ID?" The voice was harsh, challenging.

"That would be nice." Savary pulled out his notebook as the man reached around for his wallet, took out his driver's license. Savary copied down the details.

"You come around here often, Mr. Clay?"

Savary got the same answers he'd been getting since he took over the case. No one saw anything or heard anything. No matter that Jack Hudson was a neighbor, had run the neighborhood grocery store since old man Jeanfreau died in 1968. It was as obvious as the nose on the detective's face. A local boy did this, but no one was giving him up to the police. It didn't even matter if Savary was raised three blocks away on Erato Street. The day he started the police academy was the day he'd left the neighborhood—permanently.

He moved to the women. He'd spoken to some of them before, the two young men by the laundromat as well. One was the son of a fireman and was actually civil to Savary, the other barely mumbled responses. The two sitting on the dilapidated warehouse loading dock who pretended they weren't watching Savary would not even look at him as he stepped up.

"Police," he said to the taller of the two. Both were maybe twenty, both in white T-shirts and those long shorts with the crotch below the knees. "What's your name?"

Nothing.

"Stand up."

"Say what?"

"Stand up before I yank you up by your ears."

The taller one stood slowly and Savary, who towered over the man, patted him down.

"Man, you can't just search us," said the shorter one.

"I'm not searching your friend. I'm patting him down. *Terry versus Ohio*. Look it up. If a police officer has reasonable suspicion that a person has committed, is committing, or is about to commit a crime, the officer can pat that person down for weapons. For officer safety as well."

Savary found something. "That a cell phone and a wallet?"

The tall man nodded.

"Take them out. Let's see some ID."

The smaller one stood and raised his hands. Savary patted him down as well.

"What crime we did?"

Savary nodded to the large sign nailed to the wall of the warehouse which read POSTED — NO TRESPASSING.

"I don't write the laws. I just enforce them." As Savary jotted down their names, addresses, cell-phone numbers before passing their IDs and cell phones back, he asked about Jeanfreau's and received the usual information. Nothing. He called in their names, had both run through the police computer. Both had records, but no felonies and nothing around the neighborhood. "Thank you for your cooperation."

A tan Impala pulled up and Savary went around to the driver's side to speak with his sergeant. Jodie Kintyre gleeked him over her cat-eyed sunglasses. It tickled Savary, because Jodie had wide-set, hazel, catlike eyes. She claimed Scottish descent, but there had to be some Asian blood in her genes with those eyes.

"Any luck?"

He laughed, stood back as she climbed out. Unlike most women cops, Jodie liked wearing skirt suits and wore them well. This one was beige. She left her jacket in the car as well, readjusting her shoulder rig with gold badge affixed. She was a striking woman in her forties with that shock of yellow-blond hair cut in a long page-boy. Jodie stood five-seven, her heels added a good inch, but she had to crane her neck to look up at Savary, who stood six-four.

"I'll take this side of the street." She clicked her ballpoint pen, flipped open her notebook, and moved to the two outside the laundromat. Savary crossed the street. A half-block down he ran into a distant cousin, Eddie Tauzin, who worked as a caretaker at the Audubon Zoo.

"On my way to work, my man." Eddie slapped the big detective's shoulder. "You gettin' nobody to talk about it?"

Savary shook his head.

"Man, I been askin' but no one sayin' nothin'."

He got a nod in response. "I appreciate your asking around."

Eddie moved past, backing as he walked. "You know, I hear any-thing, I'll give you a call." He turned, spied Jodie across the street, and looked back at Savary. "I admire the comp'ny you keep."

Reverend Tom Milton stepped out of his chapel with a large sponge in hand, spotted Savary, and gave him a knowing smile. The Sacred Congregation of the Good Lord occupied a two-story brick building two blocks from Jeanfreau's.

"Hot enough for you, boy?" The reverend leaned over a bucket, dipped the sponge inside. Savary wiped his brow as Milton took the sponge to the picture window lining the front of his building, slapped it against the glass, and rubbed on the soapy water.

"Hear anything from your congregation?" It was the same ques-tion Savary had been asking.

"You know if I did, I'd be the first to call. You get any luck at *your* church?"

That brought a smile to Savary, a lapsed Catholic who hadn't been to church, except for weddings and funerals, since he was a teenager.

"You want a bottle of water?" the reverend asked.

"No thanks."

Milton reached over and patted Savary's back as the detective went by. Hopefully, the man of the cloth would pass any informa-tion to Savary, who had asked the reverend to talk with the chil-

dren of his congregation about the matter because kids hear and
see more than anyone in a neighborhood. When Savary was a patrolman, Milton and some kids had helped him recover two stolen
cars. But that was before Katrina.

Things were different now, AK—after Katrina. The hardcore
criminals, who were some of the first to return, had reestablished
themselves with a killing vengeance. The murder rate was back
up top as new blood carved out drug territories, and the police
department, as devastated as the neighborhoods, reeled in turmoil
from lack of manpower, lack of leadership, lack of inspiration.

Savary linked up with Jodie back at her car and she actually had
a line of perspiration on her upper lip. The fair-haired sergeant
rarely perspired, even in the sweltering summer city.

"M.F. screwed this one up from the start." She went on to her
repeated diatribe against Detective Maurice Ferdinand, who had
done absolutely nothing on the Jeanfreau case beyond overseeing
the processing of the crime scene. M.F.'s recent transfer to the
reorganized Vice Squad was welcomed by the rank and file of the
Homicide Division. M.F. in the Vice Squad, always a joke in deca-
dent New Orleans, was a classic example of the Peter Principle—a
worker rising to the level of his incompetence. So much for a man
who thought being called M.F. was cute.

"Know how I know it's somebody local?" Savary asked.

Jodie narrowed her left eye as she looked up at him.

"All these people out here and no one saw anything. No one's
heard anything. You think a ghost flittered in here and shot old
man Hudson? If it were a stranger, someone would tell me, 'I saw
him but don't know who he is.' But that's not what we're getting.
No one saw *anything* because they know who he is."

Neither detective had to say the word *retaliation*. Eyewitnesses,
especially inner-city eyewitnesses, were at the top of the endangered species list in New Orleans. So much for the vaunted witness
protection program.

Back at headquarters, Savary sat next to his Macintosh G5, donated by Apple to the department AK, typed in the hundred block
of Jeanfreau's Grocery, and searched the police database for any
incidents that had occurred there over the last five years. As a boy,
Savary had looked up the definition of *felicity*, discovering it meant
"intense happiness." Felicity Street was a real-life oxymoron.

In the five years AK, NOPD had received over one thousand calls along the twenty-four blocks of Felicity Street. In the last two years there had been two murders in the blocks around Jean-freau's—nine rapes, twelve aggravated batteries, eight burglaries, seven armed robberies, two carjackings, twenty-nine batteries . . . the list went on. Savary narrowed the search to Jeanfreau's Grocery and discovered there were nine thefts, two armed robberies, two simple batteries, four disturbing-the-peace calls, and a peeping Tom reported there.

The only arrests on-site involved the two simple batteries—fist-fights—and the peeping Tom case. A suspicious man standing outside Jeanfreau's had a warrant out for his arrest for peeping Tom from Tangipahoa Parish. Jack Hudson was the victim of both armed robberies. Of the nine theft cases, five listed young African-American males as the culprits. Two were later arrested after pulling the same shoplifting stunt at other stores.

Savary stood and stretched. Time to get home, cook something up, and call his girls on the phone. Every night between six and seven, when he wasn't working, Detective Joseph Savary called his ex-wife's number and talked to his girls. Emily was nine and Carla four. Carla thought she could show her daddy things through the phone as if he could see what she pointed the receiver at. Last night she was talking about a drawing she'd done and said, "See, Daddy?"

"Yes, baby. I see it."

Savary left headquarters, heading uptown to his small apartment near Audubon Park. He would pass his ex-wife's house, the one he still paid the mortgage on, but would not stop. Joint custody in Louisiana meant his ex was the custodial parent, but he got his girls every other weekend and every other holiday. He fought for those visits even harder than he fought to solve murders. He barely knew his father. His girls would not suffer this.

It had been a Sunday morning, just before 6 A.M., January 8, 1815, and the men lined behind the Rodriguez Canal strained to see through the heavy fog. Bagpipes echoed across the plain as the British army came at the quickstep. Major Joseph Savary, commander of the 2nd Battalion of Free Men of Color, stood near the center of the American line, not far from General Andrew Jackson. A rocket rose into the sky near the swamp to their left and the fog lifted to reveal the enemy columns in all their splendor—red coats, shako hats, steel bayonets atop their muskets.

The column near the river rushed the exposed redoubt just in front of the American line. The column coming along the swamp, closer to Savary's position, rolled toward them, sixty men abreast, the column so long its end could not be seen. It was a magnificent spectacle until the American cannons opened up.

A maelstrom of fire and shells—grapeshot, canister shot, chain shot, and black iron cannonballs—ripped through the British lines. Still they came, and Savary's men were finally able to join the firing. Major General Sir Edward Pakenham in his black commander-in-chief jacket and his best friend, Major General Samuel Gibbs, were cut down not far from Savary's position. Later, Andy Jackson would claim it was one of Savary's men who shot General Pakenham.

As the British attack faltered, eventually to fail, Major Joseph Savary learned his brother had been killed down the line. Etienne Savary was one of the eight Americans killed that morning. The mighty British army, veterans who had defeated Napoleon's finest in Spain and Portugal, suffered over two thousand casualties. Major Savary buried his brother in an above-ground tomb in the city they helped save. He had his brother's name carved into the tombstone above the words "Killed in action at the battle of New Orleans."

Nearly two hundred years later, Major Joseph Savary's descendant and namesake felt the hairs on the back of his neck stand up as he stepped away from a shotgun house in need of a paint job at the corner of Felicity and Freret Streets. The door slammed behind him. Detective Joseph Savary had just eliminated another suspect, Willie Nelson (no relation to the singer), a nineteen-year-old convicted serial purse snatcher just released after serving two years at Hunt Correctional Center. That left one name on his list of those who'd had run-ins with police around Jeanfreau's, a list Savary had made quick work of, eliminating one dead guy, one in jail in Mississippi, and the others who had fairly solid alibis. What pricked Savary's goose bumps was the fact that no one had said anything about the last name on the list, Oris Lamont, also nineteen. Every other name had come up in the interviews except Lamont's. In his short lifetime, Oris Lamont had managed to get arrested five times as a juvenile and seven times as an adult, charged with aggravated burglary, simple burglary, auto theft, simple robbery, carjacking, and a new drug charge. There was a lone conviction. Simple burglary. He served fourteen months of a ten-year sentence. Lamont had spent his entire eighteenth year in prison.

The *silence* wasn't probable cause for arrest, by a long shot, but it drew Savary to focus on Lamont, who had been arrested the previous week on Felicity Street for possession of crack cocaine with attempt to distribute. Savary hurried back to headquarters and pulled up a mug shot of Lamont, scooped up a copy of the videotape from the Jeanfreau murder, and headed straight back to his car.

On his way to the FBI Building on Leon Simon Boulevard, Savary called an old friend on his cell. Elvin Bishop had played middle linebacker at St. Augustine while Savary was the team's star defensive end. Both were good enough to bring two state championships to St. Aug, but these particular Purple Knights both passed up college ball. Bishop's knees required orthopedic surgery after their senior year, and Savary passed on playing for Southern Miss for a full academic scholarship to Xavier.

"You busy?" Savary asked when Bishop called back. He'd left a voicemail and hoped his friend was in town.

"Just got out of a meeting."

"I'm coming over."

"Now?"

"I need a favor."

The FBI compound, surrounded by a twenty-foot steel-and-brick fence, was guarded by Department of Justice police, who stopped Savary at the gate and directed him where to park his unmarked police car. The homicide detective did not have an official U.S. government "secret" clearance, so he remained in a first-floor, windowless waiting room until Bishop could come downstairs to meet him.

At five-ten, Bishop was stocky, his face filling out from his high school days. He flashed the familiar easy smile as he approached. Savary stood and they shook hands, slapped each other's shoulders.

"Glad to see you're still in town," Savary said.

Typical FBI custom was to have agents work away from their home for years before they had an opportunity to be stationed back home. Bishop spent his first five years in Baltimore but returned with the glut of special agents right after Katrina and remained.

"So, what you got?"

Savary reached into his briefcase and withdrew the videotape and the envelope with the mug shot. "Need you to send this to Quantico. See if your lab guys can do a facial comparison for me."

Bishop laughed. "You been watching too much CSI bullshit."

"I know you got the technology. This is a first-degree murder case. You gonna help me, or do I have to call Coach on you?"

They both laughed at that, although a call to Coach Washington would prod the old man to tongue-lash Bishop. Washington might be retired, but these were his boys and he was still around to coach them.

"Remember that damn hook-and-ladder play?"

"Never forget something like that."

St. Augustine Purple Knights versus their nemesis, the Archbishop Rummel Raiders, the only team to beat St. Aug both years of their back-to-back state championship seasons. Their senior year, St. Aug held on to a six-point lead. Ten seconds left, fourth and goal, and the Raiders' two sacks and a penalty had them all the way back to the St. Aug forty-yard line.

Everyone expected a Hail Mary pass. The Raiders had beat the Brother Martin Crusaders earlier in the year with one. No one expected a hook-and-ladder. Savary drew back into pass coverage. The Rummel quarterback dropped back but threw short, to their fullback, who wheeled and lateraled to their star running back, a fleet-footed, skinny white boy—they later learned he was the star of their track team and the fastest kid in the school.

"Vincent—I forget his last name," Savary said.

Vincent, the Raider running back, scampered past two linebackers, but Savary had him cut off near the sidelines with Bishop and their strong safety closing quickly.

"Still don't know how the boy got through."

They'd reviewed the videotape again and again. The four players collided at the thirty-yard line. Bishop and the safety went down, Savary pulling the Raider toward the turf, only Vincent's legs kept churning and he yanked away and hit the afterburners.

"Fastest white boy I've ever seen."

Vincent outraced the St. Aug cornerback and free safety to the end zone. Extra point good. Rummel 21–St. Augustine 20.

"I bumped into Vincent right after Katrina. He's with ATF," Bishop said. "His great-great—I don't know the number of greats —was wounded at the Battle of New Orleans."

Savary felt goose bumps again.

Both men knew the story of Major Joseph Savary and the 2nd Battalion of Free Men of Color.

Savary held up the videotape. "I need a Hail Mary on this one."

"We'll see. Wait here."

"Wait?"

"Don't have to send it to there. The meeting I was in had our two top forensic scientists from there. Let's see what they say." As he backed out of the room with videotape and envelope, Bishop pointed to the far wall. "There's coffee and muffins."

The coffee was weak but the pecan muffin quite delicious. Savary had a second and was dozing on a fairly comfortable sofa when Bishop came back in with an Asian man in a gray lab coat.

"This is Special Agent Kent Yamasaki." Bishop introduced Savary and eased behind the smallish Japanese-American, who said, "There is a ninety-seven percent probability that the man in the video is the man in the photograph. I am having a report prepared for you."

"Ninety-seven percent is good, isn't it?"

"We never go higher than ninety-eight. It's as close as you can get, Detective."

Savary called Jodie on his cell on the way back to headquarters.

"Who's the duty judge?"

"Joe Sayzo."

"Dammit."

Sayzo was as anti-police as they came. Better known as "Lack of PC Sayzo," the man rarely saw enough probable cause in officers testifying at preliminary hearings, forcing the DA to produce fact witnesses, who were hard enough to get to court for a trial, much less a hearing. Sayzo saw even less probable cause in most warrants.

"I don't have enough for an arrest warrant," Savary said. "I was thinking I have enough for a search warrant. I'll go talk to the suspect, case he wants to cop out."

"Yeah. Right."

Neither had to mention the fact that Judge Marcus Summers was next up as duty judge. That would be tomorrow. A retired state trooper, Summers understood probable cause for what it was, "a reasonable belief that an individual committed a specific crime." Far from the "beyond a reasonable doubt" necessary for conviction, PC was what every cop strived for. It was up to the DA to present a case "beyond a reasonable doubt."

Damn attorneys. Shakespeare had it right. First, kill all the lawyers.

Two sheriff's deputies brought Oris Lamont, who was young and thin, like the killer in the video, into the small, stuffy interview room at Orleans Parish Prison where Detective Joseph Savary sat behind the small table with a Miranda rights form. He'd filled out the pertinent details of name, address, date, and time.

Lamont sat in the chair across the table from Savary and reached for the mini digital tape recorder next to Savary's hand.

"Don't touch it," Savary said. He introduced himself and asked, "You have a lawyer?"

"Not yet."

Savary started reading Lamont his rights.

"I know them," Lamont interrupted.

Savary continued until he reached the waiver portion and read, "I understand what my rights are. No pressure or coercion of any kind was used against me to waive my rights. At this time, I am willing to answer questions without a lawyer present."

"What's this about?"

"It's not about any chicken-shit drug charge."

Lamont's dark brown eyes went wide. He leaned back in the folding chair. He tried smiling. Savary pulled a crime-scene photo from his briefcase, a photo of the exterior of Jeanfreau's from the afternoon of the murder. Lamont looked at it but his eyes revealed nothing, not even recognition of a place he must have passed hundreds of times in his short life.

"I don't know nothin' 'bout no murder."

"Who said anything about a murder? I could be a robbery detective for all you know."

"You got a cigarette?"

"I don't smoke." Savary pushed the waiver forward. "You'll have to sign the waiver to talk with me."

Lamont folded his arms. Savary shrugged, picked up the waiver form, and said, "You can go back inside then. With your padnas."

"I got no padnas." Lamont reached for the form, signed it, said, "I want you to tell the judge I cooperated. Damn drug charge."

"When was the last time you were in Jeanfreau's?"

"Man, I don't know. It's been a while. A year or so."

"Really? You know there's video inside. You sure you didn't drop in, get a cold drink?"

"Nope. I mean yeah. I ain't been inside."

"You remember Mr. Hudson, don't you?"

"I ain't talkin' 'bout that old man or any charge he put against me."

"I'm not here to talk about shoplifting."

Savary tried different tacks. What had Lamont heard about the murder? Was he outside when it happened, maybe saw something? Oris Lamont insisted he hadn't been at Jeanfreau's for a year. Savary turned on the tape recorder, read Lamont his rights again, and recorded the young man's statement, how he hadn't been in Jeanfreau's for a year. As he was ending the statement, Savary casually asked, "Old man Hudson"—that's what Lamont called him—"what did he mean when he touched his chin?"

"Huh?"

"When he touched his chin. Was that a signal?"

Lamont laughed. "That's no signal. Band-Aid on his chin kept comin' off, the old fool."

"When was this?"

"No time in particular. I just seen him do that."

Lamont added nothing else of value. Didn't seem overly concerned about the matter. Only added, "I need your name."

Savary passed him a business card.

"I wanna give it to the judge on this cocaine case. Show him I cooperate with the police."

Savary went to the morgue early the next morning, caught pathologist Dr. Jess Gomez before the man started on his first autopsy.

"Go back down to the record room," Dr. Gomez said. "See the investigator. I usually put everything in my notes. Only put what's

pertinent in the autopsy report, but my notes are more detailed."
Savary found it an hour later. Jack Hudson had a clear Band-Aid
on his chin on the day he was murdered.

"All this may be enough for an arrest warrant," Jodie said as
Savary typed out a search warrant on his computer. "It'll sure be
enough for a search warrant."

The right honorable Judge Marcus Summer of Criminal District
Court agreed and signed the search warrant for Oris Lamont's
shotgun single house, a block off Felicity Street at the corner of
Magnolia and Melpomene. The house smelled of burned cabbage
and creaked heavily as the detectives and uniformed officers came
through the front door. The place seemed to rock beneath their
weight.

Lamont's mama wasn't happy with all the police in her house
and being forced to remain in the living room with her five-year-
old daughter, who wore a pink dress and hugged a stuffed Sponge
Bob doll.

Savary found a Milky Way wrapper under Oris's bed, as well
as two Baby Ruth wrappers and an Almond Joy wrapper. He also
found a Ruger nine-millimeter with six rounds left in a ten-round
magazine under a loose floorboard beneath Oris Lamont's single
bed. His mama never saw the gun before. He looked at the little
girl and those big eyes stared at the semiautomatic.

"Is this your gun?" Savary asked the child.

"That Oris gun."

Her mother pulled her away from the detective and glared at
him.

"You're violating our rights, questioning a baby."

Savary gave the woman a cold smile.

A crowd had gathered outside, kept back by two Sixth District
patrol officers. Savary spotted a familiar face and went over to Reverend Milton, who moved toward him.

"Let him through."

The reverend looked Savary in the eye, but only for a moment.
He shook his head. "I figured the longer you worked on the case,
the more likely you'd figure it out."

"You knew about Oris? That he had a gun. That he did it."

"Everybody knew, 'cept y'all." The reverend looked over at
Oris's mother, now standing on the front stoop with her little girl.

"Can I go talk with her?"

Savary nodded. "We're leaving."

Reverend Milton grabbed his elbow, looked him in the eye again. "I didn't see it happen. I mean, I didn't know for sure, 'cept everyone said it and Oris asked me not to talk to the police. He acted real casual-like. You know what I mean."

A crime lab technician took the Ruger to the lab for firearms examination to check if it matched the spent casing found at the crime scene and the bullet removed from Jack Hudson's brain at the autopsy. Savary went back to Jeanfreau's and checked the candy bars. The Milky Way wrapper found under Oris's bed matched the lot number from the Milky Way bars still on the shelf at Jeanfreau's.

He wasn't at his desk ten minutes, just starting his arrest warrant, when the crime lab called. "It's a match. Casing and projectile from the crime scene came from the Ruger. *And* we got a good print from one of the cartridges. It's from your suspect's right index finger."

Savary looked at the wall clock hanging above the unofficial logo of NOPD Homicide, an art deco illustration of a vulture perched atop a gold star-and-crescent badge. Six o'clock. He should be finished with the warrant by the time he usually called his girls. Then he'd see the judge. Then go ruin Oris Lamont's evening.

Elvin Bishop smiled as soon as he spotted Jodie Kintyre with Savary in the windowless FBI waiting room. Jodie was in no smiling mood. The special agent's silver suit, coincidentally, nearly matched the color of Jodie Kintyre's skirt suit. Joseph Savary's suit was as dark brown as his eyes. Bishop brought a manila folder to Savary.

"Official forensic report on your videotape and photo comparison. SA Yamasaki wants to hold on to your evidence and will be available for court testimony."

Savary made the introductions, then gave his old friend a brief rundown on the Oris Lamont arrest as they sat, Jodie on the sofa, the two men in soft chairs.

"He lawyered up," Savary said, "but we've got a good circumstantial case against him."

"Good. Glad I could help."

Jodie held an envelope up for Bishop, said, "You can help a little more."

Bishop took the envelope, which was unsealed, removed the letter inside, and read it, slowly. He looked up at Savary afterward, for a long moment, then at Jodie.

"You serious about this?"

"Do I look like I'm joking?" Jodie's voice was low and firm, her face deadpan. "I've been a homicide detective for fourteen years. The new superintendent of the New Orleans Police Department doesn't sign a letter like that in jest."

"Misprision of felony?"

"Your boss and the U.S. attorney here in New Orleans like using this against crooked cops, don't they?" Before Bishop could answer, Jodie continued, "We have no sympathy for crooked cops either, but what's good for the goose is good for the gander."

Bishop turned to Savary, who said, in a deeper voice, "Shooting someone in a store is no different from shooting someone on a bridge."

"You're talking about the Danziger shooting?"

"No, you are. We're talking about Felicity Street. We're talking about an entire neighborhood committing misprision of felony. I have a list of names." Savary gave his old friend a hard look, then let his face relax into a slight smile.

"It has to be a federal crime," said Bishop.

"My killer committed a federal crime," Savary answered. "Eighteen U.S.C. nine twenty-two (g) makes it a federal crime for any person who has ever been convicted of any felony to ever possess any firearm regardless of whether it is inside or outside his home. This is a blanket federal ban on all felon gun possession and is punishable by up to ten years in federal prison."

Bishop looked at Jodie as she pulled out a sheet of paper and quoted, "Misprision of felony. Eighteen U.S.C., section four. Whoever, having knowledge of the actual commission of a felony cognizable by a court of the United States, conceals and does not as soon as possible make known the same to some judge or other person in civil or military authority under the United States shall be fined under this title or imprisoned not more than three years, or both." Jodie looked up, recited the rest of the statute from memory. "This offense, however, requires active concealment of a known felony rather than merely failing to report it."

"An entire neighborhood actively concealed a convicted felon with a gun, concealed a murderer from me. From justice," Savary added.

Bishop took in a deep breath. "I've been working the Danziger case."

"I know. That's why we came to you."

"Those cops met the requirement of active concealment."

"So did Oris Lamont's friends, relatives, and neighbors. I'll be happy to lay my case out to a federal grand jury."

Bishop looked at the door, started to get up, sat back down, and shrugged. "You gonna call Coach on me?"

"I'm serious about this," Savary said.

"I'll take it to the ASAC."

Assistant special agent in charge—Savary ran it through his mind.

"Indict one person for misprision of felony on this case," Jodie said, "and it'll put the fear of the Lord in people. A tool we can use."

Savary stood first, stepped toward his friend. "Tell your ASAC it's about time the FBI, with all its might and money, went after street crime here in the murder capital of America, instead of spending *all* your resources chasing politicians, bad judges, and bad cops."

Bishop stood and Savary put a friendly hand on his friend's shoulder. "We're not saying lay off crooked cops, judges, politicians."

Jodie stood. "He knows what we're talking about. *Street crime.*" She came over, extended her hand for Bishop to shake.

As he did, he narrowed his left eye, his face softening. "You know, this could work."

Savary almost reminded his friend that was what the Gene Wilder character said after reading Baron Frankenstein's secret notebook in *Young Frankenstein.*

Jodie had the last word as they were leaving. "You know how much the U.S. attorney loves being in front of TV cameras? Our superintendent intends to take this to the TV stations if you guys do nothing. Misprision of felony. It's got a nice ring to it."

As they left, back into the steamy afternoon, Savary asked his sergeant, "You think this'll work?"

"Not a chance."

"I don't think so either."

"But they'll have to think about it."

Jodie turned her face to the sun, closed her eyes, and repeated the oldest NOPD saying, one dating from the dawn of the department, back when NOPD was caught in a war between Irish street gangs, Sicilian mafiosi, wharf thugs, and a corrupt city government.

"It isn't NOPD versus the criminals. It's us against the world."

EILEEN DREYER

The Sailor in the Picture

FROM *Crime Square*

THE PHOTO IS ICONIC. A young nurse is caught in the arms of a sailor. Her leg is curled, her foot up, her head impossibly far back as people run past, laughing, waving, dancing along the black-and-white reaches of Times Square. You can almost hear the car horns blaring, the church bells, the shouts and singing and laughter. Joy, relief, triumph, a nation gone mad with giddy, mindless delight. Japan has surrendered and the world celebrates.

The photo has hung in the old woman's house as long as anyone can remember. It's a bit yellowed and spotted now, faded from years of sunlight and cigarette smoke. But wherever old Peg O'Toole has lived, the picture has hung right over the overstuffed tweed chair in the living room. And when anyone asks why, she just shrugs.

"It was the moment that changed my life," she always says.

And nobody knows how to answer, because they know what she means. At least, they think they do.

"It was an end," she says, her rheumy eyes distant and thoughtful. "And a beginning. The world changed that day."

And every time she answers, she wonders if she should tell the truth. She wonders why nobody notices that the photo she has isn't the one that is so famous. The picture Mr. Eisenstadt took when he followed that sailor who was kissing all the girls in Times Square. Peg saw the sailor, too. In fact, he kissed her on the way by. But her kiss wasn't worth capturing. She was too far away to be in the famous shot, caught only in one of the other five Eisenstadt took, her feet visible in her heavy work shoes just beyond a bystander. She was facing her own sailor, but no one could see how they met.

She doesn't have to look at the photo to remember that day, though. She carries it in her memory like a sharp shard of glass. It was the day Jimmy died.

The beginning of the end for the Japanese came on August fifth, when high above Hiroshima the bomb bay doors opened on the *Enola Gay*. The beginning of the end for Jimmy came a week earlier, when he was sent home from the Pacific because of a bad back.

It had been three years since Jim had walked through his front door to hang his cap on the hall tree and sniff the air for dinner. Three years since Peg had shared her bed or her dining room table. Three years since he'd seen the twins, then still wobbly toddlers intent on staying upright. They were in kindergarten now, bright-eyed, mischievous kids who could more often than not be found down in the super's rooms building spaceships out of the bits and pieces Mr. Peabody culled from his rounds and eating the cookies Mrs. Peabody made with the sugar she'd hoarded from combining her coupons with those of the other mothers in the building. Everyone could cook. But nobody could bake like Mildred Peabody.

"You must be so excited, Peg," Mildred said that last day of July, hands caught in the pockets of her flowered apron, the one she wore when whipping up treats for the building's children. "Just think. After all this time."

Peg's kids, Mikey and Mary Pat, were already ensconced at the Peabodys' kitchen table, the sunlight pouring in on their bent heads like butter from the barred window, beyond which a forest of ankles passed.

She'd gotten the telegram that morning. She'd opened the door to see a boy standing there in his faux uniform, his clipboard and the flimsy yellow envelope raised, as if he didn't want to hold it any longer than necessary, and she swore her heart had stopped.

Everybody knew what a telegram meant. And there had been so many in the war that the news wasn't even accompanied by someone in a real uniform anymore, or even the parish priest, his biretta clutched at his chest like a bouquet of condolence flowers. Just some pimply-faced boy rocking back and forth on his heels, a

Western Uniform cap on his head, dread tightening his shoulders. A quick stab of an envelope into your hands, a scribble for delivery, and the slam of the outside door. A gold star for a parent's window and blank silence for the wife.

The envelope crinkled in her fist. Her heart thundered as if she'd been the one to climb those four stories instead of the kid. Her first instinct had been to run down the stairs to knock on somebody's door. Collect a witness. Maybe Margie in 2B, who was waiting to hear from her own husband somewhere in the Seventh Air Corps.

It didn't matter, really. Anybody would help her. Hers was a building, a neighborhood, that stuck together. Hell's Kitchen might be poor, but Peg knew everyone in the building and the buildings around her. Often they'd sit out of an evening on the steps and talk, cigarette smoke curling from their fingers, the precious dregs of dinner coffee scenting the air, the kids shrill as a flock of starlings out in the street as they fought their own war with sticks and balls and bare hands.

Maybe she should knock on a door. Ask Mildred or Patty Devon to open the envelope for her. Face what was waiting so she didn't have to.

Could Jim really be gone? Was she alone now? Would she wake every day with only one side of the bed rumpled, no one to help when Mary Pat got sick or Mikey wanted to learn how to pitch? No one demanding an account of her hours or criticizing her food. No one else to help ease the overstretched budget or stretch it even further.

She had gotten a job the week after Jim was drafted. Day after day climbing into her sturdy shoes and work pants, tucking her hair under a net, gathering her supplies for the walk across town. Her lunch, her cigarettes, her lipstick and handkerchief and bus fare for rainy days. A book for her break and one of Jimmy's knives for protection. The small relics of her life.

"Peg?" Mrs. Peabody asked, graying head tilted. "You okay?"

Peg snapped out of her reverie. She was on her way to work, just like always, lunch pail beneath her arm, purse tossed over her shoulder, kids coloring at Mildred Peabody's kitchen table. Peg smiled at her neighbor, having no idea what it was she was supposed to say.

Was she excited? Jimmy was coming home.

"It will take some getting used to," was all she would admit to, because of course Mildred didn't know. Peg had made sure nobody in the building did. It wouldn't have done any good, only make things worse. Make her an object of pity in good people's eyes.

Mildred laughed and closed her into an overlarge, Noxema-scented hug. "You've done all you can," she said, hands on ample hips. "It's time to let a man take all this off your shoulders. Get back your real life."

And Peg felt it again. The lurch of shock when she'd opened that envelope. The flood of disbelief that seemed to engulf her, that kept her from understanding the words.

Coming home. Stop. Be there second week August. Stop. Can't wait for life to get back to normal. Stop. Jim. End.

"My real life," Peg echoed Mildred and nodded, suddenly afraid that she'd slip and tell the truth. "Yes. I imagine so."

She gave Mikey a glancing kiss, the most he would allow, and nuzzled Mary Pat like a stuffed toy, which made her little girl giggle, all red hair and blue eyes and dimples. Sweetness, baby fat, the smell of baby shampoo. Endless possibilities and the luxury of safety. Peg wanted to put down her pail and her purse and gather her children to herself, tightly, too tightly for anyone to wedge their way between them. She wanted to take them and run, but she didn't know where to go.

So she said goodbye and left for work.

She could take the bus, she knew. When she could, though, Peg preferred to walk. She loved the hard energy of New York, fighting with millions of other people for the sidewalk, dodging hats and briefcases and the swirl of wind-ruffled skirts. She loved the neon, even during the day, when it seemed no more than a vague after-image, and she loved the theaters. She loved seeing the pictures of all the actors who played there, perusing them on the way by like a family photo album of distant relatives: Ethel Barrymore, Ray Bolger, Katharine Cornell, Lunt and Fontanne, Paul Robeson.

Not that she'd seen many plays. She couldn't afford it. Peg saved up every penny she made for the day Jimmy came back. And every time anybody tried to tempt her to throw away a bit of her money to see *I Remember Mama* or *You Can't Take It with You* or *Harvey*, she reached into her purse and closed her hand around her Westside Savings and Loan book, her talisman against temptation.

She had other things to do with that money, things her mother might have done if she hadn't bought so many theater tickets. She was going to be a nurse someday, striding through a hospital like she owned it in those whispery white-soled shoes. She was going to wear a cap and a gleaming white dress and always look clean and bright, and her kids would be proud of her.

It would be so wonderful to sit in a darkened theater again, though, watching other people solve their problems, watching other women triumph. It made her believe she could, too. Oh, women triumphed in movies, and she went to see those. After all, a nickel was easier to come by. But something about live people saying those words carried portent, promise. And she needed that.

One day, she thought, *I won't have to wait for someone to give me a ticket as a treat. My problem will be choosing among the different plays I want to see. I'll step out of one of those shiny black sedans that pull up before the theater, straighten my skirt, and stroll through the door as if I belong there.*

I won't go see Mr. John Raitt in Carousel, *though,* she thought as she passed him smiling down at her from the poster, handsome in his striped shirt and cap. Not again. A few weeks ago her boss, Mr. Goldfarb, had given the two girls who worked for him the tickets he and his wife were going to use. Peg had been beside herself. The seats had been great. The music had been gorgeous and Mr. Raitt magnetic and strong. But how could anyone think Billy Bigelow was heroic? How could a hero say that he could love you so much that he hit you? Her father had loved her mother like that. He'd loved her so much he'd beaten her to death.

So Peg turned away from Mr. Raitt and she kept walking. And in another block she reached her very favorite place in New York.

Times Square.

Every time she walked out of Forty-fourth onto Broadway, she paused to take it in. Not the buildings; those were deteriorating just like Broadway. Burlesque shows were replacing legitimate theaters and seedy hotels springing up where the Astor had acted as cornerstone. Peg couldn't think of a door along Times Square she'd want to walk through right now.

But she stood there just the same, just like every other time, taking in the people. It was like reaching the delta of a river to find the sea, she always thought, a seething, flowing current of humanity, moving, moving, just like waves in a wind. She imagined Times

Square as where everything began and ended, where the energy of the city was born to stream away into the different boroughs, the tide funneled through the high walls of skyscrapers. Even on a dull day it was a place of color, people, and neon, the news ticker sliding across One Times Square so that no one could escape the moment.

Just this way had she stood with her mother, holding hands, eyes wide on the wash of energy and life that was New York. Every day they had stopped here on the way home from school. Now she knew it was so they didn't have to get home so soon. But then she was sharing magic with her mother.

"There you are, Mrs. O'Toole," a raspy voice called as she waited for the light. "Thought I'd missed you today."

Peg smiled as she turned to see a wide, smiling, graying cop head her way. His hat was pushed back on his head and his baton was in his hand, just like in the movies. Peg often wondered if the movies had copied him or he was copying the movies for the benefit of the tourists who spawned upstream to Times Square in the summer.

"Off to work," she said, smiling back at him.

He shook his head. "Still don't like you coming home after dark. Sure you couldn't get that early shift back?"

"Better pay in the evening, Officer Paretti. Besides, I like seeing the neon all lit up and sparkling when I come back."

One furry eyebrow lifted. "You can protect yourself?"

She chuckled. "You'd be surprised. Working for the butcher has built muscle."

He shook his head. "Tiny thing like you. Just not right. You should be working in a store, somethin' like that. Not choppin' up chickens and steak."

"If a store paid as much as the butcher does, I'd agree with you. But I was lucky to have Mr. Goldfarb hire me. Best surprise of my life, getting that job. After all"—she leaned closer—"my tips come in chicken livers and ham hocks."

"It'll sure be good to have all the boys home from the war, won't it?" he asked, absently nodding to a family in Bermuda shorts and cameras. "You poor ladies have been handling too much of the burden, you ask me. Ain't natural."

Peg knew she should have agreed. Should have told him that she was relieved to know that her Jimmy was coming home safe. Instead, she patted Officer Paretti on the arm and let the tide carry her across Broadway. And for another eight hours she shared a crowded, white-tiled back room with Phil Dawson, her knives flashing as she cut away steaks and roasts, ribs for barbecuing and flank for stew meat. And when the slicing was done, she grabbed the parts bucket and cranked the contents through the grinder to make hamburger. Her arms were on fire and her back ached like a sore tooth, but she actually liked what she did. There was something neat and predictable about it, a real sense of accomplishment. Mr. Goldfarb said that he would always be grateful that she was the one who answered his ad that day back in '41, because she worked hard, never complained, and never missed work. She always smiled when she came in and smiled when she left.

Peg heard about the atomic bomb, of course. Everybody did. But it didn't really make a difference to her one way or another. Jimmy was coming home whether the Japs surrendered or not. And he'd promised to be home soon.

Mildred Peabody saw that Peg was beginning to lose weight. Peg blamed it on the heat even as she spent the evening out on the street hitting fungoes to Mikey. Mr. Goldfarb noticed that Peg wasn't smiling as much. Peg told him it was because after the one telegram she hadn't heard any more from Jimmy, and it made her nervous.

"Of course," he comforted, patting her arm. "Who wouldn't be nervous, after all this time? Don't you worry, child. Your worries are over. He's coming home to you." Then, his bristly gray eyebrows drawing together like amorous caterpillars, he shook his head. "Although where I'm going to find another butcher as quick as you, I just don't know."

For the first time since she'd known him, she hugged the old man, both of their white aprons blood-spattered and grimy from the day, her own hair drooping against her sweating neck. "I'm going to miss you."

And for the first time, Mr. Goldfarb hugged her back. "You deserve better."

Surprised by a flash of anger, she leaned back. "There is nothing better, Mr. Goldfarb. I've been very happy here."

Safe. She'd been safe. It was what she felt every day when she walked down the front steps of her brownstone, when she battled the tides of Times Square. When she wielded knives as sharp as razors, mere inches from fingers and veins and faces. It didn't take Officer Paretti to tell her that New York was dangerous. Too many alleys, too many crime-thick shadows. But as often as she crossed those perilous streets late at night, as long as she'd lived without a man to protect her, she had never once felt threatened.

Mr. Goldfarb lifted a hand and patted her face. "You sure your navy boy doesn't want to be a butcher?"

She laughed. "Oh, Mr. Goldfarb, you'll have plenty of butchers coming home. Besides, Jimmy's a hod carrier."

The old man shrugged. "He couldn't lift cows instead?"

It was like an omen. A few nights later Peg was up listening to Cab Calloway on the radio. It was at least one in the morning, and the heat was still stifling in the old brick building. The kids were tumbled over the floor like puppies, the living room windows wide open to catch a breeze. The radio was playing softly into the night, and Peg was figuring out her finances at the dining room table. Jimmy still wasn't home. Peg wasn't holding her breath.

"We interrupt this program to tell you . . ."

Peg looked up.

"We've had word that Japan will sign the treaty. They will sign . . ."

That was it, then. It was truly over. No reason left for Jimmy to return to the navy. He'd loved the navy. Peg thought it was the freedom of it, the escape from wearing responsibilities. And she sympathized. But he was well and truly caught back in civilian life now. Cornered. Constrained. Committed to making a living, to being a father and a husband and a neighbor, answerable to all. Peg wondered if he'd do any better at it this time than he did before.

Peg went into work the next day just like always. She packed her purse and her lunch and when she passed Jimmy's dresser slid the drawer open and pulled out his favorite Italian stiletto. She had a feeling today. A different feeling, as if a timer had been set. As if the world was changing. Suddenly she didn't feel so safe.

She went into work anyway. Times Square was already humming when she reached it, and Officer Paretti kissed her on the cheek. The store was quiet, as everybody waited by the radio for President Truman to make the surrender official. A few car horns broke the odd hesitation, but it was as if the city waited, too, holding its breath, the jubilation corked and pressing hard.

At 7 P.M. the world went mad. Even before President Truman finished telling the nation that Japan had surrendered, New York exploded in noise. In the butcher shop Peg could hear bells and whistles and horns. Shouts, singing, feet running past. She danced a jig with Mr. Goldfarb and Phil Dawson and Susie Beilstein, who ran the cash register out front. And then, with a big smacking kiss to the cheeks of the girls, Mr. Goldfarb told everybody to go home.

"It's a day for celebrating," he said, shooing them like recalcitrant children. "Go. Celebrate." And for his contribution, he gave them all sirloin steaks for their parties.

Peg headed straight home. They'd been preparing a party on the block for the last two days, when the news seemed imminent. Peg carried her steaks as if they were the surrender agreement itself.

On her way, she shared the jubilation of her city. She laughed and danced with a couple of cops on Thirty-third and waved at the cars who passed, horns and radios blaring. She reached Times Square to see the news ticker proclaim JAPAN SURRENDERS, on a constant crawl around the building, and she stopped to savor her favorite place reacting to this moment of history. In the greater scheme of things, it didn't matter what happened to her. The war had ended, and all the boys were coming home. All the mothers and fathers, the wives and children and cousins and friends around the country could take a good breath and rejoice.

She was standing there flat-footed when the sailor caught her. He was laughing, dancing down the street like Gene Kelly, grabbing any woman he could and kissing her. Grabbing Peg around the waist, he spun her, the bag of steaks hitting him on the backside. She couldn't help laughing as she met him mouth to mouth. His hand supported her back and his nascent whiskers scraped her cheek. A puff of laughter, a cheeky grin, and he was off to another conquest.

The photographer, a tweedy, balding kind of man, flashed his own smile and followed. Peggy was still laughing.

Suddenly the laughter caught in her chest. When the photographer trotted by, she finally saw past him to where another sailor stood. But this sailor wasn't laughing or dancing. He was just looking. At her.

Jimmy.

Standing not ten feet away, smiling as if he were in better spirits than anybody in the city. Maybe Peg was the only one who saw the murder in his eyes. Maybe she was just too familiar with it to miss it. She froze, the instinctive reaction of all hunted animals. She knew better than to look away. But a shriek behind her, then laughter, told her that the sailor had captured another partner. She couldn't resist looking.

The photographer was there, too. Snapping as fast as he could, just beyond the couple. Peg couldn't blame him. It was a great picture, like ballet, that girl in all white surrounded by the sailor in his dark navy blues. It was a picture she had once kept in her own mind of the future. Jimmy home from the navy, her proud in her nursing whites. She wanted so badly to not move, not let them out of her sight. Not lose that pretty picture she knew now would never come true.

Jimmy was home.

"What the hell ya doin' here?" she heard just behind her and knew that he was there.

Run! her brain screamed. Her heart collided with her chest, right there between the fourth and fifth ribs. She had started to sweat, because she knew it was too late. It had been too late when she'd kissed that sailor.

"When did you get in, Jimmy?" she asked, turning to face him with her purse and lunch pail and sirloins clutched in sweaty hands. "I didn't get another telegram from you. I didn't know you were coming today."

He stepped closer, his nostrils flaring as if he could smell the fear on her. The sailor and the photographer had moved on. Peg couldn't hear the horns or bells anymore. She heard Jimmy's breathing. Assessing it for change.

"I sent it," he said. "And I waited for you for fuckin' hours. *Hours,* Peg."

Peg could barely breathe. "I was working, Jimmy."

"Yeah, that's what Mrs. Peabody said. So I decided to come surprise you. Give you somethin' to celebrate." He swung an arm wide to take in the humanity around him. "Seems you found somethin' else already, huh?"

It was all Peg could do to keep from flinching. Surreptitiously she looked around them, wanting only to get out of the middle of this crowd. If Jimmy really was in a mood, she didn't want to be here.

"Oh, did you see the kids?" She tried to smile. "Haven't they grown?"

But he wouldn't be distracted. "We're not talking about the kids here. We're talking about *you*. And what you've been up to since I've been gone. Whatever it is, it stops now. You hear me?"

"I haven't been up to anything but taking care of the kids and working, Jimmy. And Mr. Goldfarb already knows I'm quitting when you get home. But look." Smiling again, she held up her booty. "He gave us a gift."

He grabbed her by the arm. There would be bruises, she knew, angry red finger marks left behind on her Irish white skin. Her stomach roiled. Would he do it here? In front of all these people?

"Steaks?" he demanded, his breath accelerating, his fingers punishing. Reminding her who was in charge. Who was stronger. "Just what did you do to get those?"

He'd just gotten back, was all she could think. Couldn't he have given her a day? Maybe a week when she could believe that maybe this time it would be different?

She wasn't even going to make it home.

"I did my job," she said, refusing to cower. Not anymore. Not one more time.

He almost spit in her face. "Bullshit. Nobody gives steaks away f'r nuthin'."

He was dragging her over toward Forty-fourth. She let him. Even so, she lifted her head. Stared straight at him, where she never would have before. She wasn't going to be ashamed any-more. "I. Did. My. Job. You're the one with the dirty mind, Jimmy."

He hit her. Nobody saw it; he caught her in the kidneys. Jimmy loved the kidneys, because nobody could see those bruises but him. Peg gasped and buckled. Her lunch pail hit the ground with a clang. But she held on to her purse. She held on to the meat, as if it were more important than protecting herself.

"I'll just bet you did your job," he rasped, dragging her along the sidewalk. "I saw you with that sailor back there. I hope you got a lot of money from all the sailors who were here when I wasn't, cause you ain't gettin' any more. And if I think you're bein' free with anybody else, I'll beat the crap out of you. And then I'll take the kids away. See how you like that."

She knew better. Still, she yanked back. "You're not taking my kids anywhere."

This time he broke a rib. A couple of people paused in passing, and he glared them down before shoving her into an alley by the Majestic. It just figured, she thought, struggling to breathe past the relentless agony in her side. *He's going to beat me to death in sight of Billy Bigelow.*

"I'll do whatever I damn well please," he assured her, catching her by the hair and pulling, his mouth against her ear. "Don't you get it? They're *my* kids. You're *my* wife. *Je*-sus, Peg, did you have to make me remind you this soon? Couldn't you have let me have a little peace, a good home-cooked meal before you pissed me off?"

She tried to swing her purse at him. He belted her in the face. She could taste the blood pouring from her nose. "Don't, Jimmy. What'll the kids think?"

"They'll think that you've been stupid again and I had to come home to stop that."

She could smell the whiskey on his breath, which meant he'd been working on this mad all day. His control was already gone.

Did she have the guts to stick it out? She hurt so badly. She was so afraid.

"I've lived alone for three years, Jimmy," she said, her voice nasal and high. "I'm not going back to the way it was. I'm *not*. I'll take the kids and run if I have to."

Five minutes later she was fighting for consciousness. He hadn't just beaten her. He'd kicked her in the jaw. She wondered if it was broken. She curled into herself to try to protect her belly, her hand in her pants pocket.

"Bastard," she moaned, struggling to get up onto her elbow, her other hand tucked against her stomach. "I'm not standing for this anymore. I am . . . *not* . . . teaching my kids that this is . . . okay."

Jimmy bent all the way down and dragged her up. "You stupid bitch. Don't you get it? I could kill you and nobody would care."

Odd, she thought, blinking her one open eye. *I could do the same thing.*

So she did. Jimmy never heard the *snick* of the blade. He was focused on the hands he had around her neck. By the time he realized that this time she wasn't so helpless, Peg had driven the razor-sharp eight-inch blade deep into his chest, right between the fourth and fifth ribs as if she was cutting out a rib eye. The blade went in so cleanly she didn't even feel the scrape of a rib. She just felt a few pops, as if she'd broken through tough membranes. She hoped to hell she had.

She was holding herself up on him, and he was staring down at the knife in his chest as if he couldn't comprehend it.

"That's . . . mine."

She didn't answer. She just turned the knife and drove it in deeper. His eyes widened. His mouth opened. And then he simply collapsed in on himself.

He fell right on top of Peg. She couldn't move; not while he gasped out his last breaths or while his heart faltered to a stop, never to start again. Her face was only inches from his staring, astonished eyes, and she waited, still not sure he wouldn't wake and go after her again. She struggled to get air in past her broken nose and ribs.

She couldn't stop shaking. She couldn't believe it. She'd hoped. She'd prayed so hard that his time away would have made him a better man. Would have washed away his need to hit and hurt. She'd sure had her answer, hadn't she?

She needed to do something. The kids were waiting back at the Peabodys'. No more than half a block away, New York was dancing. And she was lying here under a man whose blood was seeping out onto the asphalt, his body a dead weight.

She could feel the bruises swelling on her face. Her right eye was completely closed, and her lip was split. Blood stained her poplin shirt all the way to her waist, and she had to struggle to get enough air in.

"Help!" she screamed, finally pushing at Jimmy. "Oh, God, help! My husband!"

With a lurch, she pulled herself free of him, only to land on her knees. Her head spun. Her heart was thumping like a bass drum. She knew she was going to be sick. But she had to get to Officer Paretti. She had to . . .

"Hey, what's going on?"

She caught a blurry glimpse of a couple of Marines shadowed at the Forty-fourth Street end of the alley.

"Please. We've been mugged. Help my husband."

Officer Paretti came running. Bending down next to her, he cradled her poor face in his hands and sighed. "I told you it wasn't safe."

"Somebody came . . . came and tried to steal . . . I think they've hurt my husband . . . with his own . . . knife."

"You sure?" one of the Marines asked. "We didn't see nobody."

Officer Paretti laughed. "You have any other ideas? You think what, that Mrs. O'Toole beat herself up and then stabbed her husband? Look at her."

And Peg felt the gaze of the Marines, who took in her tiny frame and battered features and gasping breath.

"Yeah," one of them muttered. "I guess so. Sorry, ma'am."

Peg blinked up at them. "I tried so hard," she whispered, tears streaming down her cheeks. "I really did."

"We know you did, Mrs. O'Toole," Officer Paretti said. "Now, boys, you go find me some help. And tell 'em to bring an ambulance. I'll stay with the victims."

He waited until the sound of the footsteps faded. Then he made it a point to give Peg a gentle frown. He looked over at Jimmy, who lay curled around the lethal knife that stuck from his chest. He looked at the blossoming damage on Peg's face. He took one more look at the angle of the knife, the design of the cut, the way Peg was shaking.

"I'm sorry, Mrs. O'Toole," he said, his voice even gentler than his hands. Peg could see every thought going through his head. She saw him reach over, pull his handkerchief from his pocket, and wipe off the handle of the knife. "Whoever attacked you killed your husband. Little thing like you. Lucky you're alive."

And Peg, who had survived, closed her eyes.

It was sixty years before she finally told the true story. She had just taken her granddaughter to the theater to celebrate her getting her master's degree in nursing. Her granddaughter was named after her, although this one was called Mags, a girl with Peg's red hair and Jimmy's brown eyes, who had always told Peg she wanted to be a trauma nurse just like her.

Well, she was now, and a good one. Which was why when they returned to Peg's retirement apartment in Brooklyn, Peg poured them both beers and asked Mags to listen to a story.

At first the confession was met by silence. Mags wouldn't even look at her. Peg had never felt so tired in her life.

Finally Mags looked up at the black-and-white photo that hung over Peg's head.

"*You* killed Granddad."

Peg picked up her beer with shaking hands and took a sip. "I needed somebody to know."

Somebody she trusted to understand. Somebody who saw the legacy of violence every day.

For a long moment, Mags looked out the front window. "Grams?"

"Mm-hmm."

"Did you carry that knife knowing he was coming home?"

"I did."

Her granddaughter's eyes grew pensive. "And he'd beaten you before."

"Yes."

There was a nod, and Mags took a sip of her own beer. "Then I think it was a lucky stroke that you found that butchering job. Otherwise you might not have had the strength to gut the old bastard."

Peg almost smiled. She had looked for that job for six months. "Honey," she said, the confession finally complete. "Luck had nothing to do with it."

DAVID EDGERLEY GATES

The Devil to Pay

FROM *Alfred Hitchcock's Mystery Magazine*

TOMMY MEADOWS WAS COMING back down from Riverdale, where he'd gone to see his grandma, who was up there in an assisted living facility since May. Not the worst, either, the nursing staff cheerful, familiar with everybody by name, the meals okay, even if the food was mostly stuff you could gum, and the lawns sloped down to the Hudson, so if the weather was nice, you could take the old girl outside for a turn around the grounds in her wheelchair. But when it was rainy or too cold, all the *alter kockers* were lined up in the day room, watching *Judge Judy,* with blankets over their knees and oxygen feeds in their noses.

Better than state correctional, you might say.

Tommy had just done fourteen months in Dannemora, and he was out on probation but living with his mom, so although he had to make the weekly meet with his PO, at least he didn't have to get an actual job. His old lady was letting him stay in the apartment over the garage, and as long as he forked over four hundred a month, it didn't bother her where the money came from. She was long past caring how Tommy made the vig. He'd been in and out of Juvie since he was fourteen, and done hard time twice as an adult. For his part, he let her self-medicate with Old Mr. Boston, which was her idea of a hot date, and they got along just fine.

He was in the Oyster Bar at Grand Central, the seafood pan-roast combo and a glass of white wine. He'd started out on cherrystone clams and a bloody mary shooter, and he was thinking he'd finish off with a half-dozen local bluepoints.

A couple of stools down, two guys were talking.

"You know what a pack of smokes goes for in New York these days? Ten bucks."

"You couldn't buy toenail clippers for less than ten bucks, and that's cheap," the other guy said.

"You know what a *carton* of smokes costs down South, one of the tobacco-growing states? Thirty bucks. You load up a truck, you double your money, you sell it under the counter."

"If you don't get caught with North Carolina revenue stamps on the product."

"I'm just saying."

"You just keep talking out your ass," the other guy said.

The first guy dropped his voice. "This is money in the bank," he said. "You make the investment, pay off the truck and the driver, it's gonna return fifty large, no downside risk."

If it's not your money, Tommy thought.

That's what the other guy thought, too. "Looks good on paper," he said. "But the plain fact is, you've got nothing but a handful of gimme and a mouthful of much obliged."

"Let me talk to my guy, Jack, see what he'll do for us."

"You do that," Jack said. He got up.

Tommy had made this kind of pitch himself. He knew it was a hard sell. Guys like Jack were at the top of the food chain and didn't need bottom feeders. It was the same the world over.

Tommy decided to order the bluepoints.

Tommy always had something working, nothing that was going to knock down fifty large, maybe, but it was better to stay under the radar. You got too ambitious, you attracted the wrong kind of attention. Which in fact was why he'd been inside. His brother Roy, rest in peace, had tried for a big score and gotten his dick handed to him. There was serious gang muscle involved and Tommy knew to take himself off the street until the heat blew over, so he pled to a bullshit accessory charge and went up the river for a year and change.

The thing about doing time is, your time isn't your own. In a max facility like Clinton, you're on the clock 24/7. So you get with the program. Wake up, chow line, work detail. And no such animal as privacy. Nights, there's bed check. If you got on the wrong side of the screws, you might as well kiss your ass goodbye.

It was an enormous luxury, then, for Tommy to just lie in bed in the mornings and watch the early light play off the ceiling. No bells, no PA system, nobody with a hard-on and a bad attitude ready to give him grief. He kept to a routine all the same. Brushed his teeth, started the coffee, made the bed. The studio apartment wasn't much, God's honest truth, but it was his, and he wanted his self-respect more than he wanted to hook up. Not that it was monastic, but he made the effort to keep it squared away.

The other thing he tried to keep neat was his perimeter. One of the conditions of his probation was that he not associate with known felons. This was, of course, a joke, since pretty much everybody in Tommy's circle of friends, going back to grade school, had gotten jammed up with the law, one way or another. Mostly petty theft, but a couple of guys in the heavy. He knew to steer wide of them. There was no point in giving his PO reason to violate him. Basically, he was keeping his head down.

Not that he didn't keep his ear to the ground. There was always some graft you could put your hand to. A week ago, he'd been down in Maryland. He wasn't supposed to leave the state, not without permission, but what the hey? The old lady expected her rent.

He picked up his beard in Gaithersburg, and they trawled some local gun shops. Browning nines were pricey, Glocks were a glut on the market. Gangbangers were into the Brownings, the more pimped out the better. He even found a nickeled 1911, not his own weapon of choice, if he had to choose, but covering a rough circle of two hundred miles, they picked up two dozen guns Tommy could take back to New York. He cleared fifty a pop with his wholesaler. Easy in, easy out. It wasn't up to him to meet the buyers. Shooters weren't always the most pliable clients.

On the low end, he fenced credit cards. This was only good for about forty-eight hours, until the issuing bank closed them down. Still, it was bread and butter. He knew he was coasting.

And then it fell in his lap.

Brooklyn South was sucking hind tit, and Babs DiMello was taking heat from her lieutenant.

"I'm not trying to be a complete jerk, here, Detective," he asked her, "but why are we stuck on the dime?"

Whenever somebody tells you they're not trying to be a complete jerk, they probably mean the exact opposite, Babs knew, but she was as frustrated as he was. The problem was the Russians. These days the Russian mob had their hooks into everything from white slavery to identity theft, and they took no prisoners. They were brutal with the competition. A war of attrition with a rival Jamaican posse known as the Dreads was just coming to a long and bloody close, mostly because both sides were exhausted by it, and turf wars were bad for business all around. Somebody, maybe whatever was left of one of the old Mafia families, had brokered a grudging lay-down. The *capos* had lost much of their juice, but you could still go to them for remediation. They knew from settling scores. Then there were the new kids on the block, Mara Salvatrucha, MS-13, a Salvadoran gang that had interpen-etrated the other crime syndicates, with an enormous presence in the federal prison system, where they recruited fresh meat. They hired out as muscle. Unhappily, the learning curve wasn't steep.

"Babs, tell me, please, that you've turned up something, or *any-thing*, on the hijack at Kennedy."

She understood the fork he was in. Homeland Security, the FBI, Port Authority, NYPD's counterterrorist unit. They were raking the ground. Scorched earth. A shipment of military munitions, 5.56, bound for the Gulf, had been boosted. Not an armed robbery. The entire manifest had simply disappeared. It had to be an inside job. There was a leak, obviously, but who had the ammo now? On the open market, it was worth a million bucks. And there were moti-vated buyers. But it wasn't the sellers so much that bothered the feds. The real question was the identity of the end user.

Babs wasn't the only one to think the Russians had a hand in it, and with a buyer already lined up, but she had absolutely nothing to go on.

"I'm getting hammered," the lieutenant said.

"I know that," she said.

"Sorry to take it out on you."

"Don't do it, or don't apologize," she said.

He smiled. "I should have been looking for that," he said. "You're ornery, Babs, but that's what makes you a good cop."

"I've still got diddly-squat, Lieutenant."

"I thought you had an inside guy at ATF."

It was the kind of thing the lieutenant would remember. "Treasury agent named Chapin," she said, "but he's probably been shipped off to Missoula, Montana."

"How come?"

"That thing a year and a half ago. The cell-phone scam. ATF had an oar in the water, and we stepped on their skirts. My guy took the fall for it. Senior in the office."

"There was a low-end guy, too," the lieutenant said.

"Roy Meadows."

"Which started the pissing contest between the Russians and the Dreads."

"Cleaned out the underbrush," she said.

"The way I remember it, Roy had a baby brother."

"Tommy. Went up on a minor accessory charge."

"Figure he's out by now?"

"I can find out."

"Find out first whether your guy Chapin is still assigned to the New York office."

"And if he is?"

"Oh, for John's sake. I have to spell it out for you?"

"You want me to squeeze Chapin."

"What else have we got?"

"We don't have any leverage," Babs said. "I can use him as a last resort, but it has to be a quid pro quo."

"You need something to trade?" the lieutenant asked. "Pick up Tommy Meadows, see if he'll sing for his supper."

The operation had the code name Labyrinth. Its objective was simple. Deny the enemy access. The pooh-bahs at DOD didn't have any real idea what they were up against. If radical Islam had brought the war to our shores, we were going to take it to them.

The "we" here was a private security outfit calling themselves Xynergistics. They had contracts with Defense and State as well as FBI and CIA counterterrorism. Their specialty was cyberwarfare, not physical security. They didn't provide boots on the ground. They looked for virtual footprints.

Lydie Temple was following what appeared to be an anomaly.

Lydie was one of the senior analysts, although she was only twenty-six. She'd done a tour with Naval Security Group, one of the service cryptologic agencies, and then signed on with NSA, the brass ring, but the money in the private sector was too good to turn down, push came to shove.

There was a lot of that going around. Everything was pieced out these days. GIs didn't pull KP anymore because outside contractors bid for food service to the military. Companies like Blackwater offered hazard pay to hired guns, protecting diplomats and aid workers in hot zones. CIA used what were known as proprietaries, the first of which had been Air America, in Vietnam, flying morphine base out of the Iron Triangle, to keep the Saigon regime afloat on China White. It was a turning world. Outsourcing was the rule, not the exception, and chief among its virtues was deniability, an advantage much prized by a beleaguered clandestine intelligence community.

Lydie had a marketable skill set, and the fact that her job paid her three times what she could pull down as a GS-25, major medical thrown in, didn't make her feel dirty. It made her feel necessary.

Computer traffic can be broken down and analyzed any number of different ways. Much of it is simple brute force. The big mainframes at Fort Meade, NSA headquarters, crunched the traffic wholesale. Lydie had developed an algorithm that weeded out the chatter.

Everybody was up against the same problem, the sheer volume of information. Encoded or encrypted, it presented a different set of variables, but most of it was in the clear. Trying to sort it out, classify it by timeliness or perceived risk factor, was like bailing out a sinking ship with a soupspoon. You were overwhelmed, and the boat kept getting lower in the water.

Lydie's bright idea had been to filter the communications not by red-flagging isolated vocabulary (*jihad*, say) or the user networks (Al Jazeera's blog site, for example) — not that these weren't useful — but by context. In other words, she mined the data for patterns rather than the specific. This allowed her a margin for error, but it also enabled her to build up a baseline, what was known in the trade as an order of battle. It didn't indicate the individual airline shoe-bomber, unhappily, but it mapped the links between potential events, a schematic of decentralized command-and-control. Her information had led directly to a successful Predator drone strike against a cell in Yemen, and her star was on the rise.

What she was looking at, in the event, wasn't context. It was odd in that it didn't call attention to itself. It was out of her immediate field of vision, and it was too specific.

And naturally, she followed where it led.

Tommy's PO was a hardheaded career court officer named Helen Torchio. Hardheaded, not hardhearted. She wasn't foolish enough to think Tommy could be entirely reformed, but she had hopes he might be led toward the light. It was a disappointment to her when Detectives DiMello and Beeks showed up.

Tommy's appointment that morning was at ten. The cops were there at a quarter to.

"He's no angel," Helen said to Babs DiMello.

"I was counting on that," Babs said.

"What are you after?"

"Information."

"Tommy's rolled before," Beeks said. He was the junior partner. Helen thought he was too ready to play the hard guy to DiMello's soft and easy. Not that she made Babs for soft.

"Ground rules?" she asked.

Babs nodded. "We want to know if Tommy's heard anything," she said. "I understand there's an issue. If he's hanging with other homies who've done time, you could violate him."

"I'd like not to see that happen," Helen said.

"Understood," Babs told her. "But there's the carrot, and there's the stick. Tommy gives up something useful, he's got my marker. The question might arise how he came by it."

"Makes it awkward," Helen said.

"Awkward for Tommy," Beeks said. "It gives us leverage."

"I meant awkward for me, Detective," Helen said.

Babs cut him a quick look. "Tommy knows how this game is played," she said to the PO. "He plays it like a piano, and he doesn't want to go back in the joint."

"So you're the carrot and I'm the stick," Helen said.

"I don't say I'm not trying to jam Tommy, but will you work with me on this?" Babs asked.

"We're on the same team," Helen said.

"Home-field advantage," Babs said, smiling.

Tommy was a little taken aback to see the two cops waiting in his

PO's office, but he made a quick recovery. "Hey," he said to Babs. "Detective DiMello. How you doing? Sorry, man," he said to Pete Beeks. "I forgot your name."

Beeks didn't introduce himself.

"Tommy, we could use a little help," Babs said.

"Sure." Eager, disingenuous. It was his strong suit. And it helped that they were coming to him, not the other way around.

This was the tricky part, Babs knew. She didn't want to give away all the cards in her hand, but unless she got into the details, Tommy wouldn't know what she was after.

"I'm going to get a cup of coffee," Helen Torchio said.

Tommy understood what that was about. She was telling him he wouldn't violate the terms of his release if he gave the cops any of his current criminal associations.

"The way I remember," Babs DiMello said, after Helen left the room, "your brother Roy had some kind of in with cargo handlers at JFK. Air freight, not passenger baggage. This ring a bell?"

"Yes, ma'am," Tommy said.

"I think there was some talk he knew more than he wanted to tell about the Lufthansa hit."

Tommy nodded. Six million bucks, an inside job.

"Not a major player, of course, or he'd be farting through silk," she said. "He wouldn't have been working nickel-and-dime rackets like that cell-phone scam."

"He might still be alive," Tommy pointed out.

"You want to play with the big dogs, you have to learn to piss in the tall grass," Babs said. "No disrespect, but Roy was never cut out to be a big dog. He didn't have the chops."

"Roy was only half smart," Tommy said. "We both know it."

"So don't be half-assed, Tommy," Beeks said.

"You haven't told me what you want," Tommy said.

"You still got a line into Port Authority?" Babs asked him.

"Their security's a lot tighter these days, after 9/11."

"It might leave something to be desired."

"TSA couldn't find the crack in their ass with a mirror."

Babs smiled in spite of herself. "Well, there's the crack in your ass, and then there's the mirror," she said.

"I hear stuff," he admitted.

"What kind of stuff?" Babs asked.

Tommy shrugged. "I heard of a guy wants to smuggle a tractor-trailer load of smokes up from North Carolina," he said.

"Useful, but not exactly what we're looking for."

"Hey, you wanted a for-instance."

"For instance, what do you hear about an air cargo heist at JFK?"

"Give me a what, I might know a who," he said.

So there it was. He had her in a fork. She had no choice but to spell it out. "A container shipment of 5.56 NATO. Going to Iraq. Somebody lost the manifest and made it disappear."

"That's some heavy lifting," Tommy said.

"Somebody with more muscle than brains," Beeks said. "Seem familiar?"

"I'd only be guessing, but my guess is probably the same as yours," Tommy said. "Viktor Guzenko."

No surprise there. Of the Russian gang lords, Guzenko was one of the most feared, both by the other ethnic crime families in Brighton Beach—even the Chechens, who weren't scared of much—and by the older, more established New York mobs, Irish and Italian. Like the Jamaicans and the brutally violent MS-13, Guzenko settled his scores in blood. He was reported to have survived half-a-dozen assassination attempts by rivals and his own colleagues. If anybody was contemptuous of bringing down federal heat, Guzenko was your man. But it led nowhere. It was an educated guess, as Tommy had said.

"What can you find out?" Babs asked him.

"I'm not going to wear a wire," Tommy said.

She looked at Beeks, surprised. Neither one of them had even thought to suggest it. Why so quick to say no to something they hadn't put on the table?

"You think he's blowing smoke?" Beeks asked her after they let Tommy go.

"Maybe he knows more than he's ready to tell," Babs said.

...

Of course, that was the impression Tommy wanted to leave. He'd played the cops before. They were always a handful of gimme and a mouthful of much obliged.

The question was what to give.

Not that Tommy had much to offer. He'd been bluffing Babs, and he knew better than to try and bluff the Russians. He'd gotten away with it once, and nobody had read his handwriting in it, but he didn't think he'd luck out a second time.

DiMello had given him the lead, though. He knew Brooklyn South would have already squeezed the guys working the terminal, and the feds would have put them through the wringer, too, but you couldn't get blood from a stone. Tommy figured the cops had drawn a blank, or they wouldn't be grasping at straws. Thing was, after 9/11, security had tightened up, but more often than not, the new procedures simply made everything more inconvenient and cumbersome. They didn't address the underlying problem and served to create grievances. The union rank and file didn't appreciate being taken to task for something that wasn't in fact their responsibility. Background checks were already strict. The heightened clearance requirements made for bad blood. Loss of seniority because your next of kin came from Pakistan was one step away from a class-action lawsuit.

Tommy had the one arrow in his quiver. Either the cargo handlers knew nothing or they were unwilling to speculate. You didn't give the FBI the loose end of a ball of yarn, not if you might be open to uncomfortable questions, none of which had dick to do with international terrorism, but you were vulnerable.

Tommy knew a bar in South Ozone. He took the subway out to Queens.

You spring for a round of draft beers, it's an investment.

Jeremy Chapin, she found out, was now heading up ATF regional out of Phoenix. AIC, agent in charge, so on paper it was a promotion, but if you read the runes, it might just as easily be a career ender.

"Detective DiMello," he said when Babs got him on the phone. "Good to hear from you." He sounded as if he meant it, and Babs felt a little guilty, since she'd played an inadvertent part in getting him reassigned from the New York office.

"I've got a situation here," she said. She told him about the Kennedy hijack. "There's a Russian gangster named Guzenko who might have a piece of it, but nobody's talking. They're all either bought off or scared."

"Georgian, actually," Chapin said.

"Sorry?"

"Guzenko's a Georgian, like Joe Stalin."

"You know him?"

"Not personally, but I hear he's a ruthless bastard."

"Who can he sell to, that kind of volume?"

Chapin grunted. "I could point you at some guys," he said. "Across the border from El Paso, the Juarez cartel."

"Drug lords."

"It's a free-fire zone down there, you hadn't heard. The gangs are whacking each other ten or a dozen a day. And there's a lot of collateral damage, civilian casualties."

"With all due respect, you've got a dog in the fight."

"Sure, it's my area of responsibility," Chapin said. "But you're not going to sell 5.56 NATO to the *muj* or the rebels in Chechnya. Weapon of choice in that neck of the woods is the AK, 7.62 Soviet. Down in Mexico, it's the M4."

The M4 was a slightly shortened configuration of the M16, U.S. military issue. "How come?" Babs asked him.

Chapin blew out his breath. "Think about the provenance," he said. "Where do the cartels get their guns? They don't have a source for Warsaw Pact surplus weapons."

"Right," she said, catching up. "They smuggle guns in from the U.S."

"So yeah, I've got a dog in the fight," he said. "All the border states, this is heavy traffic. The hot-button issue is illegals, but that's bullshit. What comes north is drugs, what goes south is guns and money. You want a market for ammo? You could turn that stuff in forty-eight hours, cash money."

"How do I get it there?"

"Label it plasma-screen TVs. How the hell do I know? All *I* know is, it slips through the cracks each and every day."

"Big crack, for containerized cargo to fall through."

There was a long hesitation on the Arizona end of the line. She could picture him frowning. "Containerized?" he asked.

"Yeah, we're talking a couple of million rounds."

"What was it doing at JFK?"

"Waiting shipment."

"No," he said. "You ship containers by rail or sea. You can't get something that size and weight on an aircraft, not even a C-5A Galaxy. A container would be across the river, at the docks in Jersey, or downstate, McGuire AFB. And it would be broken down into something manageable, thousand-pound pallets."

"Not my information."

"Either your information is mistaken or you're looking at this through the wrong end of the telescope," he said. "That container shouldn't have been at Kennedy. It couldn't be loaded as air freight."

She studied the problem. "It would have come in by truck."

"A semi could haul it. It could go out the same way."

"Let me get back to you," she said.

"Keep me in the loop," Chapin said. He hung up.

He had Washington on speed dial, Babs figured. Maybe this was going to break open. ATF had resources she didn't. Not that it mattered who made the case. Still, better if she stayed in front of the curve. The container. Where did *that* lead?

Xynergistics had good computer capacity, but nothing like the big arrays available to the intelligence community. Lydie Temple put her data together and ran it by her boss, and got his approval to forward the package to their NSA contact.

He e-mailed her back two hours later, which was way fast.

CALL ON THE SECURE LINE
RAPTOR

The cover name was an inside joke, a reference to Omnivore, the FBI targeted data-mining program, now on the shelf and collecting nothing but dust. NSA had newer-generation software.

Raptor was a career spook named Felix Soto.

Lydie went into the communications center and signed onto a terminal. It was a dedicated landline to Fort Meade.

Felix picked up at his end immediately. "I bow to genius," he said.

She laughed. He was teasing, but she was pleased.

"Seriously," he said. "You're onto something. I bought some time on the Cray, and we're showing consistency." He was talking about one of the half-dozen supercomputers in the bowels of the agency. "How'd you snap to this?"

"Random pattern," she said. "It was just background noise. Idle hands are the devil's plaything."

"Once you know what to look for, it's pretty hard to miss."

"How long have we been missing it?"

"You cut right to the chase, kid. We'll walk the cat back. Hopefully, we can come up with a timeline."

"It's not of purely historical interest," she said.

"You got that right," Felix said. "We're working against the clock. You know how much materiel is floating around out there, in transit, or waiting shipment? Any of it falls through the cracks, it's a raft of grief." He hung up.

Well. Out of her hands. The national security apparatus would grind into motion. It was unhappy that they were only now playing catch-up ball.

Because here was what Lydie had stumbled across. DOD, the Defense Department, contracted with common carriers, UPS and FedEx, long-haul freight companies like Old Dominion and United Van Lines and R&L, and they were on an approved list. But the other thing was that they all had websites. You could go on the Internet and schedule a pickup, a box of cookies you were sending your mom, for example, or a container cargo of 5.56 NATO, for another. Somebody had hacked into one of the websites and misdirected a shipment. Not your mom's cookies, either.

How many shipments? she wondered.

According to Tommy's guy, all you needed was a couple of cans of spray paint and some stencils.

"Containers are labeled," the guy told him. His name was Kaufman. "Originating shipper, destination, routing logs. It's written right on the box."

"Everybody knows what's inside?"

Kaufman shook his head. "They use an alphanumeric code, referencing the load ticket. The contents are on the manifest, not the container. What gets marked are the transit points. Yokohama to Los Angeles. L.A. to Biloxi. Every time that box transits a freight yard, the yard's route number goes on it, and then it gets handed off to the next station of the cross."

"What if the numbers are off?"

"Then it sits in Biloxi."

Or at JFK. "How often does that happen?" Tommy asked.

"We don't get many orphans."

"What happens if you do?"

"You get dispatch to crosscheck."

"Could something sit there for a week and not be noticed?"

Kaufman shrugged. "We move a lot of cargo," he said. "The yardmaster has a clipboard full."

"So the answer is yes."

"I'll tell you," Kaufman said. "You could put a nuclear weapon in a container. You don't ship it from Dubai, you send it through Singapore. It takes six weeks to get to New York. You fudge the numbers, it sits on a dock, unclaimed. You want I should spell it out any more?"

Tommy had been upstate when the Trade Center went down, but he didn't need it spelled out for him.

"I don't know what you're sniffing around this for, Tommy," Kaufman said, "but I smell trouble."

"You know a hood named Viktor Guzenko?" Tommy asked.

Kaufman's face shut like a door.

The agent from ATF's New York office was a woman. Babs DiMello had to wonder whether that was just the luck of the draw or they'd sent another woman to soften Babs up. The name on her ID read Phoebe Kreuz. They were about the same age.

"Jeremy Chapin's been burning up the wires," Kreuz said.

"You getting any collateralization?"

"Other agencies? Sure."

"What's the FBI given up?" Babs asked.

"Well, the Bureau . . ." Kreuz paused. "You don't change a culture overnight. They get ahold of something, if they're the lead agency, they sink their teeth into it. And they're used to protecting their turf. It's like Hoover never died."

"Like trying to turn the *Titanic* around."

"More like trying to turn the iceberg," Kreuz said.

She had a quick smile, and Babs was warming up to her.

"You'd be surprised at what turns up, if you cultivate a relationship," Kreuz said. "For instance, Jerry Chapin tells me you're the go-to gal, Brooklyn South."

"That's flattering."

"I didn't bring a box of chocolates, but I've got something to share. We've received specific intelligence."

"FBI?"

Again the quick smile. "NSA," Kreuz said. "You know what I'm talking about?"

Intercepted communications. "I hear the initials stand for No Such Agency," Babs said.

"I can't speak to sources and methods," Kreuz said. "Plain fact is, I don't *know* what their sources and methods are. But here's what they came up with. War materiel is being rerouted. Somebody's hacked the websites of the shippers."

"Chapin said there was no way a container should be at JFK, because an aircraft couldn't lift that kind of weight."

"Why did it end up at Kennedy?"

"Ease of access," Babs said.

"What happened to it?"

"It disappeared."

"Yeah," Kreuz said. "We're having the same conversation everybody else has been having for a week. What's different is, we know it's not just a target of opportunity."

"It's not accidental. It's organized."

"That's some serious diversion going on. There might be a host of corruption in Baghdad and Kabul, but we're talking about stuff that never sees the Gulf."

"Chapin says it's going to the drug lords in Mexico."

"I don't care where it's going. I want it to stay here, or we keep track of it, and it goes where it's supposed to go."

"You and me both," Babs said. She had a brother serving in the National Guard, posted to Afghanistan.

"What about this Russian gangster, Guzenko?"

"I'm hitting a wall. These guys don't rat each other out, or if they do, they're dead before it ever gets to a grand jury. People in the life are terrified of Guzenko."

"You get anything out of NYPD Organized Crime?"

"Known associates. Involvement in sex slavery, protection, identity theft. But it's a lock nobody can pick."

"Identity theft suggests some minimal computer literacy."

"I see where you're going," Babs said. "Hacking the shippers' websites. It's not that I don't make the guy for it, or that he's not capable of it. The issue is, we've got nothing we could take to a judge. There's no chain of evidence."

"So we're still sucking air."

DiMello's cell chimed. She looked at the caller ID. Tommy Meadows. "Wait one," she said to Phoebe Kreuz.

Tommy was at a Starbucks near Prospect Park.

"Be there in ten," Babs said. She broke the connection.

"Yes, no?" Kreuz asked.

"Maybe we got, maybe we don't," Babs said. She took her weapon out of the desk drawer and snapped it on her belt. She stood up. "You down with it?"

Kreuz opened her jacket to show a gun, strong-side carry. It looked to Babs like a steel-frame Sig, probably a .357 or .40 Smith.

"Let's go buy this guy a cup of coffee," Babs said.

Porfírio and Hernán were made men, MS-13, stone killers with teardrop tattoos at the outside corner of each eye, a trickle of dark ink, crocodile tears, one for every man they'd murdered. Porfírio was lean and quick, stripped down like a racecar, while Hernán was blocked out like a diesel truck, all the muscle between his ears. They'd met at Attica. They were in their late twenties, and already they had thirty years in the prison system between them, going back to Juvenile. Like other immigrants to the New World, the Italians and the Irish, Latinos and Chinese, some of them had turned to crime, muling drugs and illegals, but the Maras were enforcers. Porfírio and Hernán had never met the *Vor*, the boss of thieves, but they knew they were taking his money. Guzenko's chosen intermediary was a man named Iosif Bagratyön, another Georgian.

He gave them a name and a photograph.

"*¿Qué tan pronto?*" Porfírio asked. How soon?

"As soon as you can," the Georgian said.

"Does it matter where?" Porfírio asked.

"Near his workplace, or his family. Either one."

"Are there special instructions?"

"Make it messy," Bagratyön told them. "Make it hurt. Make it ugly. We want to send a message."

Porfírio smiled. He enjoyed using a knife.

Brooklyn South liaised with ATF and Port Authority. They didn't need a warrant. All they needed was enough people to cover the ground and maintain a security perimeter.

"Take it apart," Babs's lieutenant said. And they did.

They started at the north end of the cargo terminal and worked their way down. The paved area was three quarters of a mile deep, and the warehouse space was that again, most of it two stories. They checked all of it, cargo trailers, packed goods, pallets, and containers. If the containers were sealed, they opened the seals and locks, over the objections of the yard boss, who was responsible for the safety of shipping.

"I guess you've got the advantage of me, ma'am," he said.

"Yes," Phoebe Kreuz said. "I do."

If what Kaufman had told Tommy was right, the container was possibly hidden in plain sight, overlooked and mislabeled.

They found one at the far end of the terminal. There was no matching manifest for the routing codes stenciled on the side of the box. The yardmaster looked embarrassed.

"Where did this come from?" the lieutenant asked him.

The guy looked in his book. "If the numbers are right, the originating shipment was out of Holloman AFB, in New Mexico."

"Find out what the inventory was, and the date they shipped it."

"Right." The yard boss got on his cell phone.

"You think?" the lieutenant asked Babs.

She was looking at the numbers on the container. Holloman would be the first, then transit through Chicago or Atlanta or Louisville, which was a big repple-depple for UPS freight, and a final stateside destination before overseas delivery. It was the last number that must have been altered. You sprayed over the legitimate routing code with Rustoleum, aluminum flavor, or rust red, and stenciled in a bogus number in black. You only had to be off one digit. She didn't blame the dispatcher. It was a hole in the system. But it had been exploited by somebody on the inside.

"Pick up Tommy's source, this guy Kaufman," she told Beeks. "We need to sweat him."

The yard boss put his hand over the phone. "Four hundred thousand square feet of AM-2 matting, for temporary airstrips, a load of desert camo, tents, tarps, boots and uniforms, and five million rounds of 5.56 hardball. Shipped ten days ago by common carrier."

"Crack it open," the lieutenant said.

They got the bolt cutters.

Phoebe Kreuz was the first one inside. The box was empty.

. . .

Lydie Temple had more than one arrow in her quiver. She was gratified when Felix Soto called back from Fort Meade to tell her that her lead had panned out and NSA had developed actionable intelligence to give ATF, but she decided to follow the virtual trail. Jack knows Jill is a single link and means nothing by itself. Likewise if Jill knows Joe. But if Joe happens to know Jack, you've squared a circle.

It was an oversimplification, but crudely accurate. You could model the data footprint in any number of ways. More than a few jihadi, for example, posted on Facebook, which made it possible to penetrate their cell systems, supposedly independent of one another. Jack and Jill are careless enough to tag Joe.

Another way to model the footprint was to monitor the servers, which is what Lydie was doing. When you went online, for whatever reason, e-mail, shopping, surfing the Net, you were signed on through an interface, a commercial provider like MSN or AOL, or some other networked facility, be it government, academic, the public library, a private employer. It was open-source, the web address could be tracked. There were in fact programs that could mimic a user's individual keystrokes. Lydie was fishing in a deep pond.

Her particular target this time around was the crime ring that had hacked the freight shippers' websites. It didn't take genius, she knew that from experience. What it took was time, a feel for the world of cybersecurity, and maybe a lucky break. Lydie had the time, and an insider's confidence she could pick pretty much any lock in virtual space. She was hoping she might catch some luck, like the other guy.

She'd personalized him. It was a convenient fiction, not that he was even necessarily a *he*, but she thought of him as Little Ivan, and she'd given him a profile. Probably not a career criminal, just some kid who'd been recruited because he was a computer geek. Into video games, built his own systems from generic components, knew enough code to write basic software, had a garage or a basement full of discarded CRT monitors, blown motherboards, old memory chips. Ivan was her own mirror image, the girl she'd grown out of but not outgrown.

She approached the problem from his point of view. To penetrate the websites, you had to reverse-engineer the security protocols, so first she familiarized herself with the navigation tools and began looking for a chink in the armor, but this got her nowhere. Each site was designed around a dedicated platform, which didn't allow you to skip a step. You had to fill out a series of required fields in each window before you could access the next window. It was intended to idiot-proof shipping procedures, but it was cumbersome. Still, she had to exhaust the obvious. There might be an easy way in. Little Ivan had found it. There wasn't. Lydie shifted her sights and began the more laborious process of finding the back door.

Kaufman had been turned inside out like a sock, skinned to the bone. At some point he'd lost control of his bladder and bowels, but his bowels had been left in a slippery heap between his knees. The EMTs were shoveling him off the pavement and into a body bag. Babs DiMello had talked to the crime scene techs and gotten no joy. They could give her a time frame, but that was about it.

"No witnesses," Phoebe Kreuz, the ATF agent, said.

"Fat chance," Babs told her.

"We know this is related to the hijack."

Babs shrugged. "How not?" she asked. "Somebody's cleaning up the loose ends."

"Guzenko?"

"My guess. But here's what you have to understand. The guy doesn't sit on his hands. Even if he had nothing to do with the hijack, he'd circle the wagons. He doesn't want it walked back to him. He eliminates the chain of evidence. Anything and everybody. Nuns, pregnant mothers, you name it."

"Collateral damage."

"That's one way of looking at it."

"Who's next on his list?"

Babs glanced at the EMTs scooping Kaufman up. "If it were me they went to work on, I would have given up a name."

"Any name?"

Babs was thinking Tommy Meadows.

...

Tommy knew he was on the dime. He'd overplayed his hand with Kaufman, and if word got back to the Russians, they'd be paying Tommy a visit. Tommy didn't welcome the attention. Last time

around he'd managed to stay out of sight, but last time around
he'd had a counterweight.

What could he use this time?

Don't be half-assed, the cops had told him, meaning don't be
a wise guy who wasn't wised up, like his brother Roy, but Guzenko
was sucking all the air out of the room, and Tommy was fighting
for breath. There had to be an angle he could play, or a stalking
horse, somebody he could throw under the bus.

He caught the train into midtown and went to talk to Nico Constantine. Nico was his wholesaler, the guy he'd gone to Maryland
to buy guns for. Nico was down with the Westies, the Irish mob that
operated out of Hell's Kitchen and along the West Side waterfront,
but he was equal opportunity. You could be a Mick or an Italian, a
Latin gangbanger, a Vietnamese punk, or a Rasta. The only color
that mattered to Nico was green.

Tommy knew this was going to be delicate. Word had gotten
around about the Kennedy heist, and there was heat from the
feds, so he couldn't come right out and ask. He had to churn the
waters. Nico, like a shark, would sniff the bait.

They met at a bar on Eleventh. Tommy stood the drinks, Stoli
on the rocks for Nico, Jameson's and a bump back for himself.

Tommy eased into it. "I've got a buyer," he said. He took a sip of
his whiskey and chased it with a swallow of beer.

"Provenance?" Nico asked. He meant, how did they happen on
you?

"Couple of guys I met upriver," Tommy said. "Dirty white boys.
Took a fall on a state beef, resisting arrest, assaulting an officer."

"Retards, in other words," Nico said.

"Smart guys don't do hard time."

"Smart guys don't get caught. Who are these morons to me?"

"It's a militia group in the Adirondacks."

"Oh, *real* morons. We talking Timothy McVeigh?"

"I don't think they're looking to blow up buildings with fertil-
izer bombs. They want to stockpile guns and ammo, waiting on the
end times, civil disorder."

Nico snorted. "End times," he said. "Maybe it'll clean up the
gene pool, weed out some of those skinheads."

"Cash money, all the same," Tommy said.

"What do they want?" Nico asked him.

"M4s, modified for full auto, 5.56 hardball, mil spec."

Nico shook his head. "The guns, not that easy, but ammo, I might have a source."

Tommy veered away. "Why are the guns so hard?"

"Gimme a break," Nico said. "Selective fire? Weapons like that don't fall off a turnip truck."

"What's your price point?"

"What kind of quantity are we talking?"

"Twenty thousand rounds."

"Let me do the math," Nico said.

"Turnaround time?" Tommy asked.

Nico shrugged. "I need to call some people," he said.

"I need to get back to my guys with a ballpark."

"You need to give it a rest. We're not selling Mary Kay."

Lydie had piggybacked an Internet server that hosted a regional company called Southwest Air Cargo, out of Albuquerque. They were a subsidiary of a larger international freight carrier headquartered in Toronto. Once she'd signed on and created a dummy account, it took her the better part of the day to walk it back to an outfit called CyberResources.com, but their website was firewalled. She e-mailed Felix Soto at NSA. He flagged her back inside the hour with surveillance logs on the target, its physical location, direct contact information for ATF's New York office, and authorization for a FISA warrant.

"Ten out of ten," he added in a postscript. "How do I get you back?"

I couldn't afford the pay cut, she almost answered, but it wouldn't have been the exact truth. What she'd surrender, if she went back to Fort Meade, was her independence. Lydie enjoyed having her autonomy. She relished the occasional compliment, but she didn't miss being under NSA authority. Felix Soto was a better than decent boss. What got in the way was politics.

She called ATF. They patched her through to a cell.

"Kreuz." The voice was a woman's.

Lydie hesitated.

Agent Kreuz let her hang in the dead air.

"I've got the Guzenko computer penetration," Lydie said.

"Your place or mine?"

"Whichever works."

"Meet you at Brooklyn South," the ATF agent said. She rang off.

Not a lot of bedside manner, Lydie thought. She picked up her paperwork and downloaded the rest onto a flash drive. Push comes to shove, do a core dump. The habits of NSA culture.

Bay Ridge, just off the expressway at Sixty-fifth. A neighborhood shopping plaza, shoe repair, manicures, a tanning salon, Chinese takeout, dry cleaning, a liquor store. Mom-and-pop, generic and modest. CyberResources was an end unit. Fax and copy services, computer repair, photo and graphics, web access. The ATF agent, Phoebe Kreuz, had the lead, with Babs and her team in support. They took it down at noon.

There were three people working in the shop, one at the counter up front, for customer service, a tech at the back, trying to recover files from a damaged hard drive, and the boss, in her office. The first order of business was to deny them immediate telephone access, and the cops smothered them like a blanket, no cuffs, all courtesy, but patting them down and confiscating their cells. The woman who owned the business went through the usual boilerplate. Kreuz and DiMello ignored her.

"This isn't *Russia,*" the woman protested angrily.

Lydie Temple was fascinated. She knew this to be her Little Ivan, not the avatar she'd imagined, a college dropout obsessed with video games, but a tough, middle-aged pro. Her dossier with Homeland Security identified her as Ludmilla Shevardnadze, a legal immigrant from Tbilisi, with an MBA and a second master's in computer science. She was on the pad with Guzenko for five large a month. After her initial bluster, she folded almost immediately. She had experience of the security services in her home country, after all. They were the same the world over. You played ball or they dropped you down a well.

"Who's this guy Bagratyön?" Phoebe Kreuz asked DiMello.

"Joe Bags, he's Guzenko's *consigliere.*"

"I want witness protection," Ludmilla said to them.

"We'll negotiate," Kreuz told her. "You keep talking. The deal comes later."

"I'll stop talking."

"No, you won't. I can render you back to Georgia inside of seventy-two hours, without a hearing. You're on a felony beef, toots. You think Guzenko can get to you here? You don't figure he can get to you while you're sunbathing by the Black Sea?"

"*Suka,*" Ludmilla muttered. Bitch.

"You got that right," Phoebe said to her.

Lydie was exploring the computer array.

"What have we got?" Babs asked.

"She left a big footprint," Lydie said.

"Can you break it down?"

"Probably, given some time."

"We don't have a window," Kreuz said. "Where's the cargo?"

Nico thumped the canister on the table. Olive drab. It weighed sixty pounds. One thousand rounds of 5.56, full metal jacket.

"Three hundred dollars," he said. "Round numbers, if we're talking twenty boxes, six thousand."

Tommy looked at Beeks.

Beeks had gone white sidewall. He didn't have jailhouse tats, but he looked like a high school hockey coach from Saranac Lake, which fit the profile.

"Earnest money," Tommy said.

Beeks counted it out, uncomfortably, which fit the profile, too. He was supposed to be a rube in the big town.

"When do we do this?" Tommy asked.

"Tonight," Nico said.

"Your call," Tommy said.

Beeks had his cell phone out.

"Put that away," Nico said.

Beeks looked at him, surprised, but he folded it closed.

"No surprises," Nico said to Tommy.

"Six K, Tommy gets ten percent," Beeks told DiMello.

Babs nodded. It would be marked money, of course, and Nico wasn't going to have it for long, but they needed the full amount to make the buy or there'd be no case. "Can we shake it out of 100 Centre?" she asked the lieutenant.

Shorthand for Police Plaza, NYPD headquarters. "It's worth a shot," the lieutenant said.

Babs figured the odds were good they'd get it. If they could break the Kennedy heist, there'd be plenty of credit to go around, and everybody involved would be rolling in clover.

"You run the numbers?" the lieutenant asked.

Lydie Temple had downloaded the image from Beeks's cell. There was a control code stamped on the ammo box, and she compared it to the manifest from Holloman AFB. She got a match. Nico was fencing military supplies.

"Twenty ammo canisters out of five hundred," the lieutenant said. "Who's bidding on the rest?"

Babs looked at Phoebe Kreuz. "ATF in Phoenix thinks it's going to be sold to the Mexican cartels," she said. "That's an educated guess."

"I'm not saying Jerry Chapin's wrong," Phoebe said, "but if the cartels were the end buyer, it would be a done deal."

"I see where you're going," Babs said. "Nico Constantine's not a big enough player to swing a million-dollar sale."

"If he can lay his hands on it and piece out a part of the shipment, then it's still in New York."

"We have surveillance on Nico?" the lieutenant asked.

"*We* do," Phoebe said, meaning ATF.

"Either he picks up the munitions or, more likely, arranges a physical meet, because he can't front the money, he needs his buyer there," the lieutenant said. "So a warehouse, a pallet on the back of a truck, whatever. He has to make contact."

"Nice to get a photo op with Guzenko," Babs said.

"They won't meet face-to-face, not until the buy, if then," Phoebe said. "It'll be the other guy, Guzenko's bagman."

"Can you monitor his phone calls?" the lieutenant asked.

"Nico? Not if he's using a throwaway cell."

Lydie Temple cleared her throat.

"Ma'am?" the lieutenant asked her.

"I know somebody who might help," she said.

"And who would that be?"

"I'm not at liberty to say," she told him.

The lieutenant raised his eyebrows.

"Is this the same source that gave us Ludmilla Shevardnadze and the computer shop?" Phoebe Kreuz asked.

Lydie nodded.

"I'd trust it," Phoebe told the lieutenant.

"Okay," he said. "Now, correct me if I'm wrong, people. We've got what's-her-butt, so we know how they hacked into the shippers' websites, and she'll roll over on Guzenko to avoid deportation. We've also got Nico Constantine, who's ready to sell us stolen goods. What we're missing is a direct connection between Guzenko and the contraband. Let's find it."

They broke up to work the phones.

Nico called at seven. Tommy was at a bar off Ocean Parkway, watching a rerun of *Highlander* on cable, playing with a plate of Buffalo wings and nursing a beer. Nico gave him a location, a time, and very specific instructions. Then he hung up. The chicken wings had gotten cold and gummy. Tommy didn't have much appetite. His stomach was sour.

Truth be told, he *really* didn't want to make the meet. He was setting Nico up, and when it went down, you wouldn't have to be a particle physicist to read Tommy's part in all of it. But he didn't have a choice. The cops had him over a barrel, and who knew from the Russians? Maybe it was back to front, and Nico was the one setting Tommy up. Word on the street was already out about what had happened to Kaufman, turned skinside inside, his guts in his lap, and a Colombian necktie, his throat cut and his tongue hanging out underneath his jaw.

A lesson for a fink. If you eat with the devil, use a long spoon.

No help for it. Tommy pushed the plate of wings away uneaten and settled his tab. On the sidewalk outside, he called Beeks. They had forty-five minutes.

"Is there enough time for you to make this happen?" Lydie asked.

She was on an unsecured line to Felix Soto.

Felix wasn't happy talking on an open phone, but it was a calculated risk. Chances were nobody was intercepting their conversation, except for NSA, of course. "Satellite uplink," he said.

"Neither of these guys is going to be wearing a wire."

"Understood. All we need is a cell phone."

She gave him Beeks's number. "They'll be frisked when they go in," she said, "and Guzenko's security will disable the cells first thing. You'll lose the signal."

"It doesn't matter," he said. "Once we triangulate the meeting place, we can monitor the EM radiation. The other guys, cell or landline."

She knew Felix controlled the technology.

"Any idea of the general neighborhood?" he asked.

"Brighton Beach," she told him.

"So it's not the actual handover."

"Guzenko doesn't want to buy a pig in a poke."

"They bury their mistakes, the Georgians," Felix said.

Café Kavkaz was in the shadow of the elevated tracks, the Q line that took you to Coney Island a couple of stops down.

The restaurant on the ground floor was long and low, with pressed-tin ceilings and old wooden paddle fans that stirred the air only slightly. The lighting was subdued but not dim. At the front, there were booths along one wall, the seats furnished in worn burgundy leather, and a bar along the other. Table seating was toward the back. There was a small stage and a three-piece balalaika band. The room's acoustics were hard, and the noise level high, the place better than half full.

Nico was waiting at the bar when Tommy and Beeks walked in. He waved them over. He was drinking Moskovskaya, straight up in a chilled glass, with lemon peel. He signaled the bartender for two more. Not that it would have been Tommy's choice. His guts were churning with anxiety.

They clicked rims.

Nico knocked his drink back. "Check out those two cougars on the prowl," he said, grinning, lifting his chin.

Tommy glanced over his shoulder.

DiMello and Kreuz looked the part, he thought, sharp pants suits, good haircuts, neither one of them a dog. Kreuz was teasing the bartender, talking the virtues of a flight of vodka, a tasting. DiMello was babbling away mindlessly on her cell.

"We're not here to talk pussy," Beeks said.

Nico shrugged. "They'll still be here when we're done, and maybe drunk enough by then to handle a twofer."

If you wanted your back broken and your limp dick handed to you, Tommy thought.

The headwaiter came over. "Your table is ready," he said.

They followed him. He took them to a stairway next to the kitchen.

"Private room," Nico said.

The headwaiter tipped his head. They went upstairs without him.

The muscle was waiting for them on the second floor. They patted them down, as Lydie had predicted, and took their cell phones,

Nico's too. They shook out the batteries and handed them back. Nico suddenly seemed less confident about where this was all going. Tommy had no confidence at all.

It was a long railroad corridor. There were in fact a couple of private dining rooms to either side, which they passed, but the office was at the very back of the building, and they went in.

Bagratyön was waiting.

It was very basic. A desk, a phone. No computer. Some old oak filing cabinets that might have dated back to the Truman administration. It wasn't a command post. It was a trap.

"Your buyer," Bagratyön said. "Who is he?"

"Six thousand," Beeks told him. He put it on the table and stepped back.

Bagratyön ignored him. "That wasn't what I asked," he said to Nico.

"Tommy's never played me false," Nico said, getting some balls, finally. "He comes to me with a deal, you can take it to the bank."

Tommy wasn't sure he enjoyed the compliment. Bagratyön was leaning over the desk, his weight on his fists, but there was somebody else in the room, watching from the shadows. It had to be the *Vor*, the boss of thieves.

"Nothing's in the bank," Bagratyön said.

"The money's right there," Nico said.

Bagratyön shook his head. "We put our trust in you, Nico," he said, almost sadly, "but we punish betrayal."

"What's going on?" Beeks asked. "Are we doing the deal or not?"

"The answer is *not*," Bagratyön said.

"This isn't right," Beeks said, turning to Nico.

"We'll make it right," Nico said.

Tommy knew it wasn't going to happen.

Guzenko stepped forward, into the light. He gestured to the two bodyguards. "Take them outside and kill them," he said.

The SWAT unit went in front and back, on DiMello's signal. Babs and Kreuz were already at the head of the stairs.

There was a third bodyguard in the hallway, covering the door to the office. He barked something in Russian and drew his weapon.

Kreuz dropped to a crouch and put him down, two center chest, one to the head, the Mozambique drill, so called, in case he was wearing body armor. The shots were incredibly loud in the enclosed space. Babs slipped past Kreuz and took up position on the far side of the door. Kreuz moved up. SWAT was crowding into the stairwell.

"Federál'naya polítsiya," Kreuz called, to be heard through the closed door. *"Bez pomogí."*

It figured the ATF agent would speak Russian, Babs thought. She didn't know what it meant, but she knew it meant business.

"Sdavat'sya," a man's voice called back from inside.

Kreuz nodded to the lead SWAT uniform, who'd come up behind her, the rest of his team lining the corridor, weapons at the ready. He drove a kick at the lockset, putting his full weight behind it. The jamb splintered and the door sagged open. He ducked away, his M4 at battery, full auto, safety off. Kreuz and DiMello went in and immediately stepped back to either side of the door, so they were out of SWAT's field of fire.

There were seven guys in the room, six of them with their hands behind their heads. Even the *consigliere*, Bagratyön, was alarmed by the show of force. Only the one guy, standing a little to the left of the desk, seemed indifferent, his lizard's eyes almost sleepy. Guzenko. Babs felt a chill.

"Vnizú," Agent Kreuz snapped at them. "Down," she repeated in English.

They all hit the deck. Again, except for Guzenko.

"Sergeant," she said, over her shoulder.

SWAT used plastic flex cuffs on the three Georgians and the three Americans and got them to their feet.

"Where is it?" Phoebe Kreuz asked Guzenko. *"Gde est'?"*

"Yëb tvoyu mat'," he told her.

Babs had heard enough Russian to know what he'd said.

"We've got you for trafficking," Phoebe said. "You want to avoid the hard time and a trip back to Tbilisi, your choice."

He said the same thing again.

"Man of few words," Phoebe remarked to Babs.

The others had been led out, and the room was empty now but for the three of them.

"We've got Ludmilla," Babs said to him. "And your tough guys will crack, they always do. You give us the cargo, you can plead down. It's a one-time offer."

Guzenko didn't answer her. He stepped over to the desk and began emptying his pockets.

God save us from the hard guys, Babs thought. Usually they folded under pressure, to save their own skins, but Guzenko was immune to threat. She looked at Phoebe. Phoebe shrugged.

Guzenko patted his jacket. He looked at what he'd laid out on the desk. He leaned down and slid open one of the drawers.

"No," Babs said sharply.

He put his hand inside the desk drawer.

Phoebe Kreuz shot him before he took it out. The .40 Smith caught him in the bridge of the nose. His head snapped back. The exit wound pasted brains and bone fragments to the wall, and Guzenko dropped like a wet bag of sand.

Babs went and looked in the desk drawer. There was no gun. He'd been reaching for a disposable cigarette lighter.

Kreuz reholstered. She looked at the dead man on the floor and then into the drawer. "Oh," she said. "My bad."

Bagratyön knew where the bodies were buried, literally. He gave up everything he could in hopes of a reduced sentence. There was the money-laundering trail, and Guzenko's likely successor in the chain of command, a road map to the crew's structure and operations, even the two Maras, Porfírio and Hernán, Kaufman's killers, although they proved impossible to trace. And last but not least, a complete inventory of black-market goods.

It was in a warehouse off the Shore Parkway, near a marina out by Floyd Bennett Field. They found the ammo and the rest of the stolen cargo from Holloman, along with laptops, digital LCD monitors, computer peripherals, unlicensed software, pirated DVDs, Rolex counterfeits, generic pharmaceuticals, power tools, auto parts, and fifty cases of fruit-flavored condoms.

"It's a good bust, DiMello," the lieutenant told her.

"Thank you, sir," she said.

"Too bad we couldn't take Nico Constantine down with them."

"Fortunes of war, Lieutenant."

"There'll be a next time. Guy like that, he'll step on his dick, sooner or later."

"I'll forward his case jacket to Manhattan Midtown."

"You square things with Tommy's PO?" he asked.

She nodded.

"That kid's got nine lives," the lieutenant said.

The issue was, they couldn't pop Nico without violating Tommy, so they had to maintain the fiction that Nico and Tommy, and Beeks, undercover, in character as the upstate buyer from some Aryan brotherhood, were side cards to the main event. They got a pass. There was no other way to play it.

But it gave Babs a marker she could call in down the road. She had Tommy's balls in her pocket, and he knew it.

Not that he's worried. One thing at a time, is how Tommy deals. He's up in Riverdale again, visiting his grandmother. It's a beautiful fall day, crisp and clear, with just enough breeze off the river that she needs a lap robe. He's pushing her around the grounds in her wheelchair. The gravel on the path crunches underfoot. He's telling her a story, full of gangsters and gunrunners. She doesn't really follow it. Too complicated, too many foreign names, too many people she doesn't know.

She's happy enough with the sound of his voice.

CLARK HOWARD

The Street Ends at the Cemetery

FROM *Ellery Queen's Mystery Magazine*

AS CORY EVANS WALKED toward his car in the staff parking lot of the state prison, he had to pass the visitors' parking lot, and that was where the woman was sitting, on a cast-iron bench bolted to the ground, under a punch-press metal sign from the prison machine shop that read BUS STOP. It was cloudy and overcast, the first threatening sprinkles of rain beginning.

Cory walked past her, giving her only a glance, but a glance was enough for his trained corrections-officer mind to snap a mental picture of her: short-cropped bleached blond hair, sharp facial features, shoulders slanted a little forward from years of poor posture, slim — a little underweight — wearing jeans that had been around, high-heeled boots scuffed at the toes. A dime-store girl. Dirt-poor southern, Mississippi, maybe Alabama. A girl who could use a real good makeover.

Cory continued past her a dozen feet, then stopped. The sprinkles of rain were increasing.

"Miss the bus?" he asked the woman.

She nodded but did not look at him or speak.

"Won't be another one for an hour," he said.

She shrugged. The story of her life.

"I can give you a lift into Sacramento," he said.

"You a guard?" she asked, looking at him for the first time. Her eyes were like tracer bullets.

"I'm a corrections officer, yeah."

"Well, I'm a convict visitor," she said evenly. "Prob'ly wouldn't look too good, us driving off together, you think?"

"I'm not asking you to go to a motel with me," Cory responded, just as evenly. "Just offering you a lift into Sacramento." Now it was he who shrugged. "Take it or leave it."

He walked on away. Before he got to his car, the rainfall became steady and she was walking beside him.

On the drive in, windshield wipers slapping, she asked, "Don't you want to know who I was visiting?"

"What do you mean *who?*"

"I mean, like my husband, boyfriend, brother—"

Cory threw her a quick glance. She had a little acne scar in front of her left ear. "Look," he said, "even if you told me, I probably wouldn't know who you were talking about. We've got fifteen hundred-plus cons in there. Unless who you were visiting happened to be on my block, in my tier, which is highly unlikely, I wouldn't know him from Adam. You know who Adam was, right?"

"Were you born rude?" she snapped. "Or did you have to study it?"

At that point a cloak of silence dropped over the interior of Cory's three-hole Buick, and they rode that way, the windshield wipers seeming to keep time with their heartbeats, the rain outside heavy enough now for Cory to turn on the car's headlights. Sitting without even a glance at the other, neither spoke until they reached the city limits of Sacramento.

"Where do you want me to drop you?" Cory asked, finally breaking the uncomfortable quiet.

"The Greyhound depot'll be fine," she mumbled in reply.

Cory exited the interstate and drove to Seventh and L Streets, where he swung around to the main entrance of the ugly, uninviting Greyhound depot and pulled over and stopped with the engine idling.

"Listen, thanks for the lift," she said, getting out, her tone mellower than before.

"Don't mention it," Cory said, his own voice less disagreeable. "Have a nice trip home."

After she shut the passenger door and hurried toward the depot entrance, Cory drove away and made a U-turn into a parking space half a block down the street. He kept the engine running so the wiper blades would keep the windshield clear, but then the rain suddenly stopped completely and he shut the car down. From where he was parked, he had an unobstructed view of the bus depot entrance. He only had to wait five minutes before he saw the woman come back out of the door she had gone in, pause to glance around, then walk quickly away along L Street.

Leaving his car, Cory followed her at a discreet distance for several blocks, to a Motel 7 on the edge of a seedy downtown district. She walked directly to a room on the lower of the two floors, unlocked it with a key from her jeans pocket, and went inside. It was Room 121.

Cory returned to his car and drove to his own apartment, a little one-bedroom furnished place where he lived alone. He got a bottle of milk from his refrigerator and sat in an old club chair, drinking from the bottle and staring at the blank television screen for a long time, thinking about the woman. Later on, when he went to bed, he fell asleep thinking about her, wondering who she had been visiting, wondering even what her name was. He dreamed about her.

The next day, when Cory reported for his shift at the prison, the officer at the sign-in desk said, "You're wanted in the deputy warden's office."

Cory frowned. "When?"

"Now."

Cory made his way back out of the incoming-staff corridor to the prison's executive wing, where Deputy Warden Lewis Duffy had his office. He'd been seen, Cory thought. Seen picking up a convict visitor and driving away from the prison with her!

Well, hell, that was all she wrote. As a corrections officer, he was all washed up.

When Cory was shown into the deputy warden's office, he found himself facing not only Deputy Warden Duffy but a man he had never seen before: a conservatively dressed man in a nondescript gray suit and an out-of-style wide necktie tied in a Windsor knot on a white shirt.

"Evans," the deputy warden said, "this is special agent Roger Hardesty of the FBI." Cory nodded to Hardesty. "Sit down, Evans. We have a few questions for you. Did you pick up a woman in the visitors' parking lot yesterday, after your shift, and drive away with her?"

"Yessir, I did."

"Did you know the woman?"

"No, sir."

"Why did you drive away with her in your car?"

"It was starting to rain. She'd missed the bus and there wasn't another scheduled for an hour. There's no shelter of any kind at that bus stop." Cory shrugged. "I just offered her a ride."

"You're aware, are you not, of our fraternization rules regarding inmate visitors?"

"Yessir. But it wasn't really fraternization, Warden. I just offered her a ride. Like I said, it was starting to rain—"

"Did you exchange names with her?"

"No, sir—"

"Telephone numbers, addresses, personal information of any kind?"

"No, sir. Nothing."

"Where did you take the woman?"

"To the Greyhound depot on L Street in Sacramento."

"Where did you go then?"

"Straight to my apartment," Cory lied, shifting uneasily in his chair. "Am I being written up for this? If I am, I'd like to have a union representative present."

"There's no need for that, Evans. I don't intend to make a formal record of this meeting. Offering that woman a ride into town, even under the circumstances you outlined, was not, in my mind, very good judgment, but no report will be made if you agree to cooperate with Agent Hardesty here."

Cory looked over at the FBI man. "Cooperate with him how?"

"I'd like to give you a little information about the woman you picked up, Officer Evans," the agent said. "Her name is Billie Sue Neeley. The inmate she was visiting is Lester Dragg, serving six years for grand theft auto. He's been in two, up for parole in eighteen months. The Bureau is interested in him because we know he drove the getaway car in a bank robbery down in Modesto. The two gunmen who went into the bank grabbed one million, two hundred thousand dollars that was scheduled to be picked up by an armored truck about twenty minutes later. The robbery would have gone off perfectly except that the armored truck got there early, just as the holdup men ran out of the bank and threw the two sacks of money into the getaway car. The armored truck guards opened fire on the two men before they could get into the car themselves. In the shootout, both holdup men were killed. But the getaway car, with the money in it, got away. The armored truck guards didn't get the license number but gave a good description of the car. It turned out to be stolen. Three days later, the California Highway Patrol snagged the car in a line waiting to cross the border into Tijuana. Lester Dragg was driving; Billie Sue Neeley was a passenger. There was no sign of the money. We had no eyewitness ID that Dragg had been the driver in the bank job. All we could get him on was a state charge of grand theft auto as the driver of a stolen vehicle. And we had nothing at all on the Neeley woman; she claimed to be a hitch-hiker and Dragg backed up her story."

"So the bank robbery is why the FBI is interested," Cory guessed.

"Exactly. If we can put Dragg next to that money, we can nail him on federal bank robbery charges, and maybe get the Neeley woman for conspiracy."

"You think the Neeley woman knows where the money is?" Cory asked.

Agent Hardesty shrugged.

"Hard to say. She certainly isn't spending it if she does. She lives very frugally; the only income she appears to have is an unemployment check from the state that she gets twice a month."

So I was wrong, Cory thought. *Not dirt-poor Mississippi or Alabama. An Okie from Oklahoma. Still dirt poor.*

"There's got to be some reason she's hanging around waiting for Dragg to get out," Hardesty continued, "and we figure it's the money."

"She could just be crazy about the guy," Cory offered.

"Possibly." Deputy Warden Duffy reentered the conversation. "She's listed on his visitor card as his common-law wife."

Cory nodded thoughtfully. "So what do I have to do with all this?" he asked, looking from the agent to the deputy warden.

"That remains to be seen," Hardesty said. "You've accidentally made contact with her. We know she's living in the Motel 7 on Weed Street in Sacramento." *No kidding,* Cory thought.

"I've had her under surveillance for some time. I know where she shops, the movies she goes to, where she eats supper, everything. We thought, Deputy Warden Duffy and I, if we could arrange for you to run into her again—"

"Wait a minute," Cory interrupted, holding both hands up, palms out, deciding to play it dumb. "If you want me to be some kind of bait to trap this woman for the FBI, you've got the wrong guy. I'm a corrections officer, not some kind of undercover cop. I'm not up for anything like this."

The FBI agent and the deputy warden exchanged serious looks. "Evans," the deputy warden said, "my decision to keep this meeting informal was based on you cooperating with Agent Hardesty. You picked up this woman yesterday in violation of regulations governing your employment. Agent Hardesty's surveillance of her was compromised because of that—"

"I don't see how," Cory objected.

"I was on the bus the Neeley woman missed," Hardesty said. "By the time I got back to that bus stop, Neeley was gone. Deputy Warden Duffy had to have the prison check all of its closed-circuit security tapes to find out how she left the institution."

The deputy warden leaned forward and locked his fingers together on the desktop. "Look, Evans," he said in an even but not unfriendly voice, "you're not being asked to do anything but pursue an acquaintance with this woman and report back to Agent Hardesty anything she says to you. Just be friendly, that's all. And in exchange for that, your serious breach of regulations yesterday will not become a formal report."

"That's kind of like blackmail, isn't it?" Cory asked, his own voice equally even but not challenging.

"I'll overlook that comment," the deputy warden said. "I'll even sweeten the pot a little bit. Cooperate in this matter and the next time a sergeant's opening comes up, I'll personally see that you get on the list. *High* on the list." He sat back in his big swivel chair. "Now, what's it going to be, Evans?"

Cory managed to exhale a deep breath that sounded both weary and resigned. "I guess I'm about to make a new friend," he said.

And all the time he was thinking, *An Okie from Oklahoma. And all that money.*

After Cory left the office, the deputy warden sat forward again and silently drummed the fingers of one hand on the desktop.

"I hope to hell you know what you're doing," he said tightly to the FBI agent.

"I know *exactly* what I'm doing—or rather what *we're* doing," Hardesty said confidently. He smiled broadly. "Just play along with me, my friend, and you and I will cut up one million, two hundred thousand dollars in unmarked bills. As long as this guy Evans does as he's told and doesn't get any bright ideas of his own."

Duffy guffawed. "That guy? Hell, Roger, he's a *prison guard!* He's about as smart as a bag of nails. You don't have to worry about him."

Or you either, I hope, Hardesty thought. A million two was serious money. Serious enough to give almost any man pause for thought.

"So," Duffy asked, "where do we go from here?"

"Today's Tuesday," Hardesty said. "The Neeley woman has gone to the movies every Wednesday night for two months. We'll get Evans back in here in the morning and brief him on what to do when she goes to the movies tomorrow night. Then we'll be off and running."

"Okay," Duffy said. Then, as if to convince himself, he repeated it. "Okay."

The following night, when the first showing of the evening feature was over, Cory was waiting in the doorway of a coffee shop next to the Nugget Theater. When Billie Sue Neeley emerged in the exiting audience, he stepped out to meet her.

"Need a ride?" he asked.

She stopped, startled at having been spoken to. "What do you want?" she asked, almost demanded.

"You and I need to sit down and have a talk," Cory said. "An FBI man is watching you, and now he's watching me because I gave you a ride day before yesterday. We need to have a serious conversation."

Billie studied him for a long moment in the white glare of the movie theater marquee, with people moving past them on the sidewalk, talking among themselves, without even a glance at Cory and Billie. Presently she made her decision.

"Okay. Where?"

"There's a coffee shop around the corner."

"Let's go," Billie said. It was almost an order.

The place was called Cliff's Cafe. It had a ten-stool counter and six red vinyl booths for four, all under a sea of fluorescent lights that made its patrons look somehow ill, like they belonged in an emergency room for a transfusion instead of a café for a burger. The menus were in imitation red-leather folders that matched the vinyl booths.

"You hungry?" Cory asked conversationally when they slid into a booth.

"No," she snapped tightly.

"Well, I am."

When the waitress came, Cory ordered the Cliff's Special, a quarter-pounder with cheese, bacon, and the works, served with crispy crinkle fries on the side. With it he ordered a Dr Pepper. Billie ordered black coffee.

"Well?" she asked as they waited for their order, in the same demanding tone she had used in their encounter on the street. Cory fixed her with his flat corrections-officer stare.

"Okay, here's the story," he said.

He laid it out for her. Everything. All that had taken place in the deputy warden's office. He was straight with her, as he had earlier decided he would be. He told her everything—except the fact that he had followed her to the Motel 7 after she had left the bus depot. That was personal, he had decided. That was between him and her, and the deputy warden and the FBI had nothing to do with it. At that point he was not sure why he felt that way.

When his food was served and he began to eat, and Billie began to tentatively sip at her black coffee, she studied *him* now more than he studied her. What she saw was a guy with a pretty ordinary face: eyes a little too close together, nose slightly hooked, one ear a bit jugged.

Certainly not as handsome as her man in prison. Lester Dragg, except for a couple of crooked teeth, looked like Johnny Depp. Half the girls back in Atoka High had been crazy about him. But it was Billie Sue Neeley who snagged him. Lucky her, she had eventually thought wryly, but by then it was too late to turn back.

"So how come you're being so straight with me?" she finally asked.

Cory locked eyes with her. "I don't like being blackmailed by the deputy warden and an FBI agent," he told her evenly.

Billie gave him a knowing look. "Wouldn't have anything to do with the money, would it?" She picked up one of his crispy crinkle fries and ate it.

"They seem to think you know where it is," he told her. She took another one of his fries, salted this one, and munched some more. "Thought you weren't hungry," he reminded her.

"I *don't* know where the money is," Billie said, ignoring his last remark.

"I get the feeling that this FBI agent thinks you might be able to find out where it is."

"That agent wouldn't by any chance be named Hardesty, would he?"

"Yeah. You know him?"

"He's been leaning on me ever since Les and I got caught in that hot car trying to cross into Mexico. See, he blew it that day, big-time. If he'd let us cross, he could have paid the Mexican border cops to bump us back into the U.S. and then he'd have had Les on a federal rap, international transportation of a stolen vehicle. But he jumped the gun. Got itchy about finding the money, prob'ly. So all he could do is turn Les over to the California law and get him sent up on a stolen car rap. Once he got Les put away, he started stalking me. I told him a hunnerd times I didn't know what Les had done with that bank take, but he just never believed me." Billie sighed a weary sigh and continued to eat his crispy crinkle fries. But her eyes narrowed slightly.

"What does Hardesty expect you to get out of me?"

"I don't know." Cory finished his burger and pushed his plate with the rest of the fries over to her. "Maybe he thinks you'll fall for me, drop Lester, and decide to split the money with me."

Billie grunted softly. "Won't work. Nothing personal, but you're not my type." Her remark got no reaction at all from Cory. Billie's eyes narrowed even more, not in suspicion now but curiosity. "Well?" she finally challenged.

"Well what?"

"Aren't you going to say I'm not your type either? I mean, I'm a convict's girl and you're a prison guard, for God's sake!"

Cory finished the last of his Dr Pepper and set the bottle aside, shrugging. "I guess I don't know exactly what kind of woman *is* my type. I haven't had much luck with women."

When they left the café, Cory walked her back to the Motel 7.

"So what do you think?" Billie asked when they got to the door of her room. "Where does this go from here?"

"I don't know. I guess we just play it out and see where it takes us."

"I guess," Billie agreed.

She went on into her room and Cory walked away, toward his apartment.

Inside, Billie parted the curtains of the room's small window and watched him walking away. With the palm of one hand rubbing up and down her thigh, she watched him until he was out of sight. She had been a long time without a man.

During visiting hours the next day, an agitated Lester Dragg tapped one knuckle on the metal visiting room table that separated them. It was an open visiting room where inmates and visitors could touch, hug, kiss, snack on junk food from state-owned vending machines, and in some cases transfer drugs and other contraband. But Lester Dragg was not interested in doing any of that. Lester Dragg was only interested in the hack named Evans that Billie Sue had met.

"What else did he tell you about Hardesty?" Lester was particularly curious about the FBI agent.

"Nothing," Billie explained patiently, "except what I already told you." She sighed audibly. "Why? I mean, what's so important about him?"

"What's so important about him is that he's the fed that's been trying to cut some kind of deal with me about the money."

"You never told me about anything like that," Billie said, surprised.

"I didn't think you needed to know, Billie Sue!" he snapped. "Sometimes the less you know, the safer I feel."

Billie looked away for a moment. Lester had a way of hurting her feelings like that. It usually happened when he was upset about something. Or when he was angry. She had begun to notice that when he was upset or angry, he didn't look so much like Johnny Depp anymore.

Brushing aside her hurt feelings, Billie asked, "What do you want me to do about him? The corrections guy?"

"I don't know. Just play along with him for the time being, I reckon. See if you can figure out what Hardesty and that deputy warden are planning. But be careful what you say to him. And whatever you do"—he pointed a threatening finger at her—"don't tell *him* that you told *me* about meeting him. You got that straight?"

"I got it, Les."

He took her hands across the table, and his voice softened the way it did when he wanted something. "Listen, honey, if you should get, you know, *friendly* with this hack, to the point where he might consider doing you a favor, well, go for it, okay?"

"What do you mean?"

"I mean, if you put out to him a little, you might could ask if he could maybe get me transferred out of the goddamned laundry. All that bleach I have to handle is making my hands raw."

Billie stiffened, but only inside so he wouldn't notice. "Are you saying it's okay for me to go to bed with this guy if he'll get you transferred to a better job?"

"Well, yeah," Lester said, shrugging innocently. "I mean, it wouldn't be for real or anything. Just something you'd do for me, honey, to make my life a little easier. You understand what I mean, don't you, babe?"

"Yeah, Lester. Sure, I understand."

Walking back to the bus stop after the visit, Billie Sue felt like the back of her neck was on fire.

That evening Cory came by the motel in his car to get her and they went downtown to an Italian restaurant that was considerably nicer than Cliff's Cafe had been. Cory ordered a bottle of Barolo, and as they drank wine and waited for their dinner, Billie told him about her visit with Lester.

"I can't believe he actually asked me to do that," she complained. "I mean, I'm supposed to be his girl and he actually asked me to go to *bed* with you to get him a better job assignment!"

"Wouldn't have worked anyway," Cory said. "I'm just a level-one corrections officer. Only sergeants and higher can get an inmate transferred." He studied her for a moment, then said, "You look very nice tonight. No boots, no worn-out jeans." She was wearing dress slacks and heels, with a scooped-neck long-sleeved sweater.

She shrugged. "Well, I didn't want you to think I was a complete Okie from Muskogee. I do know *how* to dress. Lester makes me dress down when I visit the prison; he says it keeps the guards from hitting on me."

Cory smiled. "Officers aren't likely to hit on women who visit inmates. Mostly they think of them as sluts—you know, tattoos, nose rings, half a pound of makeup, trying to look good for the loser inside."

"Do you think I'm one of those?" Billie asked frankly. "A slut?"

"No, I don't." Cory looked away. "I have a confession to make. I followed you to the motel that first night, after I let you out at the bus depot. I had a feeling you'd come back out, so I waited. And I followed you."

"Why are you telling me this now?"

"I guess I wanted you to know that I was interested in you even before all this business with the deputy warden and the FBI guy started."

Billie tilted her head a bit. "Interested in me how? Getting laid?"

"No. Not at that point. Although I'm sure it would eventually have come to that. But just then I only felt that I'd like to know more about you: what your name was, where you came from, how you got to where you are now." Abruptly he stopped talking, as if unsure what to say next.

"Well, you already know my name," she told him in a throaty voice that he took notice of for the first time. "As to where I came from, we called it Dustburg. I was a sharecropper's kid. One of thirteen. Got pulled out of school when I was twelve to work in the fields. It wasn't a real fun life. One of my brothers was retarded everywhere but between his legs; me and my sisters slept with big rocks in bed to fight him off with.

"On Saturdays we'd all pile onto the back of Daddy's flatbed and go into town. That was a real big deal. We'd drive past five hundred telephone poles until we came to a sign that said city limits. After a while I got to where I'd think, so what? A tacky little one-street nothing full of dirt-poor people who lived on a steady diet of revivals every Sunday." She took a long swallow of Barolo. "So you want to know where I came from? I came from nowhere."

"That where you hooked up with Lester?"

"Yeah. When I was old enough I started slipping away from the rest of the herd on Saturday afternoons and hanging out at a juke joint. A typical Okie dive, one of those shot-and-a-beer holes in the wall with a couple of drop-pocket pool tables, an old Wurlitzer that still took nickels, a few card tables, and a steady stream of would-be Romeos trying to look like something special but coming off like nothing no-how. Lester was one of them. But somehow . . ." Her voice momentarily drifted off and she stared down at the red circle in her wineglass.

"Let me guess," said Cory quietly. "Somehow Lester was different."

Billie snapped back to real time and her expression tightened. "You making fun of me?"

Cory shook his head. "Just trying to get to know you, Billie." It was the first time he had spoken her name, and he could tell by the look on her face that it meant something to her.

It was during their dinner, well into a second bottle of Barolo, that Billie Sue seriously considered for the first time the face of the man sitting across from her: the smooth, clean angles of his jaw, the straight white teeth, lips that a woman might yearn to have all over her body—and she looked into his light blue, almost gray eyes and in an instant she was a goner. Forget about Lester, let the prick rot in prison, she was hungry for it and she was going to do it with this prison guard—excuse me, *corrections officer*—this very night. Come hell or high water, or boll weevils at harvest time.

At three o'clock in the morning, Cory and Billie sat up in her bed at the Motel 7, turned on a forty-watt light on the nightstand, and shared a bottle of warm Mexican beer from a six-pack they had picked up on the way from the restaurant where they had dinner. Billie's room was a one-star C&T: cheap and tacky. Coin-operated TV, swamp cooler instead of air conditioner, hot and cold running cockroaches.

"Christ, what a pigsty," Cory observed, looking around for the first time without raw lust on his mind. "I've seen landfills that were more appealing."

"Lester's idea," Billie said blandly. "He said if I lived anywhere more expensive, I'd attract attention."

"Good old Lester. All heart."

Billie finished the beer in the bottle they were sharing and got out of bed to walk naked over to a table to get another. Cory, seeing her undressed and upright for the first time, saw that she was a little heavy in the thighs and had a line of proud flesh across one shoulder blade.

"Don't be looking at my thighs," she chastised, walking back. "I know they're thick."

"I didn't notice," Cory lied. "I was looking at the scar on your back. How'd you get it?"

"My daddy whipped me with a bridle strap after he caught me coming out of the juke joint with Lester. Mama made him stop after he drew blood, else I'd have more scars. My sister Lillie Lee has got five of them, crisscrossed. Daddy caught her naked in the back of a pickup truck with a neighbor's boy." Billie got back in bed, took a swallow from the new bottle, and handed it to Cory. "Well, Mr. Corrections Officer, where the hell do we go from here?"

"Damned if I know," Cory said. "If you knew where that money was, we could just take it, blow a goodbye kiss to Lester, the deputy warden, and that FBI agent, and fly away to paradise." He fixed her in an unblinking stare. "But you don't know where it is, do you?"

"Nope. Wish I did." *Everything comes down to the money,* she thought.

"How'd you and Lester end up in California?" Cory asked, changing the subject.

Or *was* he changing the subject? she wondered. Was he trying to get to know her a little better or just moving the conversation around to where the money came back into the picture? Damn it all anyway.

"After my daddy whipped me," she addressed his question, "Lester said to hell with Oklahoma, we're going out to sunny California and get us jobs as movie extras. He said he looked enough like Johnny Depp that it would be a cinch for him, and he allowed that while I wasn't no raving beauty, I could prob'ly pick up a few jobs anyway. So we hopped into his falling-apart Mustang and hit the old interstate. Got as far as Joseph City, Arizona, when the car broke down. Sold it for junk and bought us Trailways bus tickets to L.A. Lester got a job at a gas station and I started waiting tables in a coffee shop. Neither one of us had a clue about becoming movie extras. It was at the gas station that Lester met the two slickers that got him involved in the bank job. One of them was a Mexican dude, the other was some kind of surfer type who had worked as a bag boy in a grocery market across the street from the bank they tried to rob. He had seen the armored truck make its pickup week after week and figured the bank must have loads of cash ready to go just before the pickups. The bank was in Modesto, a little town up north of L.A., just a branch, only four teller windows and no guard, but it was in a strip mall and had a lot of business traffic, so they figured the take would be pretty good—never *dreamed* of no million, two hundred thousand! Lester said they guessed maybe a hundred thou tops. They offered him ten thousand to wait outside and drive the getaway car. We planned to use our share and head for Hawaii. Lester wanted to get a job as a lifeguard on Waikiki Beach, and he said I could go back to waiting tables again—"

"Good old Lester," Cory said again, grunting audibly. "Always picking a glamour job for himself and waiting tables for you."

Billie grunted back. "Tell me about it. Took me a while to tumble to that, but I finally got wise. Except by then I didn't have no place to go, so I just hung with Lester."

"Too bad you and I don't have that bank money. Make life a lot different for you."

Billie sat up and twisted around on the bed until she was facing him. "You always swing back to talking about the money, don't you, honey? What's on your mind, really?"

Cory shrugged. "What difference does it make? You don't know where the money is, right?"

"Right. Don't have a clue."

Cory fell silent for several moments, eyes downcast, staring at the beer bottle it was now his turn to hold, with Billie's naked breasts prominent in his peripheral vision. His lips were pursed as he molded his thoughts for what he would say next. When he finally spoke, he looked back at Billie's face without blinking and said, "How much do you think it would be worth to Lester if I could get him out of prison?"

"Get him out when?" she asked, surprised.

"Soon," Cory told her. "Very soon."

The next morning Cory was back with the deputy warden and FBI agent Hardesty.

"I don't think the Neeley woman knows where the money is," he told them, "but I think I can get Lester to lead you to it if you can find a way to spring him. She says he wants a transfer out of the laundry detail. I was thinking maybe—the dairy farm?"

Hardesty and Duffy exchanged surprised looks. "You mean help him *escape?*" Duffy asked, aghast.

"Why not?" Cory reasoned. "He would be taken right back into custody by Agent Hardesty and returned here before there was any record that he was ever out."

Hardesty rubbed his chin. "Not a bad idea," he said.

"But what if we can't follow him once he's out?" Duffy worried. "We could lose him."

"Not a problem," Hardesty assured him. "If we provide a car for him, I'll have a silent tracker signal unit attached to it that we can follow from our own car."

"How about using my car for Lester once he's out?" Cory suggested. "The Neeley woman is familiar with it, she'll be comfortable in it."

Hardesty shrugged. "Sure, why not?"

Duffy grimaced, looking agitated.

"Look, here's how we can work it," Cory said. "I tell the woman I can arrange to get Lester transferred to the dairy farm. It's a job he can simply walk away from. I say that she and I can be parked in my car at a highway rest stop about a mile from the farm. I tell her I'll do it for, say, a hundred thousand of the bank money. When Lester gets to the car, we pick him up and head for wherever the money is. Once we get there, you two show, make the collar, and it's a done deal."

Hardesty was smiling, but Duffy was shaking his head. "I don't know," the deputy warden said. "It goes against my grain, letting a con walk away like that."

"Look," Hardesty reasoned, "you won't exactly be letting him walk away. You're giving him a short furlough is all. And technically he'll still be in custody, because Evans here is going to be with him all the time—and Evans is a corrections officer. See?" He turned to Cory. "I like it, Evans. I think it'll work. But are you sure you can set it up?"

"Positive. Actually, it was the Neeley woman's idea. She started talking about getting Lester transferred out of the laundry, and I just took it from there. I didn't even have to ask for a share of the bank money; she offered it." Cory grinned. "She thinks I'm just a dumb prison guard out to make some easy money."

"Well, won't she be surprised?" Hardesty said with a chuckle.

Won't a lot of people, Cory thought.

At a prison visiting room table, Billie Neeley and Lester Dragg leaned forward on their elbows to converse privately.

"You sure you can trust this dude?" Lester asked uneasily.

"Sure as rain, baby," Billie answered confidently. "The guy's a big hick. You should have seen his eyes bulge when I offered him a hundred grand."

"Yeah, well, he ain't gonna *get* no hunnerd grand," Lester

said, pouting. "Ten grand, maybe, if ever'thing goes smooth." He paused, then frowned suspiciously. "You go to bed with this dude to get him to do this?"

"Hell, no!" Billie declared. "Didn't have to. Oh, I let him cop a few feels, so he prob'ly *thinks* he's got something going, but he's wrong." Reaching over, she took one of Lester's hands. "You're the only one for me, sugar. Always have been."

"Well, all right then," Lester said triumphantly. "I'm counting on you, babe. Don't you let me down, hear?"

"I'd never let you down, sugar. You mean the world to me, you know that."

She squeezed his hand for emphasis.

In Cory's apartment, where Billie Sue had been spending the nights, she and Cory sat across from each other at his little dinette table.

"Okay, listen up," Cory said solemnly. "This situation is coming down to the wire. We've got to put all our cards on the table." He locked eyes with her. "I think it's about time you tell me where the money is."

Billie stiffened, biting her lower lip. Their eyes were like riveted bolts; neither of them even blinked. After a heavy moment, Billie took a deep, almost tortured breath.

"It's in a public storage facility down in Modesto, where the bank was robbed."

Cory frowned. "Why haven't you already grabbed it? Or told me about it earlier so we could grab it together? You still hung up on Lester, is that it?"

"No, damn it to hell!" She began blurting words like machine gun rounds. "Lester says the storage facility has a cyclone fence around it that's wired to a twenty-four-hour security company. There's a keyboard on the gate with a six-digit code for people to get in after hours, and Lester never told me the code. It's a great big place and I don't even know which unit he rented, and anyway he said he put this big combination padlock on the door, and Lester didn't tell me the combination either, so I couldn't get into the damned locker even if I did know which one it was."

She was crying now and pounding the table with both fists, so Cory had to reach out and grab her wrists to stop her. "Okay, okay, okay! It's okay! Calm down . . ."

It took a couple of minutes, but he managed to get her calm and got her some tissues to dry her eyes. But even so, she was still agitated, exuding a high-strung energy he had never seen in her before.

"I didn't know what to do." She seemed to be arguing with herself. "Tell you, don't tell you, lie to Lester, don't lie to Lester, try to keep all my stories straight—"

"Listen to me." He held her hands firmly across the table. "You do know where this storage place is, right?"

"Sure I do," she said irritably. "I been sending a thirty-dollar money order there every month for two damn years! I ought to know where it is! Let go of my hands, you're hurting me."

Cory released her, rose, and came around the table to kneel beside her. "Listen to me." He reached up to stroke her hair. "Everything's going to be okay. I'm going to arrange to get Lester out and the three of us are going to Modesto and get that money. And when we do get it, we're going to leave old Lester high and dry, and you and I are going to disappear together, how does that sound?"

Billie Sue sputtered a little. "Well—can we do that—I mean, can we get away with it—I mean, what about that warden and that FBI guy—and what about Lester—do we have to kill him?"

"Hell, no, baby. We're not killers. We'll just leave Lester locked in his own storage locker. Somebody will find him the next day when he makes enough noise. But we'll be long gone by then."

Gently Cory pulled her head down and kissed her tenderly on the lips, tasting the salt from her tears. He continued to stroke her hair.

"This is going to work for us, baby. I've got it all figured out."

In Duffy's office the next morning, the deputy warden and Agent Hardesty told Cory the plan was ready to be put into operation. Inmate Lester Dragg had been transferred outside the walls to the prison dairy farm.

"It's an honor assignment," Duffy reminded them. "No walls, just a cyclone fence with no razor wire across the top, and the last head count of the day is at six o'clock. Escape can be effected by going to some remote corner of the pasture, climbing over the fence, and simply walking away. Since the inmates assigned there are nonviolent first offenders with only a short time to serve, no one has ever taken advantage of that easy way out. Lester Dragg will be the first."

"Then we're all set," Cory said. "The Neeley woman is convinced that she got me to arrange his transfer to the farm for a hundred grand cut of the bank money. When she sees him tomorrow, she'll tell him it's all arranged for that night. He'll walk over to the highway and the Neeley woman and I will pick him up in my car." He looked at Hardesty. "You have that tracking transmitter?"

"I've got it in my car in the visitors' parking lot."

"Good. I'll pull my car around from the staff lot and you can put it on. You need tools?"

"No, it's magnetic. I just clamp it to anything metal on the undercarriage. The GPTS receiver sits on my dashboard."

"What's GPTS?" the deputy warden asked, frowning. Cory and Hardesty exchanged disdainful glances.

"Global Positioning Tracking System," Hardesty said. "I'll explain how it works when we're following them."

The deputy warden shook his head doubtfully. "I don't know. This thing is getting pretty involved. I mean, transferring him outside the walls with no notice, then having him just walk away —suppose somebody catches him? And this business of following him with some kind of gadget stuck to the bottom of a car—I just don't know . . ."

Hardesty rose and leaned over Duffy's desk, both hands planted palms down. "Look," he said, calmly but firmly. "This is going to work. All we have to do is stick to the plan, see? It's that simple. Relax and stick to the plan. Nothing will go wrong. Okay?"

The way Hardesty was leaning over the desk, Deputy Warden Duffy could see under his open coat front the service revolver the FBI agent carried. It was an intimidating sight. "Okay," he blurted. "Okay. We'll just stick to the plan."

"Fine." Hardesty straightened, and to Cory said, "Let's go get your car set up."

After Cory and Hardesty left his office, Deputy Warden Duffy unlocked a bottom desk drawer and removed his old service revolver, a .38 S&W Special. In case anything *did* go wrong, he didn't want Hardesty to be the only one there with a gun.

Outside the prison, when Cory and Hardesty had their cars parked alongside each other, Hardesty opened a small box about the size of a deck of playing cards and began unwrapping its contents. As he did so, he asked casually, "What's your opinion of Duffy?"

"In what way?" Cory asked back.

"You think he's up for this? He seems kind of shaky to me."

"I noticed that," Cory agreed.

"How do you feel about it? The plan, I mean."

"I think it's good. I think it'll work. There's only one thing that bothers me."

"Yeah? What's that?"

"The cut. I think I deserve a cut. All I've been promised out of this is a future promotion to sergeant. While you and Duffy divide a million two in cash. After all I've done to move this plan along, that doesn't seem quite fair."

Hardesty paused in what he was doing and fixed Cory in a flat stare. "Well, tell me, Officer Evans, what do you think *would* be fair?"

"If you and Duffy are splitting the money evenly, that's six hundred thousand apiece. If each of you kicked in a hundred grand for me, you'd both still have half a mil left—"

"And you'd have two hundred thou—"

"Plus those sergeant's stripes."

Hardesty smiled, not his professional FBI smile but a George Bush kinder, gentler smile. "I've been wondering when you'd make your pitch, Evans. I've been expecting it. You're smart. And you're reliable. Two things that Duffy isn't. How would you feel about an even fifty-fifty split between you and me?"

"How could you do that?" Cory asked with obvious interest.

"Easy. The two of us take the money and hit the road. We lock the deputy warden, the escaped convict, and his slut girlfriend in the storage garage with a new lock I'll bring with me."

Hardesty's smile now morphed into one of almost evil delight. "How Duffy will explain things when they're found will be his problem. You and I will be, as the old chain-gang song goes, long gone to Bowling Green."

"How can you manage that? You'd be a missing FBI agent."

Now Hardesty chuckled. "I resigned from the Bureau a year ago, when I first started working on this plan. I just never got around to telling Duffy about it. So nobody'll be looking for me. And if you're smart, you'll drop off your resignation at the pris-on's administrative office in the morning, effective immediately, so nobody'll be looking for you either. We just go our separate ways, me in my car, you in yours."

Now it was Cory who smiled. "Only problem with that is, you can follow me with your GPTS tracker. That would make me a little nervous."

"Hell, I'll give you the monitor," Hardesty said, shrugging. "Look, kid, we've got to trust each other to make this work. I'm not greedy. I'll settle for six hundred thou if you will. Have we got a deal?"

Cory thought about Billie Sue sitting in his apartment, and Duffy sitting back in his deputy warden's office, and Lester Dragg who had been sitting in his prison cell for two years, and all that money lying in a storage unit a hundred and twenty miles away in Modesto . . .

"Yeah," he told Hardesty, "we've got a deal."

Hardesty finished unwrapping the item he had taken from the small box and showed it to Cory. It was slightly smaller than the box, made of metal, bluish in color, and was completely covered all the way around except for a small indented switch on one edge. "This side is magnetized," he told Cory, demonstrating by laying it gently on the side of a car door, to which it attached without falling off. "The magnetized side has an ultra-high field strength which gives it a very strong resistivity once attached, so that even if your car should hit a large bump, the device will not fall off."

Hardesty got a rolled-up blanket from the back seat of his car and unrolled it under the rear of Cory's Buick. Removing his coat, he handed it to Cory to hold for him while he lay down and scooted well under the car so that only his feet remained extended. Very carefully he placed the tracking device on the side of the vehicle's muffler and switched it on.

"Go look at the monitor on the dashboard of my car," he called to Cory. "Tell me if the screen has turned from black to blue."

Hardesty watched Cory's feet at he walked round to Hardesty's car. While Cory was so occupied, Hardesty removed a second tracker, already unwrapped, from his trouser pocket, switched that one on also, and attached it to the opposite side of the muffler from the first one.

"The screen is blue," Cory called over.

"Okay, good." Hardesty scooted back out from under Cory's car and pulled the blanket out, rolling it back up and tossing it

into his car again. With his coat back on, he showed Cory how
the tracking monitor on his dashboard worked. It was about the
size of a paperback book, with most of its front being taken up
by a small screen. Slowly turning a global-assist dial, he had Cory
watch while a map materialized and a white blip blinked on and
off, indicating exactly where Cory's Buick was parked—right next
to them. "Now I'll always know where you are until this thing we're
doing is over," he said with a wink. Unless, he thought, Cory dou-
ble-crossed him and removed the first tracker. In which case, he
would *still* know where Cory was, by simply changing the monitor's
frequency to the second tracker. As a former longtime FBI agent,
Hardesty knew that a man couldn't be too careful when dealing
with dishonest people.

Billie Sue Neeley was not, as Cory imagined, sitting in Cory's apartment waiting for him, but instead was in her own shabby little Motel 7 room preparing for her part in the escape from prison of
Lester Dragg.

One of the main things in her preparation was to count how
much money she had left of the $20,000 Lester had given her to
subsist on in the event that after the bank robbery that had gone
so badly they did not successfully escape to Mexico. Immediately
following his getaway with the two canvas sacks of cash, Lester had
marshaled up a rare presence of mind and located a storage facility in which to conceal the loot, even purchasing a heavy-duty
combination padlock from a selection on sale in the rental office.

In the garage-size unit, he had used a pocket knife he habitu-
ally carried to cut open one of the locked canvas money bags and
remove $20,000 in mixed unmarked currency, which he subse-
quently boxed up at a nearby private post office and mailed to
Billie Sue Neeley care of General Delivery in Modesto. All this was
accomplished in one hour immediately following his getaway from
the bank. His hastily formed plan was to escape to Mexico, lie low
for a while on several hundred dollars he had taken for expenses,
then when things cooled down following the holdup send Billie
Sue back to Modesto to pick up the package at General Delivery.
They would then go somewhere and live off that money until it was
safe enough to retrieve the bulk of the loot from the rental facility.

It was a brilliant plan, doubly so being conceived so quickly in
the mind of an oaf like Lester. And it may well have worked had

he and Billie Sue not been stopped trying to cross into Mexico in a car stolen, unknown to Lester, by his two now deceased cohorts the evening prior to the robbery. After Lester's apprehension and subsequent conviction for grand theft auto, Billie Sue, who could not be charged with anything, moved to Sacramento to be near the prison where he was incarcerated and to live, as he sternly instructed, a very frugal, almost indigent low-profile life, so as not to suggest that she or Lester had any knowledge of the whereabouts of all that bank loot, which in fact had never left, and still remained within two miles of the bank from which it had been stolen.

Billie kept the $20,000 from General Delivery hidden in a space under the bottom drawer of a shabby dresser in the dumpy motel in which Lester insisted she lived. Access to the money, from which she removed only a pittance at a time, was by removing the drawer completely, revealing a four-inch space between the dresser and the floor upon which it stood. Billie had no qualms about the possible theft of the money; only an imbecile would think of stealing anything from the premises of a Motel 7.

Now, however, after her last visit with Lester, during which the plan for his escape had been finalized, he had given her specific instructions to take out all of the remaining money and to use part of it to buy him a handgun. He had explained exactly how she was to do it.

The name of the establishment to which Billie had been directed, on information Lester had been given by a fellow convict, located on the fringe of what passed for Sacramento's skid row, was the Three Balls Pawn Shop. It had, as was customary for such a business, an overhang above its entrance, with three shiny white balls, under which was a sign that read MONEY TO LOAN.

When Billie Sue entered, she was greeted by a smallish, balding man wearing a hearing aid. "I'd like to buy a gun," she said.

"The ones I have are back here," the pawnbroker said, with not a hint of surprise. He led her to the rear of the store. "These are the ones I have that are out of pawn and available for sale. Did you have anything particular in mind?"

"A thirty-eight-caliber."

"I have two," the pawnbroker said, opening the display case and taking out a revolver and an automatic. Billie frowned. Lester had not told her there would be a choice of models. "The Smith and Wesson revolver is seven hundred dollars," she was told, "and the Colt automatic is eight hundred."

Beginning to feel nervous, and silently thinking what a complete ignorant asshole Lester was, Billie said, "I'll take that one," pointing to the Colt.

"Of course. You realize that California has a three-day waiting period before you can actually take the weapon with you."

Now she recalled the rest of the ignorant asshole's instructions. "Oh? I was told by a friend that the waiting period could be waived for a thousand-dollar fee."

The pawnbroker frowned. "Who, may I ask, is the friend who told you that?"

"His name is Lester Dragg. He's in Folsom."

"Ah, yes. I did receive a message about him. You are, ah, prepared to pay cash for the purchase and the waiver fee?"

"Yes." Billie looked down at the display again. "What's that little one over there in the corner?"

"Oh, that. That's a Guardian twenty-five-caliber automatic. Not very powerful. Only holds six shots—"

"I'll take that also."

"It's two-fifty. And you'll have to pay for another waiting-period waiver, you know."

"That's okay. I'd like bullets for both of them, too."

"Well, I'm not licensed to sell ammunition. I have some of my own, however, and I can load each piece for you for fifty dollars. Let's see now, that comes to thirty-one hundred dollars even. You did say cash, didn't you?"

"Yes." Billie stepped over to another counter, turned her back on the pawnbroker, and counted the exact amount from her purse. Moments later she left the pawn shop with the two loaded pistols in a plain brown bag.

The night of the escape was upon them.

Cory packed a few belongings in a duffel bag and retrieved his service revolver, a .357 Ruger GP-100, which he was required to wear only when assigned to perimeter duty outside the walls of the prison or on tower duty inside.

Out at his car, he put the pistol under the driver's seat and spread a vinyl raincoat on the ground behind the car. With a pen light, he scooted under the car and located one of the tracking devices Hardesty had attached to the car's muffler. Removing it, he scooted back out, tossed the device into some bushes, and drove off to pick up Billie Sue at the Motel 7.

In her room at the motel, Billie had also packed a small overnight bag she had and put the little Guardian automatic in a pocket of her coat. She wrapped the larger pistol she had bought for Lester Dragg in a newspaper, which she put into a grocery bag that contained a six-pack of beer. Then she sat down to wait for Cory.

Hardesty, wearing his usual service revolver as well as a .32-caliber backup pistol in an ankle holster, drove his own car onto the prison staff parking lot just as Deputy Warden Duffy exited the administration building and came onto the lot to join him. As Duffy got into Hardesty's passenger seat, he unobtrusively adjusted himself to accommodate the pistol he had stuck in the waistband of his trousers.

"Everything okay?" he asked nervously.

"Everything's fine," Hardesty replied quietly. He drove off the lot and turned onto the highway toward Sacramento.

As they drove, Duffy looked off in the distance at the night lights just coming on at the prison dairy farm where Lester Dragg had started work that day and from where, with Duffy's help, he was probably blithely escaping at that very moment. Duffy's mouth went dry. From an inside coat pocket he took a flask and drank from it.

"What the hell's that?" Hardesty asked gruffly.

"Scotch," Duffy said. "Want some?"

"No thanks," Hardesty said. "But you go ahead." *Let the fool get smashed,* he thought. *Be easier to handle him that way.*

Reaching to the dashboard, Hardesty turned on the tracking monitor and watched its small screen fade from black to blue. Adjusting a dial, he watched a blip materialize on the location of the apartment building where Cory Evans lived. The blip settled and remained steady. Hardesty frowned. Cory's car was not moving yet.

Cory drove up to the door of Billie's room at the motel. Watching for him out the window, she came out at once and he opened the trunk to put her bag in with his duffel.

"What's that?" he asked, bobbing his chin at the grocery bag she carried.

"Six-pack of Budweiser," she said. "I figured we could drink one each and give the rest to Lester."

They got in the car. Billie took two bottles of beer into the front seat and set the grocery bag on the back seat. Cory started the car and pulled away from the motel. "Can't say I'm going to miss that dump," Billie muttered to herself.

Twilight had settled and low clouds were hanging in the sky like gauze. The first light raindrops hit the windshield and Cory turned the wipers on low. "Looks like Lester might get a little wet walking to the highway," he said.

Billie Sue glanced at him but said nothing.

Hardesty was watching the blip on the monitor. It was still not moving. Glancing down at the car's digital clock, he wet his lips. Something was wrong. He began turning the monitor's frequency dial.

"What's the matter with that thing?" Duffy asked testily. "Isn't it working?"

"It's working fine," Hardesty snapped. "Have another drink."

Still north of Sacramento, they now passed the rest stop where Cory and the woman were to pick up Lester Dragg. Hardesty drove another mile, then turned into a truck stop and parked.

Leaning forward, he manipulated the frequency dial more slowly and a few seconds later was able to pick up a new blip, this one moving away from Sacramento toward them. It was a signal from the second tracking device Hardesty had placed on Cory's car.

That son of a bitch, he thought. *He crossed me.* Hardesty's jaw tightened. Okay. Fine. Now there wouldn't be a split of any kind.

He would leave four people locked in that storage garage.

At the rest stop up the highway, Cory pulled his Buick into a spot next to several cement picnic benches and turned off the headlights.

"How will he know we're here?" he asked Billie.

"He'll know."

"How do we find him?"

"He'll find us."

At that moment a knuckle rapped on the passenger-side window. Billie unlocked the door and got out. In the subdued light of the rest stop, Cory saw her embrace a slim figure with a head of thick black hair combed straight back. "Hey, baby," he heard a male voice say.

"Hey, sugar," Billie answered. "Get in the back seat; there's a little surprise for you."

As Lester got in the back seat, Billie slid back in front next to Cory. "Okay, let's go," she said. "Cut over to Route 99 and head south."

Hardesty watched the blip of Cory's car as it drove away from the rest stop and swung left onto the state highway going south. Calculating that he was about six miles behind Cory, he pulled back onto the highway and eased down on the accelerator to catch up.

"That gadget working all right now?" Duffy asked edgily from the passenger seat.

"Working just fine." Hardesty threw the deputy warden a disgusted look. Couldn't depend on anybody anymore, he thought. "Have another drink, why don't you? Help you to relax."

"Don't mind if I do," Duffy said, retrieving the flask from his inside coat pocket again. As he drank, he felt the reassuring grip of the pistol sticking out of his waistband. Nobody was going to put anything over on him, he thought a little woozily. No, sir.

Outside, the pesky rain increased to a steadier downpour. Hardesty turned the car's windshield wipers on to high. The *slap-slap-slap* of the rubber blades made Duffy feel a bit drowsy. His eyelids lowered a little.

In Cory's car, the modicum of tension that had risen when Lester Dragg first got in had dissipated after they reached Highway 99 and turned south. Lester was drinking his second beer, and having found the gun Billie Sue had bought for him, had it tucked securely under his left thigh.

Billie had turned on the radio, found a country-and-western station, and was humming along to a Freddy Fender song about wasted days and wasted nights.

"How far are we going?" Cory asked Billie Sue after a bit, as if he did not already know. Lester answered for her.

"Don't you worry about how far we're going, Mr. Screw," he said with a loud belch. "Jus' keep on driving."

"Whatever you say."

"Damn straight on that. You ain't the boss out here."

The rain had increased by now to a heavy downpour, and Cory kept his speed at 55 as they kept driving, monotonously, past the next off-ramp, past the next lights up ahead in the California rural darkness, and then through stretches of nothing but the wet night.

Cory had checked his odometer at the rest stop where they picked up Lester, so he knew when they passed the off-ramp for Stockton that they were within a half-hour or so of their destination. That was confirmed by a highway sign just outside Stockton that read MODESTO 25.

Inside the car, the windshield began to steam up from the body heat of the occupants.

Hardesty by now had come up to within a dozen car lengths of Cory's Buick and was following in a trained law enforcement pattern of nondetection observance: a frequent change of lanes in the flow of traffic, occasionally exiting the highway at an off-ramp, then crossing the underpass street and reentering via an on-ramp, where he accelerated just enough to again come within range of Cory's blip on the monitor.

Next to him, Duffy's head was leaning against the passenger window and he was not quite snoring but breathing heavily. *Drunken fool,* Hardesty thought. He began to contemplate pulling over, putting a round into Duffy's temple, and dumping him on the side of the road. He even considered killing them all: four bodies in that storage garage, locked in with a bicycle lock he had purchased that morning — hell, it might be weeks before anybody noticed the stench and found them. By then he would be living easy down in Argentina, where there was no extradition treaty with the U.S. — assuming that he was ever even *connected* with the bodies.

Suddenly, as he was considering his options, Hardesty saw Cory's blip leave the highway at an off-ramp next to a sign that read MODESTO NEXT RIGHT.

I'll be damned, he thought, as he approached the same off-ramp. That was the town where the bank heist went down. *Could it be that the money never left town?*

Hardesty shook his head in disbelief.

Lester Dragg directed Cory along the outer limits of Modesto to a small industrial district of modest factories and warehouses until they came to a cul-de-sac, where he had Cory turn in.

A block down, at the dead end, was a high cyclone fence with a slider gate in its center. Above the gate was a sign: SECURITY STORAGE RENTALS. Just below the sign and to the left was a solid concrete post housing an infrared, touch-sensitive digital keypad under a two-inch-thick Plexiglas cover. All of it was brightly lit by an overhang of sulfur lights.

"Pull up to the gate, screw," Lester Dragg ordered Cory. "Keep the motor running." Stepping out of the car, he showed Cory the .38 automatic he now held in one hand. "Don't try anything funny, see? I mean business."

"I'm cool," Cory replied. "All I want is my hundred grand."

As Lester walked over to the entry post, Cory eased his left hand down to the Ruger pistol under the seat.

Billie noticed his movement but said nothing. She rested one hand on her purse, where she had the .25-caliber Guardian.

When Hardesty saw that Cory had pulled into a cul-de-sac, he immediately turned off his headlights and parked. Scoping out the situation in front of him, he made a quick, trained assessment that he had to act quickly or chance losing Cory's car inside the security fence, which might or might not have an exit gate at the rear.

Next to him, Duffy was in what looked to Hardesty to be a drunken stupor; he was slouched down in the passenger seat, wheezing quietly through his nose. Take care of him later, Hardesty decided, and got out of the car, not closing the door all the way to avoid noise.

Stealthily, in the cover of shadows, he moved in a low crouch toward the security fence, service revolver in hand.

At the gatepost Lester touched a series of imprinted squares on the Plexiglas that were directly over the infrared keyboard numbers below it. With each touch, a soft beep sounded. After selecting eight numbers, Lester touched a side key marked ENTER. As soon as he did, a buzzer sounded and the gate began to slide open.

Lester hurried back to get in the car.

Hardesty by now had moved as close to Cory's car as he could get without exposing himself to the gate's sulfur lights. The air around him was humid and he was sweating.

Taking a chance that the three people in Cory's car were all watching the sliding gate and none of the car's rearview or side-view mirrors, and crouching as low as he could, he crossed the deserted street and dashed into shadows on the opposite side. Remaining totally still, watching the car until he was certain his movement had not been detected, he took a deep breath, pulled a handkerchief from his pocket, and wiped his face clean of perspiration.

Calculating the distance to the gate, wondering how long it re-mained open after each code entry, he moved forward inch by inch toward the edge of the sulfur lights' reach.

When the gate was all the way open, Lester Dragg ordered, "Go! Inside, make a right turn!"

Cory shifted gears and eased the Buick over a speed bump on the entry drive. Once inside, as ordered, he turned right.

"Go down to Section D and turn left," Lester said. "You'll see the signs."

Cory handled the steering wheel with one hand as he slipped the Ruger up with his other and rested it against his left thigh.

Hardesty saw Cory's car make its right turn inside the fence, and seconds later he heard a buzzer again and the gate began to slide closed.

Straightening from his crouch, he broke into a run, pistol at the ready in case he was seen, and sprinted toward the moving gate. It seemed to be moving faster than he was running.

Son of a bitch! he thought. Fresh sweat broke over his forehead and ran past the corners of both eyebrows into his eyes, stinging.

The gate lumbered on, like a train.

Hardesty's heart pumped like a jackhammer.

After they'd turned into Section D of the facility's interior and driven about fifty yards past a succession of identical closed garage doors, Lester told Cory to stop.

"Pull up in front of number 276 there."

Cory eased the Buick to a stop and turned off the ignition, leav-ing the key in it.

"Okay, get out, screw." Lester touched the back of Cory's head with the gun. "Don't try nothing funny." In the rearview mirror, Cory saw Lester look over at Billie Sue. "You get out too, sugar."

As Cory opened the driver's door and slid out, he quickly slipped the Ruger under his coat into his waistband.

"Stand over there," Lester ordered Cory. "Come over here, sugar," he told Billie. He handed her his gun. "Keep him covered."

Lester turned his attention toward a large combination padlock on the garage door handle.

Billie stood with Lester's gun pointed at Cory. Her expression was stern, fixed in concentration; her eyes met with Cory's in the pale light of a single bulb above the garage door. Remaining where he had been told to stand, Cory shrugged and held his hands out, palms up. Whatever.

With a sharp click, Lester jerked the big padlock open. "All right!" he said triumphantly. Throwing the latch, he rolled open the overhang door and a light came on inside.

The eyes of all three turned to look.

Two dust-covered gray canvas sacks lay there, padlocked at one end, with one of them slit partly open to reveal bundles of bank-banded currency.

A million two.

Hardesty watched from the end of the Section D drive.

He had barely made it through the closing gate, the weight of which had impacted his right elbow, causing, he was certain, a minor fracture. It hurt like hell. But he was not about to let it bother him. Switching the gun to his left hand, he had taken off at a trot in the direction Cory's car had turned.

When he reached Section D and looked down the drive of identical garage doors, he saw Cory's car parked partway down, in front of a square of light shining out from what appeared to be an open garage door.

Bingo, he thought.

A million two.

Holding his right elbow tucked close to his side to try to relieve the throbbing pain of the fracture, he began walking at a brisk pace toward the square of light, perspiration once again wetting his forehead and his palms. When he was almost there, he paused, knelt down, placed his pistol on the ground, and briskly rubbed the palm of his left hand on his trouser leg to get it completely dry. Having to hold the gun in his left hand, he did not want it slippery as well. Having come this far, everything had to be perfect now, no slip-ups.

Pleased with himself for being so careful, Hardesty stood back up, gun in hand, and cautiously resumed his approach. But after a few steps he froze and flattened himself in the foot-deep inset of one of the garage doors.

Someone had emerged from the lighted open garage door.

Cory, ordered by Lester, came out of the garage, reached into the Buick, and pressed the button to pop open the trunk. Seeing Cory's duffel and Billie's overnight bag, Lester threw Billie a suspicious look.

"Planning a little trip with this screw, sugar?" he asked tightly. "Gonna leave poor Lester behind, maybe?"

To Cory he snapped, "Get that junk out of there — quick!" Cory removed the two pieces of luggage and set them inside the garage. "Now put the two bank sacks in the trunk and get back inside," Lester directed.

Peering from his concealment at what was going on, Hardesty saw the money sacks put into Cory's trunk and the two men move back into the garage.

Now or never, he decided.

Moving quickly, he reached the open garage door and confronted the three people inside.

"Freeze!" he shouted, leveling his gun. "FBI!" To Lester he ordered, "Drop that weapon, Dragg!"

Lester stopped cold, the gun at his side, but he did not drop it.

Hardesty stepped over to Billie Sue and jerked her next to him, pointing his gun at her head. "Drop that weapon, Dragg, or I'll kill your woman!"

Lester laughed and raised his gun. "Go ahead, kill her. I don't need the lying bitch no more." Aiming at Hardesty, he squeezed the trigger.

The automatic's hammer came down on an empty chamber.

Looking aghast at the gun, Lester rapidly worked the trigger three more times before realizing in horror that the gun was not loaded.

Then it was Hardesty who laughed. "You brainless, lowlife moron," he said, pushing Billie Sue aside. "You're too stupid to go on living."

Hardesty shot Lester twice, dead center in the chest, exploding his heart, slamming his body back eight feet, dropping him like a man hit by a truck. Then he turned his gun on Cory, who was reaching for his Ruger. But before Hardesty could fire, his head was hit at close range as Billie Sue shot him in the temple with her Guardian 25.

Cory had his Ruger out now, and he and Billie Sue faced each other with guns leveled. They stood like that for a long, taut moment. Then Billie Sue spoke.

"Let's get the hell out of here."

"Let's," said Cory.

The sliding gate opened automatically from the inside for vehicles wanting to exit. Cory eased the Buick out, their own luggage back in the trunk with the million two, the bodies of Lester and Hardesty securely locked behind them in Unit 276, the rental on which, Billie Sue pointed out, was paid up three months in advance.

We're free and clear now, Cory thought. Billie was snuggled up beside him. There was nothing else to worry about. All the pieces were now in place.

All the pieces—

Except for Duffy.

The first bullet hit the Buick's windshield, shattering glass in Billie's face. She screamed.

The second shot was low, smashing into the car's radiator. Cory swerved and slammed sideways into the back of a van parked in front of a warehouse. When the Buick came to a jolting halt, steam gushing from under the hood, a third bullet burst the driver's-side window and grazed the back of Cory's neck before plowing into a seatback.

Cory saw Duffy now, stumbling toward the car like a drunken madman, brandishing a pistol and shouting.

"You don't put anything over on me!" he yelled. "No, sir!"

Kicking open the driver's-side door, Cory rolled out, firing his own weapon. The two men exchanged shots, one of Duffy's rounds striking Cory in the right side, an in-and-out hit that spun him but did not bring him down, while four of Cory's bullets laced Duffy's chest, sending him flailing back like a rag doll.

As Cory struggled over to the car, his sense of smell was hit with the acrid fumes of gasoline. One of Duffy's shots had hit the gas tank.

In the car, Cory found Billie sobbing, hands covering her face, blood trickling down between her fingers. "Come on, baby," Cory said, taking one of her arms and dragging her across the seat.

Then another shot cracked through the silence and hit the car. Duffy, not quite dead, had managed to fire one final round, and it hit the Buick's already punctured gas tank. The rear of the car exploded in a burst of growling flame.

"Come on, baby!" Cory said again, desperately urgent now. As he got Billie almost out, another, smaller eruption of flame licked out and caught both of them, searing the sides of their faces, singeing their hair.

Limping, half dragging Billie, Cory managed to get them just far enough away not to be blown up when the rest of the Buick exploded.

Along with the million two in its trunk.

Sirens began piercing the humid air as police cruisers, fire engines, and ambulances converged on the cul-de-sac from all directions. On a narrow side street a block away, Cory managed to walk Billie along a row of older frame houses, where porch lights were being turned on and people were coming out to see what was going on.

At the end of the block, where the houses stopped and only the dark night remained, Cory paused where an old man in a wheelchair sat looking toward the fiery sky above the cul-de-sac.

"Say, mister," Cory asked, "does this street lead out of town?"

"This street?" the old man replied, peering curiously at their injured faces. "This street don't lead nowheres. This street ends at the cemetery."

Cory grunted quietly, said, "Thanks, mister," and laboriously moved on.

As he and Billie went on their way, the old man saw blood on the sidewalk and started wheeling toward a police cruiser that pulled up to block the other end of the street.

They rested on the grassy ground next to the large headstone of a grave about twenty yards inside the cemetery. There was enough light from a full moon for them to see each other.

Billie's face was shredded on both sides from the windshield glass and burned on one side from the gasoline fire, and most of her hair was burned off one side of her head.

Cory's face and hair were seriously charred on one side, his neck wound painfully seared by the fire, and his stomach gunshot wound bubbling air-blood past the hand he held pressed tightly over it in a futile attempt to stop the flow. He had looked at his bloody hand under a streetlight just before they entered the cemetery and seen that the blood was streaked with black. The bullet had nicked his liver.

As they sat with their backs against the cold surface of the headstone, two police cruisers pulled up at the cemetery entrance and four officers got out and moved cautiously onto the grounds.

"I don't want to go on, Cory," Billie managed to choke out.

"Neither do I, baby," Cory replied.

They both drew their guns.

ANDRE KOCSIS

Crossing

FROM *The New Orphic Review*

I'D BEEN WATCHING the bear from across the valley for almost fifteen minutes. I first saw him just above the last of the stunted jack pines, galloping along a snowy bench and heading for the steeps. The slope above him was corrugated by a series of narrow couloirs, and I kept the binoculars on him, wondering what he would do. He hesitated not a moment, choosing a steep, tight channel in the dark rock. The increase in incline did not perturb him; he continued motoring up at a good clip. That couloir was steep—at least forty degrees. I knew. I had skied it a few weeks before.

Where was he going? There was no food up there. And why was he not holed up in a cave, anyhow? It was March—too early for him to come out.

Sometimes bears wake up, go out to explore for a while, and then go back to sleep, but this guy looked like he was on a mission.

An eagle circled far above, soaring on thermals, king of the blue sky.

When I looked back, the bear had reached the top of the couloir, and then he disappeared over the ridge. For a moment I considered putting on my skis and trying to pick up his trail, just to see what he was up to. It would have been a lot easier if I had had a dog. Well, not easier. The bear's tracks would be easy enough to follow. But a man needs a companion to go adventuring.

Someday.

Right now it was too complicated to take care of a dog. I was up at the cabin less than half the time, and Nelson wasn't fit for humans, let alone a dog. The town was totally overrun by fat, pale tourists.

When I first moved there, in 1975, it was still a funky little place, but a third of a century has elapsed since, and a lot of things change in that much time.

On the other hand, some things don't change. The U.S. is at war again. It took just one generation to forget the lessons of Vietnam.

Ironic, that Pinto had done me a favor by ratting me out to the cops for selling him that dope. He was trying to save his own hide, but in California I still have a warrant for my arrest. I suppose I would have left anyway, when I got my draft notice.

The only thing I regret now is that I couldn't go back to see my dad before he died last year. He was eighty-one, and he had not visited me since before Mom died, six years ago.

I put the glasses down on the rock where I'd been sitting and went into the cabin, crouching to avoid hitting my head on the low doorframe. Calling it a cabin was generous. It was no more than a shack. I had dragged every log a couple of kilometers up from the tree line.

I still wonder whether the effort had been worthwhile. The cabin is on Crown land. I had camouflaged the roof to avoid detection from the air, but if any rangers wandered up into the alpine, they'd burn the unauthorized structure.

I was going to turn fifty-six soon. It was time I had a place of my own, but I could not imagine living anywhere except in the alpine. I wanted to buy some land, but my savings were not enough. Guiding was not exactly making me rich, and spending so much time chilling at the cabin pushed millionaire status further out of reach.

I picked up the little plastic baggie holding my dope and papers. It felt light. Moving back to the door, I held it up to the shaft of light and noted that the contents had definitely diminished since arriving a couple of weeks before.

Time to get a new supply. Time to go back to Nelson. Maybe even get some work.

Owen was an Englishman in his late thirties who ran a "collectibles" store on one of the side streets of Nelson. He sold comic books, hockey cards, vinyl records—anything he could buy for pennies and sell for big bucks. It was unclear whether selling dope supplemented the huge profits he made on the collectibles or whether the collectibles just served as a front.

"Hey, Sierra, you're just in time," he said as I entered the dusty, poorly lit store.

"Hi, Owen. Just in time for what?"

"A couple of blokes came in this morning. They're looking for a guide."

My clientele used to consist mainly of backcountry skiers, hunters, or fishers who wanted to spend a week in the wilderness, but in the last few years Owen had opened up a whole new market for me. The border to the U.S. is quite mountainous in this area, making it ideal for undetected transport of B.C. bud into Montana. Dope runners paid better than skiers, even after the hefty commission that Owen took. (I always suspected that he also took a percentage from the clients.)

"How do I get in touch?"

"They're coming back tomorrow. I was going to use Calvin, because I never know how to find you."

"I'm here now."

"So you are, buddy, so you are." He smiled at me, revealing the narrow gap between his two front teeth. Owen had dark, curly hair and a broad, friendly face that stood him well with the ladies. He had come to Nelson to get away from his third wife. She was still in England, working the divorce courts to squeeze more money out of Owen.

"What's been happening?"

"Same old, same old. Bush is threatening Iran to get people's minds off the fact that he ruined the U.S. economy. Hey, there is a meeting tonight to plan a demonstration. Are you coming?"

"I'm busy," I lied.

"You're constantly ceasing to amaze me, Sierra. This country gives you asylum from those warmongers and then you just turn your back on the people that saved your ass."

"Save it for someone who cares. I haven't had a toke in twenty-four hours, and I'm ready to go postal. Can you front me a baggie? I'll pay you as soon as your clients show up."

Owen went into the back for a couple of minutes. The store had a relaxing gloom, and I surveyed the racks of comics and cards, all encased in plastic. Junk. But people were willing to pay for it.

Owen came back and laid a fat baggie on the counter. I immediately rolled a joint, and we passed it back and forth.

"Tell me, Sierra, have you ever done anything to fight the imperialism of your country?"

"It's not my country, and not my business."

"Okay, have it your way, but have you ever done anything?"

"Yeah, actually, I was part of a major conspiracy to stop the Vietnam War."

Owen perked up at this. "Really?"

"Oh, yeah. There was a group of us in Berkeley. We were dangerous radicals. One time we got a bunch of identical shoeboxes, like about fifty of them. Then we took a banana, put it in a box, and sent it by first-class mail to Lyndon Johnson."

"When did you live in Berkeley?"

"After high school."

"You told me you were climbing in Yosemite after high school."

"Sometimes I'd stay in Berkeley for a couple of months."

"Oh." Owen looked at me skeptically. "So you sent a banana to the president of the United States. And that was supposed to stop the war?"

"No, no, there was more to it. The next day we took another identical box and put a banana in it and sent that to LBJ, also by first-class mail."

Owen took a deep drag on my joint and handed back to me a much-diminished version.

"We did this for over a month," I continued.

"Wow! That's perseverance."

"You don't get it. After doing this every day, we suddenly just stopped."

"So?"

I took a drag on what was left of the joint, extinguished it, and put the roach into the baggie.

"That just drove them crazy," I explained.

"Sierra, you deluded, long-haired midget, what the fuck are you talking about?"

"Well, the U.S. eventually pulled out of Vietnam, didn't it?"

*

When I showed up at Owen's store the next day, he started in on me again.

"Some people mentioned you last night. They're wondering if you support the war in Iraq."

"War is a delusion."

"What? The U.S. killing people in Iraq is no delusion."

"I'm saying that anyone who truly believes that a problem can be solved by war is deluding himself."

Owen stared at me for a second. "I don't know about that. I mean, sometimes you have to go to war. What if we hadn't stopped Hitler? Were we deluded about that?"

"The delusion started with Hitler. He thought that by eliminating the Jews he'd solve Germany's problems."

"He didn't believe that at all. The Jews were a convenient scapegoat."

"Maybe for cynical leaders war is not a delusion. They may have a personal agenda that's served by war, but for the common man, the one who has to put his life on the line, it's a delusion. The average American soldier had more in common with the average German soldier than either of them had in common with their commanders and national leaders. They just wanted to live their lives, have enough to eat, keep their families safe. Only the leaders had ideological agendas that they valued more than the lives of their country's citizens. That's the tragedy of the twentieth century —ideologies that were so important that no sacrifice was too great. It would have been different if the leaders had been asked to be on the frontlines."

"Sure, but you have to take a stand against evil . . ."

"Any individual who sacrifices himself for a cause is deluded."

Owen shook his head. "So you're a pacifist?"

"Not at all. I favor individual violence. If you attack me, I will kill you. But I will not do that for an idea."

Owen stared at me for some moments. He shook his head again. After a long silence, he said, "You can probably bump up your rate on these people."

"Yeah? How much?"

"Double."

I didn't have time to digest the implications, because just then the door opened, and two men were silhouetted against the strong sunlight from outside. The dust in the store defined shafts of light which seemed to come from their outlines. They closed the door behind them, and the gloom in the shop was restored, the grimy glass in the door effectively blocking the sun.

Introductions were made. George was above average in height, with regular features and a dark complexion. Though he was clean-shaven, black stubble darkened his strong jawline.

Thanh was short, about my height, and Vietnamese. He looked strong, packing lots of muscle on a small frame. He spoke without accent, but George had an inflection I couldn't quite identify.

They did not argue with the daily rate I proposed, but there was an issue with payment.

"You'll be paid when we meet our friends on the other side," George said.

"Sorry," I said. "I get paid up front."

George stared at me, and for a moment I felt fear. There was a ruthlessness in his gaze, something that told me that this was a man who was used to being obeyed.

"Your standard arrangement assumes half the daily rate you're charging us," he said. I was starting to get a bad feeling.

"Maybe you need another guide, someone who'll work for less."

Thanh, who had not said a word, exchanged a glance with George and then said, "We can pay half up front, half on the other side." It was hard to tell who called the shots. Many of the grow ops were run by Vietnamese, so it was likely that George was just a front. His aggressive manner was compensating for lack of real authority.

There would be six of them, and I would have to carry most of the food, tents, and communal gear, since they would be burdened with "personal baggage." Another glitch developed when they insisted that I should provide transportation to the trailhead. There was no way that seven people and all the gear would fit into my beat-up Toyota. To my surprise, Owen came to the rescue.

"If we can leave early enough so that I can get back to open the store by eleven, I'll drive you in my van."

We arrived at the trailhead around eight in the morning. It was a clear day, and the mountains to the south shone in their pristine majesty, but the usual feeling of anticipation that I experienced when heading into the backcountry was tempered by the business-like atmosphere of our expedition. Before driving off in his van, Owen pulled me aside.

"Be careful, Sierra," he said once more, as we stood on the gravel shoulder of the road, away from the others.

"Jesus, Owen, don't tell me you're developing a conscience."

"Fine. Fuck yourself, then."

"You fuck yourself, too, Owen." I smiled at him, he smiled back, and then he disappeared, trailing a cloud of blue-gray exhaust. *Needs a ring job,* I thought, and then I walked back to my new best friends.

In addition to George and Thanh, there was a burly Russian in his midforties, Yuri, and Omar, probably from the Middle East, around forty years old. The other two also looked to be from the Middle East; they were Bob, a big man, around fifty, with a scar running diagonally from his right temple across his cheekbone, and Gord, who looked soft, and much younger, no more than thirty. Their accents contradicted their names, and I decided that "Bob" wouldn't mind if, at least in my own mind, I called him Scarface.

Their ski equipment looked new and serviceable, but their packs looked like they had been picked up at an army surplus store. They were sturdy green canvas with heavy straps; not ideal for a strenuous trip in the mountains.

Since I carried our communal gear, my pack was heavy; it took a while for my muscles to adjust as we started up the steep trail. However, I quickly realized that my pace was not going to be a problem. A couple of my companions had trouble putting the skins on their skis, and Gord was in poor physical shape and had limited skiing experience. I had counted on making the crossing in three days but packed supplies for an extra day. I started to wonder whether that margin would be sufficient.

We trudged up an abandoned logging road for the first hour, and then I cut off onto an old prospectors' trail that led more directly to the alpine. Large cedars shut off the sky, and we made our way slowly in the silent gloom. I was in the lead, and my charges struggled in single file behind me. Periodically I'd hear someone stumble or curse as their ski became entangled in some underbrush. It was my policy to ignore minor problems. Anyone who ventures into the backcountry should put up with a reasonable amount of discomfort and frustration. Learning is motivated by the desire to avoid exactly such problems.

By noon the trees were getting smaller and patches of sunlight dappled the snow. I had been stopping every hour, encouraging the group to hydrate as well as to layer down to lighter clothing. Even though it was quite cold, the effort of laboring uphill with heavy packs caused the body to overheat.

Because the trail was so narrow, these stops did not allow me to observe anyone in the party except George, who followed right behind me, and Yuri, who was behind him. They appeared to be handling the pace reasonably well, though Yuri's clothing was drenched from sweat. He had ignored my suggestion to layer down.

Around one o'clock we left the tree line behind us, and we were treated to the alpine in its full magnificence. The terrain sloped off to our right, and the steep apron of Mount Veringer rose to our left. The vista ahead revealed a series of flat snowfields intersected by deep gullies, and beyond the plateau, the snow-clad peaks this side of the U.S. border.

I called a halt, and my exhausted troops gathered while I set up my small stove and made lunch. As I waited for water to boil, I tried to assess their condition.

Yuri had changed into some dry clothes, Scarface appeared to be actually enjoying the outing, and Thanh and Omar looked tired but okay. Gord, legs splayed wide, was sitting in the snow, his back against his pack, his eyes closed, his face of a deathly pallor. George was squatting on his heels next to him, speaking in low tones right into his ear. I went over, and George looked up at me in a hostile manner.

"I can take some of his load," I suggested.

"No! He'll be okay," George said roughly, staring at me.

Fine, I thought, *I don't want to touch your fucking dope.* I stood for a moment, looking down at Gord. He was panting rapidly. We were only half as high as we would eventually get, and already he was having trouble with the altitude.

"Is lunch ready?" George demanded.

I walked back to the stove.

Gord continued to sit with his eyes closed while the rest ate. He refused any food, and a couple of times he made dry retching sounds. George had a swift conversation with Yuri, and the Russian took something out of his pack and then went over to Gord with a bottle of water. I saw Gord swallow something, and within fifteen minutes he made a miraculous recovery. We set out again.

I kept the group going until sunset, to make up for our slow pace, and thus we managed to cross most of the plateau.

With help from Scarface and Thanh, I made some snow platforms for the kitchen and started melting snow to make hot tea to revive the troops. Gord was again wilting, but the others seemed in reasonable condition.

After everyone was warmed up with tea, I set up the two tents. George and Yuri hauled Gord into their tent and put him into his sleeping bag while I prepared dinner. I threw my bag into the other tent, which was occupied by Thanh, Omar, and Scarface. George insisted that all the packs be piled just outside his tent; he and Yuri made seats for themselves, with their backs resting against the pile. George was using his headlamp to read, every once in a while glancing up to observe our progress in the kitchen. Perhaps it was a trick of the light, but I detected hostility in his look.

Yuri had taken off his toque, and I noticed that he had brown hair that started low on his forehead. The hair had been cropped short, but it was very thick, and his hat had flattened it on his head. This, along with his pointed nose, gave him a distinct resemblance to a porcupine I had once known. Yuri had picked up a tree branch somewhere along the way. He now took out a vicious-looking knife and set to whittling a series of perfectly formed toothpicks. As the evening progressed, I noticed that when George was not looking, Yuri would furtively reach into his pack and take a large swig from a flask.

The sky was spangled with a profusion of stars, and our open-air kitchen was humming with activity. Thanh, it turned out, was quite the cook.

"I worked in a restaurant," he said. "That's the only job an honors degree in philosophy prepared me for."

"I keep hearing about doctors who come to Canada and end up driving a cab."

"I got my degree here."

"So you were quite young when your family came to Canada?"

Thanh did not answer. I noticed that George was glowering at him.

It took George fifteen minutes to rouse Gord so that he could come out and have some dinner. Despite having his sleeping bag wrapped around him, Gord was shivering, and to me it looked like he had a serious fever. Yuri gave him several pills to swallow with the little food that he could gulp down.

I cleaned up the kitchen while everyone went to bed, except George, who continued to read, and Yuri, who continued to turn out his perfect toothpicks. I figured that by the end of the trip he would have enough for a large tray of hors d'oeuvres. As I headed for my sleeping bag, I heard Yuri say something to George. I recognized the word *talk* in Russian, as well as Thanh's name. George quickly came over as I was preparing to enter the tent that held Thanh, Omar, and Scarface. He grabbed my shoulder. I'm somewhat vertically challenged, and as he brought his face close to mine, I had to look up to meet his glare. There was a crazy ferocity in his dark eyes, and something told me that it would take little to set him off.

"You can't sleep in there," he said, as he squeezed my left shoulder with what I thought was unnecessary force.

"You want me in your tent, George?" I smiled in what I thought was a seductive fashion. His expression indicated that the implied proposal did not appeal to him.

"We only have two tents, George," I said as I removed his hand from my shoulder.

"That's your problem," he said, and he walked back to his perch next to Yuri.

It took me less than half an hour to dig a snug snow cave. I lined it with a tarp, laid my sleeping bag inside that, put my underclothes in the bottom of my bag, and crawled in. After a few minutes I was warm, and as I lay on my stomach, I stared out the small opening of my shelter. I could see a slice of the peaks that lay to the south. They were washed in diamond moonlight, with a backdrop of velvet black sky punctured by a sprinkling of stars.

I had to revise my opinion; George was definitely in charge of this expedition. The drug industry was taking on an international flavor. Perhaps the bags were not full of B.C. bud but a more valuable cargo from the Middle East. Maybe I should have asked for a higher fee. I wondered if Owen knew.

Yuri definitely looked like Russian mafia. Where did they figure in all this? And if indeed the drugs had originated in the Middle East, why bring them in via Canada?

It seemed that my meager knowledge of Russian could prove useful in the next few days.

I wondered what Lana was doing at that moment. I hadn't thought about her in months.

Though she had escaped her Doukhobor community in the interior of B.C. when she was eighteen, Svetlana had not shed her love of Tolstoy. She taught me some Russian so that I could share her appreciation for the master, in his original language.

Lana was twenty-two and had almost finished her nursing degree when I met her in Nelson. She was petite, and her red hair reached to her waist. Her dress and her quiet manner still spoke of her rustic origins, but there was a willfulness, a rebellious defiance toward convention, a core of craggy determination that underlay her gentle exterior. By the time I realized the strength of her resolutions, it was too late.

She gave me six years, six years punctuated by my long absences for several first ascents in the Andes and for a couple of expeditions to the Himalayas, six years when she never really knew whether I'd come home in a body bag.

By that time she was twenty-eight and I was thirty-four. In retrospect, I could see that she was right, that it was time to make a decision. But I was looking at the peaks and did not notice that my companion was slipping from my side.

When I came back from that first Everest expedition, she had removed all her belongings from the ramshackle house that her presence had transformed into a home. I should have gone after her. But I didn't. I was convinced that she would be back.

I went on the second Everest trip and again failed to summit. When I came back, Lana had gone to work in the hospital in Trail. Later I heard a rumor that she got married, but didn't believe it. I was convinced that the door was still open. By this time I had developed something of a reputation as a climber, and I used that to tear a swath through the impressionable young women of Nelson.

I was thirty-seven when I returned from my last trip to Everest. I had a broken collarbone and was emaciated from two months at high altitude. While I was recovering, I drove down to Rossland. I spotted Lana entering a grocery store, holding the hand of a toddler. I was about to approach her when she was joined by a tall,

good-looking guy who had an infant with red hair in a back carrier. I heard the clerk address him as Dr. Whitmore.

I walked out of the store and drove back to Nelson at well above
the speed limit.

The next day I started breakfast before the sun rose, and we were
on the trail at dawn. Long purple shadows were cast by our figures
as we trudged across the snow, and cold pink light licked at the
peaks ahead.

My clients shivered as they warmed up from their exertion, but
seemed like they were in working condition. Even Gord moved at
a steady pace, though he appeared to be something of a zombie.
During breakfast Yuri had given him some pills again.

By midmorning we were making the first of our steeper ascents.
Even I found it difficult. My pack was much too heavy, my back was
starting to spasm, and my legs were burning. Maybe I was getting
too old for this shit. But I thought about the piece of land I'd buy,
somewhere up in the mountains, and the house I'd build.

My companions were all starting to show signs of strain. Surprisingly, Gord shuffled on much as before, his eyes glazed and with a
fixed stare ahead. Yuri was panting, and sweat poured off his face.

The slope was too steep to attack directly; our skins would
not hold at that angle, and I had to serpentine back and forth.
This served its purpose but forced us to make sharp turns every
ten minutes. As long as we were going straight, not much skill
was required to handle the skis, but turns, many of which were
almost one hundred and eighty degrees, required experience,
strength, and balance. Especially with heavy packs and in steep
terrain, it was easy to fall over. Getting up required removing the
pack, and even thus unburdened, it took a great deal of effort
to get vertical with one's tangled skis stuck in the deep snow.
Each such incident was exhausting, and my companions quickly
learned that it was best not to fall over. Omar, unfortunately, fell
regularly, and his legs were trembling after a couple of hours.
I called for a short rest stop and advised everyone to hydrate
and eat as much as they could from the snacks I had prepared
in the morning. Yuri appeared not to need the encouragement
to hydrate, as he took long swigs from his bottomless flask. I
wondered how much of his pack was composed of refills for that
little silver container.

We continued on our uphill track through the rest of the morning, and we were now getting high enough so that the view was magnificent. Behind us, the flat snowfields we had crossed the previous day; ahead, a series of peaks etched in cobalt blue. Unfortunately, along with the view came the effects of less oxygen, and now even George and Scarface were visibly panting. Thanh had pain etched on his face, and though he didn't complain, he winced with every step.

When we stopped for lunch, the others collapsed onto their packs while I cooked. I noticed that Thanh took off his boots and was examining his shins. Yuri, who seemed to be the medic, was called over for a consultation, and I joined him while I waited for water to boil.

"It's just a little bruised," Yuri said.

Both of Thanh's shins were bright red and puffy, and on his right leg lesions were starting to appear.

"Shin bang," I said.

"What?" Yuri looked at me with hostility. His eyes were bloodshot, and he stank of booze.

"Shin bang," I repeated. "If we don't take care of it, Thanh won't be able to walk by tomorrow."

"What do you suggest, genius?" Yuri challenged. His bristly hair reminded me of that of a porcupine.

"I think we'll have to amputate," I said. When I saw the expression on Thanh's face, I realized that my attempt at humor was inappropriate.

"Just kidding. The problem is that your boot is bruising your shin, and—"

"I told you, it's just a bruise," Yuri interrupted. By this time George was also standing over Thanh as he sat on his pack, with his bare feet and legs raised to keep them out of the snow.

"Yes, but we have to cushion it, otherwise Thanh won't even be able to put on his boots."

I went to my pack, took out my sleeping pad, and cut two strips from the end. I put some gauze dressing around Thanh's lower leg and used duct tape to fix the foam from my sleeping pad against his shins.

"You'll have to keep the top buckles on your boots really loose, but that foam should help," I said. Thanh looked doubtful.

*

We continued our climb for several hours, oxygen getting thinner with every step. The sky, which had been a brilliant cerulean blue, was starting to take on a hazy cast. I observed that on the high sawtoothed ridge ahead of us, major cornices had formed from the action of the wind. Plumes of snow continued to be whipped off the high points along the sharp crest. I pulled my parka a little tighter around my neck and trudged on, breaking trail in the snow, which was becoming deeper as we ascended.

We finally arrived at a bench, and I called a halt. My companions collapsed onto their packs. I went over to see how Thanh was faring.

"It's better," he said, though there was still pain etched on his thin face. His high cheekbones looked white, the skin stretched taut.

Gord looked like a zombie, staring into the distance. Yuri, who made sure that he always sat behind George, took the occasional swig from his flask. George seemed tired, but that was normal.

Scarface's pack was off to the side, but he wasn't sitting on it. I looked around and saw him standing about thirty meters away, with his back to us. At first I thought he was just being unusually modest in relieving himself, but he stood there several minutes, quite still, looking down at the snow in front of him. I walked over and stood next to him.

In the snow directly at his feet, there was a small patch of red with a few tufts of dun fur around it, and some black pellets. Aside from our footprints, there were no tracks leading to this scene of violence.

"What the fuck is it?" I said, more to myself.

Scarface turned to me; the thin scar across his cheek and temple was particularly noticeable against the deep tan of his face.

"Rabbit," he said.

I looked around. "There are no rabbits this high. How did he get here? There're no tracks."

"Eagle," Scarface said, pointing.

And indeed there was a faint impression where the feathers of one wing had brushed the snow. The raptor had probably snatched the hare below the tree line but had not completely killed it. Its struggles had forced him to drop it for an instant, while he got a better grip; he then continued on his way to his high aerie.

What terror that hare must have felt, gripped by powerful talons, its struggles futile. Then the instant of hope as the eagle dropped it, immediately dashed as the raptor took hold again. No wonder he shit himself. It was like the Angel of Death plummeting from the sky and snatching us from the life we take so much for granted.

It was a sorry-looking bunch that pulled into camp that night, but at least I was satisfied that we had a chance of getting across the border before we ran out of food. We camped at a col above a long, steep descent to the glacier below. I would have preferred to camp further down, but I was concerned about the group's ability to negotiate that difficult stretch. There were a couple of cliff bands along the way, and a stumble while skiing down could result in a disastrous plunge. It would be safer to do this when my charges were well rested.

The tents were set up, I made dinner with help from Thanh and Scarface, and Yuri kept drinking and making toothpicks. A typical evening in the mountains.

"How are your shins?" I asked Thanh after everyone had settled down.

"Better," he said.

"Let me take a look," I said.

He sat down on his pack, and I unwrapped the gauze dressing. There was some oozing of clear fluid on his right shin, but the other dressing was dry. I replaced the stained dressing with new gauze, making sure that it was quite loose, to allow a scab to form.

"Make sure we tape back the foam before we start in the morning."

"Thanks, Sierra."

"You'll be fine. You come from tough people."

"You think so?" He raised his eyebrows quizzically.

"I visited the Cuchi Tunnels, Thanh. I have some idea."

"You were in Vietnam?"

"I went there in 1995. I saw the War Atrocities Museum."

The muscles in Thanh's jaw bulged and his face hardened, but he said nothing.

"The world should know what the Americans did. They talk about what the Germans did or what happened in Rwanda, but no one speaks of the war crimes in Vietnam."

"There are some things that can't be recorded in a museum," Thanh said, and he stood up and walked to his tent.

During the night I dreamed that I was back on Everest. I tried to climb, but my legs would not move, and my lungs burned, screaming for oxygen. I woke with sweat streaming down my face.

I lay in the blackness of my snow cave, trying to get calm, but I still felt like I was suffocating. And I was hot, as if I had a fever. I groped for my headlamp under my pack, and when I switched it on, I immediately understood that I was actually suffocating. The opening to my cave was completely blocked by snow.

It took a surprising amount of effort to punch through the snow and allow some air to flow into my burrow. With the fresh air came a blast of snow and a high-pitched whine, as if a million banshees were screaming to gain entrance.

I pulled on my clothes and crawled out, to witness a scene of chaos. The wind was howling, and the snow was so thick I could barely see the few meters to where the two tents had been. In fact, I could not see the tents.

But it quickly became clear why. Thanh's tent was in tatters. He, Scarface, and Omar were desperately trying to hold on to their sleeping bags and belongings as the raging storm tried to sweep them off the col.

There was more left of George's tent, mostly because Gord was still inside it, deep in drug-induced slumber, apparently oblivious to the howling chaos around him.

The ear-splitting din and swirling snow made communication almost impossible, but I finally organized them to dig individual snow caves, using what was left of the tents to line them. George seemed more concerned about the packs than his partners, and I had to dig a larger cave in which to store their cargo. George made sure that his cave was right next to the precious burden.

Gord was housed in the same burrow with Yuri. He had slept through the whole ordeal.

Finally my charges were all settled, and with the storm still keeping up its infernal racket, I crawled back into my sleeping bag. I felt exhausted, with my whole body aching, but I couldn't fall asleep. I knew I had made several serious mistakes that had jeopardized the safety of my clients. This was no recreational outing but a drug-smuggling operation, but that did not mitigate my responsibility as a guide. First, I should have been more aware of the signs that a storm was coming, despite the fact that when we had left, the forecast had called for the persistence of the ridge of high pressure whose benign influence we had been enjoying. Second, I should never have camped on the col. It was too exposed. The choice had been forced on me, by trying to make maximum distance so that we would not run out of food yet delaying the hazardous descent while my crew was exhausted. But these were excuses. I had fucked up. To top it all off, the wind and snowfall accumulation would dramatically increase the avalanche hazard for the rest of the trip. While we enjoyed the calm weather, the snowpack had been relatively stable.

When I emerged from my lair next morning, the wind had abated somewhat, but large flakes were still pouring from the sky, and visibility was minimal. As the little group huddled in what was left of the kitchen area, I suggested that we wait out the storm.

"We have to get across the border," George said. "Arrangements have been made."

"Arrangements will have to be changed," I insisted. "You can't navigate in this visibility, and there's high avalanche danger."

The others seemed convinced by my logic, but George was not giving up.

"We can navigate by GPS. How long will the avalanche danger last?"

I had to admit that it could take days for conditions to settle down, but made it clear that I was not willing to jeopardize the group's safety just to meet some artificial deadline.

"If we don't meet our deadline, you won't be paid."

"If we all get killed, there'll be nobody to pay me."

He did not reply but stalked off toward the cave where the packs were stored. I hesitated for a few moments, as the others muttered among themselves, and then went after George to see if I could reason with him. He was on hands and knees, crawling out of the burrow backward, and I slowed when I saw that there was something black in his right hand. I froze when I realized it was a gun. George got to his feet, facing away from me, wiped the snow from the flat gun, and put it inside his jacket. Before he could see me, I quickly made my way back to the kitchen and squatted down in the same place where I had been when George left.

Just as he came within earshot, I announced, "Okay, I think the storm is settling a bit. Everyone get ready. We're leaving in half an hour." I stood up and went back to my cave to pack.

I've often wondered what causes us to compound an initial mistake with progressively greater stupidity. I had put my group in jeopardy by camping on the col, and despite the fact that I knew how dangerous it was, I had been intimidated into attempting the descent in essentially whiteout conditions. Though visibility was zero, all the indications for disaster would have been quite obvious even to a blind man.

Since most of our travel to this point had involved climbing, I did not have a clear idea of how well my group was able to ski downhill. The first part of the descent from the col was relatively gentle. Even with the large packs, George, Scarface, and Yuri were enjoying themselves, making large swooping turns in the fresh powder. Thanh and Omar were skiing adequately, though the heavy packs and the fact that they couldn't see ahead of them made them stiff and awkward.

Predictably, Gord was an utter disaster. The dosage of whatever drug they were pumping into him had obviously been reduced, in anticipation that the descent would not require as much energy as climbing. However, the man was at best a weak intermediate skier, and with the difficult conditions, this was simply not adequate. In the first hour he fell three times. Since I was leading the group, the first time I did not realize this until word had been passed up the line. I directed the others to take a rest while I climbed back up to where Gord was still floundering in the deep snow. He had exhausted himself trying to get up with his pack still on and was now lying on his side, half buried. I took off his pack, pulled him out, found one of his skis, which was buried in the snow, found his poles, supported him while he tried to put his skis back on, and then carried his pack down to where the others were waiting. I watched Gord ski down, and even without a pack he was struggling. I kept yelling at him to get forward on his skis, but after a split second he'd be leaning back again and the skis would start to run out of control. He'd then make a sharp turn to slow down. In powder, this is disastrous, and inevitably he'd fall over sideways. Without the pack, he'd manage to get up, but each time he was more exhausted. The ski to the others was short, but by the time we reached them, Gord's legs were trembling.

I decided to wait until he recovered, and made some hot tea while we waited. In the meantime, I pondered what kind of insanity had prompted George to include this novice in his group.

I also wondered why Gord's pack was so hard. It felt more like metal containers than compressed dope.

When we set off again, I gave George my GPS and charged him with staying on the route that I had planned. I stayed next to Gord and tried to coach him. He fell a few more times, but his stance was improving, and because I helped him to get up each time, this was no longer taking such a toll on his energy. As well, I noticed that Yuri had laced Gord's tea with more pharmaceutical assistance.

In this way, we managed to drop about a third of the way down. The visibility was improving, with much smaller snowflakes, and the wind had almost stopped. I could see George and the others ahead of us and was able to ascertain that he was not straying off course. I was actually starting to believe that we could make it down to the glacier below. Crossing the glacier had its challenges, but at least it was flat. Then there was one more modest ridge to cross, and we would be across the border.

We stopped for a short lunch. Food was getting low anyway.

I instructed the group to put their skins back on.

"What the fuck for?" George asked. "We're going downhill."

"There are some rocky parts ahead of us. It's easier to control your speed with skins."

"That's because you don't know how to ski," George said.

"Look, George, are you here for the turns or to get across the border?"

He glared at me but didn't reply. I saw a quick smile flit across Thanh's usually impassive face.

With the skins on, we could no longer just swoop down the slopes. We had to zigzag to make the descent gradual, and this slowed our progress dramatically.

Despite this, there were a couple of places where we had to make a traverse on a narrow ledge with a steep slope below us. I generally stuck with Gord and coaxed him through these spots. I kept telling him to look ahead, but somehow he could not resist occasionally glancing down the steep drop beside him. Sometimes his legs would begin to tremble, and then I would tell him to stop, breathe deeply, and would not allow him to go on until his legs were steady.

We were now descending through a light mist, but it had stopped snowing, and visibility had improved to the point that on occasion I could actually see the glacier below. Unfortunately, at our pace we wouldn't be able to reach it before dark, but at least I could find a more sheltered spot, in case the wind picked up. I decided to keep moving as long as possible, despite the fact that even the stronger members of our party were starting to show signs of fatigue. I called for a quick stop to allow everyone to hydrate and gulp down some food, and then we pressed on.

Gord was starting to handle the difficult parts better. Given a couple of years in the backcountry, he would probably become a competent mountaineer.

We were crossing a part that was fairly steep. I had asked the others to wait while I went ahead and packed down a firm, if narrow, traverse into the side of the steep slope. There was a cliff band above us, so there was little danger of avalanche from that direction. By cutting the snowpack with my skis, I was testing to see whether the slope below us was likely to go. If it did go, I had little hope of getting rescued by my companions. The one quick transceiver exercise we had done indicated that it would take them far too long to find and dig me out.

The slope did not slide, and I went back and instructed the group to cross one at a time and wait for me at a protected spot ahead.

They navigated the traverse, and I could see them waiting ahead. Only Gord and I were left. I had to allow him to cross by himself, because the traverse was too narrow for two.

"Keep your weight on your downhill ski," I said. He nodded, and started across. He was doing well until he came to the middle. At this spot the slope above was so steep that Gord could reach out with his left hand and almost touch the slope above him. I suppose the temptation to steady himself was too much, and he leaned in toward the mountain. Before I could warn him, his skis slid out from under him, and he started to rag-doll down the slope to his right, which was equally steep.

An experienced mountaineer would have been able to self-arrest, but Gord was anything but experienced. He kept going, flipping head over heels. While terrifying, the damage would not be severe, since the snow was soft. But as a sudden breeze blew apart the curtain of mist, I suddenly realized that there was another rock band far below us. The slope was relatively gentle there, but Gord was heading straight for it at high speed. The small figure hit the rocks and came to a stop. He did not move.

I quickly stripped off my skins and skied down at full speed. Kicking off my skis and dropping my pack, I ran out into the rocks.

Gord was unconscious, but there was no sign that he had hit his head. The pack had also protected his spine. However, his right pant leg was soaked with blood. I cut away his pants and nearly vomited. The broken end of a bone was protruding through the skin of his thigh.

I put a tourniquet on his thigh, because the blood was pulsing out of the wound. Then I used his poles, which had been clutched in his hands, to fashion a splint.

By this time the others had arrived. I don't know how they had come down the steep slope. In retrospect, I was amazed that we had not triggered an avalanche in the process.

We made camp on a flat spot nearby. While the rest retired to their individual snow caves, Yuri and George conferred in Russian about Gord. I noticed that Yuri referred to him as "professor," and I finally understood why they'd bring along someone so inexperienced. They needed him to process the drugs they carried.

I was trying to make dinner from the sparse supplies we had left. Gord was laid out on the flat platform we had dug for the kitchen. Though he was unconscious, he moaned occasionally, and his breathing seemed shallow. We had to get him to a hospital soon, or he would lose his leg. Worse, he could die from shock and infection.

Yuri injected him, and Gord's breathing became more regular, and he seemed to go into a deep sleep. George told Yuri to give him another injection, setting off a rapid discussion that I couldn't follow. Yuri injected Gord again.

It took me a long time to melt the snow required to make our evening meal. We had food enough for one more day, and at best we still had two days of travel ahead of us, possibly three. The liquid would allow me to stretch the supplies.

As I went about making dinner, I tried not to think about the events of the day. I had fucked up in so many ways on this trip! If my examiners had witnessed this disaster, they would have immediately yanked my guide's ticket for incompetence. Fortunately for me, the illicit nature of the job ruled out making a report, but that didn't change the fact that, in my own heart, I knew.

Gord had been placed into Yuri's snow cave and appeared to be sleeping peacefully. The rest of the group gathered quietly in the kitchen to consume dinner, and eventually the big Russian joined them. When he walked past me, my nose indicated that happy hour had already started.

To my astonishment, Omar spoke to him in Russian, and then Thanh joined the conversation. I finally realized that this was a Russian mob operation after all. Probably George, Gord, Scarface, and Omar were Uzbeks or something. Where Thanh fit in was puzzling, but he spoke Russian, so he was definitely part of the organization.

While my mind was occupied with trying to sort this out, the bursts of Russian became an unintelligible background noise, and thus I was surprised when Yuri suddenly jumped on Omar, bringing him to the ground, and started to pummel his face with his big fist. After a moment of shocked hesitation, I tried to pull the big Russian off, but it wasn't until Thanh helped me that we were able to stop Yuri from totally demolishing Omar's face. Even the two of us had difficulty restraining the bastard—he kept trying to break loose to get at Omar again, all the while screaming what I recognized as curses that called into question the sexual practices of Omar's mother. It took George to finally resolve the conflict. He simply pulled the gun that I had seen once before, issued a terse command in a low, guttural voice, and Yuri slunk off to his cave. The remains of his dinner lay spilled in the snow, so I suspect he supplemented his meal from his flask.

Omar sat on the snow, blood dripping between his fingers as he held his face. Thanh and I convinced him to let us inspect the damage; his right eye was swollen shut, a front tooth had been knocked out, and blood was streaming from his nose and mouth. As far as I could tell, his nose wasn't broken. I fixed him up as best I could. By this time it was dark, and everyone drifted off to their caves to sleep, except for Thanh, who stayed behind to clean up and help with preparing food for the next day.

"Where did you learn Russian?" I asked him.

He looked at me, and for a moment I thought I had made a mistake. "University," he finally said.

It seemed that getting information from Thanh was hopeless, and we finished our task in silence. I was about to go to my cave, but to my surprise, Thanh sat down on one of the seats we had carved out of the snow. He pulled something from his pocket. His headlamp revealed that it was five cigarettes inside a plastic bag. He carefully took one out, found a lighter, and lit it. There was evident pleasure in his features as he inhaled deeply.

"Why did you visit Vietnam?" he asked, looking at me through the tendrils of smoke drifting out of his nostrils.

"I was climbing in Asia, and I had always wanted to see the country. I heard about what the Americans did . . ."

His face turned hard, and he inhaled deeply. Then he turned off his headlamp, so I could no longer make out his features. His voice had a haunting quality, disembodied, as if a specter from the past had replaced the material presence that he had presented to my eyes a few moments before.

"You don't know what the Americans did. Nobody really understands."

I was standing near him. I had switched off my headlamp earlier, and I waited in silence, not moving, not even breathing. The dark night congealed around us, except for the orange glow from the tip of Thanh's cigarette. Time stood still.

"I loved my sister. She was ten years older, like a second mother. The American soldiers came to my father's restaurant, and she served them food."

There was a long silence. The cigarette glowed bright, faded, glowed bright again.

"I tried to pull him off her, but I was small, only four years old. He smelled like rotten milk. I didn't understand until I was much older what the soldier did. When my father found out, he went to the colonel. They offered him money, and my mother said to take it. Two weeks later my sister walked into the river." The orange tip of the cigarette described an arc in the blackness and was extinguished. I heard his footsteps crunching in the snow as he headed for his cave.

I stood there, motionless, for a long time.

I woke the next morning and lay snuggled in my warm sleeping bag. I could hear that the wind had picked up during the night; the storm had regained some of its fury. I turned over on my stomach and saw the weak gray light of dawn filtered by swirling snow. I could barely make out Yuri's bulky form as he crawled out of his cave and lumbered toward the cave occupied by George.

The memory of the events of the previous day shot through me as if I had just grabbed a high-voltage cable. We had to get Gord to a hospital right away. At best we were two days from civilization, considering that we would have to carry him in some kind of toboggan. We were running out of food, and the storm would make travel almost impossible. My incompetence had created this crisis.

I shot out of my cave, and was just pulling on my jacket when I saw that Yuri and George were dragging Gord out of Yuri's cave. I rushed over and immediately saw that Gord was dead.

"Froze," George said. Though Gord's face was as white as alabaster, I could still see traces of dried foam at the corners of his lips. Only once before in my life, during my druggie days in Berkeley, had I seen a face like that.

"I'll make a toboggan," I said.

"What for?" George asked.

"How else are we going to carry him?"

George and Yuri exchanged glances, and suddenly I realized how naive I had been. What did I expect? That they would take Gord to the U.S. authorities for an autopsy?

The realization that I was party to murder hit me with the force of a ten-ton truck. I stood frozen, while George and Yuri dragged the body off into the swirling snow.

I'm ashamed to say that I went back to my snow cave, took off my jacket and boots, and crawled back into the warmth of my sleeping bag. I fell asleep immediately.

When I woke again, I felt like I had been drugged. My limbs were leaden, and I had lost the desire to ever move again. I lay there for what seemed like a long time, my head pulled into the cocoon of my sleeping bag, my eyes squeezed shut. I kept hoping it had all been a bad dream, but the howling of the wind outside pulled me back to the inescapable reality of total failure, of my culpability.

When I emerged, the full force of the storm hit me. I had to lean forward to move toward the kitchen, and I couldn't see more than a couple of meters as fat flakes were whipped into my face.

As I got closer, I saw that the whole group was gathered in the kitchen, with their packs in a circle. Were these people totally insane? There was no way we could move in such a storm. I trudged toward the group, and I could hear snatches of loud conversation above the wind but could not make out any words. I noticed that Gord's pack was in the middle of the circle, and they were dividing up the contents among the other packs. George was just removing something; it looked like a blue metal canister. I stopped. Why would they have the drugs in metal containers? George carried the small canister as if it were quite heavy, in fact as if it were solid metal.

They had their backs to me and, with the wind howling, did not notice my approach. I quickly retreated to my cave, crawled in, and lay there thinking for a long time. Being an incompetent guide was one thing; there's no excuse for being profoundly stupid.

I had drifted off to sleep again, and awoke to George yelling at me to wake up. He had stuck his head into my little cave and was shaking my shoulder with a grip that was unnecessarily rough.

When I emerged, the group was assembled in the kitchen, ready to move. It was snowing, but the wind had died down. There was a small pile of personal gear—sleeping bags and clothes—which George told me to put into my pack.

I tried to talk them out of moving with such poor visibility.

"What do you suggest," George asked, "that we sit here and starve to death?"

We made slow progress for the remainder of the day. The packs were heavier, the terrain steep, and what had happened to Gord made everyone cautious. I noticed that even Scarface, who was clearly the most experienced in the mountains, was not as fluid in his motions.

Fat flakes of snow floated down steadily, creating a many-layered arras in front of us. But we managed to descend most of the way as it started to get dark. The curtain of snow had thinned out, and as we stood on a ridge, I saw the vast flat expanse of a glacier below us. Beyond that, I knew, was one more range, and then the U.S. border. With any luck, our ordeal would be over in two days.

I woke the next morning to find that a dense fog had settled onto the landscape. The view of the glacier from the previous evening had been replaced by a claustrophobia-inducing closeness.

We had to make do with a sparse breakfast, and I could not hide from the others that beyond that evening, we would be running on empty. Yuri was particularly vocal in his complaints, and he no longer hid his drinking.

Because of the fog, it took us much longer than I had anticipated to descend to the glacier. Dusk caused the mist to congeal around us; we were now on the glacier, but still had most of it to cross.

The setting of the invisible sun was marked only by a gradual attenuation of the already meager light. I dropped my pack, and the others came up behind me and unloaded their burdens as well. George, who had been at the back of the line, saw us standing there and said, "It's not time to stop yet."

"It's getting dark. I can't see where we're going," I pointed out.

"We have GPS. We gotta keep moving."

"Go ahead, George. You can lead the way."

"How much longer to the border?"

"At this rate, two more days." This raised a chorus of groans.

"Two more days, two more days. You always say two more days. Are we even going in the right direction?" George asked.

"You have the GPS. You tell me."

"We're out of food," Yuri put in.

I turned to him. "Going ahead in the dark is suicide. The glacier is full of crevasses. Better to go slow and get there alive."

I used up the last of our food to make a thin, confused stew that night. Yuri supplemented his portion with his inexhaustible supply of vodka. He sat there, whittling on some wood that he had picked up the day before. His drinking had never created any signs of inebriation in the past, but tonight the strokes of his knife became more and more savage, and an insane expression gradually suffused his face.

I was cleaning up the dishes and had my back to the group, but listened to the conversation, trying to pick out words from Russian that would at least indicate the general topic of the discussion. Omar drifted over to help me; his face was still a mess from the beating Yuri had administered.

"What kind of name is Sierra, anyway?" he asked at one point.

"I changed it when I came to Canada. My original name is James."

"You're not Canadian?"

"Nah. I'm a draft dodger."

"From the States?" I turned to look at him. He seemed quite agitated.

"From the States?" he repeated.

"Well, yeah."

"You're American!"

"I've been here thirty-seven years. I'm a Canadian citizen."

Omar stared at me from the one eye that wasn't swollen shut and then walked back to the others, who were still conversing in Russian. I was about to head off to sleep when I was confronted by George, Omar, and Thanh.

George started. "You're American."

"No, I'm a Canadian citizen. What the fuck's the difference, anyway?"

Their angry expressions told me that there was a difference.

"I came here a long time ago so I wouldn't be drafted."

"But you're American," George insisted.

I decided to change tack. "Look, I have a warrant for my arrest in the U.S. for selling dope, in addition to being a draft dodger. That's why I can only take you a short way past the border. But I'll get you and your cargo there. I don't care that you're carrying drugs. I used to be a dealer myself." I had never before exaggerated my involvement with drugs.

The three of them exchanged glances. Whatever it was that they were going to do next, it didn't happen, because suddenly there was a burst of loud Russian from behind them. Yuri was half standing, knife in one hand, wood in the other, roaring at Scarface. I could make out only one word of his tirade—*Taliban*. The insane expression on Yuri's face was terrifying, even from where I stood. His face was a deep red, glistening with sweat, and his eyes were tiny brown spots. His bristly hair stood on end like threatening porcupine's quills.

Scarface was sitting, impassive, except that the scar was like a white lightning bolt against the livid color that suffused the rest of his face.

Though he was in a posture to spring on Scarface with the knife, it was unclear whether Yuri actually intended to do so. Nevertheless, in a motion that my eyes could barely follow, Scarface reached inside his parka, pulled out a black gun, and shot Yuri square in the forehead. The bullet went out the back of his skull with a spurt of blood, and Yuri, still in a squat, tumbled over backward.

For a moment it was as if I were in a wax museum that was displaying a tableau frozen in time. Only the crimson stain seeping from Yuri's head into the snow got larger. Scarface sat rigidly pointing his gun to where Yuri had been, and my three interrogators, half turned toward him, looked like statues with their torsos awkwardly twisted.

Then everyone exploded into action. George confirmed that Yuri was dead, kicking the knife in his hand away from the body, and then started shouting at Scarface, who stood with his right arm hanging limply but still clutching the gun.

They ignored me while they stripped Yuri's body. His skin was as white as the snow around him, but I noticed a large reddish area on his back, as if he had a sunburn. Omar and Thanh burned the bloodstained clothes while Scarface and George dragged the naked body off somewhere into the darkness. The red stain in the snow was covered up, and by the time those two returned, the camp looked entirely normal. Scarface sat down and rapidly disassembled and cleaned his gun and put it back together. This was a man who knew his weapon.

Suddenly I was the one who felt out of his depth, as a military atmosphere suffused the camp. George issued terse orders, and the others carried them out without question. They soon turned their attention to me. My ankles and wrists were tied, and George decided that he liked my company after all, because he crawled into my cave with his sleeping bag next to mine. He had a rope tied to his wrist, the other end of which was looped around my throat. I awoke several times during the night to the sensation that I was suffocating; whenever George turned over, the loop would tighten around my neck, and I'd be forced to turn with him. Needless to say, I did not get much sleep. I guess Lana was right—I have issues about getting close.

When George and I did our synchronized crawl out of the snow cave the next morning, we were greeted by fog that was, if anything, more dense than the day before. This was surprising. It was rare for conditions to stay stable for such an extended period, because weather systems in the mountains tend to evolve rapidly. True, we were on the glacier, which forms an extended flat area and is more conducive to allowing a stable system.

Not that I could even tell that we were on the glacier. I could barely make out the openings to the snow caves where the others were sleeping, just five meters from me.

Our remaining provisions consisted of some coffee and a tiny bag of oatmeal, and George let me off my leash only long enough so that I could melt snow and prepare this travesty of a breakfast.

As I went about my tasks, I pondered my situation. I thought seriously about just making a break and leaving them. Surviving without my pack would have been difficult, but not impossible. In any case, I had little doubt that George would dispose of me once I led them across the border.

However, even if I abandoned the group, there was a chance that they would survive to carry out their mission. Scarface clearly had mountaineering skills. I had to chuckle at my dilemma. Owen and the other self-righteous activists always said that we all have to choose sides at some point. Circumstances sometimes force us to make surprising choices.

As I ruminated on this, my foot came in contact with something hard that was wedged into the crack under a block of snow that I was using as a makeshift counter. I bent down. In the dim light of dawn I saw the dark handle of Yuri's knife that George had kicked away from that inert body. Looking around to make sure no one observed me, I tucked the knife inside my parka.

Later, the process of dividing up the contents of Yuri's pack took place. George tied me up again, leaving me inside my snow cave, but even in the mist it was pretty obvious that it wasn't drugs they were transporting. As I peered out the opening, I could make out another blue metal canister, and something square that must have been a piece of electronics inside a layer of cushioning.

Soon we were under way again. Even under less bizarre circumstances it would have been advisable to rope ourselves together. If any of us fell into a crevasse, the others would prevent him from falling too far.

The storm a few days previously had dumped a large amount of snow over the area. This meant that the crevasses were difficult to detect. Over the winter, a snow bridge often forms over a crack in the ice. As long as it's cold, these snow bridges are strong enough to support a person crossing them. In spring, the bridges melt, revealing the gaping openings in the deep ice of the glacier. The most dangerous time is in between. The snow hides the traps but is not strong enough to support someone crossing over them.

We trudged along almost in lockstep, one long rope looped through the climbing harnesses that we all wore. I was in the lead, with George behind me, followed by Omar, Thanh, and then Scarface at the back.

Progress was slow, because of the poor visibility. Scarface had the GPS, and he occasionally shouted to me if I wandered too far from the correct heading. His voice sounded as if it came from another world, muffled by the fog. I could see no more than a couple of meters ahead, and when I looked back, I could see George, but Omar was a dark blur, and my eyes could not penetrate to see Thanh or Scarface.

George called for frequent stops. Their packs were obscenely heavy, having increased 50 percent as their numbers dropped. Mine, in contrast, got lighter as we used up all our food, since they were unwilling to trust me with their lethal cargo.

In the dull rhythm of putting one ski in front of the other, I had lots of time to consider exactly what these men were carrying. The red marks on Yuri's back looked like radiation burns to my inexperienced eye.

We stopped again after a while, sitting in a circle, sipping from our water bottles. There was some discussion in Russian, which may have concerned sharing the load with me. The only decision made was to put Scarface immediately behind me, thus leaving Thanh at the end. There was a fair amount of loose snow from the storm, and breaking trail made the going harder. The farther back in the line one was, the more packed the trail.

"How much longer until we get out of this fog?" George asked.

"It looks like it's settled onto the glacier for good. Once we start climbing, we'll probably get above it."

"How long?"

"Maybe seven kilometers. Depends on how fast we go."

He scowled, and then gave the order to move.

About a half-hour later, as my right ski slid forward, I thought I heard a soft crunch in the snow under me. My numbed brain took a moment to decipher the meaning of this sound, but my body kept its rhythm, one ski ahead of the other, and an instant later I heard a louder crack behind me. Instinctively, I threw myself to the ground, kicked off my skis, and dug my heels into the snow; at the same time, both of my hands grabbed the rope connecting me to the others. There was a violent yank on the rope, only a little of which I was able to absorb with my arms. I was being pulled back, my heels making deep grooves in the packed snow as I slid toward a wide black opening. On the other side of the gap I could make out Thanh, in much the same situation. We continued to skid, from opposite sides, toward the edge of the crevasse, pulled by the weight of the three men dangling on our rope.

For a moment the mist thinned, and I could clearly see the horror in Thanh's eyes as I swiftly pulled out Yuri's knife and cut the rope. Thanh struggled, but even for the two of us the weight had been too much. Thanh's face had a look of reproach as he disappeared over the lip of the crevasse.

I scrambled farther away from the edge, taking my skis with me. I dug a trench parallel to the opening, tied another rope to my skis, and then buried them to form an anchor. Using the rope as a belay, I crawled on my stomach until I could look over the lip.

The crevasse was very deep, and the walls were almost vertical. Not even Joe Simpson could climb out of it. I could barely see Thanh lying face-down deep below, on a narrow ledge. He looked to be unconscious, and there was a red smear near his face. I couldn't even see the others.

I crawled back to my pack, dug out the skis, put them on, and started trudging toward the border. I could sneak into some small town, pick up a few supplies, and then head back to Nelson.

The rhythm of my motion provided a hypnotic background to the thoughts swirling around in my head. I had deliberately killed four people, yet I felt no guilt. For one thing, Thanh and I could not have held the other three, so the alternative was that all five of us would die.

But I had to admit that even if there had been a way to save the others, I would not have done it. Like Oetzi, their bodies, along with their lethal cargo, would be spit out by the glacier in a few thousand years. I wondered if any humans would be left to find them.

As a kid, during the Cold War, I had lived with the constant threat of nuclear war. It had been averted, and we believed we had emerged into a new era of tranquility, where we would not have to be thinking about death from an outside, impersonal force. But we were wrong.

Terrorism became the new boogeyman. It made me think of

Orwell's *1984;* our government always finds some outside threat, so that we stay docile.

I'm tired of being held hostage to someone else's fanatical ideas, whether it's some desperate character in the Middle East or some religious zealot in Washington. I'd rather face any danger in the wilderness than be hostage to their insanity.

I thought about what had held those six disparate men together. After all, Yuri and Scarface had most likely fought on opposite sides in Afghanistan. And how did Thanh fit in?

There was only one logical explanation. Their blind hatred of the U.S. was the bond that could overwhelm even their own natural antipathy toward each other.

I wondered what Owen would say now about my lack of political commitment.

Sometimes we're forced to take sides, even if it's just for a few split seconds. But that doesn't obligate me to buy into the rest of the bullshit.

As soon as I get back to Nelson, I'm heading for high ground. If I'm lucky, I'll have a few years before the serious shit begins.

KEVIN LEAHY

Remora, IL

FROM *The Briar Cliff Review*

WE WERE DESPERATE, it's true. That doesn't excuse what happened, but we don't know what we could have done differently. As soon as the last car rolled off the line, the owners shuttered the plant, sold the machinery, and returned to Europe. To this day, the mention of it turns a heart to lead. The kids weren't scared, though. The night the plant closed, a handful of them drove to the property's edge with cases of beer. Girls danced in headlights while the radio blared from open doors. Boys carved doughnuts in the Blooms' nearby cornfield until Kyle Rouse's pickup got stuck in mud. They laughed it off. All their lives they'd been told the plant would be waiting for them with a good job once they turned eighteen. Now they'd be spared the fates of their parents, who had built boxy, affordable sedans and carried a vague unease in the lines around their eyes.

But to everyone else it seemed like a bomb had gone off in the center of town — the shock wave knocking down stores all through the summer. Hal's Bakery went first, followed by the record shop and the Bailey Café. By the time the leaves changed colors, even the grand old Cineplex was hollowed out, its marquee denuded of the letters we sometimes found rearranged into profanities. Sheets of plywood with spray-painted *X*'s blinded its windows, and tufts of crabgrass reclaimed its parkway. The town manager shifted public workers to a four-day week and promised to do everything he could to attract business.

We all hoped things would return to normal and tried to get by. We flushed our cars' engines and scoured the sediment from our hot water heaters, hoping both would last another winter. We bought dry beans instead of canned, and canned vegetables instead of fresh. Our wallets grew fat with coupons.

It would not be a stretch to say those first hard months made us closer, as a town. We stopped feeling sorry for ourselves, and lingered in the church basement after services for crumb cake and coffee. Helen Bree, whose late husband had worked at the plant for thirty-eight years, organized a clothing drive. Parents tutored each other's children when the schools closed on Fridays. People invited out-of-work friends to dinner, and they pretended not to notice their gratitude, or their envy. And when they left, the hosts lay in bed and prayed that the spirit that had claimed their guests would pass over them.

No one recalls who came up with the prison. It might have been Herman Floss, who had sold life, car, and homeowner's insurance to nearly the whole town, and who was given to making uncomfortably deep and probing eye contact with each of us at town meetings. It could have been Deputy Ken Dufresne, who muttered to anyone who would listen that the uptick in unemployment meant a looming epidemic of bar fights, drunk-and-disorderlies, and what have you. In any case, around the first of the year the council invited a consultant from a private prison company to lay out our options.

Not that there weren't objections. At the town meeting, the Bloom family, who came from Quakers, spoke against it right in front of the consultant, who sat behind the dais at the front of the hall with the selectmen and manager. Herman Floss said that the Blooms had farm subsidies to fall back on, so why didn't they tend to their soybeans and keep out of it? Helen Bree stood and declared it "unseemly." We loved Helen Bree, and we had nothing against the Blooms, but by then the town was so mired in debt that we canceled the Christmas parade and cut our trash collection to twice monthly. All winter the town lay dormant, the trees along the main thoroughfare naked—no lights, no foil Santas or tinseled candy canes. Parents bought dollar-store toys for their children and baked gingerbread for relatives. Husbands and wives surprised each other with nothing, and were disappointed and glad in equal measure. The weather was likewise stingy. Though the ground was packed hard with frost, little snow fell, and rows of desiccated cornstalks, ordinarily invisible under a blanket of white, thrust up from the Blooms' fields like grave markers.

"There's real opportunity here," said the prison consultant. "This would mean jobs not only in the facility but for the shops that serve visitors."

Ed McConnell, who owned a ranch not far from the abandoned plant, stood to speak. "The plant bought meat from me for twenty years. What kind of guarantees can you give us that you'll do like-wise?"

We hated McConnell for asking that, as if the wrong question might blow our chances. We'd become shy about making demands. But the consultant nodded and said, "I don't think that'll be a problem. We usually make use of local producers." He gestured to the screen on the stage, where a chart was projected from a device he'd hooked to his laptop. "There are ancillary benefits, too," he said, scanning our faces. "Each prisoner counts as a resident. That means more dollars for your district."

Most of us didn't need persuading. We were using one credit card to pay off another. We ransacked our filing cabinets and dresser drawers for half-remembered savings bonds. People looted their pensions and college funds and spent the inheritances they'd hoped to leave their children. Young couples postponed their wed-dings. Though we weren't supposed to know, we heard whispers that Grace Chilton, the kindergarten teacher whose unemployed husband, Robert, once worked double shifts between the record shop and the Cineplex, had stopped her fertility treatments. We were ready for something good to happen, and we hoped this was it.

Corvus Correctional won the bid, with construction to begin after the first thaw.

On a cold March morning we watched a wrecking ball punch through the plant's façade. The structure collapsed on the fourth swing, coughing up plumes of dust we could taste from a quarter mile away. It fell so easily—we had no idea how frail it was. For a while a great number of us worked as unskilled laborers, heaving broken pieces of the building into dumpsters. Rumor had it that Kyle Rouse smuggled out all the copper pipes that first night and sold them for scrap two towns over, but nothing came of it. Who could blame him? We would have done the same, if we'd thought of it. Those first paychecks were intoxicating. We'd forgotten the feel of having money, and were starving for it.

After work we were exhausted but happy. There was pleasure in our aching shoulders, in the newfound roughness of our hands. On paydays some went to Barry's Tap to drink. Those who'd worked at the plant confessed to feeling funny about Corvus using that space. They'd be loading a wheelbarrow with cinder block when a remnant of floor tile signaled they were standing in the old break room, where Bill Bree had hustled them and many of their fathers in penny-ante poker. The banks of lockers they hauled away were the same ones in which they'd hung their coveralls and filter masks, glittering with metallic dust, at the end of a shift. It wasn't that the plant had been problem-free. There'd been strikes and wage freezes and every so often an accident that claimed a limb. But day by day, as they dismantled what was left of their old workplace, they marveled that anyone had looked at that site and imagined a prison.

Then there came a need for construction workers and tradesmen—welders, pipefitters, laborers, and the like. But only the skilled among us could do that work, and a fresh wave of discord passed through as we were sorted yet again into those with jobs and those without. From the ground rose a fortress of towers joined by ramparts, its perimeter enclosed by a cursive scrawl of razor-wire fence. Inside, men slotted together racks of iron bars. They partitioned the floor into six-by-eight-foot cells, which everyone deemed both too small and entirely appropriate. They studded common areas with concrete embankments to disrupt foot traffic and minimize opportunities for mayhem. They painted lines that prisoners would not be allowed to cross.

With thousands of inmates arriving in a year, we expected a boon from the prisoners' relatives and police who would eat in our restaurants, gas up at our filling stations, and shop in our stores. The council rezoned everything, which would allow us to rent out unused bedrooms to overnight visitors. Real estate speculators from upstate bought foreclosed businesses and leased them out. The Baileys reopened their café, though they rented the space they once owned. Robert Chilton, Grace's husband, found occasional work.

The Sunday after the grand reopening of the Bailey Café, only three people stayed after church for Helen Bree's crumb cake social. As if relieved of a great burden, her heart stopped until Pastor Kimble shocked it back to life with the portable defibrillator the church had bought during fatter times. Few of us visited her in the hospital, we're embarrassed to say, though once she returned home the Bloom boy trekked over from the farm twice a week to deliver groceries, remove her trash, and sit on her couch watching the Nature Channel, which she was immensely fond of.

As the third Christmas since the plant closing approached, workers put the finishing touches on the prison. In each cell they installed steel toilets that were, strangely, also sinks. They wired up a network of cameras and reinforced the doors with metal plates. In the hallways they passed burly men in shirts embroidered with the Corvus Correctional logo, who stocked the armory with shotguns, rifles, batons, tear gas, and pepper spray. On their belts the Corvus people wore plastic zip cuffs resembling the six-pack rings that poisoned sea turtles or ensnared gulls, and which Helen Bree had once led a campaign to ban. Corvus was hiring soon, was the word.

"You have no idea what you're in for," said Ken Dufresne to a group of young men at Barry's. They'd applied to be guards. *"Corrections officers,"* he said, and looked away with a slow shake of his head. The group left soon afterward. Our town hadn't had a murder in eight years, not since Gene Shipsky, Dufresne's old fishing buddy, shot his wife and her lover dead in the Shipskys' bedroom. He then put the pistol to his own temple and pulled the trigger. Ken had been first on the scene.

There was no horsing around during guard training. The new hires knew what they were up against. They learned the basics of the daily prison routine, the rules for visitors, and how to search a cell for contraband. They had a classroom refresher on the criminal justice system. None of them could exactly remember what the Fourth Amendment was. They wrestled each other until the veins in their necks threatened to burst. Kyle Rouse volunteered to be shocked for the taser demonstration, but then again, Kyle always had been a crazy son of a bitch. They learned how to club an aggressive prisoner—on the biceps, on the legs, but never the skull, which lawyers would eat them for. They were divided on their preferences for straight or side-handled batons. The weapon's weight on their belts was strange at first. But they got used to it.

One winter morning a caravan of buses with waffled grating over their windows came plowing down the highway. Those of us who lived within sight of the road watched from our windows as the chain of buses carved a trench in the gray slush, carrying their freight of human cargo to the prison, where so many of our husbands and sons, our friends and neighbors, waited to receive them. The buses were only the beginning—soon retail stores and good service jobs would follow. To the extent that we thought about the men in those buses, we imagined them as one type, multiplied: sullen, dangerous, and deserving of punishment, but potentially redeemable, through faith and good works. Even from afar, they radiated menace. We were thrilled and terrified to see them.

Slowly, money began to circulate. We drew paychecks instead of unemployment. To our children's dismay, the town could afford teachers on Fridays again. Ed McConnell's ranch did well enough that he had to hire a dozen more people. Perhaps best of all, Grace and Robert Chilton were finally expecting a baby. We splurged on $20 bottles of Zinfandel to celebrate our good fortunes, but we still clipped coupons.

A number of Corvus people moved into town, and while we were friendly with them, we couldn't say we were friends. The men had a stiffness to them; the women, brittle smiles. We asked them how they were and they always seemed miffed by the question, hiding the answers in their cheeks before spitting them out. Some guessed privately what they thought of us: bumpkins, hicks, rednecks. We chafed at that. We were a distinguished enough bunch. Joshua Bloom, not even in high school yet, was a state fair prizewinner in canning and preserving. We had an active community theater and a two-wing library. Many of us had been to college. To the extent that we had an idea of ourselves as a town, it was as families and good neighbors. The newcomers had pronounced a silent judgment upon us, made sharper by the fact that many of them were our bosses. It almost made us miss the light touch of the German plant owners who ruled our parents and grandparents.

If we were unprepared for anything, it was the number of visitors. They trickled in at first, women and the occasional child, mostly, until it seemed they were everywhere. A group of us would be holding a book club at the Bailey Café and a red-eyed stranger would order a coffee and sit at the window for an hour, steeling herself for whomever she was about to see. Three blocks and one diner booth away, an unfamiliar mother and her teenage son chewed sandwiches in silence, then departed in a car with Kentucky plates. We saw couples at the gas station on the outskirts of town, buying trail mix for the squalling children on their hips as we stood in line for cigarettes, their faces washed free of any emotion but a trace of shame.

On the street, we snuck glances at the young women coming to visit their husbands and boyfriends. They wore painted-on jeans and shirts with plunging necklines, and if a group of us happened to catch an eyeful, we weren't above a murmured joke about conjugal visits. Other times we saw older women, who we guessed were the mothers of inmates, in floral-print dresses and hats piled with elaborate confections of silk, wool, and felt. Sometimes we saw strangers in sweatpants and T-shirts, and we imagined that they dressed modestly so as not to make the prisoners feel shabby.

On summer weekends we hosted a parade of cars with license plates from Missouri, Indiana, Kentucky, and as far away as Wisconsin. We were grateful for the business, but we weren't prepared to handle the busload of suited and gowned seniors from a charismatic church in Missouri, who arrived without fanfare and stayed for three days to minister in the prison. Nor were we prepared for the hundred-odd carousing attendees of the Corrections Officers Convention, whose location was changed to our town with little notice. We were not prepared for the mothers and wives who lodged in our attics and spare bedrooms, whose footsteps creaked above our heads when they were unable to sleep, who sobbed into our guest pillows, who filled our houses with their grief.

Oh, to hell with that, some of us said. We were decent people, faithful to our wives and husbands. We tithed and donated sweaters and jeans to the Salvation Army. We flew the flag from our porches and took it inside when it rained. We visited Helen Bree, whose heart was failing, which marooned her indoors most of the time. Were these things not proof of our largesse, our essential goodness?

On a trip to Helen Bree's house, Pastor Kimble and the church vocal quartet sat with her to watch a nature documentary. It concerned a fish that attached itself to a shark's skin and lived off scraps by cleaning the shark's teeth. They left after the first commercial break, which in retrospect was a shame. Some of us would have liked to learn how those fish managed to avoid being eaten.

When Grace Chilton gave birth to a boy three months prematurely, Pastor Kimble collected donations to help with the family's hospital bills. By that time most of the town had reconnected their satellite TVs, so it was no great burden to pitch in a twenty for little Anthony's medical fund. During those months it wasn't uncommon to see Robert Chilton walking around ashen-faced with worry, until he took a job as a prison guard.

Those of us who worked as guards wondered whether he had it in him. We'd developed something of an edge, a hyperalertness that was lacking in gentle Robert. Corvus paid well enough, we couldn't complain there. But just being in that place chiseled away at our composure. The smell of sweat permeated the building. It was worse after lights-out, as if the concrete walls and floor had absorbed the stench all day only to release it all night long. Sometimes we'd catch a group of prisoners staring at us, and flowers of ice would bloom in our chests. Never for a second could we forget they would kill us, given the chance.

That was a hard notion to shed after work, when the same dozen or so of us gathered at Barry's for drinks before going home to our families. We made overtures to the Corvus people, the more senior guards, but they never joined us. You could tell by looking that they never would. We became body-language experts, sizing up everyone we met. We instinctively looked for the half-closed fist hanging at someone's side, a slight bunch in the shoulders, tense little pulses in the jaw and temple. Even a cleancut prisoner like Howard Albright—White Bright, other inmates called him—all downcast eyes and mumbled *Yessirs*, set our hearts racing if he shuffled by too close or approached from behind. We couldn't turn it off, that hypervigilance. The best we could do was manage it.

There was another issue brewing, one that we mostly didn't talk about: the town was nearly all white, and the inmates were nearly all not. Likewise, many of the visitors were black or Hispanic, and their skin announced them as citizens of Chicago, or Joliet, or Plano, or any of the other towns up north from which we siphoned and warehoused young men. It was Isaiah Bloom who first spoke about it, at a town meeting where a revitalization of the town square was under debate.

Bloom was tall and rangy, perpetually sunburned, with sandy blond hair and a chinstrap beard. "You know how I feel about this prison," he said, quietly enough so that we had to strain to hear him from the back of the hall. He put his hands—large, gnarled mitts—on the podium, his pale eyes casting about for a sympathetic face. "And I know a lot of you don't feel the same. But this money—it's not rightly ours."

It turned out that the census counted every prisoner as one of us—two thousand extra unemployed men. Our swollen ranks earned us more federal dollars. To hear Isaiah Bloom explain it, we were the beneficiaries of a cruel trick played on poor blacks and Latinos. It was true that among many of us, a mental shorthand had developed: if we saw white strangers, we assumed they were police, or lawyers, or with Corvus. If they weren't white, we assumed they were visiting an incarcerated friend or family member. This mental routing, this either/or, was so fast and seemed so natural that its profound weirdness didn't really register with us until Bloom went on to point it out. It wasn't clear whether these kinds of thoughts had always been with us or we'd been tainted by the prison's arrival.

The prison was segregated, too. Out in the yard, surrounded by towers with riflemen silhouetted against the sky, inmates broke into racialized clusters. Gang fights erupted in brief but frequent bursts, like chamber musicians tuning their instruments before the commencement of some terrible overture. Even unaffiliated prisoners got caught up. During one of these fights, another inmate punctured Howard Albright's thigh with a sharpened toothbrush before we pulled him to safety.

"I mean, Christ," said Kyle Rouse, three beers deep at Barry's. "Puerto Rican, Mexican, what's the difference?"

Robert Chilton looked as uncomfortable as some of us felt, but with Kyle paying for round after round, we said nothing. With his clear, open face and Cupid's bow mouth, Robert looked much younger than the dozen or so of us, despite being a few years older. We could only imagine how he must have looked to the prisoners.

"I heard that Corvus is looking to build another facility," said Kyle, who labored under the impression that he'd purchased our ears along with our drinks. "They're closing some place in Indiana and shipping everyone here."

"Eh," said Herman Floss, curled over his drink at the next table over. "Put a bullet in each of their heads and be done with it."

There were times when we all came to feel that way. A few weeks later, a prisoner known as Skinny Charles flung a slurry of fluids at Kyle, who ducked the missile but still wound up with foul-smelling flecks spattered across his shoulder. It took three of us to hold Kyle back—carefully, so as not to get any stains on us—while all of C block laughed and hollered.

We rousted everyone after that. We shoved inmates against the walls chest-first, kicked their legs apart, and patted them down. Flicked open personal switchblades and Leathermen and ripped through mattresses. We left boot prints on pictures of their families. We tore apart their cells, looking for contraband, and boy, did we find it: razor blades, screwdrivers, shivs. Plastic bottles of pruno fermenting in toilet bowls. An exquisitely detailed portfolio of hand-drawn pornography. A tattoo gun cobbled from a Bic pen, an eraser, the motor from an electric toothbrush, and a length of guitar string for the needle. In Howard Albright's cell, shears and actual needles. We marveled at their stupidity: how could they have imagined they could keep anything from us, some of whom had built those very cells? So no—whatever it might have meant for the town, we guards were not looking forward to another thousand Skinny Charleses coming in.

"He knows what he did," said Skinny, when questioned about the attempted sliming of Kyle Rouse. "That motherfucker's gonna get got."

In three cells on C block, we found knotted condoms filled with brittle rocks. In Skinny's cell we discovered an empty condom with traces of powder, which the lab confirmed was cocaine. As soon as that news came through, he couldn't stop talking.

"What the fuck?" said Kyle, when he happened into the changing room as two guards rummaged through his locker.

There was nothing in his locker, but word went out that Kyle was being watched. He stopped going to Barry's for a few months. When we patrolled the upper tier of cellblocks with him, we could feel CentCom watching us through the compound eye of cameras, noting whose cells we lingered at, how long it took us to complete a loop. We'd always watched out for each other—maintaining sightlines with fellow guards was crucial to making sure you were covered—but now we watched each other.

Early one morning, while the prison slept, our supervisor tacked the following month's schedule to the locker room's corkboard and announced extra shifts. We didn't know it at the time, but Kyle had been in custody for hours, and his pickup—one of the models built at the plant, a lifetime ago—had been impounded by Corvus's investigators, after they'd found a dozen condoms filled with rock cocaine in its glovebox. But we didn't know that yet. We finished dressing and signed our names in the empty boxes, grateful for the overtime. Once we'd divided up Kyle's hours, we secured our batons to our belts, stepped out onto the tier, and threw the power switch, flooding the prison with light.

While it was probably no comfort to his wife and young son, it was a small mercy that Kyle got sent to a facility a few hours north. In the months he'd been selling drugs in the prison, passing them between a visiting gang contact and a crew inside, he'd begun to adulterate the shipments, diluting them so much that he'd earned the enmity of casual users and addicts alike. It wasn't hard to find inmates willing to testify against Kyle, and he wound up pleading out for eight years. Some of us heard rumors that Sheila knew about his dealing the whole time, but we were in no mood to cast aspersions.

In hindsight, we'd felt it building all through the end of that year. The gen pop had been on edge since the drugs dried up, though the occasional shipment managed to slip in. All it took was one sign of disrespect—cutting in line, a walk-by shoulder check —and though none of us knew what the exact offense was, the prison cafeteria exploded at dinner a week after Thanksgiving. A scrum of men tackled two lone prisoners, bringing them to the ground with a flurry of little jabs. They dispersed, leaving growing blots of red on the chest of each twitching victim.

At that, the cafeteria broke into waves of scrambling bodies. Most of the inmates flattened themselves against the wall. Others bellowed as they kicked and punched and choked each other. Skinny Charles took a tray to the jaw and went sprawling. Howard Albright fell backward and skittered into a corner, arms braced over his head. Prisoners pinned one another to the ground and pummeled away.

The adrenaline hit like a shock wave, made our eyeballs throb. Someone's tear-gas canister struck the floor with a dull metallic *thunk*. We shouted and swore as we rushed to seal our helmets, the canister belching smoke. Prisoners stopped fighting and fell to their knees, wheezing. We waded into the thick of it, bleary-eyed, the sound of our own rasping breath deafening in our helmets. Images swam through the haze—an outstretched hand, a face twisted in pain. Fear deformed every thought in our heads. We unsheathed our batons and laid waste to anything in a blue jumpsuit. We let the full force of our rage find expression at the end of those clubs. We split open scalps, made men spit teeth.

A quarter-hour later, when the last inmate had been carted off to the medical wing, we received word that both stabbing victims would live. Robert Chilton was in the infirmary, scrubbing off blood with soap and saline. A trace of gas lingered in the air, sour in our throats. Our hands trembled. But there was no time to consider what had happened. A caged light bulb above the cafeteria door flashed red, and the lockdown alarm rang.

One of the inmates lapsed into a coma and stayed under for weeks. When he awoke, he couldn't walk or talk, and the right side of his face was slack. Robert Chilton quit that day. By then he looked as if he hadn't slept in forever. The inmate was transferred to a state hospital soon afterward, where someone could help him eat and bathe.

After that, a parade of lawyers came through. Groups of them came and went in shifts, day after day, men in discount suits carrying thick file folders, conferring with inmates in low voices so we couldn't overhear. A kind of submarine pressure began to fill the prison walls. We felt fragile and exposed, ignorant of what was happening up on the surface, afraid that depth charges could detonate at any moment.

No one remembers which guard announced we were one inmate short. But we all remember the jolt at finding out it was Howard Albright. His cell empty, except for the scraps of prisoner's blues tucked beneath his mattress. Later on, it came out that he'd stitched together a jacket and slacks from chalk-dyed jumpsuits and walked out the front gates with a forged lanyard. We watched it over and over on video, Albright passing through the checkpoint with four other men in suits. Just another lawyer. The state police had set up roadblocks as far north as Bloomington. They needn't

have bothered. Deputy Ken Dufresne followed Albright's footprints in the new snow. Footprints that led, with almost comical
traceability, to the Blooms' neighboring farm.

Over the next two weeks, a clique of professionally coiffed men
and women descended upon our town. They shot bleak snow-
scapes that framed the prison building and the Bloom farmhouse,
which was quarantined by yellow tape, and they said grave things
into cameras: how Albright had broken into the Blooms' garage,
how young Joshua Bloom had interrupted Albright as he tried to
hotwire the Blooms' truck. In somber tones they recounted the
struggle in which Albright fatally stabbed Joshua, only to be killed
moments later by a blast from Isaiah Bloom's shotgun. We turned
off our televisions and let our newspapers molder on our porches.
We didn't need to be told who the Blooms were, or who we were,
for that matter.

The week before Christmas we held a memorial service at
church. Neither Isaiah nor Annalee Bloom attended. Pastor Kimble did his best, but most of us barely heard a word. We were sick
with grief for the two of them, but they wanted nothing to do with
us. They'd spoken to no one, refused every interview, rebuffed
even the pastor. They made private arrangements for their son's
body, and some months later left for Pennsylvania.

It was those killings that put us on the map, but not in the way
we'd expected. For years afterward, our town couldn't be mentioned without them. When people moved away, their new neighbors would bring it up as soon as they found out where the movers
had come from. When we traveled across the state for our children's cross-country meets and wrestling championships, fellow
parents would squint through pained smiles when we told them
where we lived. Huh, they'd say. That's the prison town, isn't it?
The shopping malls and processing plants we'd hoped for never
materialized. Instead, once a respectful amount of time had
passed, Corvus quietly purchased the Blooms' farm and started
building an expansion.

The cohort of guards who survived the cafeteria melee began
drinking nightly at Barry's. They didn't talk about it, but they'd all
been changed by what happened. Certain vivid thoughts boiled
up with greater and greater frequency. They'd be sitting at dinner with their families when the images surfaced, uninvited. They

couldn't look at their children without flashing on batons striking their skulls, the *thwock* they'd make ringing out in their own heads. That summer the group of them took turns building decks around the pools in each other's yards. Amid the camaraderie and coolers of beer on those long weekend afternoons, it occurred to more than one that his hammer had the same heft as his club.

Everyone thought the warden would resign after the killings, but instead he gave a pep talk and promised to support the guards, whether that meant more training, more staff, or better weapons. There was a new generation of tasers coming to market that promised to "revolutionize compliance management." Another flurry of media attention fell on us during the DOC inquiry, once a dozen inmates' lawyers raised hell. But after a few days of anemic coverage, the story disappeared. The inquiry faded, too. All eyes turned overseas, where news had leaked that American forces were operating a vast network of secret prisons across the globe. To the town's great relief, we were forgotten.

From the looks of things, the town is back to normal. The Cineplex has reopened, and the manicured lawns and flower boxes along the thoroughfare are flush with color. The smell of fresh asphalt cuts the air. Not a single building in our modest downtown remains empty. And all the while, everything outside of town decays. The state teeters on the edge of bankruptcy. We hear rumors of cutbacks and shutdowns—schools, hospitals, fire departments, police. Everything but the prisons, those marvelous engines that run on damaged men. We should feel lucky.

Our parents' faces have become our own. Maybe, for all their talk about the permanence of the plant, they knew all along just how precarious our arrangement was. The plant offered a good job, but there was risk there, too. Every so often, someone got caught in the gears.

Over drinks at Barry's, Ed McConnell brought news of the Chiltons, who had moved away after Robert quit. Little Anthony—healthy and strong, according to McConnell—had started school, and Grace had found work as a teacher again. Robert was working as an undertaker's assistant after being unemployed for the better part of a year. "Hell of a way to earn a living," said McConnell.

Yeah, we said. But then again, what isn't?

NICK MAMATAS

Thy Shiny Car in the Night

FROM *Long Island Noir*

Northport

MY FATHER TOLD ME around the time I seriously started reading books as a teenager that he used to know Jack Kerouac. "When
I was a young man, he was living right here in Northport," he said.
When we were next on Main Street, he pointed to Gunther's Tap
Room as we passed it and said, "Petey, Kerouac used to play pool
in there all the time, and sometimes he'd hold court on whatever
subject bubbled up in his writerly brain." There were even a few
photos of Kerouac in the window, and a sign reading KEROUAC
DRANK HERE, which I'd never noticed before. I was a kid; I had
eyes only for Lic's Ice Cream, the Sweet Shop, and the little news-
stand that carried comic books alongside *Newsday* and car magazines. But then I started noticing the other Northport, the one
day-trippers don't see.

That's about when I figured out what my father did for a living. "Waste management, middle management," he'd tell me,
"boss of all the garbage men on the North Shore." I'd repeat that
line in school, knowing it wasn't quite the whole story. I knew we
were semiconnected, since Uncle Peter, for whom I am named,
couldn't stop talking about it. He was a cliché, central casting for
The Sopranos, with a thick-tongued accent my father didn't have, a
penchant for tracksuits, a ridiculous silvery Cadillac, and rings too
gaudy for even the pope to wear.

I'd be working on my Commodore 64 or have my nose in a book
when he'd come over for dinner and say, "That's right. You do good

in school, you hear me, and get a good job. A *career.*" *Career* was a three-syllable word to Uncle Peter. "Work to get laid," he'd say. "Not to get made. It's no life." Even I knew what getting made was.

Uncle Peter said he knew Kerouac, too. "That guy? Ha! Jim said he knew him?" Granted, my father was a little man, balding with a bundt cake of hair around the back of his head, and he dressed like an accountant. Not the kind of guy you'd think would be hanging out with the king of the Beats.

"Yeah," Uncle Peter continued, all wistful. "Me and this friend of mine, we'd seen Kerouac on TV, then two days later in his garden, wearing coveralls like some kid, then that night wandering down the street like a real stumblebum. The guy was *stunad,* so I thought we'd give him a shakedown."

"Why, Uncle Peter?"

"Eh, we were just dumb kids. We thought writers had money! Anyway, he was a pretty big dude. A lot of muscle, and he could take a punch. I was waling on him, my friend was holding—"

"Who? Dad?"

"Pfft, no way. Nah, you don't know this guy. He was my friend who died before you were born. Anyway, Kerouac was just standing there. It was like punching a car through a pillow. There were definitely muscles under all that fat, and he was just going on about Buddhism and how he was a pacifist. Anyway, your *nonna* had sent Jim to go find me, and he pulls me off and tells me that writers don't have any money, and plus Jack is the only one left to take care of his old mother, so don't hurt him, and especially don't break his thumbs as he won't even be able to do any writing if we did. Kerouac looked like a friggin' bum—unshaved, ratty old navy coat, smelled like a vineyard, so I felt bad and I ended up putting fifty bucks in *his* pocket." Uncle Pete ran his big palms over his face. "Man, that was a time." Then, conspiratorially, "Don't tell Elaine about any of this."

Elaine was Uncle Peter's fiancée. The wedding took place a week after that conversation, in Queens where they lived. We had to park four long Queens blocks away from the church because every spot on the street was taken up by a sedan—some belonged to guests, others to pairs of men who sat in their cars the whole time, eating sandwiches, writing down notes on little pads, and occasionally taking photos of the church, the street, or one of the other cars.

My mother fixed my tie, put a tired smile on her face, and said, "Stand up straight. Pretend that you're famous and that the men across the street are paparazzi." Left unspoken was *and not federal agents.*

It was a great wedding. Tons of food, and dancing, and all sorts of guys coming up to my father at our table and shaking his hand, telling me what a good guy my dad was, how fair and honest and sweet, and that I'd be lucky to grow up to be like him. "Keep that nose clean! In the books!" My father bragged to them about my grades and that I had free access to the adult section at the public library. "Adult, eh?" a few of them said, snickering.

That was a Saturday, June 16, 1984. Back in Northport Ricky Kasso was torturing and killing Gary Lauwers out in the Aztakea Woods. Kasso was the high school "Acid King," a drug dealer and user who was into heavy metal and, supposedly, Satanism. Kasso stabbed Lauwers over a dozen times, demanding that he say, "I love Satan!" Lauwers was the good boy of the story—he would only say, "I love my mother!" The body wasn't discovered till the Fourth of July, his eyes ruined, maggots in the wounds, animals picking at scraps of flesh. Kasso, who had been bragging to his friends about "human sacrifice," killed himself in jail three days later. Then Northport really went crazy.

Uncle Peter cut his honeymoon to the old country short. He was now always at our house, going off on sudden errands my father needed done. And Dad was on the phone constantly, talking to guys in the city. "Satanists in the fucking woods!" he bellowed, angry for the first time ever as far as I knew. "We got to get them out of there."

The local priest came over for dinner; I had to wear my wedding suit again. We'd only ever gone to church on Christmas Eve, but Father Ligotti was attentive to my father's questions about Satan and "today's kids" to the point of seeming frightened. Then it clicked—my father wasn't just some pencil pusher in an office in charge of waste management, he was definitely part of the Mothers and Fathers Italian Association, and probably pretty high up. The town longhairs—that's what they called themselves; us normal kids called them dirtbags—didn't spend much time outside that summer, but when I'd see one on Main Street or over by the harbor or in the rich neighborhood pushing a mower across the lawn of someone else's house, they'd be sporting black eyes, a missing tooth, or a broken hand. They never walked alone. There were strange things happening in the woods, all right, and soon enough every kid in town knew to stay the fuck away from Aztakea.

I was too young to know the older kids except by face and reputation. They'd picked on a lot of us freshmen, but I never had any problems, thanks as I now know to Dad. I heard all the Kasso stories, most of which were just hysterical rumors. But one was true —Kasso was probably on drugs when he committed the murder. There was a boulder by the scene where he, or someone anyway, had tried to scrawl *SATAN LIVES*. But he spelled it wrong; it read *SATIN LIVES*.

We had an assembly when school started that year to talk about drugs and watching out for one another. There was a big sheet hung in the hallway by the principal's office and we were told we could write whatever we liked on it, as long as it was positive. No pentagrams, no band names, nothing like that. I wrote, *Whither goest thou, America, in thy shiny car in the night?* from *On the Road*. My English teacher that year, Mrs. Hartman, congratulated me on my "apropos epigram." I ate lunch in the library every day, so it was easy for me to look up *apropos* once I figured out how to spell the word.

My mother went through my records and tapes, demanding answers. "What's this?" she asked. "More heavy metal?" It was Van Halen's *1984*.

"Mom, that music's on the radio all the time! It's not Satanic. There's even an angel on the cover," I said, probably whining, definitely embarrassed.

She snorted. "An angel! That's just the Devil's way to lure you in." The Stephen King paperbacks went into the trash; so did *The Savage Sword of Conan* back issues. She had her hands on *Desolation Angels*, too, but my father slid into the room and grabbed her wrist, my hero. "Mary. Maria. That one's fine. That one's okay. It's a college-level book."

I read a lot of college-level books. They were still allowed; fantasy novels, Dungeons & Dragons, Freddy Krueger, Rambo, that was all contraband. I started reading *real* books, literature, more intently than ever, so looking back I guess I don't mind. My parents, ever overprotective, didn't want me to go away for college, or even to the city. "Between the *mulignan* in the projects and the fruitcakes in the Village, you'll end up a vegetable if you go to

NYU," Uncle Peter said. My father told him not to talk that way at the table, but he agreed with the sentiment.

So I went to Hofstra and did well, then hit the road. I did a lot of scut work — janitor; a baton-twirling Wackenhut security professional for a town dump in New Jersey (my surname helped); out to Chicago as an SAT tutor; then on to California to work in a bookstore. And I wrote. I always wrote. I got over romanticizing poverty, and the road, but I never got over Kerouac. Like the book says, *I knew there'd be girls, visions, everything; somewhere along the line the pearl would be handed to me.*

I got a few things published, too — poems in a haiku journal, stories in *Oakland Hills Review* and one in a C-level men's magazine about D cups that ran the occasional lurid fiction feature. It was called "Satin Lives," that story, and it was about a thinly veiled Ricky Kasso. I'd turned into what Uncle Peter called a "real smartass," and over late-night coffees during Christmas when I visited for a week or three I let my father know what I thought of his work. My mother was already in bed. Cooking for forty fat cousins and their kids always took a lot out of her, especially after the lumpectomy. Nobody would lift a finger to help her either, not even me, I'm ashamed to admit.

"I don't hurt anyone, Petey. If not for me, there'd be a lot more people hurting, I'll tell you that much," my father said. "It's what we call *property rights.* There's a lot of money to be made hauling trash on Long Island. People here are pigs; they certainly generate enough garbage. The island used to be beautiful, all trees and little towns. Now it's just a hundred-mile-long dump for hamburger wrappers and toxic waste. A lot of people want in on sanitation, and I keep everyone happy, working a certain territory."

"And if someone steps out of line?" I asked. "Or wants to just run an honest business?"

He snorted. My family was full of snorters. My mother was the champion, but Dad was a top contender. "Honest business? Good luck. Look at Wall Street. And anyway, you weren't complaining about ethics when I paid your college tuition; when you were able to gallivant around the country without a penny of debt thanks to me."

"What about the government? What about the law?"

"Listen, if the government cared, they'd just municipalize garbage collection and put us all out of business. We're more efficient than they are, even with the occasional *present* we have to buy, or a labor action here and there. You think garbage men could afford to live out here if Suffolk County paid them? Pfft."

"That doesn't mean what you're doing isn't illegal. The law, the American way—"

He laughed. He had a great laugh, my father. "You sound like Kerouac now. He was a real Republican near the end, all that beatnik business aside. He *hated* hippies, hated liberals. Let me tell you, what does the government do? It organizes property rights just like I do. And yes, it threatens violence when it has to. The difference is that the government doesn't care about the people—they're a violence monopoly, they don't have to. We have to watch out for ourselves; we can't just go crazy and invade the next town over for no reason, not like the Bushes invading Iraq whenever they want to feel tough." George W. Bush was rattling the saber just then for what would be the 2003 invasion, just like his own father had back when I was in college.

"It's not the same, it's just not the same." I was tired, itching for a fight. "The government . . ." What? I thought to myself. The government doesn't bully people? Doesn't tax the hell out of them? Doesn't dump toxic waste out in Aztakea Woods and pollute water tables and give nice suburban mothers breast cancer? The rest of my sentence hung in the air like steam from my mouth. Dad knew where we could take the conversation if I wanted, and so did I. It was nowhere good. I went outside to smoke a cigarette and stare up at the Long Island sky. *The stars were pinpricks in the woolen blanket of the night here, but not in the metropolises of America, where you never dare look up.* I wrote that down, and put it in an (unpublished) poem.

I don't know exactly what happened; it surely wasn't our arguments. But the following summer my dad went to the DA and turned rat. He wasn't offered a deal or pressured. He just showed up with a zip drive full of evidence and an eagerness to explain where "all the bodies are buried"—as it read on the front page of *Newsday*—right after he buried my mother. It was the breast cancer that killed her, like so many ladies from Long Island. *No cancer cluster on LI, my prostate!* Listen to that. Here I am, turning into Uncle Peter, who was coming tonight to kill my father, his own brother. Uncle Peter was always a kidder, always ready with a joke or a smart remark. But he took his oath seriously, more seriously than marriage or blood. Not like my dad, not like me.

I was waiting outside, on the porch. I didn't smoke anymore, but I smoked that night to keep my lungs warm. The sky was brighter than when I was a kid, thanks to the big-box stores and strip malls dotting the highway. My father didn't rate any police protection—though it took a few months, the government got all they wanted out of him, and the local uniforms could be bought off with grocery money. He was inside, drinking his best wine, the stuff he used to kid he was saving for my wedding, and waiting to join his Maria. Uncle Peter's giant boat of a Caddy, still all polished and gleaming, drove up the curve of the driveway. My mother always loved this house.

"Hey, kid," he said conversationally. "When'd you get in? Haven't seen you since your poor mother, bless her in heaven, passed." Uncle Peter wasn't as huge as he used to be. He looked partially deflated, like a Macy's Day parade balloon half an hour after the crowds left.

"I just got here this morning. Took in the sights. Had some fresh snapper; the fish are better out here than in California, you know. Had a Crazy Vanilla ice cream down at the store, went to Gunther's, that sort of thing."

"Gunther's, eh? You a pool hustler now?" He edged forward, keeping his hands in front of him. Maybe he wouldn't kill me here on this porch. Maybe Northport was still a nice small town, where a gunshot wouldn't be written off as a car backfiring, where porch lights might blink on and screen doors swing open at one in the morning.

"Nah, they had a reading tonight. I was one of the readers." I lit another cigarette. "It was even listed in the paper; they ran my picture. *Homecoming for Local Author*."

"A reading?" He was confused. Good. Maybe a little drunk, too. I hoped he'd have to be to kill his own brother in cold blood, never mind having to kill me, too. "Like, people just sit there and read?"

"No, Uncle Peter; we read aloud. It's like a show. It's for Kerouac's memorial anniversary. They do one every October at Gunther's."

"Was Louie there? Jess?"

I shook my head. "Nah, the regulars clear out when the poets hit the stage. You know how Northport is . . ." I waved my right hand, the cherry of my cigarette bobbing along in the shadows, so he didn't see what I reached for until my old extendable baton telescoped out and smacked him right in the shin. Uncle Peter was still a large man — it's like trying to chop down a tree with a baseball bat. *Something he would say!* But he was old and slow, and I got up and swung the baton down on his head three, four times, and I shouted. I shouted, "I love my mother! I love my mother! I love my mother and father!" No porch lights went on. No screen doors swung open, except for the one behind me.

"Pete . . ." my father said, his mouth heavy with wine. I didn't know which of us he meant.

The Cadillac is eating Pennsylvania for breakfast by the time the sky lightens. My father's next to me, leaning his head out the window like a dog. His son's crazy, the craziest man he's ever known, but he's alive. Alive and free and on the road. Forget property taxes, chemicals on the lawns to keep them green. Forget the police, forget the families of New York, who are all dying or senile or in prison or watching better versions of themselves on the television and saying to themselves, *Yeah, yeah. Al Pacino, that's me.* Forget Long Island, that little turd hanging off the end of America. *California, here we come!* We have a suitcase full of unmarked bills my father had hidden behind the drywall in the garage, my bandaged-up uncle in the trunk banging away on the lid. We have nothing to lose, everything to live for, my father and I. Dad figures his brother will calm down by the time we get to Ohio; then we can let him out and have a little "sit-down" about his future. I hope Uncle Peter decides to come with us. We'll fall asleep and wake up again a million times. In the West, the sun peeks out distantly on the horizon, a great white pearl.

EMILY ST. JOHN MANDEL

Drifter

FROM *Venice Noir*

Ponte dei Sospiri

WHEN ZOË'S HUSBAND DIED she decided to travel. She was twenty-eight years old and had seen very little of the world, and this seemed like the best possible moment to leave Michigan. A friend from art school had been to the Arctic in the summertime once and she'd told Zoë about the landscape's clear beauty, the wildflowers, ice-blue lakes, and slate mountains. Now it wasn't summer, but that was almost the point. Zoë boarded a series of flights to the Northwest Territories and found herself in a lunar kingdom of shadows and ice, scoured landscape. The sun behaved strangely. The days were short.

"Trying to lose yourself?" Zoë's brother asked, when she called from a hotel in Inuvik to tell him where she'd gone. Zoë's husband, Peter, had been dead for four weeks. She had given up the apartment, sold or given away all of her belongings. People were concerned.

"Trying to find myself," she said, which wasn't at all true but had the desired effect of slightly reassuring her family. Losing herself wasn't enough. Zoë wanted to erase herself. She wanted extremity. She wanted to be eradicated, but she didn't want to die. When she left the hotel she felt swallowed up by the landscape, by the absolute cold. By night she stared through the hotel room window at the northern lights, colors shifting across the breadth of the sky. She liked it here, but she was restless and she'd heard of a town that was even farther north: Tuktoyaktuk, on the edge of the Beaufort Sea.

"The ice road just opened," a man behind the counter in a coffee shop told her when she asked about it. "Should have no problem getting up there." He looked at her doubtfully. "You got a four-by-four?"

"No," Zoë said. She'd sold her car before she left Michigan.

"I know a guy who's going up tomorrow. Probably take you with him if you split the cost of gas. I'll ask him if you want."

"Thank you. I appreciate it." What she truly appreciated was the way the man in the café didn't ask why she'd want to go to Tuktoyaktuk this time of year, or what she was doing in the far north in the first place. Over the weekend she agreed on a fee for gas expenses and got into a truck with a silent man in his fifties who navigated them seamlessly down a ramp onto the frozen MacKenzie River.

Zoë had heard the phrase *ice road* in the café without thinking about what it might mean. It meant driving on ice. Driving in slow motion with chains on the tires, fifteen kilometers an hour with the lights of enormous rigs shining ahead and behind them in the four P.M. darkness. They drove up the river to the northern edge of the world and then turned right and drove for a time over the frozen Beaufort Sea.

The village itself was like Inuvik, only smaller, darker, more utilitarian, little windows shining bright in the permanent twilight. Daylight lasted four hours, but the stars here were brighter than any she'd ever seen. She felt that she'd traveled beyond the edge of the world and landed on some colder planet farther from the sun. Aurora borealis in the sky most nights, shifting vapors of green and yellow that she watched by the hour, sitting alone by the hotel window wrapped in blankets with the lights out. On the third day she rented a snowmobile, got a cursory driving lesson from the man who ran the rental business, and drove a little way out of town.

Zoë liked the sound of the machine, the din and the forward momentum, but it wasn't a smooth ride and she felt as if her bones were rattling. She stopped by the sea. She could go no farther. She climbed off the machine and walked a few paces to look out at the horizon, blue shadows of icebergs. The sun was low above the ice, the few scattered lights of Tuktoyaktuk shining in the near distance.

"I am not unafraid," she whispered, to Peter, to herself. She had said this first, in the dazed weeks just after the diagnosis, when they were trying to come up with words to frame the catastrophe. They had repeated it to each other in the final nine months that followed, a private phrase that conveyed hope and stoicism and terror in equal measure. The cold was getting to her now, her fingers numb inside her gloves. She turned, and for a fraction of a second Peter was standing there beside the snowmobile, smiling at her in the fading light. He was gone in less than a heartbeat, less than a blink.

"Oh God," Zoë whispered, "oh no, please, please . . ." It took a moment to restart the snowmobile; she kicked at it frantically, not daring to look up. There was movement at the edge of her vision, faint as a curl of cigarette smoke. She heard Peter's voice as though from a long way off, but couldn't make out what he was saying. The cologne he used to wear on special occasions hung sweet and clear in the freezing air. The snowmobile jerked into motion and her tears froze on her face. She left all the lights on in the hotel room that night and packed up to leave the north in the morning, a slow process at this time of year, performed in increments over a number of weeks. There were several runways that had to be navigated to get from the Arctic Circle to the warmer parts of the continent, and most of them were frozen over. There were long delays in northern airports, sometimes for days at a stretch. She slept on benches, ate out of vending machines, washed in public restrooms, and felt somewhat deranged. Her reflection was pale and hollow-eyed in mirrors and darkened windows, hair standing up in all directions. It wasn't until she was sitting in the airport in Edmonton two and a half weeks later, drinking coffee after a sleepless night and staring out at an airplane that would take her farther south as soon as a storm cleared, that it occurred to her to wonder why she'd been afraid of Peter's ghost.

Zoë arrived in the Toronto airport and spent some time considering flights back to Michigan, but she had no desire to return just yet, and the situation seemed to call for a new continent. Zoë and Peter had made a good living dealing coke to college students and she still had a few thousand dollars at her disposal, so she flew from Toronto to Paris and lived for some time in a marginal neighborhood, trying unsuccessfully to learn French. But the lines and

beauty of Paris reminded her too much of the architectural paintings Peter had been working on when they'd met at art school and
her money dwindled rapidly there, so she left France and began a
slow, directionless slide across the continent, heading mostly south
and east.

Zoë didn't have much money now. There were dark little places
in winter where she didn't speak the language, and she occasionally forgot which town she was in. She found a job busing tables
in Slovakia for a while. She heard there were resort jobs to be
had on the Croatian coast, so she made her way through Hungary
and then worked for some months as a waitress near the Adri-
atic Sea. On the day she saw Peter walking across the town square
she packed her things and resumed a halting eastward migration,
through Bosnia and Herzegovina, across a corner of Serbia and
through Albania, toward Greece. It was important in those days to
keep moving. She saw Peter sometimes, always at a slight distance,
moving through crowds in various countries. Not looking at her,
not sick anymore, seemingly in somewhat of a rush. She was perfectly aware every time that it couldn't possibly be him — Peter was
buried in her family's plot in Ann Arbor — but that didn't make
her see him any less often.

"I'm worried about you," her brother said. He persisted in keeping in contact, which was thoughtful but also somehow annoying.
She was trying to drift across a landscape without remembering
and he kept pinning her to home.

"There's no need to worry," she replied. "I'm just traveling a
little."

"When are you coming home?"

"I don't have a home," she said. "I'm like that song. I'm a rolling stone."

"Have you been drinking?" he asked.

She didn't see that this was any of his business. She took a long
pull of whiskey before she answered him. "Of course not. And
even if I *was* drinking, what difference would it make? Haven't I
always been the black sheep?" This was in Albania, at a pay phone
in the lobby of a rundown hotel near the Greek border. The clerk
glared at her from behind the front desk but said nothing.

"It doesn't matter what you've always been," her brother said.
"All that matters is that everyone's worried, Zoë, we all love you,"

and she understood from his voice how tired she'd made him. "We all want you to come home."

"I'm sorry," she said. "I lost Peter there."

In Greece, after two years of travel, she discovered that she could sell landscape paintings to tourists. Zoë disliked painting landscapes. She had other interests. On the days when she painted landscapes she spent a lot of time swearing at the canvas. In her last three years in the United States she'd taken to painting extreme close-ups of liquid in glasses, and she'd felt that she'd found something, if not her mature style, then the style that might lead to it. She'd loved the way glass and ice and liquid caught the light, the warmth of red wine in a low-lit room, the suspension of bubbles in champagne, in seltzer, lime slices trapped among ice cubes with tiny bubbles clinging silver to the peel. Her work had been shown in galleries. She'd entertained thoughts of a brilliant future. It was difficult to paint landscapes again after all these years of ice cubes and extreme martini-glass close-ups, after the two years of traveling and not painting at all, but on the other hand she was nearly out of money.

She lived in a dilapidated inn by the sea, where she cleaned and helped the cook in exchange for a room and sold paintings to tourists for food money. Her life wasn't unpleasant. She had come to realize the value of southern countries: she would never have imagined this quality of sunlight, the way it bleached the landscape, the way it seemed to pass through her, the way it burned away the darkest parts of her thoughts. She spent a lot of time on the beach with a fifth of whiskey, disappearing into brilliant light. She attracted frowns from passersby, but she didn't think it was such a terrible thing, actually, drinking a little by the sea. She didn't see why people had to be so judgmental about it.

Zoë had been in Greece for six months when she decided to keep moving. She knew she wanted to remain in a southern country and she spent a long time studying maps of India, but she was afraid of malaria and she wasn't sure how a person would go about getting vaccination shots in Greece. She'd always wanted to see Venice, so she spent two weeks trying to sell the last of her landscape paintings, abandoned the ones she couldn't sell along the beach in the early morning, took a bus to Athens and then a cheap flight to Rome. She did crossword puzzles and read the *International Herald Tribune* all the way to Italy, where she found upon arrival that she had just enough money left to get to Venice by train.

It was September and a tide had overtaken the city. The water had risen over the streets and tourists moved slowly on walkways, wearing strange boots that looked like bright plastic shopping bags tied up to their knees. In a doorway near the train station she counted the last of her money. Eighteen euros and eighty-seven cents. Her bank account was empty, and she had no credit cards. She didn't want to spend money on a vaporetto, so she made her way on foot through the drowning city, trying not to think about how little money she had or what might become of her now. There was an unexpected pleasure in wading through the water and getting her shoes wet, childhood memories of splashing in puddles with her dog.

Zoë came upon St. Mark's Square, turned now into a shallow lake. She waded out over the cobblestones in water up to her knees and stood before the domes and archways of St. Mark's Cathedral, pigeons wheeling through the air above her, and this was when she realized that she'd had it wrong: it wasn't that she'd always wanted to come to Venice, it was that Peter had always wanted to come to Venice. He had painted this cathedral from photographs a dozen times. He was everywhere.

She turned away and left the square, but within minutes she had landed in another of Peter's paintings. She looked up from a bridge and was ambushed by memory. Detroit, the year before Peter got sick, their apartment filled with canvases, a Sunday afternoon: "It's called the *Bridge of Sighs*," Peter said, and stepped back from the easel so she could see what he'd done. All this time later here it was before her, an enclosed white bridge with two stone-grated windows high over the canal, somehow dimmer in life than it had been in her husband's luminous painting.

She crossed the bridge and spent some time wandering, watching the movement of boats from the flooded sides of canals, from the arcing bridges, these crafts gliding on the water streets. She came upon a narrow canal that Peter had never painted, a place where the water hadn't reached the level of the promenade, and for the first time all day she was perfectly alone. She had lost track of where she was. A residential quarter far from St. Mark's Square, houses crowded tall and silent on either side. The water of the canal was almost still.

Zoë sat on a step and pulled her knees in close to her chest. She would have to buy food soon, and then the eighteen euros would deplete still further. She'd been dimly aware of how little money she had when she'd bought the train ticket, but it somehow hadn't registered, all she'd really thought of was the next destination, and now she didn't have the money to either get out of Venice or stay here. She could call her family, but she knew they'd only buy her a plane ticket back to Michigan. She could go to the American consulate, but what would they do except return her to the United States? She was looking at the rippling shadows the houses cast on the canal in the end-of-afternoon light, thinking of how she'd paint this water if she still had money for paint, and this was when she became aware of footsteps. A tall man in jeans and an expensive-looking sweater, dark curly hair and sunglasses that reflected her own pale face when he looked at her. He stopped before her and said something that she didn't immediately comprehend.

"Parla inglese?" she asked, in what was meant to be a steady voice. It came out wavery.

"Can I be of any help at all?" he asked.

There was a fleeting second when she thought she smelled Peter's cologne in the air.

"I don't know," she said. No one else was on the street, and she wondered if he'd followed her here.

"You're quite wet," he said gently.

Her jeans were in terrible condition, now that she looked at them—soaked past the knees and filthy. Her tennis shoes were waterlogged.

"I went wading," she explained.

He extended a hand. "Rafael."

"Zoë."

"Zoë, may I buy you a cup of coffee?"

"You may," she said. There was no reason why not. She wasn't one to decline offers of coffee from strange men. She hadn't had coffee all day, or food for that matter, and it was nearly evening. "Would you mind buying me dinner instead?" she asked.

*

"Tell me about yourself," Rafael said. He had taken her to a small dark restaurant not far from where he'd found her, a place so narrow that she might have walked past it without noticing. The street outside was shadowed and still. He'd led her to a table in a far back corner, and now he was sipping red wine while she attacked a plate of pasta.

"I'm a painter," she said. "I *was* a painter, I mean."

"I see. And where are you from?"

"The United States. But I've been traveling for a long time."

"You're traveling alone?"

"I am," she said.

"Do you have any family?"

"A brother. I haven't spoken to him in a while." Memories of a pay phone in a hotel lobby in Albania, the desk clerk glaring as she capped the whiskey.

"There's no one else?"

"My parents died in a car accident when I was little." This wasn't at all true — her parents were a seldom-thought-of presence in the suburbs of Ann Arbor, probably worried about her, faded to shadows now — but wasn't she free to reinvent herself? This wasn't her continent. "I have no children."

"But you're married," he said. She still wore the ring.

"He's dead."

"I'm sorry. How long have you been traveling, Zoë?"

"Two years? Maybe three. I haven't really kept track."

"A drifter." Rafael smiled to soften the blow of the word.

She had been reaching for her wineglass but found herself stilled by the idea. Memories of Greece, of Slovakia, of the Arctic, dark cities. "I suppose," she said. "Yes, I suppose you could say that."

"I have a confession to make." Rafael had taken off his sunglasses. His eyes were blue, and she thought him handsome; there was an easy grace in every movement, a confidence in his gaze. She liked his smile.

"What sort of confession?" She was interested in the confession, but more interested in her pasta. It was the first time she'd eaten that day and she was having a hard time chewing slowly.

"I followed you for a while before I approached you."

A quick bright star of light caught in an ice cube as she raised her water glass to her lips.

"Really," she said.

"And my interest, if I may be entirely candid, was partly economic in nature. You appear to be—forgive me for speaking so bluntly—a girl of limited means."

"You could say that." Zoë was aware of her appearance. She knew she hadn't been paying enough attention to it. The cuffs of her sweater were fraying and a seam was coming apart at the shoulder. It had been some time since she'd washed her hair.

"It happens," he said, "that there's a job I need done. It would take no more than an hour of your time."

She had all at once the same feeling she'd had those years ago on the ice outside Tuktoyaktuk, when for an instant she'd thought she'd seen Peter standing on top of the snow and she'd been seized by a desperate desire to flee. Rafael's questions, she couldn't help but notice, seemed designed to establish that she was alone in the world. *Put down your glass,* she told herself. *Stand up from the table, thank Rafael for the meal, and walk out of the restaurant.*

"What kind of job?" she asked, instead of doing any of these things.

"A simple delivery."

"Of what?"

"A small package," he said. "It happens to be a matter of the utmost delicacy. You'll deliver a small package to an address near here, and in return I'll pay you a hundred euros."

"In advance."

"Half in advance, half when you return." He glanced at his watch. "I'll be waiting for you here, at this table."

"We're doing this now?" she asked.

"In thirty minutes," he said.

"Why would you send someone you don't know, if it's a matter of utmost delicacy?"

"You're at hand," he said. "All you have to do is knock on the door and tell whoever answers that you have a message from Rafael. You'll step into the building, give them the package, and you'll be on your way."

"And you'll pay me a hundred euros for that?"

"It's important to me to see that the package gets delivered, but it isn't possible for me to do it myself."

"I see." There were things she could accomplish with a hundred euros. She could pay for a hostel for a few nights, and perhaps that would be long enough to find a new job. It was suddenly possible that she hadn't reached the end after all. She wanted very much not to go home.

The package was a rectangular box no larger than a deck of playing cards, wrapped neatly in brown paper. Rafael slid it across the table following the dessert course, extracted fifty euros from a wad in his pocket, and pressed the money into her hand. "The rest when you return," he said. He nodded at someone behind her, and when she looked up a man who had been sitting at the bar when they came in was standing by her side. "My friend will walk you to the address."

She felt unsteady as she stood. Perhaps she'd had slightly too much wine. Rafael's friend said nothing, only nodded to her and set off for the door.

"Goodbye, Zoë," Rafael said. He winked at her. She looked back as they left the restaurant, and he was speaking softly and urgently into a cell phone.

Zoë held the package in both hands. It was curiously light. She was worried that it might be fragile, and it was certainly important; Rafael's friend kept glancing at it as they walked. She wondered if it could possibly be jewelry—a blood diamond? She wanted to ask, but she feared the question was indiscreet, and he seemed to be a man not given to talking. Her feet were cold and wet in her sneakers. At least the tide had receded. They were in a corner of Venice that seemed all but deserted, buildings pressed close on either side of the street. Night had fallen, and the streetlamps were few and far between, pools of light spilling over cobblestones and walls.

"Here," Rafael's friend said. It was the first word he had spoken to her. They had stopped before a narrow stone building. He rang the doorbell and was gone almost instantly, sliding into the shadow of a nearby doorway. She knew he hadn't gone far, but she felt acutely alone on the silent street. The graveyard stillness of a city without cars.

The man who opened the door was very old, stooped and blurry-eyed in an impeccable black suit. It seemed to Zoë that he couldn't see her very well.

"I have something for you," she said. "A message from Rafael."

He considered this for a moment before he stepped back to let her enter. She found herself in a dimly lit foyer, wall-mounted lamps casting shadows on the walls, a black lacquered sideboard with a potted white orchid gleaming in the half-light. She was painfully aware of how dirty her clothes were, how ragged and wet. He closed the door behind her.

"Here," she said, and tried to give him the box, but he shook his head and gestured for her to follow him. She thought about turning and slipping back out into the street, leaving the box by the orchid and running away, but she was seized by curiosity. She wanted to see what came next. She wanted to do the job correctly and return to Rafael for the other fifty euros. It had perhaps been a mistake to leave her backpack with him, in retrospect. The wine she'd had with dinner was wearing off quickly.

The butler moved slowly down the hallway before her, his thinning hair soft and wispy at the back of his head. She wondered who he was, if he had a family, if he knew Rafael. Her shoes were making embarrassing squelching noises on the carpet. He opened the last door on the right and she stepped into a long, low room, a study. There was a massive black desk at one end, chairs and a sofa at the other. A man in his early thirties sat in an armchair reading *La Repubblica.* Everything about him looked expensive, from the high shine of his shoes to his carefully tousled hair. His shirt was pink. He made a show of folding his newspaper unhurriedly when he saw her, but she noticed that his hands were shaking.

An older man was walking away from her, and she had the impression that he'd been pacing. He pivoted sharply when the door closed behind her, but said nothing. The butler had retreated into the hall.

"Hello," Zoë said, but the two men only looked at her. "I have a message from Rafael," she said.

She held out the box. The older man came toward her, and she saw the strain he carried, bloodshot eyes and slumped shoulders, a two-day beard. His suit was expensive, but his collar was in disarray, he'd pulled his tie loose, nails bitten to the quick. He took the box from her hands and held it for a moment as if weighing it. She watched the color leave his face. He set the box on a low marble coffee table before the man in the pink shirt, sank down into the sofa, and closed his eyes.

The man in the pink shirt glanced at Zoë. He unwrapped the box carefully and removed the lid, pulled back the layer of gauze within. He let out a strangled sound in his throat.

The box contained a human ear. It had been washed clean of blood and it was small and waxy, blue-white, a porcelain seashell with a pink stone earring in the shape of a rose still attached to the earlobe. As she stared, the man in the pink shirt put his hand on the other man's shoulder and murmured something to him. The older man was still for a moment, as if it took two or three heart-beats for the words to absorb, and then he began a slow down-ward movement that reminded Zoë of a marionette being lowered on its strings; he slumped forward on the sofa until his head was nearly at his knees, curling in on himself; he pressed his hands to his face and began silently weeping.

The man in the pink shirt sat still for a moment, looking at the ear. He carefully replaced the gauze, set the lid back on the box, carried it away to the far end of the room, and put it high on top of a bookshelf. Zoë stared at him, waiting, trying to guess what might happen now. His face was expressionless when he turned to her.

"I didn't know," she said.

"It's a beautiful night," he said. His voice was hoarse. "Let's go for a walk."

He opened the door and ushered her out into the dim corri-dor. When she glanced back into the room, the older man hadn't moved. The back door of the building opened into an empty courtyard, houses silent all around them. She breathed the cool air and thought about running — but where could she go? The courtyard was enclosed, and anyway, they were already in motion, the man in the pink shirt holding her arm. He was leading her to a wooden door in the far wall, their shadows moving black over the cobblestones. Light escaped here and there through the cracks between shutters. She could hear a television somewhere, voices rising and falling, canned laughter. When she stepped through the wooden door she found herself on the edge of a canal, water lapping near her feet. The man in the pink shirt stepped through behind her and closed the door. Something caught the light just then, the quick sharp gleam of a gun in his hand. She wasn't sure where it had come from.

There was no one else by the canal, and the buildings on the other side were dark. He took her arm again and they walked to-gether, an unhurried stroll down the length of cobblestones with the water rippling black beside them. The slight pressure of the handgun against her ribs. She felt strangely detached, a sleep-walker in a long dream. Her thoughts wandered.

Once in Michigan she'd been held up at gunpoint. This was when she was dealing coke to art school students, and she knew it was dangerous, but no transaction had ever gone bad before and her guard was down. She knew as soon as she walked into the apartment that everything was wrong: the squalor, the way the girl sitting on the sofa was staring at her, the cigarette burning in an overflowing ashtray, the way the door closed just a beat too quickly just as someone said her name— *Zoë, I'm real sorry about this, we're just going to take the money and the coke, no one's going to hurt you—* and then she'd heard the click of the safety catch. *Okay,* she said quietly. *Okay.* She raised her hands. The colors of the apartment were florid, a fever dream of red and purple and orange, and she found herself staring at the curtains and trying not to look at the girl on the sofa, who smelled bad when she leaned in close to pull the wad of money out of Zoë's jacket pocket, and then later out on the street, unharmed, she'd felt so alive, so giddy that she started laughing even though she'd just been robbed and snow was falling through the haze of streetlights; she looked up and she felt it, felt it fall on her face—

"I told Rafael that if he did this, I would kill the messenger," the man said softly. He sounded apologetic, but he wouldn't meet her eyes when she glanced at him. His grip tight on her arm, their footsteps quiet on the stone promenade. Time was moving very strangely. She felt that perhaps she'd always been walking beside him.

"But I didn't know what was in the box." She heard her own voice as if from a long way off.

"It is a request for payment," he said. "It's an escalation. It's a message that demands a reply."

"Whose ear is it?" she asked, but he didn't answer.

In Greece she bought a postcard of her village by the sea, the little place where she was living with the white buildings and the church and the endless light, and she sat on the beach at the end of a difficult day and wrote a note to her brother: *Jon, it's Zoë. I'm sorry for your worry and I just wanted you to know I'm still alive, I hope you're alive, too, I wish I knew you better, I'm sorry we were never close—*

"We're close now," the man said. They were nearing a dead end. A boarded-up restaurant with a wide awning that reached across the width of the promenade, where once there must have been café tables shaded from the sun, and on the other side of the awning the promenade ended in a brick wall. They stepped into the awning's ink-black shadow, and Zoë realized that they were all but invisible to anyone who might be watching from a window, now that they'd passed out of the light.

She'd had a dog when she was little, Massey, a cocker spaniel with ears like silk who quivered with joy when she came home from school, and when it rained they splashed in puddles together—

"Here," the man said.

They had stopped by the brick wall. Zoë turned to look at the canal, all rippling moonlight and black. Darkened buildings rising up on the far side, moored boats. What was strange was that she wasn't frightened. She could hear nothing outside of herself but the sound of the man in the pink shirt breathing beside her, the movement of water. Both of them were waiting, but especially her.

"Step forward," the man said softly, "toward the water," and she inched toward the canal until her shoes were at the very edge. She felt the metal against the back of her head, the click of the safety catch being released. There was an instant when it seemed that nothing had happened, but then the moonlight expanded and became deafening and there was only pure sound, the gunshot flashing into blinding light—

Her brother making a snow angel in the playground—

Massey chasing a squirrel in the grass—

"It's cancer," the doctor said, and Peter gripping her hand so tight—

Prom night in Ann Arbor, the headlights of cars pulling up in front of the auditorium, the slippery tightness of her green silk dress—

Blue ice shadows on the Beaufort Sea—

"You have a fever, sweetie, no school for you today," and a cool hand on her forehead, her mother's voice—

"Stand up," Peter murmured. His hand on the back of Zoë's head, where the bullet had entered her. "Stand up, my love. Let me look at you."

DENNIS MCFADDEN

The Ring of Kerry

FROM *New England Review*

As A GIRL, Eena one day heard someone make mention of the
Ring of Kerry. To her childish mind then, a title so grand could
never be given to a thing so ordinary as a route for tourists to
traipse; a magnificent name such as that could only be fit for a
splendid piece of jewelry, a ring that might grace the finger of a
queen. Even after the mundane truth became known to her, there
was always a spot set aside in her heart for the *real* Ring of Kerry,
the genuine, golden, gem-laden article of fabulous beauty and im-
ponderable worth.

And so the first time she laid eyes on her grandmother's ring,
there it was. "You should have seen the thing, Mister," she told Lafferty. They were in the bed of her room above the restaurant, she
with the sheet up to her chin to hide the flatness of her chest. She
was a stray, a mutt, skinny as a reed, unruly red hair immune to
the brush, ears that stuck out like the handles on a jug, and brown
eyes so big they could occupy her face entirely. Thin light from the
cloudy afternoon squeezed through the blinds of the window, and
he could hear the warble of a tin whistle from the Commodore
Pub across the street. "The grandest thing I ever seen," she said.
"Fine, delicate carvings, little circles and twirls all around it, they
might have been etched there by the angels. Lovely emeralds like
clusters of green stars, and gold thick and shiny as the icing on a
cupcake."

"The Ring of Kerry," said Lafferty. "Old, was it?"

"Ancient. My great-great-grandda discovered the thing one day
in the bog when he was gathering turf for his fire. In a rotted

old leather packet, as though it had been hid there long ago and somehow forgot."

"Whatever become of it?"

"That's the thing of it, Mister. My grandda buried it with her."

He caught his breath. "In the ground?"

She nodded. "Like the bloody Egyptians. He said how she loved it, her only treasure in the world, and he buried the bloody thing with her in her grave."

"Surely someone would have . . ."

She shook her head. "He told no one, you see. Folded her hands just so."

"He told you."

"I was a lass on his knee. Forever talking about the Ring of Kerry. And doesn't he let it slip out of himself one day when he was well in his cups."

At that moment the possibility had already unfurled itself before him. He could persuade her to go away with him, to retrieve the ring from the grave of her granny, and they'd run off together, just the two of them. He could do it, he was certain, easy as persuading a flea to hop, for he was aware of his own powers of persuasion with members of the gentler gender, attributable largely to the sincerity of the dimple on his chin.

But would it be right? He was not keen to use the innocent young thing for his own greedy gain. She was a waitress, or tried to be. After his meal at the Sugarshack Restaurant, the first time in the spring he'd ever laid eyes on her, she'd followed him out into the street. "Wait, mister," she'd called. Ever since, he'd been Mister. "Wait—you're after leaving your money on the table in there."

"Why, that's yours," Lafferty had said. "That's your tip."

"Tip?" she'd said, her freckles all up in a bunch.

There were other considerations as well. His wife, Peggy, for example. The degree of their estrangement notwithstanding, they were still man and wife, and for all the cause he might have given her, she'd never once betrayed him. Lafferty drew the line at betrayal.

And there was a man, Lafferty had learned, an abusive man by the name of Ray, from Dublin, a criminal of some sort, though the exact nature of his criminality remained a bit of a mystery. What Eena was was on the run from him, which would account for how she'd ended up in godforsaken Kilduff, in the heart of County Nowhere. Ray was in Portlaoise Prison, she'd told him, and Lafferty, aware of the high-security nature of the place, concluded that he was not your garden-variety shoplifter.

Destiny struck one day late in the summer when Jelly Roll in the eighth at the Curragh came in at fifty to one. There was no reason on God's green earth he ever should have, and Lafferty never would have given the horse the time of day, but Eena liked the name. She was fond of strawberry jelly. Lafferty's turf accountant, Mickey G, was suspicious and reluctant, his nose bright red with worry, but he forked over the tidy sum, and Lafferty headed off to fetch Eena for a proper celebration. The timing was serendipitous, as Peggy was off on her monthly shopping trip to Dublin with her girlfriend Judy, leaving Lafferty free to borrow her little brown Ford, Peggy being reluctant to lend it. She was fiercely possessive of the thing, owing no doubt to the time Lafferty'd borrowed it, unbeknownst to herself, and the unfortunate incident with the innocent donkey. Eena was reluctant to miss her shift at the Sugarshack, displaying what Lafferty considered an unreasonable degree of loyalty toward the pitiful place. "Tell 'em your granny passed away," he said. "You won't be lying at all."

He knew of a place in Naas, not far from Dublin, scarcely more than an hour's drive, a place called the Oyster Tavern, where he'd celebrated a similar stroke of good fortune a number of years before with Peggy. It seemed proper and poetic. Eena wore a pair of high heels and a cocktail dress, the likes of which he'd never seen on her before, the likes of which he was surprised she possessed. She looked like a schoolgirl dressed up for show, and she was giddy as a schoolgirl, forever wanting to peek at the big wad of bills Lafferty had stuck in his pocket, wanting to touch it and smell it, the brown eyes of her filled with the wonder. In possession of a small fortune they were, high on the wings of escape, and her dear old dead granny having played a part—Lafferty allowed the notions to entangle themselves, just as he knew Eena was doing, and sure enough, nearly to Naas, doesn't she come out with it.

"Mister," said she. "If we could think of a way to get the ring up out of my granny's grave, we could go to the Oyster Tavern anytime we pleased."

He'd been waiting the months for her to suggest it. "And how might we go about that?"

"Why, we'd have to dig it up, I suppose."

Lafferty pulled in the reins on his smile, which was chomping quite fierce at the bit. "But wouldn't that be . . . I don't know . . . sacrilegious?"

He glanced away from the road to see her eyebrow go up. "Oh, I don't think so, Mister," said she. "Only a wee desecration is all."

They laughed. She'd come far since the spring, when she'd been incapable of deciphering his humor at all. The deal was all but sealed. All that remained was for Lafferty to decide how best to accommodate the matter of Peggy. Betrayal was not his currency, but there were degrees of betrayal, and accommodations could often be reached, given the right rationale.

The Oyster Tavern was a splendid old stone edifice with a doorway of dark heavy oak and, inside, a grand dining hall with beams in the ceiling, a magnificent stone fireplace at the far end. Crisp white linens, waiters in black jackets, and the finest steaks within a hundred miles of Dublin. Candles on the tabletops, music in the air. They settled in to study the menu, Eena hanging on his every word and wisdom, just as she always did, full of trust, safe in his hands. Lafferty was up to high living when he had to be, and he ordered a rare Merlot, had it opened by the table to let it breathe. He couldn't escape her eyes in the candlelight. He held her hand on top of the tablecloth, where it squirmed like a tiny bird.

When the soup arrived steaming hot, he asked her what she judged the ring to be worth—had her grandda ever mentioned it in passing? In response her hand darted from beneath his own to hide in the shadows of her lap. "Mister," she whispered.

"What is it?"

"Over there. Is it not herself?"

Back over his shoulder he looked. Herself it was indeed. Peggy across the crowd, Peggy and a man, a man he'd never before set eyes on, leaving the place together, a couple, laughing, tipsy, her arm about his back as she smooched his cheek, his hand on the full of her fine, round rear.

Lafferty listened to the blood clambering in his ear, the sound of a deal being sealed.

He parted the coarse green curtain, raising up a cloud of dust. Rattigan's Motor Court, an apt appellation. He was accustomed to cheap rooms, some of the happiest moments of his life had been squandered in cheap rooms, and he could only hope this would prove to be another. The hardest part was the waiting. Keeping the girl on an even keel. Keeping himself on one as well, his heart still smarting at the revelation of his wife's perfidy. But Lafferty, ever the optimist, viewed it as motivation, pure and simple. Opportunity beating his door in. Outside the twilight lingered till he thought it would never come to an end.

The little motorway in front led into Ballybeg, on the outskirts of which lay the church of St. Brigid, behind which lay the moss-covered graveyard, within which lay Mrs. Bernadette Moore, the granny of Roseena Brown. They'd driven by so he could see for himself the lay of the land, exactly as she'd described, the isolation of it, isolation enough at any rate, after midnight. Now the trick was getting midnight here. And Lafferty with his bowels raging perilously.

As great and tempting as the reward might be, the cost was steep. There was, for one thing, the matter of the manual labor necessary to dislodge six feet of good, solid Ballybeg earth; Mrs. Lafferty had not raised her boy to work with his hands, and he'd always found hard labor distasteful. Not to mention the grisly and ghastly nature of communion with a corpse.

"Mister." Eena curled on her side in the bed, blanket pulled up to her chin. Underneath she was naked, quiet and still and lost in her thoughts, every bit the opposite of himself, pacing the floor in his boxers. "Maybe it isn't such a good idea at that. Maybe we should call the whole thing off."

Lafferty paused at the window, giving the twilight another dusty glimpse. The first notion that popped into his mind, he was not proud to admit, was of himself carrying on, on his own, without her assistance at all. He knew everything he needed to know, the ring was there waiting like a potato in the ground, and how much assistance could she offer at any rate, wee little thing that she was. He would have to do the heavy lifting. But he overcame his selfish inclination. He was nothing if not a moral man. He looked at her there curled in the bed, the size of an orphan. "In for a penny, in for a pound," he said, crawling into the bed behind her, gathering her up in his arms.

"I'm scared," she said, her heart pounding the cage of her ribs.

"Aren't you after telling me your granny would want you to have it? That she'd give it to you herself if she could? After all your troubles, all you been through, all the torment your man Ray has caused you, look at it as your just deserts."

She was still, a captured kitten.

"Think past today. There's a good girl. Think past the unpleasantness to the rewards that'll follow. Think of us free and easy on our own, living the good life."

She was quiet for a long while, and he hoped the idea was soothing her, though still he could feel the working of her heart. "And what about Peggy, Mister?"

What about Peggy indeed. His face began to burn. "Her just deserts as well," he said.

"How did you end up with the likes of her in the first place?"

"Young and ignorant, I suppose. Seemed at the time like the proper thing to do. She was up the pole, so it was the honorable thing."

"And where's the child then?"

"After all that, she lost it."

Eena never turned. Her ear sticking up through her hair like a cookie there for him to nibble on. "Lost it," said she, "or told you she lost it?"

In the shadows of the hedgerow Peggy's little brown Ford was invisible from the motorway. He wondered if she'd called the cops to report it stolen. Behind the church of mossy stone, the steeple glimmering in the black of the night with the light of a hidden moon, the graveyard climbed along a sloping hill. Beside it a row of trees all slanted and hunched from the wind through the years, like fingers pointing in from the sea. Lafferty waist-deep in the grave of Mrs. Bernadette Moore, his shirt clinging to his chest with the sweat, stinking of it, his hands on fire from the handle of the spade — Peggy's spade he borrowed from her garden. Eena perched on a neighboring stone, sitting morose and worried, knees clapped together, fiddling with the torch in her hand she never once lit, like the candle on the chest in her room.

"Could you spell me a minute, love?" said Lafferty, wiping the sweat from his face.

She tried, but she was useless as tits on a bull, every other shovelful tipping and falling back into the hole. The spade was lanky in her hands, and she wielded it as though she were uncertain which end to stick into the ground. Reminded Lafferty of her awkward and clumsy way with a tray full of dishes, or how she was in the bed whenever he tried to teach her a new trick, forever shy and clumsy, ill-equipped for the task at hand. But by God earnest and eager. When she was embarrassed, or hard at work, or deep in thought, the tips of her ears became red.

He caught his breath, looked up at the sky, gray notions of clouds scudding across it. Down across the slope past the church the village lay dark and quiet, save for the odd barking of a dog. A spot of light here, another there. Lafferty was soon impatient to take the spade from her hands. So close he could nearly taste it, the gold like icing on a cupcake, the sticky star clusters of emeralds. He considered she might be wrong, that maybe her old grandda was a liar—for wasn't it after all too easy? A blow to his dreams to be sure, but he found, nearly to his surprise, the shattering of her dreams his foremost concern. He could imagine her all hollow and sad, imagine her shrinking, drying up, blowing away. And he found the oddest thing happening to his train of thoughts, found it twisting and heading down the side track. For it was this thing, the shattering of her dream, he was bound to deter, for if the worst were to happen he would take her, hold her, find the joy for her, somewhere, somehow. He was nothing if not an optimistic man, and in all his exhilaration, perched here on the verge of joy, Lafferty felt such a love for the girl struggling in the hole he wanted to pick her up and squeeze her. So there it was. The fortune scarcely in his mind at all, the joy the ring would bring her having surpassed the worth in value, and so he took the spade from her hands, helped her up out of the hole, and set about his business. He'd never felt more noble, and the feeling of it brought a shiver to his skin, a tear to his eye.

By the time he was up to his chin in the dirt, nobility was fading fast. Exhaustion was only the half of it. The unholiness of the whole bloody project, the graveyard, the smell of earth and sweat, the girl on the stone, the half-lit sky, the wind twisting through the trees, wasn't it all beginning to play on his mind. Wasn't he beginning to worry there was no one buried at the bottom of this hole at all, that he could dig all the way to Pakistan and come up empty. Wasn't he beginning to feel the panic of being down in the grave, the prospect grabbing him by the throat and squeezing tight that he might never come up out of it again. *My mam always told me I'd end up digging dirt for a living,* he said. But Eena up above never uttered a word of response, causing Lafferty to wonder if he'd really said it aloud or only thought it, or maybe only dreamt it. And then to wonder if his mam had in truth ever uttered the words, though he was fairly certain she had, as she'd never had a good word to spare him or his da, when indeed his da was home with them at all. For a long time he pictured her there in front of the stove in the dark tenement, the smoke lifting the smell of frying rashers, her back to him, her hand clenched up in a fist on the side of her apron, and the sight of it stayed with him till his shovel knocked on wood.

"Are you there, Mister?"

Lafferty might have grunted. The exhilaration was back, jumbled up with a grand dollop of apprehension, as he cleared off the top of the box. He knelt on the lid, on the lower half, and when he reached up to swing it open, he hesitated. He found he couldn't lift the thing up. There was no physical barrier to him doing so, but he found he couldn't lift the thing up at all.

"Mister?" The whispered word sweet as an onion. Lafferty looked up at the head of her peering down. "What are you waiting for?"

Lafferty stood. "Could you give us a kiss for courage?" She had to lie on the ground to do so, and that was the way they held one another, both perpendicular against the dirt, arms embracing, cheeks touching, tears mingling. He wasn't surprised to find her weeping, too, for now the circuit was joined, the electricity coursing through them, locked there together and for good. "Okay then," said he. "Okay."

He looked down at the box beneath his feet. "Will the smell of it be something awful?"

"I shouldn't think so. She's been down there so long."

"Will she be dreadful? All rotted and the like?"

"I shouldn't think so. All dried up by now, I'd suppose."

Nevertheless he held his breath and closed his eyes and pulled up the top of the lid. Warm air rose up to his face. It was the bravest thing he ever did. It was an inanimate object in the box, he told himself, and he did what he had to do. Finally he stood, turning his face up again toward Eena, standing up looking down. "I have it."

"From off her finger?"

"Of course from off her finger. From right where your grandda placed it."

"That one's the fake."

"What fake?"

"That's not the real one. That's the replica, crafted to look like the genuine article."

"You never mentioned a fake."

"The real one's tucked beneath her. Underneath her arse."

Lafferty's mind stalled in the processing of the words, as he stared at the black of the dirt, the fake ring clutched in his fist.

"Just grab it, Mister. I'll explain it to you later."

And so he did. He took a deep breath, diving in again. Never let the air out of him till he was standing once more. Dizzy, his mind still spinning. "Got it?" said she. He nods. "Hand it up then," and so he did.

She tilted her head as she took it, sticking it straight in the pocket of her jeans. He drew in a great chestful of air, all the dread leaking out of him, and, reaching up to take her hand, doesn't he glimpse the oddest flash, too feeble for lightning, and doesn't he hear the faintest roar, too weak for thunder, a sight and a sound he could put together only after the fact as the back of the shovel coming barreling gangways toward his face at great velocity, behind which was Eena, the wee girl swinging the thing for all she was worth, like a champion hurler on the pitch.

Was he ever truly out? He was never truly certain, for it seemed as though no time had passed at all till he found himself slumped in the corner of the hole, on the lid of the box, white stars in his head drifting away, slowly letting blackness seep back in. And all the while the sight of Peggy in his mind, standing over him with her frying pan. He crawled up out of the hole, dirt crumbling back in with a rattle on the lid. Felt the lump on the side of his head, hair matted down in the dampness there. Down across the graveyard by the hedgerow, Peggy's car was gone. A light or two down across the village. No sounds at all now, the dog having gone to sleep, or having been murdered, just the whisper of a breeze restless through the trees. Lafferty picked up the shovel, wondered what the bloody thing was doing in his hand, and dropped it into the hole with a clatter.

He didn't head down toward the road. He went up higher instead among the gravestones, resting himself up a ways by a mossy Celtic cross, not far from the hunched-over trees.

There he waited. Not another five minutes gone by till he saw the headlamps. Sure enough, turning into the car park. Peggy's little Ford, the girl climbing out, Eena. Scrambling up toward the grave of her granny. If indeed it was her granny at all.

"Mister?" she cried. "Mister! Where are you? Jesus, I'm sorry!"

Down the hill, down his nose, Lafferty watched her panicky antics. Lighting the torch, she pointed it down in the hole, the beam bounding up again as if swatted away, and then all about the graveyard in a skelter of bedlam. Far too feeble to reach him. Lafferty watched, breathing in the cool night air.

"Where are you? Mister? Terrence? I don't know whatever come over me."

He watched. Watched the spirit seeping out of her. Saw the torch beam droop and falter, then fail altogether. Watched the shadow of her trailing away back down across the graveyard to the car. He considered showing himself, confronting her, but in the end he couldn't do it. In the end he couldn't be certain the passenger seat of the car was empty.

So he watched. She climbed into the car and drove away, tail lamps disappearing down the road. When they were gone, when the sound of the engine had trailed off altogether in the still night air, not until then did he unclench his fist, no easy feat, so cramped was it from the work and the will. He held the thing up. Beheld it there. Even in the black of the night it gleamed against the sky, the genuine article, the real glimmering thing, the actual Ring of Kerry.

Mrs. Lafferty had not raised her son to work with his hands. He'd always found manual labor distasteful, and so it was with travel by foot. So it came to pass an hour or two later, maybe more, when the eastern sky was beginning to give in to gray and the car came up the motorway, that Lafferty changed his plan and stuck out his thumb.

For a long while the magic of the ring on his finger had sustained him, the heft and history and beauty and sheer gold lifting him above his weariness, and he'd vowed to trek on till morning, get as far away as he could on foot, then find shelter, rest, then plan out the rest of his life. He'd have put the ring in his pocket in the first place, only there were holes there, bloody holes his bloody wife could never be bloody bothered to sew, so he'd slipped it on his pinkie instead, where it fit snug as a rubber. But the weariness at last overcame him, that and the ache of his head, and after first determining that the car in question bore no resemblance to the little brown Ford of his erstwhile wife, Lafferty stuck out his thumb.

It was a big black car, posh and polished to a gleam, that came to a stop on the side of the road. Lafferty hustled up, climbing in. A man was behind the wheel, a man all dressed to the nines with his vest buttoned up, a man with a face full of smiling teeth, his hair pulled back in a ponytail and gleaming as bright as the car. "Lonely night for thumbing," he said.

"It is," said Lafferty.

"Where to?"

He was totally unprepared for the question. "Which way are you heading?"

The driver had to smile again, leaning up to the wheel. "West."

"West it is, then," Lafferty said, pointing like a cowpoke. "West across the island."

There came a loud metallic click, the sound of the doors being locked, and Lafferty felt a jolt. The driver wasn't driving. He nodded toward Lafferty's lap, where his hand lay. "Lovely ring you're wearing."

The first thing he was was surprised. The last thing he supposed was the thing could be seen in the dark. He was about to respond with the first inanity that popped into his head, *nothing special,* when he looked at the lap of the driver, where a gun was quietly glinting.

"You'd be Ray, then," he said.

Ray smiled even broader. "And you'd be Mister Lafferty." He nodded again toward the ring. "Hand it over."

"I can't get it off."

"What do you mean you can't get it off?"

"I mean it won't come off."

The gun twitched up with impatience. "Give it a yank then."

"I'm after giving it a yank. I'm after giving it a yank and a tug and a jerk and a pull. The bloody thing won't budge."

"Try spitting on it."

"I'm after spitting on it, too—do you think I'm a bloody eejit?"

"Try it again with the spit. Only wipe it off good before you hand it over."

To no avail again. Lafferty nearly pulling off the skin.

"Stick it over here." Lafferty did, and Ray grabbed and yanked, yanking the finger nearly out of the socket, the shoulder nearly out of its own. Nor did twisting, prying, cajoling, and cursing do any good at all. Ray sat back and slapped the wheel, twisting his head to glare out the window at the sky growing bright. "You're spoiling my morning, Mister Lafferty."

"Get some butter," Lafferty suggested. "Butter always works."

"Mister Lafferty," said Ray, leaning over calm and peaceful. "I have no butter. Do you see any butter? Do you think I'm carrying butter in my fucking pocket?" The volume gradually increasing, as was the redness of his face. "Do you think there's butter in the glovebox? There is no bloody butter! No butter on my person, in the car, lying out by the road, no butter within miles of this godforsaken shithole! There is no fucking butter!"

"I should have known butter," said Lafferty. Why, he didn't know.

Nor did Ray. He glared a moment, then started the car with a roar, turned, heading back toward Ballybeg. He settled into silence for a while, though it was a fierce silence to be sure, the ferocity of which was exhibited by his reckless driving, the likes of which would have caused Lafferty to fear for his life, had that fear not already been in place.

Finally he slowed to a civil speed. "Mister Lafferty. Reach into the glovebox there. A celebration, a wee drop to the recovery of the ring."

Lafferty, leery, did as he was told. It was a bottle of Powers, clear and gold.

"Well?" said your man, glancing askance at the faltering Lafferty. "Not thirsty?"

"Awfully early," said Lafferty.

"Give it over," Ray said. Lafferty handed him the bottle, and he took a gurgling draft, handing it back to Lafferty. "There. No poison. Now drink."

Lafferty shrugged. "To the Ring of Kerry," he said, tipping it up.

Ray looked at him, puzzled by the mention of the tourist trap. "Take another," he said, and so Lafferty did. "There's a lad," Ray said, smiling now. He'd the face of a child, Lafferty noticed, the face of a child of the streets. Dangerous to be sure, but innocent as well, with a certain capacity for compassion. They drove for a while in time to the gurgles and swallows, Ray seemingly pensive, peering out through the windscreen at the windy little road. Nearly back to Ballybeg, he spoke. "Do you like puzzles, Mister Lafferty?"

Lafferty, puzzled, neither nodded nor spoke.

"Have another," Ray said, "and I'll tell you a puzzle. Eena—our mutual friend—calls me up in Dublin, what, not three hours ago, and isn't she crying, full of grief and misery to tell me what's happened, how Mister Lafferty has absconded with our ring. And what do you suppose is the story she tells me?" Looking Lafferty's way again, drawing a blank again. "No guess in you then at all? Not very keen at the puzzles, are you?

"Why, she'd wanted to surprise me. To fetch the ring back to me all on her own, to atone for all the harm she done me back then." Glancing again at Lafferty. "You'd be unaware of the harm, then? How she cost me four bloody years of my life?" And so Ray told him. How Eena, five years before, had brung the ring to his attention in the first place. How Eena, who'd been a domestic for the wealthy Mrs. Moore, owner of said ring, had botched the simple snatch-and-switch late at night when the old lady was laid out at home for the wake. How just as Ray was about to do the switch, Eena knocked over a tray full of dirty saucers and such, alerting the family, who apprehended your man beating feet down the lane with the replica, which of course they mistook for the real thing. And Eena meanwhile fleeing under cover of the ruckus, having stashed the real McCoy under the old lady's dead arse. And how her clumsiness cost him four years in Portlaoise—from which he'd been sprung but a few days before.

"So here's the puzzle then. Am I to believe she was going to fetch the ring back to me? Or was she planning to make off with the bloody thing all along, go off on her own, and myself left in the proverbial lurch? What am I to believe, Mister Lafferty? Do you yourself believe little Eena Brown to be capable of treachery and betrayal? For I understand you've got to know her well since the day you left her the stinking little two-punt tip."

Lafferty was stung, though he kept it to himself.

"But the thing of it is, Mister Lafferty," said he, "the thing of it is, she could well be telling me the truth. That's the nature of her.

That's Eena. She might well have been planning to bring me a get-out-of-jail present. Or she might have been planning to fuck me. With Eena, you just never know."

Lafferty didn't know, couldn't even think about sorting the thing out in his mind. Ray nodded. "Take another drink," he said, and Lafferty did, thankful for small blessings.

At Rattigan's everything was gray, everything from the sky right down to the pavement beneath his feet when he stepped from the car. Something moved in the window—Eena peeping through the ratty green curtain. Peggy's car nowhere to be seen, and only one other car in the car park, several doors down, Lafferty concluding that the owner of a rusty yellow Fiat with a dent in the fender would not possess the formidability needed to come to his aid at all.

Eena rushing to Ray where she buried her face in his shoulder left Lafferty more stricken than ever. Wounded and hollow, and lightheaded from the whiskey, not to mention the thump on the noggin. Shot through with fear and sorrow. Though how much of the burying of her face was out of love for your man, how much out of not wanting to look Lafferty in the eye? Ray gently stroked the nape of her neck under the rowdy red hair.

"Mister Lafferty," said Ray, pointing the gun toward the bed. "Sit."

Lafferty did. Ray handed the gun to Eena, who held it in both of her hands like a foreign object, like a spade or a tray full of dishes. Ray took off his jacket, hanging it neatly on the rack. He unbuttoned his vest, removing it as well, hanging it beside the jacket. From the pocket of his trousers, he withdrew an object that Lafferty at first couldn't identify. When he placed it by the car keys on the rickety table, he saw it was a knife. A long knife. A long, shiny knife, and this before the blade was ever out of it. Ray removed his trousers, lined up the creases, hung them neatly over a hanger. Unbuttoned his shirt, hung it by the rest of his clothes, then stood there in his boxers and undershirt, Lafferty noticing the round pucker of a scar above his knee.

Eena looked at him as well, puzzled as well.

"The ring won't come free of his finger, love," said Ray. "I have to perform surgery, and I don't fancy ruining a good suit of clothes with the blood."

"Butter," Lafferty said.

"Butter works," said Eena.

Ray stamped his foot on the threadbare rug. "There is no butter!"

"There's always butter somewhere," said Lafferty, his mouth dry
as a cobweb.

Ray took the gun. "Into the bathroom," he said, taking Lafferty
by the collar. "Eena, love, bring the knife. Gather up the towels."

Lafferty naturally resisted. Ray naturally pressed the gun to his
cheek. "Mister Lafferty. I'm not a heartless man. I'm after allowing you your anesthesia—here, have another." He handed Lafferty the bottle of Powers from the nightstand. "Now I intend to
cut the pinkie from your hand to take possession of the ring that's
rightfully mine. I paid four years of my life for it. I intend to cut it
off you and leave you alive, without a pinkie, which, in your line of
work as I understand it, will not be much of a hindrance. However,
if I must, I will cut the finger from a dead man. It would, in fact,
be a far easier trick."

The bathroom was small, a sink with a little glass shelf and
smeared mirror above it, a standing shower stall and the toilet with
the lid up. "Would you like to sit then, Mister Lafferty? You might
be needing to."

Lafferty shook his head. His voice had deserted him.

"You wouldn't have an apron in your bag, would you, love?" said
Ray, looking down at his undershirt.

Eena bit her lip and shook her head, the tips of her ears going
red.

"Pity," said Ray. "Hold his hand there, love, tight to the side of
the sink."

"Wait," said Eena. "Let me try."

"You'd like to carve?"

"Let me try to get it off. I used to be able to get the things off
my own finger when they were stuck."

Ray nodded.

She came to Lafferty, her brown eyes big and close. She took his
hand in both her own, raising it up to her face, taking his pinkie
into her mouth.

"Easy, love," said Ray. "You're getting me all up."

She didn't hear him. Lafferty watched her eyes that never left
his own, feeling his pinkie in her mouth so warm and moist it

nearly stopped him trembling. Nearly. He watched her lips at their work, lips he'd never seen so skillful before, watched her cheeks suck in, felt her tongue laboring every bit as hard, the ears of her going redder and redder, his pinkie wanting to disappear down her throat. He felt the ring loosen. Felt it loosen then come free, sliding quickly away down his finger, too fast, away from his finger and into her throat, too deep, into her throat where it caught.

She drew away quickly, coughing, choking. Ray clapped her on the back, hard, once, twice, a third time, and the ring came shooting up out of her, lifting through the air, arching straight toward the toilet, where it landed with a neat little splash. Settling down to the bottom, lying there gleaming in all its golden splendor, beneath the foul water on the stained and dirty porcelain.

The three of them stared at the thing. "Get it," said Ray.

"You get it," Eena said.

"I'm not putting my hand in that," Ray said. "Mister Lafferty, you do it."

Reaching over, Lafferty flushed the toilet.

The ring disappeared, sucked down a different throat. Lafferty looked at Ray. Eena stepped back. Ray trembled, the tremble going to quaking proportions, red all over with the boiling blood, and he sputtered unintelligible syllables, and the gun in his hand came up, pointing at Lafferty, his finger on the trigger twitching. Lafferty felt his knees buckle and go under, and he was falling toward the floor.

"No!" said Eena, stepping in to knock it away, but doesn't the bloody thing discharge with a bang that shook the shower curtain. Lafferty, concussed by the sound and the shock, took a moment to divine what was happening, for it was the oddest dance they were doing, Ray and Eena, clutched together there swaying, Ray's little-boy face over her shoulder all white and grim and pulled back tight, and the head of Eena flopping loose and lolling.

And the red splash of blood coming down.

"God!" said Ray. "God, help me—Lafferty! Help me! Get something!"

Lafferty reached up, handing him a cheap scrap of a towel that Ray pressed to her chest. He lowered her to the floor, her eyelids fluttering, looking up from one of them to the other. "Get help," Ray said. "Hurry—get help!"

Lafferty arose, riding his rubbery legs.

Eena, surprise lingering on her face, stared up past Ray, straight into the eyes of Lafferty. *"Hurry,"* said Ray. "Get help."

Snatching the car keys from the rickety table, Lafferty galloped out the door, pulling it shut behind him. The car park was empty, no one out from the office, nor from the room near the Fiat, no one roused by the gunshot, no one wondering as to the mortal goings-on in the room at the end of the court. The morning was sleepy, motionless, as if he'd stepped into a painting, a still life, a landscape, all the trees arranged alongside the road, the house across the way with the tidy blue shutters, the clean gleaming glass of the petrol station next door, the letters on the sign so bold and red. The Audi started up in a fine, smooth purr, hitting on all cylinders, unlike his mind, for hadn't he been sleepless the whole of the night, engaged in the most desperate of physical labors, thumped about the head, his finger nearly cut off him, his very life in mortal jeopardy. He squealed away out of the car park, heading west, west across the island, the countryside sweeping by, the rock walls and hedgerows, the tumbledown cottages, leaving it all behind him, the cold awful touch of the dead woman, the porcelain white face of Ray, the blast of the gun and the blood.

But even as he crested the hill and flew toward the next, the eyes stayed with him, the lying eyes of Eena, full of hope and truth at last, going bigger and browner as the color leached from her face. The eyes stayed with him, and the ring, the dreadful, awful, never-ending ring.

MICAH NATHAN

Quarry

FROM *Glimmer Train*

SAM SAW THE OWL a day earlier, resting in the eaves of the barn. Their father had left for market, and so Henry got the Browning and stood on a hay bale, stock set against his bony shoulder; he squeezed the trigger between breaths like his father had shown him. The owl fell in a storm of feathers and Henry set down the gun. He grabbed the bird by its tiny, curled feet.

"It didn't hurt anybody," Sam said. He stared up at the motes swirling in stalks of morning light.

"We lost eight chickens last month," Henry said. "And it wasn't from a fox."

"How do you know?"

"Dad said a fox leaves a trail, but a bird of prey takes the whole damn thing."

"You said damn."

"So. You just said it, too."

Henry inspected the owl. The twenty-gauge had made holes in the rump and neck, but the face was unspoiled; he would clean and stuff it, and have it ready for his father.

Sam smoothed the tail feathers. They were soft as velvet and left a dusty sheen on his fingers.

"Maybe Dad will let you have it, when I'm done," Henry said.

"I'd put it over my door."

"That would look good," Henry said.

"Can I help?"

"No. There's other things that need finishing."

"But you—"

"But nothing. Fetch me the arsenic soap, if you want."

Sam crossed his arms. "Fetch it yourself."

Henry shrugged and left the barn, owl in hand, shotgun propped against his shoulder. Sam glared at his brother's back, and shivered even though he tried not to; the morning was bitter cold.

Henry set the bird on his desk. Through his bedroom window he could see the field where Sam now worked, digging out rocks from the ground softened by Indian summer and carrying them to the well near the forest's edge. The well was dry, and they'd been dumping rocks in it for as long as they could remember. Years before, peering over the edge with Sam, his brother had asked him if the well had a bottom, or if it just kept going.

Henry watched Sam kneel on the dirt and figured he was playing with the sluggish beetles he'd uncovered, using his finger to make them crawl in circles around the sockets of earth. Henry wanted to start work on the owl, but it would have to wait. First a cup of coffee, and then he'd lift the heavy rocks his brother could not.

Henry frowned and set the water to boil; he sighed as he sat at the kitchen table with a steaming mug. He was fourteen and believed this ritual set him on the correct path to adulthood, because his father did the same thing every morning, preparing his coffee with great seriousness. Sometimes his father talked about common cattle diseases, sitting at the table with the mug held in both hands under his chin. Multiple abortions in the breeding herd usually meant lepto. Lameness and spongy swellings along the shoulders and hips often indicated blackleg. Henry kept quiet during his father's lectures; his sonorous voice and the thick smell of coffee were conversation enough.

Sam banged through the front door and ran into the living room, shouting Henry's name. Henry set down his mug and whistled for him.

"There's a man," Sam said, breathing hard. "In the forest. I think he's dead."

They found the man in a shallow trench along a stand of bare maples. He was missing one shoe and his toenails were dirty. Henry saw a dark hole in the man's thigh, black trails snaking down to the bottom of his blood-stiffened cuff. His brown hair was mashed to his forehead, and bits of dirt stuck to the tips of his eyelashes. His lips were almost white.

Sam picked up a stick and poked the man's shoulder. "Is he dead?"

Henry put his ear to the man's chest. "He's alive. Stop poking him."

"I'm just trying to wake him up."

"You can't. He's hurt bad. We need to bring him inside."

"Why?"

"Because he'll freeze out here. Now hold his arms, and I'll grab his feet."

"What happened to his leg?"

"Doesn't matter."

Sam sniffled. "It's from a bullet. Don't tell me it isn't."

"So what. He was hunting and had an accident."

"He doesn't look like a hunter."

"You don't know a damn thing about anything." Henry grabbed the man's ankles. "If you won't help, I'll do it myself."

The boys worked quickly and quietly. They dragged him from the forest and across the bumpy field. They rested near the broken tractor, the man lying between their feet. Henry wiped his forehead with his sleeve and spat.

"Ready?" Henry said, and Sam nodded.

By the time they'd put the man on the living room couch, Henry thought he might throw up. He ran to the bathroom and waited by the toilet. Sam knocked on the door.

"Go away," Henry said. "I'm sick."

"Is it because of the man?"

"It's because I'm sick. Hurry up and fetch a hot compress for him, and make some tea."

"Dad says that tea is for guests."

"Well, he's a guest, isn't he?"

Henry waited until he heard Sam walk into the kitchen. Then he flushed the toilet, rinsed his face, and took the necessary tools from the medicine cabinet.

Cleaning the wound wasn't as hard as he'd expected; he plucked bits of pant cloth from the clotted hole and poured alcohol until the blood dissolved and soaked into the gauze like watered-down wine. The man moaned and shifted when Sam put the hot compress on his forehead, and Sam drew back.

"I bet you he's a criminal," Sam said.

"He might be," Henry said.

"Do you think he lost his shoe before he got shot, or after?"

"I don't know."

"If it's before he got shot, then he's just a bum," Sam said. "Walking around with one shoe. Dad won't care if we brought in a bum. Dad likes bums. Remember when we gave that smelly old man a ride to town?"

Henry probed with the tweezers; the man grunted and gripped the couch. His hands reminded Henry of his father's—large and rough, with fine black hairs.

"He looks kind of young for a bum," Henry said, and he pointed to the man's scarred knuckles. "Those are boxer's lumps. Uncle Frank had them."

They ate an early dinner in the kitchen while the man slept. Sam drank his milk and licked froth off his upper lip, then set the glass down with a bang.

"He's probably hungry," Sam said.

Henry cut a piece of chop. "When he wakes up I'll give him some pork, if he wants. Whose turn is it to scrub?"

"Yours."

"I hate scrubbing."

"Me, too."

Sam pushed his corn around on his plate, fork tines scraping.

"Henry?"

"What."

"You think we should get the doctor?"

"Not tonight," Henry said. "It's too cold, and I'm not leaving you here alone."

The man cried out, and the boys ran into the living room to find him sitting upright, glassy-eyed, the front of his shirt soaked with sweat. His hair stuck up at odd angles. He was shivering.

The man dragged his gaze across the room and stopped at Henry.

"Did I yell something?" the man said.

Henry nodded.

"What'd I say?"

"Nothing. You just yelled."

The man coughed. "Am I in a yellow farmhouse?"

"You are," Henry said.

"Is your father home?"

"He's at market."

"What's he doing there?"

"Selling cattle."

Sam stood by Henry's side, holding his arm. The man smiled at Sam. His left eyetooth was missing.

"Hello. I'm Jacob."

"I'm Sam Beasley."

"You scared of me, Sam Beasley?"

"Yes, sir."

Jacob slid back down, rested his head on a bolster pillow, and held his wounded leg.

"I couldn't find the bullet," Henry said.

"You dressed it all right." Jacob closed his eyes. "Will one of you boys fetch me something I left in the woods?"

Henry and Sam looked at each other.

"I might," Henry said, but Jacob was asleep.

Cort sat in a booth, sipping coffee thick with sugar and cream. He dumped a handful of coins on the table and watched the diner's parking lot through the window. A week of Indian summer had melted all the snow; now the cold wind returned. The pavement glittered with frost, and car windows reflected the moon. Fields across the road were spiked with broken stalks.

He pondered what had gone wrong. He'd kept it simple, as always—stand in the middle of the road, wait for the bank truck, and level the sawed-off when the driver gets close. But Jacob hadn't frisked the guard properly, and the guard pulled a Chief's Special from his boot, popping off two shots before Cort leaped on him and plunged the blade into his eye. Jacob limped into the woods with the sack of money banging against his side. He moved fast despite being wounded; Cort tracked him until leaves swallowed the blood trail.

Even if the shots proved fatal, Cort figured Jacob was at least a few miles away from where they'd left the truck, and he wouldn't be dead yet. He knew if Jacob was going to come anywhere, it would be someplace like this. A friendly spot, where he could tie off his wounds and ask for a doctor. There would be questions, but Jacob wouldn't care—he was weak, and frightened, and he'd probably confess the world in exchange for a warm bed.

"More coffee?"

Cort looked away from the window. His eyes were small and dark, his black hair cut short. He had thin lips and a thin nose.

"No, ma'am," he said.

The waitress smiled. "We got some fresh pie. Apple and pumpkin."

"Apple'd be nice."

"Whipped cream?"

"Yes, ma'am."

She smiled again and walked away. Cort stared at her back, wondering what she smelled like up close and in the dark. Then he returned to the window and waited.

Jacob woke in the middle of the night. Sam was upstairs, awake in bed, but Henry sat in the living room chair. His father's shotgun lay across his thin thighs. In the dark room lit by the moon, Jacob looked like a dead man, his face drawn, eyes sunk behind large black circles. He moved his hand to the wet, sticky gauze laid over his wound.

"You been sitting here all night?" Jacob said.

"I have."

Jacob grinned. "Watching over me."

"Just watching," Henry said.

"You're being smart. You'd be even smarter if you got my bag from the woods. It's near that old well."

Henry nodded at the bloodied sack sitting on the floor. "I got it."

"Finders keepers," Jacob said.

"I don't want it."

"Your father might."

"He won't."

"We'll see about that."

"We will. He comes back Friday."

"Friday?" Jacob winced and drew in a deep breath. "You don't have that long."

"There's a doctor ten miles south," Henry said. "Our tractor's broke, but I can send Sam first thing. The doctor is good. He fixed my arm a few years back."

"Do you have a phone?"

Henry shook his head. "The lines haven't made it out here yet. They were supposed to have them done by last year."

"Goddammit." Jacob rested his arm over his eyes and sighed.

Henry waited. He heard the kitchen faucet dripping into the sink.

"I'm sorry," Jacob said.

"For what?"

"For not dying in a ditch, far from this place."

Henry gripped the butt of the shotgun.

"You know, I killed a woman in Litchfield," Jacob said. "Six months ago. She was young. Younger than me."

Henry imagined his father driving back home, through the night, gripping the steering wheel and staring ahead. *It's just a feeling I got,* his father would say. *My boys are in trouble. I couldn't sleep. Saw their doom in a nightmare.*

That's not how life works, Henry told himself. *Stop thinking like a child all the time.*

"Funny thing about that woman," Jacob continued. "Wasn't what I expected. You ever watch *Death Valley Days?*"

"We don't have a television."

"Well, that's good. Nothing about it is real. Makes everything look clean. I shot that woman in the throat, and she flopped around for a full minute. The worst thing I ever saw, swear to God. She made these *noises.*" Jacob paused. Then he uncovered his eyes and looked straight at Henry. "Take your brother and leave."

"Why?"

"You have to. He's coming."

"Who is?"

"He's looking for his money."

"Who?"

"Goddammit," Jacob said, and that's all he would say, no matter how many times Henry asked.

Ed's Bar was dim and quiet, the sort of bar Cort preferred because it reminded him of his youth, when he'd sit at a corner booth with a pint of cheap beer and watch the crowds until closing. Now a small scattering of men sat along the bar and at tables pushed against the rough plank walls. Cort ordered a beer and took a seat in the back. He sipped and waited.

After an hour, Cort approached a man seated in the far corner.

"You ever make it down to New Haven?" Cort said.

The man glanced up. He wore a baseball cap pulled low and a felted sweater. Years of farm sun had creased his face. His nose looked like it had been broken several times.

"I'm certain I've seen you there," Cort said. "At Charlie's Tavern. Am I right?"

"Never been to Charlie's," the man said. "Nor New Haven."

"My mistake."

"No harm." The man tipped back his beer and smacked his lips.

Cort sat down and rested his elbows on the table. "I'm just passing through. Selling watches, if you can believe that."

"You should keep passing. Nothing here except dogs and ditches. Couple of farms still trying to make it, but give them time. They'll suffer, just like the rest."

"Does that include you?"

"It does."

Cort grinned. "I wonder what our wives would think of us now. Wasting our days."

The man held up his left hand. Cort held up his own ringless hand.

"Only way to go," the man said.

"You know it."

"I got close, once."

"I didn't," Cort said.

The man looked at Cort.

"What was it you came over here for?"

"A ride," Cort said. "My transmission dropped."

"I thought you were selling watches."

"I am. Selling other things, too."

"What sort of things?"

"That all depends on what you need."

The man paused, glass held in midair. "I might help you, provided one of them watches looks good enough."

Cort grinned. "It all looks good."

The man finished his beer and wiped his mouth with the back of his hand. He looked over his shoulder at the shadowed room. Everyone sat with their heads down.

Cort followed him to the parking lot. He retrieved his shotgun from a stand of weeds, tucking it under his coat. The man drove a blue Chevy sedan, rust spots over the wheel wells and a long crack across the windshield. They pulled onto the main road and Cort rested his head against the window. He stared at the pale morning sky.

After a few miles Cort said, "I have to piss. You mind pulling off somewhere?"

The man slowed near an elm with a scarred trunk and killed the engine. He looked in the rearview, at the empty road.

"Bit public for my tastes," the man said. He dropped his hand to his crotch and left it there.

"I'll be careful," Cort said. He reached into his boot and withdrew a short blade. He turned and thrust it into the man's throat. The man grabbed Cort's arm. He kicked and gurgled as blood streamed down the front of his shirt. Cort pulled out the blade, watched the pump of blood slow to a trickle, then hauled him across the seat and switched places.

After he'd dumped the man by the side of a pond and covered him in a loose scab of leaves and twigs, he rinsed his hands in the icy water and looked to the cloud-covered sun. He walked back to the blue Chevy, drove to the main road, and found the first farm within minutes.

Two men worked in front of a red house; a dog loped across the yard. Cort crept through the bare woods, shotgun low and ready, white breath rising above his head. He didn't mind if the dog smelled him—he figured he could shoot the thing and get back to his car before the owners knew what had happened. Cort sat on a crumbling stone wall and watched the men work, one pushing a wheelbarrow and the other walking in and out of the barn. The scene was perfectly normal, he decided, so he got back in the Chevy.

Before dawn Henry felt better, but Jacob's breathing had turned ragged. Sam stood at the end of the couch and pressed a cool cloth to Jacob's forehead. Henry left the shotgun on the floor and waited by the window, for what he didn't know—he just felt like staring at the frost-covered fields still lit by the moon.

"I shouldn't have fought with you," Sam said to Henry. "I should have hurried up and helped you carry him."

"You did."

"But I didn't want to."

"It doesn't matter, Sam."

"It does. He's real sick. Is he dying?"

"I think so."

"We should go for the doctor."

"Not until the sun's up. It's too cold."

"But he's dying."

"I know."

"Don't you care?"

"I do." Henry continued staring out the window. "We'll leave at sunrise. I promise."

Sam eyed the bloody bag sitting on the floor. "What's in the bag?"

"Money," Henry said. "Don't touch it."

"I shouldn't have poked him with that stick."

"It wasn't your stick that hurt him. He was *shot.*"

Sam started to cry. Henry stared at the floor. He heard the rattle in Jacob's lungs and remembered the same sound at his mother's side, when Sam was a baby sleeping in the other room.

"Minute the sun comes up," Henry said, "we'll head out."

"Promise?"

"I promise. And after Doc fixes him, we'll finish hauling those rocks. Everything will work out just right. Now go on and take a bath. Make the water good and hot. We got a long walk ahead of us."

Sam glanced at Jacob.

"He'll be okay," Henry continued. "I'll change his bandage and make more tea."

Sam frowned. "Are you just saying this to make me feel better?"

"No."

"Swear?"

"I swear."

Sam inhaled deeply and scratched his head. "You call me back in if anything happens?"

"I will."

Sam wiped his cheeks and ran upstairs.

This is how it should be, Henry thought, and he picked up the compress. *This is what men do for each other.*

He wrung the compress into a bowl and resoaked it. He laid it on Jacob's forehead; the man groaned and opened his eyes.

"Told you to leave," Jacob said. He started to say something else, but his voice caught; he coughed and whooped. He inhaled once more and fell slack, mouth open, hands twitching. Henry scrambled back and tripped over the bowl of cold water. He crashed on the floor. The room smelled of shit and sour sweat.

"Pardon me?"

"I said I'm looking for a man. Brown hair, big eyes, young face. Might have a limp."

The woman with her hair in a tight gray bun looked past Cort's shoulder to the blue Chevy parked in front of her porch. She drew in her robe and shivered. The living room felt warm at her back, but far away.

"Well, I haven't seen anyone fits that description," she said.

"You sure, ma'am?"

"Of course I'm sure. What kind of silly question is that?"

"It's not silly if you're standing where I'm standing."

Cort narrowed his eyes toward the living room, the warm house, the sound of children playing upstairs. The porch felt small and confining.

"Where's your husband at?"

"He's on a job," she said.

"What's he do?"

"That's none of your business."

"I'm just curious. This is a fine home. Looks like a man of great care lives here."

"He's a carpenter."

"Like Jesus."

"If that's how you want to put it."

"That is how I'm putting it. You checked your barn this morning?"

"Every morning," she said. "Now if you'll excuse me—"

Cort stepped forward, boot toe knocking against the threshold. He stared at a strand of gray hair that had fallen across her forehead. It waved in the cold wind, inquisitive-like.

"Something about my car interests you," Cort said.

"No, sir." Her voice quivered.

"Go on. Tell me."

"I'd rather not."

"Rather doesn't enter into it. Tell me."

The woman drew in a sharp breath. Her daughter squealed up-stairs.

"That's Ed Dobber's Chevy," she said.

It was late afternoon and the boys had cleared the rest of the rocks, letting Jacob cool in the living room because they didn't know what else to do with him. For a few hours Henry almost forgot what was waiting for them back in the house. When they'd dumped the last of the stones, Henry squatted on his heels and looked up at the sky. Sam stood near him, breathing hard in the cold.

"Tomorrow we'll dig a grave with Dad," Sam said, and he sniffed and put his hands on his hips.

They walked back to the house. Sam fetched the good sheets from the linen closet while Henry stripped Jacob to his underwear and sponged his legs clean. He bundled the soiled jeans into a paper bag and set them by the front door. Sam combed Jacob's hair, slicking it back with some of their father's pomade. Then he wiped Jacob's ears with a washcloth and folded his arms across his chest. They finished covering Jacob with a sheet when Henry spot-ted someone walking up the driveway.

The man stopped in front of their house. He wore a long black coat and narrow boots. His eyes were small and dark, like a doll's eyes.

"Get upstairs," Henry said to Sam. "Wait in my room, and don't come down until I call for you. No arguing this time. Just *go*."

Sam ran up the stairs as Henry picked the sack off the floor. He spotted the Browning, leaning against the old china cabinet. The man knocked, sharp and loud.

Henry opened the door. Cort stood on the porch, hands in his pockets, eyes narrowed.

"Your father home?"

"No, sir. He's out back."

Cort glanced at the driveway, at the rusted tractor sitting in the field. A cluster of sparrows sat huddled on its hood, chests puffed against the wind.

"Maybe you could go get him for me," Cort said.

"He's working. I'm not supposed to bother him when he's work-ing."

Henry saw a fine spray of dried blood on Cort's neck and a spot of blood in his ear.

"I'm looking for someone," Cort said. "Might have come this way."

"I haven't seen anyone."

"Let me finish. He's about yay tall, may have a limp."

"No, sir. It's been me and my brother all day."

"And your father."

Henry nodded. "That's right."

Cort looked back at the driveway. Henry wondered if the man could hear his heart pounding. It was the loudest thing he'd ever heard. It drowned out the wind and everything else. Just his heart, running fast and hard.

"I did find this, though," Henry said, and he grabbed the sack from behind the door and held it out for Cort.

Cort smiled slightly and opened the sack while Henry held it. Then he took the bag and pulled the sawed-off from underneath his coat. He leveled it at Henry, tilting his head to one side.

Henry stood, frozen.

"You had me fooled," Cort said.

"Take the money."

"Oh, I will."

"Just remember I didn't have to give it to you."

"Yes, you did." Cort rubbed his forefinger against the double triggers. "Where's Jacob?"

"He's dead. We found him in the woods."

"And your brother?"

"In the house."

"Call him."

"I will not."

Cort smiled again. "Call him, son."

Henry tightened his lips.

"You know, when I was your age, this was something I wondered about every day," Cort said. "How often you get a chance to see the end before it comes. You ever wonder about that?"

"Sometimes."

"Now that's a shame."

Cort settled back on his heels and lowered the shotgun level with Henry's chest. Something flashed and boomed behind Henry; his right arm stung like hornets and he cried out. Cort stumbled sideways. He squeezed both triggers of the sawed-off. A chunk of the porch exploded. Splinters peppered Henry's legs. The air smelled like firecrackers.

When Henry looked up from his bleeding arm he saw Sam standing on the porch, holding the Browning, smoke curling from the mouth of the barrel. Cort had fallen onto the front gravel path; he lay there, coat shredded and blood blooming across his white T-shirt. Henry knelt by Cort's side and inspected his face. His breathing was shallow. A few pellets were embedded in his cheek.

"You got him," Henry said.

Sam dropped the shotgun and ran to his brother. Henry let him hug as he gazed across the field, toward the edge of the woods. His arm throbbed and he didn't know how he felt. Sick, or sad, or maybe even excited. Maybe all three.

"Fetch the wheelbarrow," Henry said.

Sam stared down at Cort.

"Sam."

Sam blinked.

"Go on and fetch the wheelbarrow," Henry said.

"But he's still breathing."

"Don't you worry about that."

They pulled Cort out of the wheelbarrow. Henry grabbed him by his belt with his good arm and hauled him over the lip of the well as Cort groaned and his eyes fluttered beneath his lids. Sam dropped the sack of money into the yawning hole, watching the white disappear.

"On my count," Henry said.

Sam pressed his hands against Cort's warm side.

"One. Two. Three."

Cort fell. The two boys peered over the edge, staring into the dark, waiting to hear the sound of his body. They waited a long time.

JOYCE CAROL OATES

So Near Any Time Always

FROM *Ellery Queen's Mystery Magazine*

OH! HE WAS SMILING at me.

Was he smiling—at *me*?

Quick then looking away, looking down at my notebook— where I'd been taking notes for a science-history paper—while spread about me on the highly polished table were opened volumes of *Encyclopedia Britannica, World Book of Science, Science History Digest.*

A hot blush rose into my face. I could not bring myself to glance up, to see the boy at a nearby table, similarly surrounded by spread-open books, staring at me.

Though now I was aware of him. Of his quizzical-friendly stare.

Thinking, *I will not look up. He's just teasing.*

In 1977: still an era of libraries.

In the suburban branch library that had been a millionaire's mansion in the nineteenth century. In the high-ceilinged reference room. Shelves of books, gilt-glinting titles, brilliant sunshine through the great octagonal window so positioned in the wall that, seated at one of the reference tables, you could see only the sky through the inset glass panes like an opened fan.

Will not look up, yet my eyes lifted involuntarily.

Still he was smiling at me. A stranger: a few years older than I was.

Never smile or speak to strange men, but this was a boy, not a man.

I wondered if he was a student at St. Francis de Sales Academy for Boys, a private Catholic school where tuition was said to be as high as college tuition and where the boys, unlike boys at my school, had to wear white shirts, ties, and jackets to class.

Smiling at me in a way that was so tender, so kindly, so *familiar.*

As if, though I didn't know him, he knew me. As if, though I didn't know him, yet somehow I did know him, but had forgotten as you feel the tug of a lost dream, unable to retrieve it, yet yearning to retrieve it, like groping in darkness, in a room that should be familiar to you.

He knows me! He understands.

I was sixteen. I was a high school junior. I was *young for my age,* it was said—not to me, directly—which translated into an adult notion of *underdeveloped sexuality, emotional immaturity, childishness.*

It wasn't so unusual that a boy might smile at me, or a man might smile at me, if I was alone. A young girl alone will always attract a certain kind of quick appraising (male) attention.

If whoever it was hadn't seen my face clearly, or my skin.

Seen from a little distance, I looked like any girl. Or almost.

Seen from the front, I looked like a girl of whom relatives say, *Her best feature is her smile!*

Or, *If only she would smile just a little more—she'd be pretty.*

Which wasn't true, but well-meaning. So I tried not to absolutely hate the relative who said it.

This boy was no one I'd ever encountered before, I was sure. If I had, I would have remembered him.

He was very handsome! I thought. Though I scarcely dared to look at him.

Mostly I was conscious of his round, gold-rimmed glasses, which gave him a dignified appearance. Inside the lenses his eyes were just perceptibly magnified, which gave them a look of blurred tenderness.

His face was angular and sharp-boned and his hair was scrupulously trimmed with a precise part on one side of his head, the way men wore their hair years ago; unlike most guys his age, anyway most guys you'd see in Strykersville, he was wearing an actual shirt, not a T-shirt—a short-sleeved shirt that looked like it might be expensive.

Smiling at me in this tentative way to signal that if I was wary of him, or frightened of him, it was okay—it was cool. He wouldn't bother me further.

He'd been taking notes in a notebook, too. Now he returned to his work, studious and intense, as if he'd forgotten me. I saw that he was left-handed—leaning over the library table with his left arm crooked at the elbow so he could write with that hand.

A curious thing: he'd removed his wristwatch to position it on the tabletop, so that he could see the time at a glance. As if his time in the library might be precious and limited and he feared it spilling out into the diffuse atmosphere of the public library, in which, like sea creatures washed ashore, eccentric-looking in-dividuals, virtually always male, seemed drawn to pursue obsessive reference projects.

So I continued with my diligent note-taking. *Amphibian ancestors. Evolution. Prehistoric amphibians: why gigantic? Present-day amphibians: why dwindling in numbers?*

Trying not to appear self-conscious. With this unknown boy less than fifteen feet away facing me as in a mirror.

A hot blush in my cheeks. And I regretted having bicycled to the library without taking time to fasten my hair back into a pony-tail so now it was straggly and windblown.

My hair was fair brown with a kinky little wave. Very like the boy's hair, except his was trimmed so short.

A strange coincidence! I wondered if there were others.

My note-taking was scrupulous. If the boy glanced up, he would see how serious I was.

. . . *environmental emergency, fate of small amphibians worldwide* . . .

. . . *exact causes unknown but scientists suggest* . . .

. . . *radical changes in climate, environment* . . . *invasive organisms like fungi* . . .

Then, abruptly—this was disappointing!—after less than ten minutes the boy with the gold-rimmed glasses decided to leave: got to his feet—tall, lanky, storklike—slipped his wristwatch over his bony knuckles, briskly shut up the reference books and returned them to the shelves, hauled up a heavy-looking back-pack, and without a glance in my direction exited the room. The soles of his size-twelve sneakers squeaked against the pol-ished floor.

There I remained, left behind. Accumulating notes on the trag-ically endangered class of creatures *Amphibia* for my earth science class.

*

Did it occur to you to exit the library at the rear? Just in case he was wait-
ing at the front.

Did it occur to you it might be a good idea not to meet up with this boy?
Of course it didn't occur to you he might be older than he appeared.
He might be other than he appeared.
Of course it didn't occur to you, and why?
Because you were sixteen. An immature sixteen.
A not-pretty girl. A lonely girl.
A desperate girl.

"Hey. Hi."

He was waiting for me outside the library.

This was such a shock to me, a relief and a wonder — as if nothing so extraordinary had ever happened and could not have been
predicted.

I had assumed that he'd left. He'd lost interest in me and he'd
left and I would not see him again, as sometimes — how often, I
didn't care to know — male interest in me, stimulated initially, mysteriously melted, evaporated and vanished.

But there he was waiting for me, in no way that might intimidate
me: just sitting on the stone bench at the foot of the steps, leafing
through a library book he was about to slide into his backpack.

Seeing the look of surprise in my face, the boy said "Hi!" a
second time, smiling so deeply that tiny knife cuts of dimples appeared in his lean cheeks.

Shyly, I said hello. My heart was beating in a feathery light way
that made it hard for me to breathe.

And shyly we stared at each other. To be *singled out* was such an
unnerving experience for me, I had no idea how to behave.

To feel this sensation of unease and excitement, and so quickly.

Like a basketball tossed at me without warning, or a hockey
puck skittering along the playing field in the direction of my feet
— I had to react without thinking or risk getting hurt.

Boldly, yet not aggressively, he asked my name. And when I told
him he repeated "Lizbeth."

He told me his name — Desmond Parrish.

Amazingly, he held out his hand for me to shake — as if we were
adults.

He'd gotten to his feet, in a chivalrous gesture. He was smiling so hard now, his glittery gold glasses seemed to have become dislodged and he had to push them against the bridge of his nose with the flat of his hand.

"I wondered how long you'd stay in there. I was hoping you wouldn't stay until the library closed."

Awkwardly I murmured that I was doing research for a paper in my Earth science class . . .

"Earth science! Quick, tell me, what's the age of Earth?"

"I—I don't remember . . ."

"Multiple-choice question: the age of Earth is a) fifty million years, b) three hundred sixty thousand years, c) ten thousand years, d) forty billion years, e) four point five billion years. No hurry!"

Trying to remember, and to reason: but he was laughing at me.

Teasing-laughing. In a way to make my face burn with pleasure.

"Well, I know it can't be ten thousand years. So we can eliminate that."

"You're certain? Ten thousand years would be appropriate if Noah and his ark are factored in. You don't believe in Noah and his ark?"

"N-No . . ."

"How'd the animals survive the flood, then? Birds, human beings? Fish, you can see how fish would survive, no problem factoring in fish, but mammals? Nonarboreal primates? How'd they manage?"

It was like trying to juggle a half-dozen balls at once, trying to talk to this very funny boy. Seeing that I was becoming flustered, he relented, saying, "If you consider that life of some kind has been around about three point five billion years, then it figures—right? —the answer is e) four point five billion years. That's a loooong time, before October ninth, nineteen seventy-seven, in Strykersville, New York. A looong time before *Lizbeth* and *Desmond*."

Like a TV standup comic, Desmond Parrish spoke rapidly and precisely and made wild-funny gestures with his hands.

No one had ever made me laugh so hard, so quickly. So breathlessly.

As if it was the most natural thing in the world, Desmond walked with me to the street. He was a head taller than me—at least five feet eleven. He'd swung his heavy backpack onto his shoulders and walked with a slight stoop. Covertly I glanced about to see if anyone was watching us—anyone who knew me: *Is that Lizbeth Marsh? Who on earth is that tall boy she's with?*

It seemed natural, too, that Desmond would walk me to my bicycle, leaning against the wrought-iron fence. Theft was so rare in Strykersville in those years, no one bothered with locks.

Desmond stroked the chrome handlebars of my bicycle, which were lightly flecked with rust—the bicycle was an English racer but inexpensive, with only three gears—and said he'd seen me bicycling on the very afternoon he and his family had moved to Strykersville, twelve days before: "At least, I think she was you."

This was a strange thing to say, I thought. As if Desmond really did know me and we weren't strangers.

Somehow it happened Desmond and I were walking together on Main Street. I wasn't riding my bicycle; Desmond was pushing it while I walked beside him. His eyes were almond-shaped and fixed on me in a way both tender and intense, which made me feel weak.

Already the feeling between us was so vivid and clear—*As if we'd known each other a long time ago.*

People scorn such an idea. People laugh, who know no better.

"Lizbeth, you can call me Des. That's what my friends call me."

Desmond paused, staring down at me with his strange wistful smile.

"Of course, I don't have any friends in Strykersville yet. Just you."

This was so flattering! I laughed, to suggest that if he was joking, I knew he'd meant to be funny.

"But I don't think that I will call you Liz—Lizbeth is preferable. Liz is plebian, Lizbeth patrician. *You* are my patrician friend in plebian western New York State."

Desmond asked me where I lived and where I went to school; he described himself as "dangling, like a misplaced modifier, between academic accommodations" in a droll way to make me smile, though I had no idea what this meant.

At each street corner I was thinking that Desmond would pause and say goodbye, or I would summon up the courage to interrupt his entertaining speech and explain that I had to bicycle home soon, my parents were expecting me.

On Main Street we were passing store windows. Pedestrians parted for us, glancing at us with no particular interest, as if we were a couple — *Lizbeth, Desmond.*

Desmond's arm brushed against mine by accident. The hairs on my arm stirred.

I saw a cluster of small dark moles on his forearm. I felt a sensation like warmth lifting from his skin, communicated to me on the side of my body closest to him.

Though I was sixteen I had not had a boyfriend, exactly. Not yet.

I had not been kissed. Not exactly.

There were boys in my class who'd asked me to parties, even back in middle school. But no one had ever picked me up at home; we'd just met at the party. Often the boy would drift off during the course of the evening, with his friends. Or I'd have drifted off, eager to summon my father to come pick me up.

Mostly I'd been with other girls, in gatherings with boys. We weren't what you would call a popular crowd and no one had ever *singled me out.* No one had ever looked at me as Desmond Parrish was looking at me.

Walking along Main Street! Saturday afternoon in October! So often I'd seen girls walking with their boyfriends, holding hands; I'd felt a pang of envy, that such a thing would never happen to *me.*

Desmond and I weren't holding hands, of course. Not yet.

Beside us in store windows our reflections moved ghostly and fleeting — tall lanky Desmond Parrish with his close-trimmed hair and schoolboy glasses, and me, Lizbeth, beside him, closer to the store windows so that it looked as if Desmond were looming above me, protecting me.

At the corner of Main Street and Glenville Avenue, which would have been a natural time for me to take my bicycle from Desmond and bicycle home, Desmond suggested that we stop for a Coke, or ice cream — "If this was Italy, where there are *gelato* shops every five hundred feet, we'd have our pick of terrific flavors."

I'd never been to Italy, and would have thought that *gelato* meant Jell-O.

In the vicinity there was only the Sweet Shoppe, a quaint little ice cream–candy store of another era, which Desmond declared had "character"—"atmosphere." We sat at a booth beside a wall of dingy mirrors and each of us had a double scoop of pistachio butter crunch. This was Desmond's choice, which he ordered for me as well and paid for, in a generous, careless gesture, with a ten-dollar bill tossed onto the table for the waitress: "Keep the change for yourself, please."

The waitress, not much older than I was, could not have been more surprised if Desmond had tossed a fifty-dollar bill at her.

In the Sweet Shoppe, tips were rare.

For the next forty minutes, Desmond did most of the talking. Sitting across from me in the booth, he leaned forward, elbows on the sticky tabletop, his shoulders stooped and the tendons in his neck taut.

By this time I was beginning to feel dazed, hypnotized—I had not ever been made to feel so *significant* in anyone's eyes.

Kindly and intense in his questioning, Desmond asked me more about myself. Had my family always lived in Strykersville, what did my father do, what were my favorite subjects at school, even my favorite teachers—though the names of Strykersville High School teachers could have meant nothing to him. He asked me my birth date and seemed surprised when I told him (April 11, 1961) —"You look younger"—and possibly for a moment this was disappointing to him; but then he smiled his quick dimpled smile, as if he were forgiving me, or finding a way he could accept my age —"You could be, like, thirteen."

This was so. But I had never thought of it as an advantage of any kind.

"Life becomes complicated when living things mature—the apparatus of a physical body is, essentially, to bring forth another physical body. If that isn't your wish, maturity is a pain in the ass."

I laughed, to show Desmond that I knew what he meant. Or I thought I knew what he meant.

Though I wasn't sure why it was funny.

I said, "My mother tells me not to worry—I will grow when I'm ready."

"When your genes are ready, Lizbeth. But they may have their own inscrutable plans."

Desmond told me that his family was descended from "lapsed WASP" ancestors in Marblehead, Massachusetts; he'd been born in Newton, and went to grade school there; then he'd been sent to a "posh, Englishy-faggoty" private school in Brigham, Mass.—"D'you

know where Brigham is? In the heart of the Miskatonic Valley."
Yet it also seemed that his family had spent time living abroad
—Scotland, Germany, Austria. His father, Dr. Parrish—Desmond
pronounced "Dok-tor Parrish" in a way to signal how pompous he
thought such titles were—had helped to establish European research institutes connected to a "global" pharmaceutical company,
"the name of which I am forbidden to reveal, for reasons also not
to be revealed."

Desmond was joking, but serious, too. Pressing his forefinger
against his pursed lips as if to swear me to secrecy.

When we parted finally in the late afternoon, Desmond said he
hoped we would see each other again soon.

Yes, I said. I would like that.

"We could walk, hike, bicycle—read together—I mean, read
aloud to each other. We don't always have to *talk*."

Desmond asked me my telephone number and my address but
didn't write the information down. "It's indelibly imprinted in my
memory, Lizbeth. You'll see!"

I have a boyfriend!
   My first boyfriend!

A passport, this seemed to me. To a new wonderful country only
glimpsed in the distance until now.

He hated the telephone, he said: "Talking blind makes me feel
like I've lost one of my senses."

He preferred just showing up: after school, at my house.

For instance, on the day after we'd first met, he bicycled to
my house without calling first, and we spent two hours talking together on the rear redwood deck of my house. So casually he'd
turned up, on a new-model Italian bicycle with numerous speeds,
his head encased in a shiny yellow helmet—"Hey, Lizbeth, remember me?"

My mother was stunned. My mother, to whom I hadn't said a
word about meeting Desmond the previous day, for fear that I would
never see him again—clearly astonished that her plain-faced and
immature younger daughter had a visitor like Desmond Parrish.

When my mother came outside onto the deck to meet him, Desmond stood hastily, lanky and tall and "adult." "Mrs. Marsh, it's
wonderful to meet you! Lizbeth has told me such intriguing things
about you."

"Intriguing? Me? She has? Whatever—?"

It was comical—cruelly, I thought it was comical—that my mother hadn't a clue that Desmond was joking; that even the gallant way in which he shook my mother's hand, another surprise to her, was one of his sly jokes.

But Desmond was sweet, funny, *affectionate*—as if the adult woman he was teasing on this occasion, and would tease on other occasions, was a relative of his: his own mother, perhaps.

"D'you believe in serendipity, Mrs. Marsh? A theory of the universe in which nothing is an accident—nothing *accidental*. Our meeting here, and the three of us here together, two twenty-four P.M., October eleventh, nineteen seventy-seven, was destined to occur from the start of time, the Big Bang that set all things in motion. Which is why it feels so right."

Charmed by her daughter's new friend, like no other friend Lizbeth had ever brought home, female or male, my mother pulled up a deck chair and sat with us for a while; clearly she was impressed with Desmond Parrish when he mentioned to her, as if by chance, that his father was a "research scientist"—with an "M.D. from Johns Hopkins"—the new district supervisor of a "global" pharmaceutical company with a branch in Rochester, a forty-minute commute from Strykersville.

Immediately my mother said, "In Rochester? Nord Pharmaceuticals?"

Desmond seemed reluctant to admit a connection with the gigantic corporation that had been in the news intermittently in the past several years, as he seemed reluctant to tell my mother specifically where his family had moved in Strykersville, in fact not in the city but in a suburban-rural gated community north of the city called Sylvan Hills.

"It must be beautiful there. I've seen some of the houses from the outside . . ."

"That might be the best perspective, Mrs. Marsh. From the outside."

My mother was a lovely woman of whom it would never be said that she was in any way socially ambitious, or even socially conscious; yet I saw how her eyes moved over Desmond Parrish, noting his neatly brushed hair, his clean-shaven lean jaws and polished eyeglasses, his fresh-laundered sport shirt with the tiny

crocodile on the pocket; noting the handsome wristwatch with
the large, elaborate face (Desmond had shown me how the watch
not only told time but told the temperature, the date, the tides,
the barometric pressure, and could be used as a compass) and his
close-clipped, clean nails.

"You should come to dinner soon, Desmond! It would be nice
to meet your parents sometime, too."

"Yes. You are right, Mrs. Marsh. It would be."

Desmond spoke politely, just slightly stiffly. I sensed his rebuff of
my mother's spontaneous invitation, but my mother didn't seem
to notice.

He'd brought with him, in his backpack, a Polaroid camera
with which he took several pictures of me when we were alone
again. As he snapped the pictures he was very quiet, squinting at
me through the viewfinder. Only once or twice he spoke—"Don't
move! Please. And look at me with your eyes—fully. Straight to the
heart."

I was very self-conscious about having my picture taken. Badly I
wanted to lift my hands, to hide my face.

Nearby on the deck lay our golden retriever, Rollo, an older
dog with dun-colored hair and drowsy eyes; he'd regarded Desmond with curiosity at first, then dropped off to sleep; now, when
Desmond began taking my picture, he stirred, moved his tail cautiously, came forward, and settled his heavy head in Desmond's lap
in an unexpected display of trust. Desmond petted his head and
stroked his ears, looking as if he were deeply moved.

"Rollo! 'Rollo May' is enshrined in my DNA. This is why fate
directed me to Strykersville, Lizbeth. From the Big Bang—onward
—to *you*."

We hiked in Fort Huron Park. We bicycled along a towpath beside
the lake. And there was a boat rental, rowboats and canoes, and
impulsively I said, "Let's rent a rowboat, Des! Please."

The lake was called Little Huron Lake. Long ago my father had
taken Kristine and me out in a rowboat here and the memory was
still vivid, thrilling. But I had not been back in years and was surprised to see how relatively few boats there were in the rental.

Desmond spoke slowly, thoughtfully. As if an idea, like a Polaroid print, were taking shape in his mind.

"Not a rowboat, Lizbeth—a canoe. Rowboats are crude. Canoes are so much more . . . responsive."

Desmond took my hand as an adult might take a child's hand and walked with me to the boat rental. It was the first time he'd taken my hand in this way, in a public place—his fingers were strong and firm, closed about mine. With a giddy sensation I thought, *This is life! This is how it is lived.*

There was a young couple in one of the canoes, the girl at the prow and the man at the stern wielding the paddle. The girl's red-brown hair shone in the sun. As the canoe rocked in the waves the girl gave a frightened little cry, though you could see that there was little danger of the canoe capsizing.

"I'm afraid of canoes, I think. I've never been out in one."

"Never been in a canoe!"

Desmond laughed, a high-pitched sort of laugh, excited, perhaps a little anxious. Clearly this was an adventure for him, too. Squatting on the small dock, he inspected each of the canoes, peering into it, stroking the sides as a blind man might have touched it, to determine its sturdiness. At least, that's what I thought he must be doing.

"The Indians made canoes of wood, of course. Beautifully structured, shaped vessels. Some were small, for just two people—like these. Some were long, as long as twenty feet—for war."

The boat-rental man came by, a stocky bearded man, and said something to Desmond which I didn't quite hear, which seemed to upset Desmond, who reacted abruptly, and oddly—he stood, returned to me and grabbed my hand and again hauled me forward, this time away from the boat rental.

"Some other time. This is not the right time."

"What did the man say to you? Is something wrong?"

"He said, 'Not the right time.'"

Desmond appeared shaken. His face was ashen, grave. His lips were downturned and twitching.

I could not believe that the boat-rental person had actually said to Desmond "Not the right time"—but I knew that if I questioned Desmond, I would not find out anything more.

"If I died, it would be just temporary. Until a new being was born."

"That's reincarnation?"

"Yes! Because we are immortal in spirit, though our bodies may crumble to dust."

Desmond removed his gold-rimmed glasses to gaze at me. His eyes were large, liquidy, myopic. There was a tenderness in his face when he spoke in such a way that made me feel faint with love for him—though I never knew if he was speaking sincerely or ironically.

"I thought you were a skeptic—you've said. Isn't reincarnation unscientific? In our earth science class our teacher said—"

"For God's sake, Lizbeth! Your science teacher is a secondary public-school teacher in Strykersville, New York! Say no more."

"But if there's reincarnation"—still I persisted, for it seemed crucial to know—"where are all the extra souls coming from? The earth's population is much larger than it ever was in the past, especially thousands of years ago . . ."

Desmond dismissed my objection with an airy wave of his hand.

"Reincarnation is de facto, whether you have the intellectual apparatus to comprehend it. We are never born entirely new—we inherit our ancestors' genes. That's why some of us, when we meet for the first time, it isn't the first time—we've known each other in a past lifetime."

Could this be true? I wanted to think so.

As Desmond spoke, more and more I was coming to think so.

"We can recognize a soul mate at first sight. Because of course the soul mate has been our closest friend from that other lifetime, even if we can't clearly remember."

Desmond had taken out his Polaroid and insisted upon posing me against a backdrop of flaming sumac, in a remote corner of Fort Huron Park, where we'd bicycled on a mild October Saturday.

Each time Desmond and I were together, Desmond took pictures. Some of these he gave to me, as mementos. Most he kept for himself.

"A picture is a memento of a time already past—passing into oblivion. That's why some people don't smile when they are photographed."

"Is that why you don't smile?"

"Yes. A smiling photograph is a joke when it's posthumous."

"Posthumous—how?"

"Like, above an obituary."

It was so; when I tried to take Desmond's picture with my little Kodak camera, he refused to smile. After the first attempt, he hid his face behind outstretched fingers. "*Basta*. Photographers hate to be photographed, that's a fact."

Another time he said, mysteriously, "There are crude images of me in the public world, for which I had not given permission. If you take a picture, someone might appropriate it and make a copy —you're using film. Which is why I prefer the Polaroid, which is unique and one time only."

When Desmond photographed me, he posed me, gripping my shoulders firmly, positioning me in place. Often he turned my head slightly, his long fingers framing my face with a grip that would have been strong if I'd resisted but was gentle since I complied.

More than once, Desmond asked me about my family—my "ancestors."

I told him what I knew. I'd wondered if he was teasing me.

Several times I told him that I had just a single, older sibling —my sister, Kristine. Either Desmond seemed to forget this negligible fact or he had a preoccupation with the subject of siblings.

He was curious about Kristine—he wanted to see her (at a distance), "not necessarily meet her." And just once did Desmond meet Kristine, by accident when he and I were walking our bicycles across a pedestrian bridge in the direction of Fort Huron Park and Kristine with two of her friends was approaching us.

Kristine was twenty years old at this time, a student at Wells College, home for the weekend.

"Kristine! I've heard such great things about you," Desmond said, shaking my sister's hand vigorously. "Lizbeth talks about you all the time."

This remark, which had so charmed my mother, fell flat with Kristine, who stared at Desmond with something like alarm.

"Yes? I'll bet."

Kristine spoke coolly. Her smile was forced and fleeting. She made no attempt to introduce Desmond to her friends (girls she'd known in high school), who also stared at Desmond, who loomed tall and lanky and ill at ease, smiling awkwardly at them.

I was furious with Kristine and her friends: their rudeness.

They're jealous of me. That I have a boyfriend.

They don't want me to be happy, they want me to be like them.

Afterward, Desmond asked about Kristine: was she always so *hostile?*

"Yes. I mean, no! Not always."

"She didn't seem to like me."

Desmond spoke wistfully. Yet I sensed incredulity, even anger beneath.

I said, "We get along better now that she's away at college, but it used to be hard—hard on me—to be her younger sister. Kristine is so critical, bossy—sarcastic . . . Always thinks she knows what's best for me . . ."

Maybe this wasn't altogether true. My older sister was genuinely fond of me, too, and would be hurt to hear these words. My face smarted with embarrassment, that Kristine hadn't been nearly so impressed with Desmond as I'd hoped, or as Desmond might have hoped.

She had to be jealous! That was it.

Desmond said, "She looked at me as if—as if she knew me. But she doesn't know me. Not at all."

Later he said, "I'm an only child. Which is why I'm fated to be an outsider, a loner. Which is why my favorite writer has always been Henry David Thoreau—'The greater part of what my neighbors call good I believe in my soul to be bad.'"

At home, Kristine said, "This Desmond Parrish. Mom was telling me about him, and he isn't at all what Mom said, or you've been saying—it's all *an act.* Can't you see it?"

"An act—how? What do you mean?"

"I don't know. There's something not right about him."

"Not right—how? He's a wonderful person . . ."

"Where did you meet him, exactly?"

I'd told Kristine where I had met Desmond. I'd told her what he'd explained to me—he'd been offered a scholarship at Amherst, his father's college, but had deferred it for a year, at his request.

Kristine continued to question me about Desmond in a way I found offensive and condescending. I told her that she didn't know anything at all about Desmond, what he was like when we were alone together, how smart and funny he was, how thoughtful. "I think you're just jealous."

"Jealous! I am not."

"I think you are. You don't like to see me *happy.*"

Kristine said, incensed, "Why would I be jealous of *him?* He's weird. His eyes are strange. I bet he's older than he says he is—at least twenty-three."

"Desmond is nineteen!"

"And you know this how?"

"He told me. He took a year off between high school and college—he deferred going to Amherst this year."

"This year? Or some other year?"

"I think you're being ridiculous, and you're being mean."

"Also I think—I wouldn't be surprised—he's *gay*."

This was a shock to me. Yet in a way not such a shock.

But I didn't want Kristine to know. I nearly shoved her away, furious.

"You know, Kristine—*I hate you*."

Later, to my chagrin, I overheard Kristine talking with my mother in a serious tone about this "weird boy" who was "hanging out" with Lizbeth, who seemed "strange" to her.

Mom objected: "I think he's very nice. He's very well-mannered. You want your sister to have friends, don't you?"

"She has friends. She has great girlfriends."

"You want her to have a boyfriend, don't you? She's sixteen."

"Just that he'd be attracted to Lizbeth, who looks so young, and"—here Kristine hesitated; I knew she wanted to say that I wasn't pretty, wasn't attractive, only a weird boy would be interested in me—"isn't what you'd call 'experienced'—that seems suspicious to me."

"Kristine, you're being unfair. I've spoken with Desmond several times and he's always been extremely congenial. He's nothing like the high school boys around here—thank God. I'd like to have him to dinner sometime, with his parents. I think that would be very nice for Lizbeth."

"Not when I'm here, please! Count me out."

"I'd almost think, Krissie, that you're a little jealous of your younger sister. Among your friends there isn't anyone I've met who is anything like Desmond Parrish . . ."

"He's *weird*. I think he's *gay*. It's okay to be weird and to be gay but not to hang around with my sister, please!"

"All right, Krissie. You've made your point."

"I'm just concerned about her, is all."

"Well, I think that Lizbeth can take care of herself. And I'm watching, too."

Kristine laughed derisively, as if she didn't think much of my mother's powers of observation.

*

"Dreams! The great mystery within."

On the redwood deck a few feet from us Rollo lay sprawled in the sun, asleep. His paws twitched and his gray muzzle moved as if, in his deep dog-sleep, he were trying to talk.

"Animals dream. You can observe them. In his dream Rollo thinks he's running, maybe hunting. Retrievers are work dogs, hunting dogs. If not put to the use to which they've been bred, they feel sad, incomplete. They feel as if part of their soul has been taken from them."

Desmond spoke with such certainty! I had never thought of Rollo in such a way.

He said, "Dreams are repositories of the day's memories. Or dreams are wish fulfillment, as Freud said. In which case there is a double meaning—a dream is the fulfillment of a wish, but the wish can be just a wish to remain asleep. So the dream lulls us into thinking we're already awake."

"Then what's the purpose of nightmares?"

"Must be, obviously—to punish."

To punish! I'd never thought of such a thing.

"Tell me about your dreams, Lizbeth. You haven't yet."

In this, there was an air of slight reproach. Often now Desmond spoke to me as if chiding me; as if there were such familiarity between us he had no need to explain his mood.

I wondered if the meeting with Kristine was to blame. He knew that my sister wasn't *on his side.*

I had no idea what to say. Answering Desmond's questions was like answering questions in school: some teachers, though pretending otherwise, knew exactly what they wanted you to say; if you veered off in another direction, they disapproved.

"Well . . . I don't know. I can't make much sense of my dreams, mostly. For a while, when I was little, I thought they were real—I'd remember them as if they were real. I have a recurring dream of trying to run—stumbling, falling down. I'm trying desperately to get somewhere, and can't."

"And who is in your dreams?"

"Who? Oh—it could be anyone, or no one. Strangers."

We were sitting close together on a wicker sofa-swing on our redwood deck. Desmond's closeness was exciting to me in contemplation, when I was alone; when we were together, always there was something awkward about us. Desmond never slipped his arm around my shoulder or took my hand, except if he was helping me on a steep hiking trail; he hadn't yet brought his face close to mine, though he "kissed" me goodbye, brushing his (cool, dry) lips against my cheek or my forehead as an adult might, with a child.

I didn't want to think that what Kristine had said might be the explanation—Desmond wasn't attracted to me in that way.

But then, why was he attracted to me at all?

Interrogating me now about my dreams as if this were a crucial subject. Why?

I told him that there was nothing special about my dreams that I could remember. "They're different every night. Sometimes just flashes and scraps of things, like surfing TV. Except if I have a nightmare . . ."

"What kind of nightmare?"

"Well . . . I don't know. It's always confusing and scary."

Desmond was staring at me so intently, I was beginning to feel uneasy.

"What sort of dreams have you been having recently? Has there been anything specific about them?"

How to answer this? I wasn't sure. It was almost impossible to remember a dream, which evaporated so soon when you awoke.

"Well, I think that a few times I might have dreamed about—you . . ."

I wasn't sure if this was true. But it seemed to be the answer Desmond was hoping for.

"Really! Me! What was I doing?"

"I—I don't remember . . ."

The figure had been blurred. No face that I could see. But the hand had been uplifted, as if in greeting, or in warning. *Stay away. Don't come near.*

"When did you have this dream? Before you met me, or after?"

Desmond was gripping my arm at the wrist, as if not realizing how he squeezed me.

So it was not true that Desmond Parrish rarely touched me: at such times, he did.

Except this did not seem like *touch* but like . . . something else.

I wished that my mother would come outside to bring us something to drink, as she sometimes did. But maybe Mom wasn't in the kitchen but in another part of the house.

Because Desmond dropped by without calling first, there was no way to know when he might show up. There was no way to arrange that someone else might be in the house, if I had wanted someone else to be in the house.

In our friendship, as I wanted to think of it, Desmond was always the one who made decisions: when we would meet, where we would go, what we would do. And if Desmond was busy elsewhere, if from time to time he had "things" to do in his own, private life, he just wouldn't show up—I didn't have a phone number to call.

He'd taken out the Polaroid camera, which I'd come to dislike.

"Did you have that dream before you met me? That would be wild!"

"I—I'm not sure. I think it was just the other night . . ."

"Talk to me, Lizbeth. Tell me about your dreams. Like I'm your analyst, you're my *analysand*. That would be cool!"

As I tried seriously to recall a dream, as a submerged dream of the night before slowly materialized in my memory, like a cloudy Polaroid print taking a precise shape, Desmond took pictures of me, from unnervingly close by.

". . . there was a lake, a black lake . . . there were strange tangled-looking trees growing right out into the water, like a solid wall . . . we were in a canoe . . . I think it might have been you, paddling . . . but I'm not sure if it was me with you, exactly."

"Not you? What do you mean? Who was it then?"

"I—I don't know."

"Silly! How can you have a dream in which you are not you? Who else would it be, paddling in a canoe at Lake Miskatonic, except me and you? You're my guest at our family lodge there —must be."

Desmond's voice was distracted as he regarded me through the camera viewfinder.

Click, click! He continued questioning me, and taking pictures, until I hid my face in my hands.

"Sorry! But I got some great shots, I think."

When I asked Desmond what his dreams were like, he shrugged off the question.

"Don't know. My dreams have been taken from me, like my driver's license."

"How have your dreams been taken from you?"

"You'd have to ask the Herr Doktors."

I remembered that Desmond's father was a *Doktor.* But here was a reference to *Doktors.*

I wondered if Desmond had taken some sort of medication? I knew that a category of drugs called "psychoactive" could suppress dreams entirely. The mind became blank—an emptiness.

Desmond peered at the Polaroid images as they materialized. Whatever he saw, he decided not to share with me this time and put the pictures away in his backpack without a word.

I said it seemed sad that he didn't dream any longer.

Desmond shrugged. "Sometimes it's better not to dream."

When Desmond left my house that day, he drew his thumb gently across my forehead, at the temple. For a moment I thought he would kiss me there, my eyelids fluttered with expectation—but he didn't.

"You're still young enough, your dreams won't hurt you."

I thought it might be a mistake. But my eager mother could not be dissuaded.

She invited Desmond to have dinner with us and ask his parents to join us, and with a stiff little smile, as if the first pangs of migraine had struck behind his eyes, Desmond quickly declined: "Thanks, Mrs. Marsh! That's very generous of you. Except my parents are too busy right now. My father may even be traveling. And me—right now—it's just not a—not a good time."

My mother renewed the invitation another time, a few days later, but Desmond replied in the same way. I felt sorry for her, and unease about Desmond. Though when we were alone he had numerous questions to ask me about my family, as about myself, clearly he didn't want to meet them; nor did he want his parents to meet any of us, even his dear soul mate Lizbeth, whom he claimed to adore.

It was near the end of October that Desmond brought his violin to our house and played for my mother and me.

This magical time! At least, it began that way.

In Desmond's fingers the beautiful little instrument looked small as a child's violin. "A little Mozart—for beginners."

Curious, too, and somehow touching, was the way in which Desmond played the instrument as left-handed, the violin resting against his right shoulder.

Desmond bit his lower lip in concentration as he played, shutting his eyes. He moved the bow across the strings at first tentatively and then with more confidence. The beautiful notes wafted over my mother and me as we sat listening in admiration.

We were not strangers to amateur violin-playing—there were recitals in Strykersville in which both Kristine and I had participated as piano students.

Possibly some of Desmond's notes were scratchy. Possibly the strings were not all fine-tuned. Desmond himself seemed piqued, and played passages a second time.

My mother said, "Desmond, that's wonderful! How long have you had lessons?"

"Eleven years, but not continuously. My last teacher said that I'm gifted—for an amateur."

"Are you taking lessons now?"

"No. Not here." Desmond's lips twitched in a faint smile, as if this question were too naive to take seriously but he would take it seriously. "I'm living in Strykersville now, not in Rochester. Or in Munich, or Trieste."

Meaning that there could be no violin instructor of merit in Strykersville.

My mother lingered for a while, listening to Desmond play. It was clear that she enjoyed Desmond's company more than the company of many of her friends. I felt a thrill of vindication, that my sister was mistaken about Desmond. I thought, *Mom is on our side.*

When my mother left us, Desmond played an extraordinarily beautiful piece of music. "It's a transcription for violin. The 'love-death' theme from *Tristan und Isolde.*"

Though Desmond didn't play perfectly, the emotional power of the music was unmistakable. I felt that I loved Desmond Parrish deeply—this would be the purest love of my life.

Desmond lowered the bow, smiling at me. His eyes behind the gold-rimmed lenses were earnest, eager.

"Now you try, Lizbeth. I can guide you."

"Try? To play—what?"

"Just notes. Just do what I instruct you."

"But—"

"You've had violin lessons. The technique will come back to you."

But I hadn't had violin lessons. I'd mentioned to Desmond that I had had piano lessons from the age of six to twelve, but I hadn't been very talented and no one had objected when I quit.

I protested, I couldn't begin to play a violin! The instrument was totally different from a piano.

"You've had music lessons, that's the main thing. The notes, the relationships between them—that's the principle of music. C'mon, Lizbeth—try!"

Desmond closed his hand around mine, gripping the bow. As he positioned the fragile instrument on my left shoulder.

"You are right-handed—yes? It's a little strange for me, this reversal."

Awkwardly Desmond caused the bow to move over the strings, gripping my fingers. The sounds were scratchy, shrill.

"Desmond, thanks. But—"

"I could teach you, Lizbeth. All that I know, I could impart to *you*."

"But—that isn't very realistic . . ."

Sternly Desmond said, "Look. Playing a musical instrument requires patience, practice, and faith. It doesn't require great talent. So don't use that as an excuse—you aren't talented. *Of course you aren't talented*—that's beside the point." He spoke as if explaining something self-evident that only obstinacy prevented me from accepting.

"We could play together. Each with a violin. We could have a recital—people would applaud! But it requires patience."

The scraping noises of the violin, and Desmond's abrasive voice, caused Rollo to glance up at us from a few feet away, worriedly.

Desmond was wholly focused upon "instructing" me. This was a side of him I hadn't seen before—there was nothing tender about him now, only an air of determination. A smell of perspiration lifted from his underarms; there was an oily ooze on his forehead. He breathed quickly, audibly. Our nearness wasn't a comfort but intimidating. It was beginning to be upsetting that I couldn't seem to explain to this adamant young man that I really didn't want to take violin instructions from him, or from anyone.

When I tried to squirm away, he squeezed my hand, hard—he was looming over me, and his smile didn't seem so friendly now.

"You're not even trying, for God's sake. Why do you just *give up?*"

Hearing Desmond's voice, my mother appeared in the doorway.

Quickly then Desmond stammered an apology, took back the gleaming little violin from me, and left.

Mom and I stared after him, shaken.

"That voice I heard, Lizbeth—I'd swear it wasn't Desmond."

Following this, something seemed to have altered between Desmond and me.

He didn't call. He began to appear in places I would not expect. He'd never made any effort to see me before school, only after school, once or twice a week at the most, but now I began to see him watching me from across the street when I entered school at about 8 A.M. If I waved shyly to him, he didn't wave back but turned away as if he hadn't seen me.

"Is that your boyfriend over there? What's he doing there?" my girlfriends would ask.

"We had a disagreement. He wants to make up. I think."

I tried to speak casually. I hoped the tremor in my voice wasn't detectable.

This was the sort of thing a girl would say, wasn't it? A girl in my circumstances, with a *boyfriend*?

I realized that I had no idea what it meant to have a *boyfriend*.

Still more, *had a disagreement*.

And after school, Desmond began to appear closer to the building. He didn't seem to mind, as he'd initially minded, mingling with high school students as they moved past him in an erratic stream—Desmond a fixed point, like a rock. Waiting for me, then staring at me, not smiling, with a curt little wave of his hand as I approached—as if I might not have recognized him otherwise.

I'd gotten into the habit of hurrying from school, on those days I didn't have a meeting or field hockey. It seemed urgent to get outside soon after the final bell. I didn't always want to be explaining Desmond to my friends. I didn't want always to be telling them that I had to hurry, my *boyfriend* wanted to see me alone.

Where Desmond hadn't shown any interest in watching me play field hockey, now he might turn up at a game, or even at practice, not sitting in the bleachers with our (usually few) spectators; he preferred to remain aloof, standing at the edge of the playing field, where he could stroll off unobserved at any time—except of course Desmond was observed, especially by me.

"When are you going to introduce Desmond to us, Lizbeth?"

"Is he kind of . . . the jealous type?"

"He looks like a preppy! He looks rich."

"He looks a little older, like . . . a college guy, at least?"

It was thrilling to me that my friends and teammates knew that the tall lanky boy who kept his distance was my *boyfriend*—but not so thrilling that they must have been talking behind my back, speculating and even worrying about me.

There's some secret about him, Lizbeth won't tell.

Maybe Lizbeth doesn't know!

You think he's abusing her? You know—it could be mental, too.

Lizbeth is kind of changed lately.

Does anybody know him? His family?

They're new to Strykersville, Lizbeth said.

She's crazy about him, that's obvious.

Or just kind of crazy.

You think he feels the same about her?

"I'm thinking maybe I will defer again—and wait for you. I have plenty of independent research I can do before going to college. And if you couldn't get into Amherst, or couldn't afford it, my dad could help out. What d'you think?"

For the first time, I lied to Desmond.

Then, for the second time, I lied to Desmond.

He hadn't been waiting for me at school but he'd come over to our house at about 6 P.M., rapped on the back door, which led out onto the redwood deck, as he usually did, and when I came to the door I told him that I couldn't see him right then: "My mom needs me for something. I have to help her with something."

"Can't it wait? Or can't I wait? How long will this 'something' require?"

I was so anxious, I hadn't even invited Desmond inside. Nor did I want to go outside onto the deck, which would make it more difficult for me to ease away from Desmond and back into the house.

A thin cold rain was falling. A smell of wet rotting leaves.

Desmond had bicycled over. He was wearing a shiny yellow rain slicker and a conical rain hat, which made him look both comical and threatening, like an alien life form in a sci-fi horror movie.

"I said I can't, Desmond. This isn't a good time . . . Daddy will be home soon, we're having dinner early tonight. There's some family crisis kind of thing going on I can't tell you about—my elderly grandmother, in a nursing home . . ."

This was enough to discourage Desmond, who had no more questions for me but backed off with a hurt smirk of a smile.

"Goodnight then, Lizbeth! Have a happy 'family crisis.'"

This sarcastic remark lingered in my memory like a taste of something rotten in my mouth.

I thought, *He hates me now. I have lost him now.*

I thought, *Thank God! He will find someone else.*

It happened then; Desmond Parrish drifted to the edge of my life.

He ceased coming to the house. He ceased waiting for me after school. His telephone calls, which had been infrequent, now ceased.

I felt his fury, at a distance.

He'd been insulted by my resistance to him. So subtle, another boy would scarcely have noticed. But of course Desmond Parrish wasn't *another boy.*

I regretted turning him away. I thought it might be the worst mistake of my life. When I received my amphibian paper back, in earth science, seeing a red A+ prominent on the first page, my first wish was to tell Desmond, who'd helped me with the paper.

So long ago, that seemed now! But it had been less than a month.

Desmond had read a draft of the paper for me and made just a few suggestions. He'd encouraged me to explore the theme of *amphibian* in a way not exclusively literal. "'Ontology recapitulates philology.' If you don't know what that means, I can explain."

Now all that was changed.

Now I couldn't predict when I might see Desmond. He had removed himself from my life, decisively—but he was still *there,* observing.

In the corner of my eye I would see him. And in my uneasy dreams I would see him.

Walking with friends. Driving with my mother in her car.

One afternoon at the mall, with Kristine.

And another time with Kristine, driving to a drugstore a half-mile from our house, in a shopping center, and there I saw, about thirty feet away, Desmond Parrish observing us: in his shiny yellow cyclist's helmet and a nylon parka and arms folded tight across his chest, and when I stopped to stare, the figure turned quickly away and vanished from my sight.

Seeing the look on my face, Kristine said, "Are you all right, Lizzie? You look kind of sick."

I was so stricken by the sight of Desmond, I had to sit down for a few minutes.

Kristine asked, concerned, if I wanted to go home; but I said no, I did not want to go home. I did not!

"You've seemed kind of quiet lately."

I told her I was all right. But I had things to think about that couldn't be shared.

"About Des? Something about Des?"

Kristine knew that Desmond wasn't dropping by the house any longer. Nor did I speak of Desmond to her now, or to my mother.

"What's happened to him? Did you two break up?"

In Kristine's voice there was the equivalent of a smirk.

Break up. Your weird boyfriend.

My sister's condescending attitude made me want to slap her. For what did Kristine *know*?

It was so, Desmond frightened me now. Since he'd squeezed my hand so hard, gripping the violin bow, and since I'd sensed in him a willfulness that had no tenderness for me but only a wish to subjugate, I did not want to be in his presence: I began to tremble thinking of him.

Yet, perversely, I cherished the memory of my *boyfriend*. The memory of Desmond Parrish was more thrilling to me than Desmond himself had been in recent weeks.

"You didn't . . . make any mistakes with him, did you? Lizbeth?"

Kristine spoke hesitantly, embarrassed. We were not sisters who confided in each other about intimate things, and we were not about to start now.

Gritting my teeth, I told her no.

"He didn't coerce you into—or force you into—anything you didn't want to do, did he?"

Muttering no, I walked away from Kristine.

I wasn't sure if I wanted to shove her from me or, ridiculously, push into her arms so she could comfort me as she'd done when I'd been a little girl.

"Maybe you thought you loved—love—him. But you didn't— you don't . . ."

When we left the drugstore to cross the parking lot to my mother's station wagon, which Kristine was driving, in the corner of my eye I saw a tall lean figure wearing a yellow helmet, in the rear exit of another store. It was the very figure I dreaded seeing, and dreaded not seeing.

I collapsed into the station wagon, my knees weak. I didn't turn to stare at the figure on the pavement; I didn't say a word to Kristine, who reached out wordlessly to squeeze my hand.

Wistfully my mother said, "Lizbeth, what has happened to Desmond? Has he *disappeared?* He seemed so—devoted . . ."

I knew that Mom was thinking, *So devoted to both of us.*

YOU CAN'T JUST SHUT ME OUT OF YOUR LIFE LIZBETH
YOU KNOW THAT WE ARE SOUL MATES FROM THAT OTHER
LIFETIME

This message was left for me, in felt-tip black ink on a scroll of gilt paper, inside a plain white envelope thrust into my high school locker.

I opened the gilt paper and read these words, stunned. I could not believe that Desmond had actually come into the school building, where he didn't belong; that he'd risked being detected in order to observe me, at least once, who knows how many times, at my locker.

Then, to slip the envelope into my locker, he must have come after school, when the corridor was deserted.

My hand trembled, holding the gilt scroll that looked like some kind of festive announcement.

Many times I would reread it. Many times in the secrecy of my room.

The message held a threat, I thought—or hinted at a threat.

I must tell my parents, I thought.

But they might try to contact Desmond's parents or, worse yet, the Strykersville police . . . I did not want this.

Yet it wasn't clear how Desmond expected me to contact him.

He had never given me his telephone number or his address. It was as if we were gazing at each other across a deep ravine and had no way now of communicating except in broad, crude gestures, like individuals who did not share a language.

"Please! Just leave me alone."

He did call. I think it had to be him.

Late at night, and just a single ring, or two—if someone picked up the phone, silence.

A taunting sort of silence into which words flutter and fall: "Hello? Hello? Who is this . . ."

He bicycled past our house, I think.

I think it was Desmond Parrish. I couldn't be sure.

A car pulled into our driveway, headlights blinding against our windows. There was a rude blast of music. Then the car pulled away again.

Then Rollo disappeared.

One night he failed to appear at the back door when we called him, where usually Rollo was pawing the door to be allowed back inside.

(Our acre-sized back lawn was fenced in, so that Rollo could spend as much time outdoors as he wanted. Usually he just slept on the deck.)

We scoured the neighborhood, calling "Rollo! Rollo!"

We rang doorbells. We photocopied fliers to staple to trees, fences. We checked local animal shelters. Kristine came home from Wells to help us search. We were distraught, heartbroken.

I thought, *Desmond would not do this. He would not be so cruel, he liked Rollo.*

I thought, *Maybe he is keeping Rollo. Until I see him again.*

Now Desmond was *the stalker*—this was Kristine's term.

Suddenly it happened, he was always *there*. And others saw him, too.

Where previously, before Desmond, I'd often been alone, and comforted myself with self-pity, that I was alone, now I could not ever be alone; I could not ever assume that I was alone. For I knew that Desmond Parrish was thinking about me obsessively, even when he wasn't actually watching me.

. . . Can't just shut me out. Soul mates from that other . . .

Hockey season was ending. This was a relief. For Desmond had begun showing up at practice, which was Thursdays after school. A lone lanky figure now behind the chain-link fence at the very rear of the playing field, arms uplifted and fingers caught in the links so that a quick glance made you think that whoever this was, he'd been crucified against the fence.

My teammates nudged me in the ribs, whispered to me.

"Hey, Lizbeth, is that your *boyfriend?*"

Or, "Looks like Lizbeth's *boyfriend* is stalking her."

Our coach called me into her office and spoke with me frankly. She said that my *boyfriend* was causing distraction and disruption. "You aren't playing very well, which is why I haven't sent you in much lately. And your distraction is bringing your teammates down."

Weakly I said, "He isn't my boyfriend. We broke up, I guess . . . I don't know why he's doing this."

"How close were you two? Were you . . . intimate?"

The question was like a slap in the face. To answer *no* seemed pathetic. To answer *yes* would have been more pathetic.

I told Ms. DeLuca *no*. Not *intimate.*

"You're sure?" Ms. DeLuca regarded me suspiciously.

Yes, I was sure. But I spoke slowly, uncertainly. For just to speak of Desmond with a stranger was a betrayal of our true intimacy, which was like nothing else in my life until that time.

"Lizbeth? Are you listening?"

"Y-yes . . ."

"There has certainly been a change in you. Your eyes look *haunted*. Did this boy abuse you in any way? Did he take advantage of you?"

I shook my head wordlessly. How I hated this woman who wanted only to protect me!

"Well, do your parents know about him? They've met him — have they?"

I murmured *yes* ambiguously. For after all, Mom knew Desmond well — or would have claimed that she did.

I'd never told my father. I was terrified of what my father might say and do, for I believed that in his alarm at what was happening, my father would blame *me*.

Finally I left Ms. DeLuca's office. I wasn't sure if our awkward conversation had ended; I just left.

In a plain manila envelope addressed to "LIZBETH" at my street address, he sent me photographs of myself taken with a zoom lens. These were not Polaroids but small matte photos: there I was, oblivious of the camera eye, climbing out of my mother's car, walking with friends on the sidewalk near school, playing field hockey. The most disturbing photo was of me inside our house, after dark in our lighted kitchen, talking with a blurred figure who must have been my mother.

On the back of this photo was written in block letters:

SO NEAR ANY TIME ALWAYS

I did not show anyone. I was terrified how my family would react.

You did this! You invited this person into our lives.

How could you have been so careless? So blind, ignorant?

Terrible to see myself, a figure in another's imagination, of no more substance than a paper doll.

A figure at the mercy of the invisible/invincible photographer.

I stood at the window, staring out into the darkness of our backyard. At the farther end of our property were trees, a thick stand of trees, impenetrable in darkness as a wall.

I thought that Desmond must hide inside these trees, with his remarkable zoom lens.

He was a hunter. I was in his crosshairs.

I wanted to scream out the back door *I hate you! I wish you were dead! Give Rollo back to us! Leave us alone.*

Desperately I wanted to wake up and it would be six—seven? —weeks ago.

Before the library. Before I'd bicycled into town on a Saturday afternoon to take notes on the evolution of amphibians in a way to make of myself a *good dutiful student.*

And I would wake up to the relief that no one was following me —no one loved me.

Then one day when I was leaving school late, after a meeting, at dusk, there stood Desmond Parrish waiting for me.

"Hey, Lizbeth! Remember me?"

Desmond was smiling at me, in reproach. The muscles of his face were clenched, he was so angry with me.

"Haven't forgotten me, have you? Your friend Des."

I stammered that I didn't want to see him. I would have turned to run back into the school building, but I didn't want to insult him.

I didn't want to anger him further.

I could not move: my legs were weak, paralyzed.

"Know what I think, Lizbeth? I think you've been avoiding me. We've had a misunderstanding. I want to honor that—I mean, your wish to avoid me. I am all for the rights of women—a female is not *chattel*. But since your behavior is based upon a misunderstanding, the logical solution would be to clear it up. We need to talk. And I have a car, I can drive you home."

"You have a car? You have a license to drive?"

"I have a *car*. My father's car. I'd only need a license to drive if I intended to have an accident or to violate a traffic law, which I don't intend."

"I—I can't, Desmond. I'm sorry."

Still, I couldn't move. My knees had lost all strength.

Desmond loomed above me, smiling so hard that the lower part of his face appeared about to crack.

His jaws were unshaven. His smart gold-rimmed glasses were askew on his nose. His hair hadn't been cut in some time and had begun to straggle over his collar.

"Just come with me, Lizbeth. We'll take a little drive—to the lake—the lake right here—remember, the canoes? You wanted to go out in a canoe, but then you were afraid? You were silly—you were afraid. But there's nothing to be afraid of. We can go there—we can try again. Then I'll drive you home. I promise. We need to talk."

Desperately I said that it was too late in the season, the boat rental wouldn't be open in November. And it was too late in the day, it was dark . . .

Foolishly, I was protesting. As if renting a canoe was the point when clearly Desmond wanted to take me with him—wherever he had in mind.

*

There was in fact a vehicle parked nearby; headlights on, motor running, and driver's door flung open as if the driver had just leaped out.

Desmond dared to come forward and take hold of my arm.

Desmond dared to taunt me, in a mock tender voice.

"I've heard your dog is lost. That's a tragedy—you love that dog. All of you love that dog. Might be I could help you look for him. Was it Rollo? Named for Rollo May? Cool!"

I had no idea what Desmond was saying, just that he had Rollo. He knew where Rollo was.

Yet he was pulling me toward the car. Instinctively I resisted.

"No. I don't want to go with you!"

"Don't be ridiculous, Lizbeth. Of course you want to come with me if I can lead you to Rollo. And we can go to the lake—Little Huron Lake. In less than an hour this will all be cleared up and we will be friends again."

I tried to disengage my arm from Desmond. His fingers gripped me tight.

My voice was pleading. "What do you want with me? Why are you doing this?"

"What do I want with you! What do you want with *me!* We are destined for each other, as I knew at first sight, Lizbeth—and so did you."

Panicked, I thought, *This is not real. This is not happening.*

I thought, *The boyfriend!*

Even with the lure of finding Rollo, I knew that I must not get into that car with Desmond Parrish.

Desmond cursed me, as I'd never heard him curse before. I was reminded of my mother remarking that the voice she'd heard on our deck hadn't been Desmond's voice but the voice of another.

Desmond was grappling with me, pinning my arms against my sides, half carrying me to his car. I could feel his hot breath in my face. I could smell his body—the hot sweaty urgency of a male body. I was too frightened to scream. I could not draw breath to scream.

Then someone saw us, shouted at us, and Desmond quickly released me, ran to his car, and drove away.

"Who was that? What was he trying to do to you?" one of the vocational arts teachers was asking me.

I told him it was all right: I told him it was a misunderstanding.

"Should I call 911?"

"No! No, please. It's just my boyfriend—but things will be all right now."

I was upstairs in my room when my mother called up to me, sounding hysterical.

On the local ten o'clock news it was announced that a Strykersville resident, Desmond Parrish, had died in a single-vehicle accident on the thruway. His car, driven at an estimated eighty miles an hour, had crashed into a concrete overpass six miles south of Strykersville.

We stared at film footage of the wreck, partly obscured by the flashing lights of medical vehicles and flares set in the left lane of the interstate highway. A young woman newscaster was saying solemnly that death was believed to have been instantaneous.

We stared at a photograph of Desmond Parrish looking very young, with schoolboy eyeglasses and a knife-sharp part in his hair.

"That can't be Desmond! I don't believe this . . ."

My mother was more upset than I was. My mother was gripping my hands to console me, but my hands were limp and cold and unresponsive.

I was too shocked to comprehend most of the news. The breaking-news bulletin passed so swiftly; within a few seconds it had ended and was supplanted by an advertisement.

My mother embraced me, weeping. I held myself stiff and unyielding.

I was waiting for the phone to ring: for Desmond to call, a final taunting time.

That night I dreamed of Little Huron Lake rippling in darkness.

In the morning we read in the Strykersville paper a more detailed account of how Desmond Parrish had died.

The front-page article contained another photograph of Desmond taken years before, looking very young. Again, Desmond wasn't smiling.

The photograph ran above the terrible headline:

STRYKERSVILLE RESIDENT, 22, DIES IN THRUWAY CRASH

Witnesses of the "accident" reported to state troopers that the speeding vehicle seemed to have been accelerating when the driver "lost control," slammed through a guard rail, and struck the concrete abutment head-on. No signs of skidding had been detected on the pavement.

The wrecked automobile, a 1977 Mercedes-Benz, was registered in the name of Gordon Parrish, Desmond's father.

Desmond Parrish had been driving without a license. At the time of the crash, his parents had not known where he was: he'd been "missing from the house" since the afternoon.

Again it was stated, "Death is believed to have been instantaneous."

New York State Police would be investigating the crash, which occurred outside the jurisdiction of the Strykersville police department.

Soon after, a woman who identified herself as a detective with the New York State Police came to our house to speak with me and my parents.

The detective informed us that a "cache" of photographs and "journal entries" concerning me had been recovered from the wrecked car.

Police were investigating the possibility that Desmond Parrish had committed suicide. The detective asked me if I had been intimate with Desmond Parrish; how long I had known Desmond Parrish, and in what capacity; when I had seen him last; what his "state of mind" had been when I'd seen him.

Calmly I replied. Tried to reply. I was aware of my parents listening to me, astonished.

Astonished and disapproving. For I had betrayed them, in not sharing with them all that had passed between my *boyfriend* and me.

Never after this would they trust me wholly. Never after this would my father regard me, as he'd liked to regard me in the past, as his *little girl*.

For instance, my parents hadn't known that Desmond had been stalking me—that he'd left a threatening message in my locker at school. They hadn't known that I'd seen Desmond so recently, on the very day of his death.

They hadn't known that he'd wanted me to come with him in that car, to drive to Little Huron Lake.

I would give a statement to police: Desmond had confronted me behind our school building at about 5:20 P.M. By 9:20 P.M. he had died.

The vocational arts teacher who'd come up behind us, who'd surprised and frightened Desmond away, would give a statement to police officers also.

There'd been an "altercation" between Desmond Parrish and the sixteen-year-old high school sophomore Lizbeth Marsh. But Ms. Marsh had not wanted the teacher to call 911, and Mr. Parrish had driven away in his father's Mercedes.

It was believed that prior to the crash he'd "ingested" a quantity of alcohol. He had been driving without a license.

The detective told us that the Parrishes refused to believe that their son may have caused his own death deliberately. At the present time, they were not speaking with police officers and were "not accessible" to the media.

It would be their theory, issued through a lawyer, that their son had had an accident: he'd been drinking, he had not ever drunk to excess before and wasn't accustomed to alcohol, he'd had "personal issues" that had led to his drinking and so had "lost control" of the car and died.

He had not been suicidal, they insisted.

He had so much to live for, since moving to Strykersville.

He was seeing a therapist, and he'd been "making progress." He had not ever spoken of suicide, they insisted.

He'd had a "brilliant future," in fact. A scholarship to Amherst College, to study classics.

"You know, I hope, about Desmond's background? His criminal record?"

Criminal record?

We were utterly stunned by the detective's remark.

She told us that Desmond had been incarcerated from the age of fourteen to the age of twenty-one in the Brigham Men's Facility for Youthful Offenders in Brigham, Massachusetts. He'd pleaded guilty to voluntary manslaughter in the death of his eleven-year-old sister in August 1970.

All that was known of the incident was that Desmond, fourteen at the time, had been canoeing with his sister, Amanda, on Lake Miskatonic, where the Parrishes had a summer lodge, when in a "sudden fit of rage" he'd attacked her with the paddle, beat her about the head and chest until she died, and tried without success to push her body into the lake without capsizing the canoe. No one had witnessed the murder, but the boy had been found in the drifting canoe, with his sister's bloodied corpse and the bloodied and splintered paddle, in a catatonic state.

Desmond had never explained clearly why he'd killed his sister except she'd made him "mad"; he'd had a quick temper since early childhood and had been variously diagnosed as suffering from attention deficit disorder, childhood schizophrenia, Asperger's syndrome, even autism. He'd been "unusually close" to his sister and had played violin duets with her. His parents had hired a lawyer to defend him against charges of second-degree homicide. After months of negotiations he'd been allowed to plead guilty to a lesser charge of manslaughter and was sentenced to seven years in the youth facility, which contained also a unit for psychiatric subjects, from which offenders were automatically released at the age of twenty-one.

This was a ridiculous statute, the prosecution claimed—anyone who'd committed such a "vicious" murder should not be released into society after just seven years. But Desmond was too young at fourteen to be tried as an adult. He'd been diagnosed as undeniably ill—mentally ill—but in the facility he'd responded well to therapy and was declared, by the time of his twenty-first birthday, to pose no clear and present danger to himself or others.

The family had relocated to Strykersville, within commuting distance of Rochester. It was hoped that the family, as well as Desmond, would make a "new start" here.

The Parrishes had never lived in Europe. Mr. Parrish had never helped to establish branches of Nord Pharmaceuticals in Europe. His position with the corporation was director of research in Rochester, exclusively.

The detective showed me a photograph of Amanda Parrish. Did she resemble me, did I resemble her? I don't think so. I heard my mother draw in her breath sharply seeing the photograph, but I did not think that we looked so much alike; this girl was very young, really just a child, with a plain sweet hopeful face, unless you could call it a doomed face, those eyes, haunted eyes you could call them, that set of the mouth, a shy smile for the camera which might even have been held by her murderous older brother.

I thought of Desmond's warning about smiling for the camera. How foolish, how sad you will appear, when the smiling photograph appears posthumously.

The child/sister murder had been a celebrated case in the Miskatonic Valley since the Parrish family was well known there, had owned property in the region since Revolutionary times.

"A tragic case. But these cases are not so rare as you might think."

It was a curious remark for the New York State Police detective to make to us, at such a time.

My father became livid with rage. My mother was upset, incredulous. They wanted to immediately confront the Parrishes, to demand an explanation.

"Those terrible people! How could they have been so selfish! They allowed their sick, disturbed son to behave as if he were normal. They must have known that he was seeing our daughter! They must have known that the medications he was taking weren't enough. They couldn't have been monitoring their son . . ."

It was chilling to think that the Parrishes had been willing to risk my life, or to sacrifice my life, the life of a girl they didn't know, had never met but must have known about—their son's *girlfriend.*

They would never consent to speak with us. They would consent only to communicate through lawyers.

At that time I could not answer any more of the detective's questions. I could not bear my parents' emotions. I ran away from the adults, upstairs to my room.

I hid in my bed. I burrowed in my bed.

So often I'd dreamed of Desmond Parrish in this bed, it was almost as if he were here with me: waiting for me.

I thought, *He wanted to take me with him. He loved me—he would not have hurt me.*

In Strykersville today there are too many memories; I never remain more than a night or two, visiting my parents.

I try to avoid driving in the vicinity of Fort Huron Park. Never would I revisit Little Huron Lake.

The remainder of my high school years is a blur to me. In the summer I went to live with my grandmother in White Plains, and there I took summer courses at Vassar; my senior year, I'd transferred to a private school in White Plains, since my parents thought it might be best to remove me from Strykersville, where I had "emotional issues."

My old life was uprooted. My old "young" life.

I thought of wasps in our back lawn, their nests burrowed into the ground into which my father would pour liquid insecticide. In terror, wasps would fly out of the burrow, fly to save their lives, dazed, desperate. I wondered if the wasps could reestablish a nest elsewhere. I wondered if the poison had seeped into their frantic little insect bodies, if mere escape were enough to save them.

I missed my friends, my family. I missed the life we'd had there, our sleepy old dog stretched out on the redwood deck at our feet. But I could not have remained in Strykersville, where there were too many memories.

The other day I saw him. Across a busy street I saw his hand uplifted and in his face an expression of reproach and hurt, and without thinking I began to cross the street to him, and at once horns sounded angrily—I'd stepped off the curb into traffic and had almost been killed.

So near any time always.

Rollo's body was never recovered.

NANCY PICKARD

Light Bulb

FROM *Kansas City Noir*

The Paseo

IT TOOK JUDY HARMON fifty-eight years to wonder about the other children. Maybe it was the deluge outside her apartment that reminded her of the flooding that summer in Kansas City back in the '50s. Maybe it was the lightning flashing over downtown Detroit that jogged her memory. Whatever the cause, the epiphany struck her all of a nasty sudden while she was doing nothing more than watching a crime show on TV and drinking her supper of wine and more wine.

Oh my God, there must have been other children.

Judy sat up so fast that she spilled wine and didn't care: pink blotch on white pants, new stain on her conscience seeping through to soak her in dismay. Only now, fifty-eight years later, did her unconscious pull a light cord to force her to look — *Over here, Judy!* — at the decaying fly in the spidery corner of her psyche's forgotten basement.

How could I have failed to realize it for so long?

It felt like her boss coming in to tell her she was fired, which he had done last week. It felt like not being able to pay her mortgage, which she couldn't next month. It felt like watching her retirement slip away as CEOs bought yachts and stockbrokers sent their kids to private schools. It felt like when she'd realized that she was never getting married, or having children, or doing anything but working all of her life, and it felt like not even being able to

do that now. It was a sinking in her stomach, a sick feeling in her
heart, a setting of a match to an unburned pile of regret.

I was a child myself! I couldn't have known!

She defended herself to herself and to the other—possibly
other, probably other—children who might have been hurt,
might have been scarred, by the man.

Outside, rain plunged down her windows in the same waterfall
way it had poured that July in Kansas City. That summer, the Missouri River drowned the industrial districts of both Kansas Cities—
the Missouri one, where she spent her childhood, and the smaller,
poorer one in Kansas. She remembered staring at the frightening water from the back seat of her parents' '47 Chevy. The river
made a washing sound, like surf where there wasn't supposed to
be a beach. Judy remembered a green car, brown water, and a dull
bright sky that looked like the dirty chrome on the car's bumpers
before her daddy washed them in the parking lot behind their
apartment on Paseo. The air that summer smelled wet—not the
fresh, clean wet of ordinary summers, but the wet of dirty dishrags,
drowned rats, overflowing sewers. She'd been excited to see the
flood, wanted to get near enough to watch it rising up the floors of
the buildings, and then got scared when her father inched the car
close enough to spy the river's currents. They bubbled ugly brown
and sudsy white; they surged and swirled in boat-sucking eddies.

"Back up, Daddy! Back up!" she had yelled in panic from the
back seat. That had made her father smile, but he slid the gearshift into neutral and didn't tease the Chevy any closer.

"I swear that river could shoot us all the way to St. Louis!" her
mother had said.

Now, fifty-eight years later, Judy berated herself: *I should have
told them about that man. Why didn't I tell my parents?*

Judy Harmon picked up her cell phone to call her mother.

Judy was eight years old that summer.

While the two Kansas Cities were flooding, she went to Vacation
Bible School at a Presbyterian church on Linwood Boulevard near
their home. She and her parents lived six blocks south, on the
white side of the city's "color line," Twenty-seventh Street. Blacks
who ventured in that direction generally needed the passport of a
job.

Theirs was a block of red-brick apartment buildings and old

homes converted into rentals. There was a synagogue catty-cornered to their building. It was safe to play outside or walk home alone from school in her neighborhood, even though it wasn't a rich one. The only bad things that had ever happened to her on her own block were getting stung by a wasp and falling off her bike. Once she'd watched her mother give a hobo a half-empty box of powdered doughnuts after he knocked on their door and asked for something to eat. When he left, he had confectioners' sugar on his whiskery chin, as if he'd dipped it in a snowdrift, but she didn't have the nerve to tell him.

There were many things she'd never had the nerve to say.

That day, when she walked to the babysitter's by herself from Bible school, Judy carried an umbrella that was too big for her. She had to fight it to keep it up. Judy remembered feeling nervous when she started out—it was five blocks to the sitter's and she'd never walked so far alone. Her father was at work at the factory; her mother had a summer job at Katz Drug Store. Usually Judy went with a little friend; years later she couldn't remember why she walked by herself that day. She remembered hearing thunder rumble, though. Her too-big umbrella was black with a wooden handle, and it didn't keep her dry. The backs of her calves got spotted with raindrops, her dress clung to her legs, her fingers got wet and slipped up and down the handle so she had to carry it in both hands.

"Why didn't you tell us?"

Judy's mother lived in a retirement home in Arkansas. Judy had just told her about that day in the rain.

"I told the babysitter, didn't she tell you and Daddy?"

"She never said a word."

Her mother was angry, as if it had happened only yesterday. Judy remembered her mother as she'd looked in those years—young, harried, smelling of cherry-scented Jergen's hand lotion and dressed in a cotton shirtwaist, with hose and pointy high heels that caused bunions and bent her big toes sideways.

"Nobody would have believed me, anyway," Judy said.

"I would have! Your dad would have gone over there."

"But then what would have happened? People would have hated us."

Her mother fell silent.

"You know they would have, Mom, for saying bad things about a churchman. Maybe that's why I didn't tell you—because I didn't want to cause you and Daddy any trouble."

Her mother couldn't let it go. "I can't believe she didn't tell me. You were just a child, and she was the grownup. And I'm your mother. She should have told me."

The man was white, tall, and thin.

In Judy's memory, he wore black trousers, a white dress shirt buttoned to his neck, with a thin black tie, although she might have invented the tie. As she walked home alone from Bible school she passed another church, where she heard someone call out to her.

"Little girl!"

Startled, she paused and looked left. The rain had slowed a bit, so she could see the man from under her umbrella. He stood just inside an open door. He could have been the minister or janitor, he could have been a deacon. She didn't know who he was, but she had a sense of what he was even though she couldn't name it.

She saw a ladder in front of him.

"Little girl, come help me change this light bulb."

She glanced up and saw a light fixture above the ladder.

She was an obedient child, respectful to grownups, but something inside of her didn't like this. Nobody had ever warned her; nobody ever warned any children about anything like this in those days, but still, she knew.

She shook her head and gave him a small, stiff smile.

"Come in here and help me," he called out to her. "Don't you want to come in out of the rain?"

He wasn't attractive. He had dark hair that looked thin and greasy, which was how his voice sounded to her, too. She had a crush on the handsome husband of one of her mother's friends, but this man didn't look like that. She wouldn't have wanted to laugh at his jokes, or take any lemonade he handed her.

She shook her head again. "I have to go."

"What? Come closer so I can hear you!"

"No," she whispered, her heart pounding as she started walking away from him. "No thank you."

"But I need help. It will only take a minute. You should help me, little girl. Don't you want to help me?"

He wasn't much of a salesman, she thought years later, or he'd have known never to ask a question that could be answered no.

She walked faster. Why would a grown man need to have a little girl help him put in a light bulb? She felt shaky and afraid and embarrassed without knowing exactly why. Nobody had told her anything about sex, but she'd seen her parents kiss, she'd been to an Elizabeth Taylor movie, and she blushed when her mother's friend's husband was nice to her. She didn't know anything, and yet she knew. She wanted to run, but she had an instinct like a little animal that knows that if you run you'll look even more like a rabbit. She walked awkwardly, as if she'd forgotten how to move her legs; she walked quickly, longing for the end of the block, longing to turn the corner and get out of his sight, afraid to look back. She kept her face pointed straight ahead, as if nothing were amiss, as if she didn't think he was scary. When she was sure he couldn't see her any longer, she finally did run, releasing the handle of the umbrella when it pulled against her hand, letting it fly off behind her.

"I was so mad at you for losing that umbrella."

"What if he's still out there, Mom?"

"After all these years? Judy, he's dead by now. Or he's as old as I am." She was ninety-three. "He could have Alzheimer's. He could be in prison."

"I think he was about thirty. That would put him near ninety now. He could still be in pretty good shape. Look at you. You're as smart as you ever were, and you'd still be walking a mile a day if your back didn't hurt so much."

"I want him to be dead," her mother said. "Judy, tell me the truth, are you sure he didn't hurt you?"

"He never touched me. Truly, Mom. He never got close."

"You were smart."

"I was lucky."

She didn't tell her mother there was another Judy, an imaginary one who had developed in her mind over the years, a little girl who obeyed him even though she didn't want to, a child who did go up that walk, who entered the dark hallway and started to climb the ladder, a little girl he grabbed when she was halfway up. Judy thought of her as Alternate Reality Judy. Sometimes Alternate Reality Judy made it home and told her parents and they got him arrested and thrown in jail, sometimes she bit him and hurt him, and sometimes nobody ever saw that little Judy again. She'd had nightmares about imaginary Judy. And now she realized there could be real children, other Judys out there, and maybe she could have saved them.

"How's your job?" her mother asked.

"Okay," Judy lied, and then quickly got off the phone.

Two more glasses of wine later, she looked at her calendar, and then she looked up airfares to Kansas City.

This is crazy.

But it wasn't only that she hadn't told her parents about a child molester. It was that she had kept silent about a lot of things throughout her life. She didn't say a word when a popular boy in high school mocked an old black man and called him nigger. Cringing on the inside wasn't courage, and neither was shame. Sympathy, alone, was not integrity. Moving to Detroit, where she was in the minority, wasn't anything noble either; she'd been chasing jobs, not racial equality. She hadn't ridden a Freedom Bus or marched in Selma, or even in Kansas City. She hadn't crossed lines, not literal ones like Twenty-seventh Street, nor metaphorical ones. Once she'd had a boss who cheated customers, but she'd never reported him. She'd seen car accidents where people could have used a witness, and she'd driven on. She felt as if she'd spent her life with tape over her mouth, one word written on the tape in black and permanent ink — *coward.* It was why she liked mystery novels with strong female detectives; she could feel their courage without having any herself.

"Little girl! Don't you want to help me?"

"I did help you," she murmured as she clicked her payment through for a flight. "I helped you to keep doing it."

In a rental car she picked up at the Kansas City airport, Judy drove into downtown and then cut east to Paseo, where she turned south toward Linwood. What she saw along the way seemed to confirm what she'd heard: the city of her birth was still segregated. She drove past her old address, but the building was gone. The Presbyterian church was still there on Linwood, but it stood empty, truncated, half of it vanished, leaving only bare ground in the place of three stories of brick that she would have sworn could never fall.

And then, there it was — the corner with the church where he had stood in the doorway calling to her. It was an African American Methodist congregation now, she saw from its sign. It looked as deserted as her own old church. She parked anyway, and walked over to the side door. How many times had she sent Alternate Reality Judy up this walk? she wondered. How many other children had crossed that distance?

"That church is closed."

She turned and saw an elderly black woman coming slowly down the sidewalk. Judy walked toward her.

"Hello. I used to live around here," she said, "back in the fifties." She wanted to defend herself: *I was just a child.* "This was a different church then, and I can't remember the name of it. You wouldn't happen to know what it used to be, would you?"

"Well, it wouldn't have been like this one," the woman said. It wouldn't have been African-American, she meant. She looked permanently tired; the circles under her eyes were twice as dark as the rest of her face. "It's been a lot of different churches."

"Do you remember any of them?"

She appeared old enough to remember when she herself wouldn't have been allowed to sit in the pews of any church along the boulevard.

"Not from when you would have lived here. Sorry, I can't help you." She started again on her slow perambulation over the buckling cement. But then she turned back: "You might try looking it up on the Internet, honey. That's what I'd do."

"I did look it up, but I couldn't find it."

"This where you went to church when you were young?"

"No. It's where a man tried to molest me."

It felt liberating to say it out loud to a stranger.

"Lot of that going around," the woman said, with a headshake and a look of disapproval. "Good luck to you, although I don't know why you'd want to find that man again."

"I want to stop him."

That felt good to say, too.

"A little late, aren't you?"

Judy felt herself flush, the good feeling dissolving into shame.

"If it was that long ago," the woman said with a shrug, "then I expect God's already stopped that man by now."

Judy glanced up the impoverished block and saw no sign of any deity's beneficence to children.

"Do you know where the nearest police station might be?"

"Police? We don't need no police around here," the woman said, in the tone of a wry joke. But then she raised her right arm and pointed. "Go on up west on Linwood, honey."

At the police station, a young black female officer sent Judy back north to the Crimes Against Children Division. The detective who took her to an office there was also Afro-American, also a woman. Changes, Judy thought, and was grateful for them. The expression in the cop's brown eyes blended wary attention with a willingness to listen. "I don't know if the archives go back that far," she said, "but I'll check." Her tight-lipped smile reminded Judy of salespeople who didn't have what she wanted but promised to let her know if anything came in, and then she never heard back from them.

"Why now," the cop asked, "after all these years?"

"It finally dawned on me there might be other kids that he did worse things to than what he did to me. He only scared me. I don't think that was his first time. I doubt it was his last time, either. I just thought, maybe I can still do something. Maybe he's a grandfather now, maybe he has grandchildren . . ."

The cop nodded. "If I find out anything, I'll call you."

Judy felt her hope fall.

They traded cards with phone numbers.

Judy got into her rental car, knowing nothing was going to come of this. She had thought she'd feel better for the effort, even if it was too little, too late, but she only felt worse for trying and failing.

Why did I waste all this money I don't even have?

She was sixty-six years old, alone, out of work, at the limit on her credit cards, soon to be out of her house.

Feeling despairing and adrift, she checked her cell phone and saw there'd been a call from her mother.

"Judy, I've remembered the name of that babysitter," her mother said when Judy called. "Or, rather, I didn't remember it, but I've found it."

Judy felt queasy in the hot car. "I didn't know you were looking for it," she responded slowly, and then tried to swallow away the sick feeling in her mouth. She turned on the ignition and the air conditioning, rolled down all the windows, and waited for a chance to tell her mother goodbye.

"Well, the more I thought about how she didn't tell me, the

madder I got. So I looked for my old phone directory, and there it was. I guess personal phone books have gone out of style now that people have those fancy cell phones to keep track of everything, but I've still got mine from every place we ever lived. So, if she's still married to the same man, her name is still Mary Lynn Whelan, and his name was Sidney, and their daughter's name is Sue."

"Wait. What? She had a daughter?" With her free hand, Judy plucked at her lower lip.

"A year younger than you."

"I don't remember."

"I'm not surprised. She didn't have much personality, and what little there was of it wasn't all that great." Her mother laughed a little. "We called her dishwater girl, because she had a kind of bland and dirty look."

"That was mean of us. Mom, I'd better go."

"If you talk to Mary Lynn Whalen," her mother suddenly blurted, "you tell her that she should have told me!"

"I won't be talking to her, Mom."

But after Judy got off the phone, a breeze kicked up. She was still depressed, though her stomach had calmed down. Curiosity got the best of her, and she looked up Sidney Whalen on the Internet on her cell phone—thinking that the old black woman would approve—and shocked herself by finding the listing: *Sidney and Mary Lynn Whalen.* While she stared at it, she got another call, this one from the local area code, 816.

The detective.

"I made a call," she told Judy, "and I've got you some information on a cop who used to cover that beat, back in the day. Do you want it?"

Judy felt her pulse jump with surprise and anxiety.

"Oh. I . . . sure . . . yes. Thank you!"

"I probably should tell you . . ."

When the detective didn't say anything for a moment, Judy said, "What?"

"He's a mean old bastard, and he says there were other children."

He was old, fat, bad-tempered, cancerous, and unreasonable, and he lit into her the moment she entered his room in his nursing home. He was in a wheelchair, and he said, "Come over here where I can see the person who might have saved those children and didn't. It was you, was it? You knew what he was doing, you could have been a witness. All I needed was a witness, somebody he'd molested or tried to molest, some kid to say what he did and how he did it, and you could have been that girl, but you didn't do it. Why didn't you? Do you know how many children he hurt after you? Before you? Because of you?"

"You can't blame me for what he did—"

"Of course I can, you goddamned little coward."

She recoiled. He was her own conscience reviling her.

"I was eight years old, for heaven's sake."

"Well, you're not now, are you? And you haven't been that young for how long? Fifty years, sixty years? All that time you could have come forward. All that time you could have done some good. Go away. I don't even want to see your goddamned face. Now you come? Now you say there was a bad man in that church? What the hell good did you think this was going to do?"

"Who was he? Is he still—"

"His fucking name is James Marway, and he is a senile old pervert, vegetating away in the Greenly Nursing Home, and they treat him nice and gentle instead of poking him with hot irons the way they ought to do, and he doesn't even know what he did to those little kids. I kept hearing about it, rumors, and I finally figured out it was him, but nobody would talk, nobody would accuse him, and there wasn't anything I could do to get him. With you, maybe I could have got him. I could have stopped him, or at least got him moved out of my streets. Get out of here! You're too late, you're too damn many years late!"

She fled, and it felt familiar.

"I'm surprised you remember me."

"My mom asked me to say hi."

Judy didn't know why she was sitting in Mary Lynn Whalen's living room. She barely remembered driving there, ringing the doorbell, stumbling over "Hello, I'm Judy Harmon, and you used to be my babysitter." *Maybe I want a babysitter right now,* she thought. *Maybe I want somebody to take care of me and sing me a lullaby and tell me I'm not a horrible person.*

"Well, that's so nice of her."

Mary Lynn looked a little confused as she sat at the opposite end of her very nice couch. Sidney must have done all right over the years, Judy thought, thinking of how her own parents had been upwardly mobile, too. In her own generation, people were only moving on down.

Mary Lynn said, "How are your folks?"

"Dad died ten years ago. Mom lives in Arkansas, and really likes it. I'm in Detroit. I had a job in accounting with General Motors."

"I can't believe a girl I babysat is old enough to be retired."

Judy didn't correct the impression. She wondered if she looked as wild-eyed, shocked, and besieged as she felt. Probably not, or this woman, this stranger now, wouldn't have let her inside. "What about your family?"

"Oh, Sid and I are okay, I guess. We lost our daughter—I doubt you'd know about that."

"Sue? No, oh, I'm so sorry. When did she die?"

"Oh, not that kind of lost, although honestly sometimes I think it might be better. I mean lost as in meth addict, all kinds of problems, prostitution, in and out of jail."

"Sue?" This time the single syllable held a new world of shock.

"I know, who'd have suspected she would turn out like this . . ." She trailed off, stared down at the carpet.

"I'm so sorry, Mary Lynn. I had no idea." After a moment she said, abruptly enough to feel rude, "I want to ask you about one of the times you babysat for me."

"Okay." Mary Lynn looked up, clasping her hands in her lap.

"I came in late one day, from Bible school. It was raining really hard, and I'd lost my umbrella. And I told you that a man had scared me. That I'd run away from him because he tried to get me to go inside his church."

"What?" Her hostess seemed to pull herself together, and then she startled Judy by laughing. "Oh my gosh, I do remember. Didn't I tell you not to worry?"

"I don't remember."

"Well, I should have, because that was just Sue's uncle."

"Sue's uncle?"

"No, wait, I wouldn't have told you that, come to think of it."

"Excuse me. It was some man I'd never seen before."

"No, I suppose you hadn't ever met him, but yes, that was my husband's brother. I'm sorry I couldn't tell you. I should have, so you wouldn't be scared. He was custodian at that church, and we didn't like to tell people that. So silly. We should have been open about it, but we were embarrassed. If we'd only known the humiliating things we'd have to tell people about our own daughter later . . . Sue wasn't supposed to tell anybody about him, either."

"About him?"

"That he was a janitor."

"Are you sure we're talking about the same man? What was his name?"

"Well, it still is his name, though he has forgotten it." She shook her head. "James Marway was, is, his name, because he had a different father from my husband. Sidney's dad died in World War II and his mom got remarried to Jim's dad. I never liked him very well, to tell you the truth. Jim, I mean. There was just something about him, you know? He always loved children, though. So that was a point in his favor. His own kids are incredibly screwed up, though, so it wasn't just us that ruined our kid."

Her eyes had endless regret and bafflement in them. "I think that's why Sue didn't come home with you that day, wasn't that right? I think she stopped off to help her Uncle James with something."

"Changing a light bulb," Judy said, her mouth dry.

"Was that what it was?" Sue's mother smiled, breaking Judy's heart. "You really do have a good memory, to be able to recall a little thing like that."

Judy told her everything else she remembered of that day.

She had to see him.

"I'm his niece," she told the nurse in his room.

The overhead light was on, making the room unpleasantly bright, but it allowed her to see clearly the old man under the sheets. He wore white pajamas, and the blanket and sheets were tucked up neatly under his armpits, as if the nurse had just performed that service and then placed his long arms over the top of them. He looked grizzled, with white whiskers and long strands of white hair over his skull. "He needs a shave," the nurse said, sounding apologetic.

"Don't worry," Judy said, thinking of straight-blade razors.

The nurse walked out of the room.

Judy went up to the bed and stared down at him. His eyes were closed, and she wanted him to open them, so she said his name several times.

"James. Jim Marway!"

When he didn't respond, she raised her hand and slapped his face so that his eyelids popped open and he looked around, confused.

"That was for your niece," she told him.

He seemed to peer into her face without seeing her.

"Sue," she repeated.

She was shocked at herself, and then momentarily scared that somebody might have seen her slap him. She turned to check if anybody was in the hallway and shielded her eyes from the overhead light. The part of her that was still scared and reticent felt as if it was crawling to the back of her being, and a new, bolder, furious Judy seemed to be taking over.

She let it in, let it flood her with confidence.

"I hate this light," she said, and then walked over and flipped it off, throwing the room into dimness, and closed the door. "Oh look!" she exclaimed in a mocking little-girl voice. "The bulb has gone out! I think this light bulb needs changing, don't you? Don't you want to help me change this bulb, little boy?"

The old man's eyes cleared for a moment, and he stared at her with panic. She crossed back to his bed and jerked a pillow out from under his head and then put it onto his face and pressed.

"And this is for the other children."

Just northwest of downtown, where the Kaw River flows into the Missouri and they start riding on east together, there is an overlook that wasn't there when Judy was a child. If it had been there in the early '50s, it would have been underwater. She stood with her arms crossed over a railing to watch the rush of muddy water below.

She thought she remembered the river as having been busy with barges and tugs, but there were none that she saw now. It was as treacherous-looking as she recalled, however, full of rough current and dangerous eddies. She watched a big log pop up and down, get caught, sucked under, and then turn up again downstream. It made her stomach feel funny, like being on a roller coaster, as if she'd ever been brave enough to actually ride one.

I'm braver than that now, she thought.

She leaned harder against the railing so she could stare deeper down into the river. In the back of her mind she heard her own scared, childish self, yelling, *Back up, Daddy! Back up!*

Judy put her right foot on the lower bar of the railing.

"I swear that river could shoot us all the way to St. Louis!" her mother had exclaimed that day in the Chevy, during the great flood in Kansas City.

Judy climbed to the top rung and brought her legs over until she could sit on the railing. The bar was slick with moisture, and it was easy to lose her grip.

BILL PRONZINI

Gunpowder Alley

FROM *Ellery Queen's Mystery Magazine*

FROM WHERE HE SAT propped behind a copy of the *San Francisco Argonaut,* Quincannon had an unobstructed view of both the entrance to the Hotel Grant's bar parlor and the booth in which his client, Titus Willard, waited nervously. The Seth Thomas clock above the back bar gave the time as one minute past nine, which made the man Willard was waiting for late for their appointment. This was no surprise to Quincannon. Blackmailers seldom missed an opportunity to heap additional pressure on their victims.

Willard fidgeted, looked at the clock for perhaps the twentieth time, and once more pooched out his cheeks—a habitual trick that, combined with his puffy muttonchop whiskers, gave him the look of a large rodent. As per arrangement, he managed to ignore the table where Quincannon sat with his newspaper. The satchel containing the $5,000 cash payoff was on the seat next to him, one corner of it just visible to Quincannon's sharp eye.

The *Argonaut,* likc all of the city's papers these days, was full of news of the imminent war with Spain. The Atlantic fleet had been dispatched to Cuban waters, Admiral Dewey's Asiatic Squadron was on its way to the Philippines, and President McKinley had issued a call for volunteer soldiers to join Teddy Roosevelt's Rough Riders. Quincannon, who disdained war as much as he disdained felons of every stripe, paid the inflammatory yellow journalism no mind while pretending to be engrossed in it, and wondered again what his client had done to warrant blackmail demands that now amounted to $10,000.

He had asked Willard, of course, but the banker had refused

to divulge the information. Given the fact that the man was in his midfifties, with a prim socialite wife and a grown daughter, and the guilty flush that had stained his features when the question was put to him, his transgressions likely involved one or more young and none-too-respectable members of the opposite sex. In any case, Willard had shown poor judgment in paying the first $5,000 demand, and good judgment in hiring Carpenter and Quincannon, Professional Detective Services, to put an end to the bloodletting after the second demand was made. The man may have been worried, frightened, and guilt-ridden, but he was only half a fool. Pay twice, and he knew he'd be paying for the rest of his life.

Quincannon took a sip of clam juice, his favorite tipple now that he was a confirmed teetotaler, and turned a page of the *Argonaut*. Willard glanced again at the clock, which now read ten past nine, then drained what was left of a double whiskey. And that was when the blackmailer — if it was the blackmailer and not a hireling — finally appeared.

The fellow's entrance into the bar parlor was slow and cautious. This was one thing that alerted Quincannon. The other was the way he was dressed. Threadbare overcoat, slouch hat drawn low on his forehead, wool muffler wound up high inside the coat collar so that it concealed the lower part of his face. This attire might have been somewhat conspicuous at another time of year, but on this damp, chilly November night, he drew only a few casual glances from the patrons, none of which lingered.

He paused just inside the doorway to peer around before his gaze locked in on his prey. Out of the corner of one eye Quincannon watched him approach the booth. What little of the man's face was visible corroborated Willard's description of him from their first meeting: middle-aged, with a hooked nose and sallow complexion, and average to small in size, though it was difficult to tell for certain because of the coat's bulk. Not such-a-much at all.

Titus Willard stiffened when the fellow slipped into the booth opposite. There was a low-voiced exchange of words, after which the banker passed the satchel under the table. The hook-nosed gent opened it just long enough to see that it contained stacks of greenbacks, closed it again, then produced a manila envelope from inside his coat and slid it across the table. Willard opened the envelope and furtively examined the papers it contained — letters of a highly personal nature, judging from the banker's expression.

They would not be the sum total of the blackmail evidence, however. Finding the rest was one part of Quincannon's job, the others being to identify and then yaffle the responsible party or parties.

While the two men were making their exchange, Quincannon casually folded the newspaper and laid it on the table, gathered up his umbrella and derby hat, and strolled out into the hotel lobby. He took a position just inside the corridor that led to the elevators, where he had an oblique view of the bar entrance. His quarry would have to come out that way because there was no other exit from the bar parlor.

The wait this time was less than two minutes. When Hook-nose appeared, he went straight to the swing door that led out to New Montgomery Street. Quincannon followed twenty paces behind. A drizzle of rain had begun and the salt-tinged bay wind had the sting of a whip. It being a poor night for travel by shanks' mare, Quincannon expected his man to take one of the hansom cabs at the stand in front of the Palace Hotel opposite. But this didn't happen. With the satchel clutched inside his overcoat, the fellow angled across Montgomery and turned the far corner into Jessie Street.

Quincannon reached the corner a few seconds later. He paused to peer around it before unfurling his umbrella and turning into Jessie himself, to make sure he wasn't observed. Hook-nose apparently had no fear of pursuit; he was hurrying ahead through the misty rain without a backward glance.

Jessie was a dark, narrow thoroughfare, and something of an anomaly as the new century approached—a mostly residential street that ran for several blocks through the heart of the business district, midway between Market and Mission. Small, old houses and an occasional small business establishment flanked it, fronted by tiny yards and backed by barns and sheds. The electric light glow from Third Street and the now steady drizzle made it a chasm of shadows. The darkness and the thrumming wind allowed Quincannon to quicken his pace without fear of being seen or heard.

After two blocks, his quarry made another turning, this time into a cobblestone cul-de-sac called Gunpowder Alley. The name, or so Quincannon had once been told, derived from the fact that Copperhead sympathizers had stored a large quantity of explosives in one of the houses there during the War Between the States. Gunpowder Alley was even darker than Jessie Street, the frame buildings strung along its short length shabby presences in the wet gloom. The only illumination was strips and daubs of light that leaked palely around a few drawn window curtains.

Not far from the corner, Hook-nose crossed the alley to a squat, dark structure that huddled between the back end of a saloon fronting on Jessie Street and a private residence. The squat building appeared to be a store of some sort, its plate-glass window marked with lettering that couldn't be read at a distance. The man used a key to unlock a door next to the window and disappeared inside.

As Quincannon cut across the alley, lamplight bloomed in pale fragments around the edges of a curtain that covered the store window. He ambled past, pausing in front of the glass to read the lettering: CIGARS, PIPE TOBACCO, SUNDRIES. R. SONDERBERG, PROP. The curtain was made of heavy muslin; all he could see through the center folds was a slice of narrow counter. He put his ear to the cold glass. The faint whistling voice of the wind was the only sound to be heard.

He moved on. A narrow, ink-black passage separated R. Sonderberg's cigar store from the house on the far side—a low, two-storied structure with a gabled roof and ancient shingles curled by the weather. The parlor window on the lower floor was an uncurtained and palely lamplit rectangle; he could just make out the shape of a white-haired, shawl-draped woman in a high-backed rocking chair, either asleep or keeping a lonely watch on the street. Crowding close along the rear of store and house, paralleling Gunpowder Alley from the Jessie Street corner to its end, was the long back wall of a warehouse, its dark windows steel-shuttered. There was nothing else to see. And nothing to hear except the wind, muted here in the narrow lane.

A short distance beyond the house Quincannon paused to close his umbrella, the drizzle having temporarily ceased. He shook water from the fabric, then turned back the way he'd come. The woman in the rocking chair hadn't moved—asleep, he decided. Lamp glow now outlined a window in the squat building that faced into the side passage; the front part of the shop was once again dark. R. Sonderberg, if that was who the hook-nosed gent was, had evidently entered a room or rooms at the rear—living quarters, like as not.

Quincannon stopped again to listen, and again heard only silence from within. He sidestepped to the door and tried the latch. Bolted. His intention then was to enter the side passage, to determine if access could be gained at the rear. What stopped him was the fact that he was no longer the only pedestrian abroad in Gunpowder Alley.

Heavy footsteps echoed hollowly from the direction of Jessie Street. Even as dark and wet as it was, he recognized almost immediately the brass-buttoned coat, helmet, and handheld dark lantern of a police patrolman. Hell and damn! Of all times for a blasted bluecoat to happen along on his rounds.

Little annoyed Quincannon more than having to abort an investigation in midskulk, but he had no other choice. He turned from the door and moved at an even pace toward the approaching policeman. They met just beyond the joining of the saloon's back wall and the cigar store's far side wall.

Unlike many of his brethren, the bluecoat, an Irishman in his middle years, was a gregarious sort. He stopped, forcing Quincannon to do likewise, and briefly opened the lantern's shutter so that the beam flicked over his face before saying in a conversational tone, "Evening, sir. Nasty weather, eh?"

"Worse coming, I expect."

"Aye. Heavy rain before morning. Like as not I'll be getting a thorough soaking before my patrol ends."

Quincannon itched to touch his hat and move on. But the bluecoat wasn't done with him yet. "Don't believe I've seen you before, sir. Live in Gunpowder Alley, do you?"

"No. Visiting."

"Which resident, if you don't mind my asking?"

"R. Sonderberg, at the cigar store."

"Ah. I've seen the lad a time or two, but we've yet to meet. I've only been on this beat two weeks now, y'see. Maguire's my name, at your service."

Before Quincannon could frame a lie that would extricate him from Officer Maguire's company, there came in rapid succession a brace of muffled reports. As quiet as the night was, there was no mistaking the fact that they were pistol shots and that the weapon had been fired inside the squat building.

Quincannon's reflexes were superior to the patrolman's; he was already on the run by the time the bluecoat reacted. Behind him Maguire shouted something, but he paid no heed. Another sound, a loudish thump, reached his ears as he charged past the shop's entrance, dropping his umbrella so he could grasp the Navy Colt in its holster. Seconds later he veered into the side passage. The narrow confines appeared deserted, and there were no sounds of movement at its far end. He skidded to a halt in front of the lighted window.

Vertical bars set close together prevented both access and egress. The glass inside was dirty and rain-spotted, but he could make out the figure of a man sprawled supine on the floor of a cluttered room. There was no sign of anyone else.

The spaces between the bars were just wide enough to reach a hand through; he did that, pushing fingers against the pane. It didn't yield to the pressure.

Officer Maguire pounded up beside him, the beam from his lantern cutting jigsaw pieces out of the darkness. The bobbing light illuminated enough of the passage ahead so that Quincannon could see to where it ended at the warehouse wall. He hurried back there while Maguire had his look through the window.

Another short walkway, shrouded in gloom, stretched at right angles to the side passage like the crossbar of the letter *T*. Quincannon thumbed a lucifer alight as he stepped around behind the cigar store, shielding it with his hand. That section was likewise empty, except for a pair of refuse bins. There was no exit in that direction; the walkway ended in a board fence that joined shop and warehouse walls, built so high that only a monkey could have climbed it. The match's flicker showed him the outlines of a rear door to R. Sonderberg's quarters. He tried the latch, but the heavy door was secure in its frame.

Maguire appeared, his lantern creating more dancing patterns of light and shadow. "See anyone back here?" he demanded.

"No one."

"Would that rear door be open?"

"No. Bolted on the inside."

The bluecoat grunted and pushed past him to try the latch himself. While he was doing that, Quincannon struck another match in order to examine the other half of the walkway. It served the adjacent house, ending in a similarly high and unscalable board fence. The house's rear door, he soon determined, was also bolted within.

The lantern beam again picked him out. "Come away from there, laddie. Out front with me, step lively now."

Quincannon complied. As they hurried along the passage, Maguire said, "Is it your friend Sonderberg lying shot in there?"

No friend of mine or society's, Quincannon thought. But he said only, "I couldn't be sure."

"Didn't seem to be anybody else in the room."

"No."

"Well, we'll soon find out."

When they emerged from the passage, Quincannon saw that the elderly woman had left her rocking chair and was now standing stooped at the edge of her front window, peering out. One other individual had so far been alerted; a man wearing a light overcoat and high hat and carrying a walking stick had appeared from somewhere and stood staring nearby. Quincannon knew from rueful experience that a full gaggle of onlookers would soon follow.

No one had exited the cigar store through the Gunpowder Alley entrance; the door was still locked from within. Maguire grunted again. "We'll be having to break it down," he said. "Sonderberg, or whoever 'tis, may still be alive."

It took the combined weight of both of them to force the door, the bolt finally splintering free with an echoing crack. Once they were inside, Maguire flashed his lantern's beam over displays of cigars and pipe tobacco, partly filled shelves of cheap sundries, then aimed it down behind the low service counter. The shop was cramped and free of hiding places—and completely empty.

The closed door to the rear quarters stood behind a pair of dusty drapes. "By the saints!" Maguire exclaimed when he caught hold of the latch. "This one's bolted, too."

It proved no more difficult to break open than the outer door had. The furnished room beyond covered the entire rear two thirds of the building. The man sprawled on the floor was middle-aged, medium-sized, and hook-nosed—Quincannon's quarry, right enough, though he no longer wore the overcoat, muffler, and slouch hat that had partially disguised him in the Hotel Grant. Blood from a pair of wounds spotted the front of his linsey-woolsey shirt; his open eyes glistened in the light from a table lamp.

Maguire went to one knee beside him, felt for a pulse. "Dead," he said unnecessarily.

Quincannon's attention was now on the otherwise empty room. It contained a handful of secondhand furniture, a blanket-covered cot, a potbellied stove that radiated heat, and a table topped with a bottle of whiskey and two empty glasses. The whole was none too tidy and none too clean.

Another pair of curtains partially covered an alcove in the wall opposite the window. Quincannon satisfied himself that the alcove contained nothing more than an icebox and larder cabinet. The only item of furniture large enough to conceal a person was a rickety wardrobe, but all he found when he opened it was a few articles of inexpensive clothing.

Maguire was on his feet again. He said, "I wonder what made him do it."

"Do what?"

"Shoot himself, of course. Suicide's a cardinal sin."

"Is that what you think happened, Officer?"

"Aye, and what else could it be, with all the doors and windows locked and no one else on the premises?"

Suicide? Faugh! Murder was what else it could be, and murder was what it was, despite the circumstances. Three things told Quincannon this beyond any doubt. Sonderberg had been shot twice in the chest, a location handgun suicides seldom chose because it necessitated holding the weapon at an awkward angle, and one of the wounds was high on the left side in a nonlethal spot. The pistol that had fired the two rounds lay some distance away from the dead man, too far for it to have been dropped if he had fired the fatal shot. And the most damning evidence: the satchel containing the $5,000 blackmail payoff was nowhere to be seen here or in the front part of the shop.

But Quincannon shrugged and said nothing. Let the bluecoat believe what he liked. The dispatching of R. Sonderberg was part and parcel to the blackmail game, and that made it John Quincannon's meat.

"I'll be needing to report in to headquarters," Maguire said. "The nearest callbox is on Jessie, two blocks distant. You'll stay here, will you, and keep out any curious citizens until I return, Mr. — ?"

"Quinn. That I will, Officer."

"Quinn, is it? You'll be Irish yourself, then?"

"Scotch-Irish," Quincannon said.

Maguire hurried out. As soon as he was alone, Quincannon commenced a search of the premises. The dead man's coat and trouser pockets yielded nothing of value or interest other than an expired insurance card that confirmed his identity as Raymond Sonderberg. The pistol that had done for him was a small-caliber Colt, its chambers fully loaded except for the two fired rounds; it bore no identifying marks of any kind. The $5,000 was not in the room, nor was whatever blackmail evidence had been withheld from Titus Willard tonight.

The bolt on the rear door was tightly drawn, the door itself sturdy in its frame; and for good measure a wooden bar set into brackets spanned its width. Sonderberg had been nothing if not security-conscious, for all the good it had done him. The single window was hinged upward, the swivel latch at the bottom of the sash loosely in place around its stud fastener. Quincannon flipped the hook aside and raised the glass to peer again at the vertical bars. They were set tightly top and bottom; he couldn't budge any of them. And as close together as they were, there was no way in which anything as bulky as the satchel could have passed between them.

Sonderberg had brought the satchel inside with him, there could be no mistaking that. Whoever had shot him had made off with it; that, too, was plain enough. But how the devil could the assassin have committed his crime and then escaped from not one but two sealed rooms in the clutch of seconds that had passed between the firing of the fatal shots and Quincannon's entry into the side passage?

The night's stillness was broken now by the sound of voices out front, but as yet none of the bystanders had attempted to come inside. Muttering to himself, Quincannon lowered the window and made his way out through the cigar store to stand in the broken doorway.

The parlor of the house next door, he noted, was now dark and the white-haired occupant had come out to stand, shawl-draped and leaning on a cane, on the small front porch. The others gathered in Gunpowder Alley numbered less than a dozen, drawn from nearby houses and the Jessie Street watering hole, among them the man in the cape and high hat, who now assailed him with questions. Quincannon provided only enough information, repeating Maguire's false theory of suicide, to dampen the bystanders' enthusiasm; shootings were common in the city, and there was not enough spice in a self-dispatching to hold the jaded citizens' interest. He then sought information of his own, but none of the crowd owned up to seeing Sonderberg or anyone else enter the cigar store after its six o'clock closing.

Some of the men were already moving away to homes and saloon when Maguire returned. The bluecoat dispersed the rest. The elderly woman still stood on the porch; it was not until the alley was mostly deserted again that she doddered back inside the darkened house.

Quincannon asked Maguire if he knew the woman's name and whether or not she lived alone. "I couldn't tell you, lad," the patrolman said. "I've not seen her before—the house has always been dark when I've come by."

The morgue wagon and a trio of other bluecoats arrived shortly. None of them was interested in Quincannon. Neither was Maguire any longer. San Francisco's finest, a misnomer if ever there was one, found suicides and those peripherally involved to be worthy of little time or attention. While the minions of the law were inside with the remains of Raymond Sonderberg, he remembered his dropped umbrella and mounted a brief search, but it was nowhere to be found. One of the onlookers must have made off with it. Faugh! Thieves everywhere in this infernal city!

He crossed to the adjacent house. The parlor window was curtained now, no light showing around its edges. The bell pull beside the door no longer worked; he rapped on the panel instead. There was no immediate response. Mayhap the white-haired woman wanted no truck with visitors after the night's excitement, or had already retired—

Neither. Old boards creaked and a thin, quavery voice asked, "Yes? Who's there?"

"Police officer," Quincannon lied glibly. "A few questions if I may. I won't keep you long."

There was a longish pause, followed by the click of a bolt being thrown; the door squeaked open partway and the old woman appeared. Stooped, still bundled in a shawl over a black dress, she carried her cane in one hand and a lighted candle in the other. A cold draft set the candle flame to flickering in its ceramic holder, so that it cast patterns of light and shadow over her heavily seamed face as she peered out and up at him.

"I know you," she said. "You were here before all the commotion next door."

"You spied me through your parlor window, eh? I thought as much, Mrs. —?"

"Carver. Letitia Carver. Yes, I often sit looking out in the evenings. A person my age has little else to occupy her attention."

"Did you see anyone enter or leave the cigar store at any time tonight?"

"No, no one. What happened to Mr. Sonderberg?"

"Shot dead in his quarters."

"Oh!"

"Possibly by his own hand, more likely by an intruder. You heard the shots, did you?"

"Yes. I thought that's what they were, but I wasn't sure."

"You live here alone, Mrs. Carver?"

"Since my husband passed on, bless his soul."

"And you've had no visitors tonight?"

She sighed wistfully. "Few come to visit me anymore."

"Did you hear anyone moving about in the side or rear passages, before or after the pistol shots?"

"Only you and the other policeman." She sighed again, sadly this time. "Such a tragedy. Poor Mr. Sonderberg."

Poor Mr. Sonderberg, my hat, Quincannon thought. Poor Titus Willard, who was now bereft of $10,000. And poor Carpenter and Quincannon, Professional Detective Services, who were out a substantial fee if the mystery of Sonderberg's death remained unsolved.

The woman said in her quavery voice, "Is there anything more, young man? It's quite chilly standing here."

"Nothing more."

She retreated inside and he returned to the boardwalk. R. Sonderberg's body was in the process of being loaded into the morgue wagon. None of the policemen even glanced in Quincannon's direction as he crossed the alley and made his way to Jessie Street, his thoughts as dark and gloomy as the night around him.

*

Sabina was already at her desk when he walked into the Market Street offices of Carpenter and Quincannon, Professional Detective Services, the next morning. She was a handsome woman, his partner and unrequited love—the possessor of a fine figure, eyes the color of the sea at dusk, and sleek black hair layered high on her head and fastened with a jeweled comb. Today she wore one of the leg-of-mutton blouses which he usually found enticing, but his mood was such that he took only peripheral notice of her. His night had been a mostly sleepless one in which he'd wrestled unsuccessfully with the problem of how R. Sonderberg had been murdered and by whom. His lack of success was all the more frustrating because he prided himself on having an uncanny knack for unraveling even the knottiest of seemingly impossible problems.

Sabina said, as he shed his umbrella and rain-spotted overcoat, "Titus Willard telephoned a few minutes ago. He was upset that you failed to contact him last night."

"Bah."

"Well, he asked that you get in touch with him as soon as you arrived."

"I'll see him later this morning. He won't be pleased to hear the news I have for him at any time."

"You weren't able to identify the blackmailer, then?"

"On the contrary. The blackmailer's name is, or was, Raymond Sonderberg, the proprietor of a cigar store in Gunpowder Alley. He was murdered in his locked quarters before I could confront him and recover the blackmail evidence and payoff money."

"Murdered? So that's why you're in such a foul humor this morning."

"What makes you think my humor is foul?"

"The scowl you're wearing, for one thing. You look like a pirate on his way to the gibbet."

"Bah," Quincannon said again.

"Exactly what happened last night, John?"

He sat at his desk and provided her with a detailed summary. They often shared information on difficult cases in order to obtain a fresh perspective. Sabina's years as a Pink Rose, one of the select handful of women operatives hired by the Pinkerton Agency, plus the four years of their partnership had honed her skills to a fine edge. He would never have admitted it to her or anyone else, but she was often his equal at the more challenging aspects of the sleuthing game.

"A puzzling series of events, to be sure," Sabina said when he finished his account. "But perhaps not as mysterious as they might seem."

"What do you mean?"

"You know from experience, John, that such mysteries generally have a relatively simple explanation."

He admitted the truth of this. "But I'm hanged if I can see it in this case."

"Well, the first question that occurs to me, was the crime planned or committed on the spur of the moment?"

"If it was planned, it was done in order to silence Sonderberg and make off with the five thousand dollars."

"By an accomplice in the blackmail scheme."

"So it would seem. The accomplice must have been waiting for him in his quarters. The stove there was glowing hot, and there was not enough time for Sonderberg to have stoked the fire to high heat, even if he'd built it up before he left for the Hotel Grant."

"Then why all the mystification?" Sabina asked. "Why not simply shoot Sonderberg and slip away into the night with the loot?"

"To make murder appear to be suicide."

"That could have been accomplished without resorting to such elaborate flummery. Locked rooms and mysterious disappearances smack of deliberate subterfuge."

"Aye, so they do. But to what purpose?"

"The obvious answer is to fool someone in close proximity at the time."

"Who? Not me, surely. No one could have known ahead of time that I would follow Sonderberg from the hotel to Gunpowder Alley."

"The bluecoat, Maguire, then," Sabina said. "From your description of him, he's the sort who makes his rounds on a by-the-clock schedule. Still, it seems rather an intricate game just to confuse a simple patrolman."

"*If* the whole was planned ahead of time, and not a result of circumstance."

"In either case, there has to be a plausible explanation. Are you certain there was no possible means of escape from Sonderberg's building following the shooting?"

"Front and rear entrances bolted from the inside, the door to his living quarters likewise bolted, the only window both barred and locked. Yes, I'm certain of that much."

"Doesn't it follow, then, that if escape was impossible, the murderer was never inside the building?"

"It would," Quincannon said, "except for three facts that indicate otherwise. The missing satchel and greenbacks; the presence of the whiskey bottle and two glasses on the table; the pistol that dispatched Sonderberg lying at a distance from the body. There can be no doubt that both killer and victim were together inside that sealed room."

"The thump you heard just after the shots were fired. Can you find any significance in that?"

"None so far. It might have been a foot striking a wall—that sort of sound."

"But loud enough to carry out to Gunpowder Alley. Did you also hear running steps?"

"No. No other sounds at all." Quincannon stood and began to restlessly pace the office. "The murderer's vanishing act is just as befuddling. Even if he managed to extricate himself from the building, how the devil was he able to disappear so quickly? Not even a cat could have climbed those fences enclosing the rear walkway. Nor the warehouse wall, not that such a scramble would have done him any good with all its windows steel-shuttered."

"Which leaves only one possible escape route."

"The rear door to Letitia Carver's house, yes. But it was bolted when I tried it, and she claims not to have had any visitors."

"She could have been lying."

Quincannon conceded that she could have been.

"I don't suppose there's any chance that she herself could be the culprit?"

"She's eighty if she's a day," he said. "Besides, I saw her sitting in her parlor window not two minutes before the shots were fired."

"Lying to protect the guilty party, possibly. Perhaps a relative. In which case the murderer was hiding in the house while you spoke to her."

"A galling possibility, if true." Quincannon paused, glowering, to run fingers through his thick beard. "The crone seemed innocent enough, yet now that I consider it, there was something . . . odd about her."

"Furtive, you mean?"

"No. Her actions, her words . . . I can't quite put my finger on it."

"Why don't you have another talk with her, John?"

"That," Quincannon said, "is what I intend to do straightaway."

Gunpowder Alley was no more appealing by daylight than it had been under the cloak of darkness. Heavy rain during the early morning hours had slackened into another dreary drizzle, and the buildings encompassing the alley's short length all had a huddled appearance, bleak and sodden under the wet gray sky.

The cul-de-sac was deserted when Quincannon, dry beneath a newly purchased umbrella, turned into it from Jessie Street. Boards had been nailed across the front entrance to the cigar store and a police seal applied to forestall potential looters. At the house next door, tattered curtains still covered the parlor window.

He stood looking at the window for a few seconds, his mind jostled by memory fragments—words spoken to him by Maguire, others by Letitia Carver. Quickly, then, he climbed to the porch and rapped on the front door. Neither that series of knocks nor two more brought a response.

His resolve, sharpened now, prodded him to action. In his pocket he carried a set of lock picks which he'd purchased from an ex-housebreaker living in Warsaw, Illinois, who manufactured burglar tools, advertised them as novelties in the *Police Gazette,* and sold them for ten dollars the set. He set to work with these on the flimsy door lock and within seconds had the bolt snicked free.

In the foyer inside, he paused to listen. No sounds reached his ears save for the random creaks of old, wet timbers. He called loudly, "Hello! Anyone here?" Faint echoes of his voice were all the answer he received.

He moved through an archway into the parlor. The room was cold, decidedly musty; no fire had burned in the grate in a long while, certainly not as recently as last night. The furniture was sparse and had the worn look of discards. One arm of the rocking chair set near the curtained window was broken, bent outward at an angle. The lamp on the rickety table next to it was as cold as the air.

Glowering fiercely now, Quincannon set off on a rapid search of the premises upstairs and down. There were scattered pieces of furniture in two other rooms, including a sagging iron bedstead sans mattress in what might have been the master bedroom; the remaining rooms were empty. A closet in the foyer contained a single item that brought forth a blistering, triple-jointed oath.

He left the house, grumbling and growling, and stepped into the side passage for another examination of the barred window to Sonderberg's quarters. Then he moved on to the cross passage at the rear, where a quick study confirmed his judgments of the night before: there was no possible exit at either end, both fences too tall and slippery to be scaled.

Out front again, he embarked on a rapid canvass of the immediate neighborhood. He spoke to two residents of Gunpowder Alley and the bartender at the saloon on the Jessie Street corner, corroborating one fact he already knew and learning another that surprised him not at all.

The first: The house next to the cigar store had been empty for four months, a possibility he should have suspected much sooner from the pair of conflicting statements he'd finally recalled—Maguire's that in the two weeks he'd patrolled Gunpowder Alley the parlor window had always been dark, the woman calling herself Letitia Carver's that she often sat there at night looking out.

And the second fact: Raymond Sonderberg, a man who kept mostly to himself and eked out a meager living selling cigars and sundries, was known to frequent variety houses and melodeons such as the Bella Union on Portsmouth Square.

The mystery surrounding Sonderberg's death was no longer a mystery. And should not have been one as long as it had; Quincannon felt like a damned rattlepate for allowing himself to be duped and fuddled by what was, as Sabina had suggested, a crime with an essentially simple explanation. For he knew now how and why Sonderberg had been murdered in his locked quarters. And was tolerably sure of who had done the deed—the only person, given the circumstances, it could possibly be.

Titus Willard was alone in his private office at the Montgomery Street branch of Woolworth National Bank when Quincannon arrived there shortly before noon. And none too pleased to have been kept waiting for word as long as he had.

"Why didn't you contact me last night, as we agreed?" he demanded. "Don't tell me you weren't able to follow and identify the blackmailer?"

"One of the blackmailers, yes, the man you paid. Raymond Sonderberg, proprietor of a cigar store in Gunpowder Alley."

"*One* of the blackmailers? I don't understand."

"His accomplice shot him dead in his quarters and made off with the satchel before I could intervene."

Willard blinked his surprise and consternation. "But who . . .?"

"I'll have the answer to that question, Mr. Willard, after you've answered a few of mine. Why were you being blackmailed?"

". . . I told you before, I'd rather not say."

"You'll tell me if you want the safe return of your money and the remaining blackmail evidence."

The banker assumed his habitual pooched rodent look.

"A woman, wasn't it?" Quincannon prompted. "An illicit affair?"

"You're, ah, a man of the world, surely you understand that when one reaches my age—"

"I have no interest in reasons or rationalizations, only in the facts of the matter. The woman's name, to begin with."

Willard hemmed and hawed and pooched some more before he finally answered in a scratchy voice, "Pauline Dupree."

"And her profession?"

"Profession? I don't see—oh, very well. She is a stage performer and actress. Yes, and a very good one, I might add."

"I thought as much. Where does she perform?"

"At the Gaiety Theater. But she aspires to be a serious actress one day, perhaps on the New York stage."

"Does she now."

"I, ah, happened to be at the theater one evening two months ago and we chanced to meet—"

Quincannon waved that away. No one "happened to be" at the Gaiety Theater, which was something of a bawdy melodeon on the fringe of the Barbary Coast. The sort of place that catered to middle-aged men with a taste for the exotic, specializing as it did in prurient skits and raucous musical numbers featuring scantily clad young women.

He asked, "You confided in her when you received the first blackmail demand?"

"Of course," Willard said. "She had a right to know . . ."

"Why did she have a right to know?"

"It's . . . letters I wrote to her that are being held against me."

Highly indiscreet letters, no doubt. "And how did the black-mailer get possession of them?"

"They were stolen from her rooms last week, along with a small amount of jewelry. This man Sonderberg . . . a common sneak thief who saw an opportunity for richer gains."

Stolen? Sonderberg a common sneak thief? What a credulous gent his client was! "Was it Miss Dupree's suggestion that you pay the initial five thousand dollars?"

"Yes, and I agreed. It seemed the most reasonable course of action at the time."

"But when the second demand arrived two days ago, you didn't tell her you'd decided to hire a detective until *after* you came to me."

"That's so, yes. Engaging you was a spur-of-the-moment decision—"

"And when you did tell her, you also explained that I'd be present at the second payoff and that I intended to follow and confront the blackmailer afterward?"

"Why shouldn't I have confided in her? She—" Willard broke off, frowning, then once again performed his rodent imitation. "See here, Quincannon. You're not suggesting that Miss Dupree had anything to do with the extortion scheme?"

It was not yet time to answer that question. "I deal in facts, as I told you, not suggestions," Quincannon hedged. "Where are you keeping her?"

"Her rooms are on Stockton Street," the banker said stiffly.

"Is she likely to be there or at the Gaiety at this hour?"

"I don't know. One or the other, I suppose."

"Come along, then, Mr. Willard," Quincannon said, "and we'll pay a call on the lady. I expect we'll both find it a stimulating rendezvous."

They found Pauline Dupree at the gaudily painted Gaiety Theater, primping in her backstage dressing room. She was more or less what Quincannon had expected—young and rather buxomly attractive, with dark-gold tresses and bold, smoke-hued eyes wise beyond her years. Her high color paled a bit when she saw Quincannon, but she recovered quickly.

"And who is this gentleman, Titus?" she asked Willard.

"John Quincannon, the detective I told you about." The smile the banker bestowed on her was fatuous as well as apologetic. "I'm sorry to trouble you, my dear, but he insisted on seeing you."

"Did he? And for what reason?"

"He wouldn't say, precisely. But he seems to have a notion that you are somehow involved in the blackmail scheme."

There was no need to hold back any longer. Quincannon said, "Not involved in it, the originator of it."

Pauline Dupree's only reaction was a raised eyebrow and a little moue of dismay. A talented actress, to be sure. But then, he'd already had ample evidence of her skills last night.

"I?" she said. "But that's ridiculous."

Quincannon's gaze had roamed the small dressing room. Revealing costumes hung on racks and an array of paints and powders and various theatrical accessories were arranged on tables. He walked over to one, picked up and brandished a long-haired white wig. "Is this the wig you wore last night, Mrs. Carver?" he asked her.

There was no slippage of her composure this time, either. "I have no idea what you're talking about."

"Your portrayal of Letitia Carver was quite good, I admit. The wig, the shawl and black dress and cane, the stooped posture and quavery voice . . . all very accomplished playacting. And of course the darkness and the candlelight concealed the fact that the old-age wrinkles were a product of theatrical makeup."

"And where was I supposed to have given this performance?" Pauline Dupree's eyes were cold and hard now, but her voice remained even.

"The abandoned house next to Raymond Sonderberg's cigar store in Gunpowder Alley. Before and after you murdered Sonderberg in his quarters behind the store."

"Murder?" the banker exclaimed in shocked tones. "See here, Quincannon! An accusation of blackmail is egregious enough, but murder—"

Pauline Dupree said, "It's nonsense, of course. I have no idea where Gunpowder Alley is, nor do I know anyone named Raymond Sonderberg."

"Ah, but you do. Or rather, did. Like Mr. Willard, Sonderberg was drawn to melodeons such as this one. My guess is you made his acquaintance in much the same way as you did my client, and used your no doubt considerable charms to lure him into your blackmail scheme."

"Preposterous!" Willard cried. "Outrageous!"

"But you never intended to share the spoils with him," Quincannon said to the actress. "You wanted the entire ten thousand dollars. To finance your ambition to become a serious actress, may-hap? A trip east to New York?"

An eye-flick was his only response. But it was enough to tell him that he'd guessed correctly.

"I give you credit, Miss Dupree," he went on. "You planned it well enough in advance. You had two days to make your arrange-ments, after learning from Mr. Willard that I would be at the Hotel Grant last night. You found out, likely from Sonderberg, about the abandoned house next to his building; he may even have helped you gain access. Sometime yesterday evening you went there and made final preparations for your performance—applied makeup, arranged a rocking chair near the window, created the illusion of an old woman seated there."

"Yes? How did I do that?"

"By placing a dressmaker's dummy in the chair, covering the head with the white wig, and draping the rest with a large shawl. This morning I found the dummy where you left it, in the foyer closet."

Willard made disbelieving, spluttering sounds. The actress said, "And why would I have set such an elaborate stage?"

"To flummox me, of course. You knew I would follow Sonder-berg from the hotel and that I would be nearby after he arrived home with the satchel. Your plan all along was to eliminate him once he had outlived his usefulness, and to do so by making cold-blooded murder appear to be suicide and staging an apparent van-ishing act must have seemed the height of creative challenge."

Willard should have been swayed by this time, but he wasn't. His feelings for Pauline Dupree were stronger than Quincannon had realized. "My dear," he said to his paramour, "you don't have to listen to any more of this slanderous nonsense—"

"Let him finish, Titus. I'd like to know how he thinks I accom-plished this creative challenge he speaks of."

"It wasn't difficult," Quincannon said. "So devilishly simple, in fact, it had me buffaloed for a time—something that seldom happens." He paused to fluff his freebooter's beard. "Your actions from the time you set the scene in the house were these: You left the same way you'd entered, by the rear door, crossed along the walkway, and were admitted to Sonderberg's quarters through his rear door. Thus no one could possibly have seen you from the alley. How you explained the old crone's makeup to Sonderberg is of no real import. By then I suspect he would have believed anything you told him.

"You waited there, warm and dry, while he went to the Hotel Grant. When he returned with the satchel, he locked both the entrance to the cigar store and the inside door leading to his quarters. You made haste to convince him by one means or another to let you have the satchel. Then you left him, again through the rear door, no doubt with instructions to lock and bar it behind you."

"Then how am I supposed to have killed him inside his locked quarters?"

"By slipping around into the side passage and tapping on the window, as if you'd forgotten something. When Sonderberg opened it, raising it high on its hinge, you reached through the bars, shot him twice, then immediately dropped the pistol to the floor. Naturally he released his grip on the window as he staggered backward, and it dropped and clattered shut—the loudish thump I heard before I ran into the passage. The force of impact flipped up the loose swivel catch at the bottom of the sash. Of its own momentum the catch then flipped back down and around the stud fastener, locking the window and adding to the illusion.

"It took you no more than a few seconds, then, to run to the rear walkway and reenter the house, locking that door behind you. While the patrolman and I were responding to the gunshots, you drew the parlor drapes, removed the dressmaker's dummy from the rocking chair, donned the wig, and assumed the role of Letitia Carver. When I came knocking at the door a while later, you could have simply ignored the summons; but you were so confident in your acting ability that you decided instead to have sport with me, holding the candle you'd lighted in such a way that your made-up face remained shadowed the entire time."

A few moments of silence ensued. Willard stood glaring at Quincannon, disbelief still plainly written on the lovesick dolt's pooched features. Pauline Dupree's expression was stoic, but in her eyes was a sparkle that might have been secret amusement.

"Utter rot," the banker said with furious indignation. "Miss Dupree is no more capable of such nefarious trickery than I am."

"Even if I were," she said, "Mr. Quincannon has absolutely no proof of his claims."

"When I find the ten thousand dollars, I'll have all the proof necessary. Hidden here, is it, or in your rooms?"

Again her response was not the one he'd anticipated. "You're welcome to search both," she said. Nor did the sparkle in her eyes diminish; if anything, it brightened. Telling him, he realized, as plainly as if she'd spoken the words, that such searches would prove futile, and that he would never discover where the greenbacks were hidden, no matter how long and hard he searched.

Sharp and bitter frustration goaded Quincannon now. There was no question that his deductions were correct, and he had been sure he could wring a confession from Pauline Dupree, or at the very least convince Titus Willard of her duplicity. But he had succeeded in doing neither. They were a united front against him.

So much so that the banker had moved over to stand protectively in front of her, as if to shield her from further accusations. He said angrily, "Whatever your purpose in attempting to persecute this innocent young woman, Quincannon, I won't stand for any more of it. Consider your services terminated. If you ever dare to bother Miss Dupree or me again, you'll answer to the police and my attorneys."

Behind Willard as he spoke, Pauline Dupree smiled and closed one eye in an exaggerated wink.

"Winked at me!" Quincannon ranted. "Stood there bold as brass and winked at me! The gall of the woman! The sheer mendacity! The—"

Always unflappable, Sabina said, "Calm yourself, John. Remember your blood pressure."

"The devil with my blood pressure. She's going to get away with murder!"

"Of a mean no-account as mendacious as she."

"Murder nonetheless. Murder and blackmail, and with her idiot victim's complicity."

"Unfortunately, there's nothing to be done about it. She was right—you have no proof of her guilt."

There was no gainsaying that. He muttered a frustrated oath.

"John, you know as well as I do that justice isn't always served. At least not immediately. Women like Pauline Dupree seldom go unpunished for long. Ruthlessness, greed, amorality, arrogance . . . all traits that sooner or later combine to bring about a harsh reckoning."

"Not always."

"Often enough. Have faith that it will in her case."

Quincannon knew from experience that Sabina was right, but it mollified him not at all. "And what about our fee? We'll never collect it now."

"Well, we do have Willard's retainer."

"It's not enough. I ought to take the balance out of his blasted hide."

"But you won't. You'll consider the case closed, as I do. And take solace in the fact that once again you solved a baffling crime. Your prowess in that regard remains unblemished."

This, too, was true. Yes, quite true. He *had* done his job admirably, uncovered the truth with his usual brilliant deductions; the lack of the desired resolution was not his fault.

But the satisfaction, like the retainer, was not enough. "I don't understand the likes of Titus Willard," he growled. "What kind of man goes blithely on making a confounded fool of himself over a woman?"

Sabina cast a look at him, the significance of which he failed to notice. "All kinds, John," she said. "Oh, yes, all kinds."

RANDALL SILVIS

The Indian

FROM *Ellery Queen's Mystery Magazine*

HARVEY SHOVES OPEN the door of the bar and comes striding
in the way he always does, walking fast, angry, lips moving as he
mutters to himself. His brother Will, who owns the bar and at forty-
one is two years younger than Harvey, reaches for an icy Schlitz at
the bottom of the cooler, gives it a wipe with the bar towel, twists
off the cap, and sets the bottle on the bar just as Harvey gets there.
Harvey doesn't reach for the bottle right away because he's too
angry to drink, too angry to do anything but stand there gripping
the curved edge of the cool wooden counter. His fingers knead the
scarred mahogany.

"I swear to God I am going to kill that pasty-faced weasel once
and for all," he says.

Will has been standing behind the bar with nothing much to do
and thinking about Portugal. In his mind he has been standing on
a bluff overlooking the glittering Atlantic, while behind him on a
sun-bleached plateau lies a small, well-ordered city with wide clean
streets and whitewashed buildings and the dome of a mosque
glowing golden in the sun.

It takes Will a moment to adjust to this sudden migration
back to his bar and the heat of his brother's anger. Then Howard down at the end of the bar clears his throat. Will takes a
frosted glass out of the other cooler and fills it from the plastic
jug of daiquiri mix he makes just for Howard, who comes in four
nights a week and sits primly at the far end of the bar. Between
six and eight each night he drinks four lime daiquiris without
uttering a word unless another customer or Will addresses him

directly. He is a small man who, according to Will's wife, Lacy, looks the way Tennessee Williams might have looked had he lived to be seventy-eight instead of choking on the bottle cap from a bottle of eye drops. For thirty-seven years he worked at the local driver's license center, where he failed both Harvey and Will upon their first attempts many years ago, Harvey for roll-stopping at an intersection and Will for bumping the curb while parallel parking.

Tonight is a steamy Tuesday in baseball season, but the Pirates are off until Thursday, so the only other customers are four golfers, who came in for burgers and beer. Will is grateful for the golfers because on nights when there isn't a televised sporting event he doesn't sell enough alcohol to cover his electric bill. The big-screen TV at the rear of the room is only two years old, but unfortunately it hasn't helped him to compete with the motel bars out by the interstate. He can't compete with the live bands and free munchies and the college girls in their short skirts. All he has to offer is a clean, quiet place to spend an hour or so with friends without having to shout to be heard, a place where for $14 you can quietly submerge yourself in enough lime juice and rum to soften the edges on some undisclosed misery.

Will looks toward the golfers now and asks with a lift of his eyebrows if they are ready for another pitcher. "We're good," a golfer says. The TV is tuned to *CNN Headline News* but nobody is paying any attention to it. The air conditioner is working hard to counteract the sticky August heat. There is something loose inside the air conditioner, and every once in a while Will can hear it rattling around in there.

Harvey wraps both hands around his beer bottle but doesn't take a sip. "I mean it," he says, only loud enough for Will to hear. "So I need to borrow your .357 for a while."

Will fills a small wooden bowl with salted peanuts and sets it on the counter. "Stevie's upstairs watching TV with Lacy," he says. "Go ahead and go on up if you want."

"I mean it, Will. I am seriously going to do it this time."

Will would say something if he knew what to say. He isn't exactly sure what his brother's troubles are, and he suspects that Harvey isn't sure either. All Will knows is that even in Harvey's lighter moods there seems to be something eating away at him, some worm of bitterness gnawing at his gut. It might have to do with his job as a truck driver for Jimmy Dean Sausage, but Will doubts it. There can't be much stress involved in humping sausage around to regular customers on a regular route. It might have to do with Harvey's marriage, but Will doubts that, too. Harvey and Jennilee have been married for seven years, and Will knows for a fact that his brother is still madly, even desperately, in love with Jennilee.

"I'm going to need that .357," Harvey says again. Will flinches a little and looks toward Howard. Howard stares straight ahead at the bottles on the shelves, he sips his daiquiri, and he waits without complaint for a streetcar that will never arrive.

Will tells his brother, "Hold on a minute." He goes to the kitchen, checks the deep fryer, lifts out a basket of wings and another of fries, drains them, dumps each into a separate wicker basket lined with napkins, sprinkles them with salt. He carries these to the bar and hands them to Harvey. "Take these upstairs to Stevie, will you? I'll be right behind soon as I check on those golfers. Lacy and me are splitting a pizza. You want anything?"

Harvey says, "I'm not kidding this time. You might think I am, but I'm not."

"I'll be up in a minute," Will says.

In the kitchen he tries to get back to Portugal, but Portugal has been burned away in the sizzle and stink of the deep fryer's fat.

At the top of the stairs Harvey kicks the door a couple of times. Five seconds later Stevie, his youngest brother, yanks open the door, reaches for the wings and fries, and says, "About time. I'm starvin' to death here." To Lacy he says, "Look who the delivery boy is tonight."

Lacy, seated on the sofa in the middle of the living room, looks over her shoulder. "Hey, Harvey, how ya doin'? Jennilee come with you?"

Harvey doesn't answer. There is a movie on the television, something with Nicolas Cage and Meg Ryan, and Lacy's police scanner on the mantel is crackling with static-filled voices. A floor fan in the corner of the room makes a constant clicking whir. After a moment Harvey asks, "Molly around?"

"At the library with some friends. Library closes at seven, so she'll be home before long. Why do you ask?"

Instead of explaining, Harvey glares at the TV. Even with all the windows open and the fan on high, the room pulses with damp heat. "It's like trying to breathe through a wet towel in here," he says.

Lacy smiles up at him. "What has you so agitated?"

"How do you guys even sleep at night? I can't breathe in here."

"We take the fan into the bedroom. Molly's got a little one of her own."

"Make Will buy you an air conditioner, for chrissakes."

Lacy blushes and looks away. "The heat only lasts a couple of weeks."

Stevie says, "I'd still like to know who you're so pissed at."

"Wait for Will. I'm not telling this story twice."

"Whatever," Stevie says.

Harvey stands there beside the sofa and watches the color in Lacy's cheeks, sees the way the rubied glow spreads down her neck when she blushes. What kind of life is this, Harvey wonders, when a man who works as hard as Will can't even afford an air conditioner for his wife.

Then Stevie says, "You ask around for me yet over at Jimmy Dean?"

"I already told you. Nobody is ever going to hire you as a driver. Not with your record, they're not."

Unlike his brothers, Stevie passed his driver's exam on the first attempt and was even graced with a handshake from Howard afterward. But in the twenty years since that accomplishment Stevie has amassed several thousands of dollars in fines for various driving violations. He has twice had his license revoked, for three months each time. One more violation and he will lose his license for a year.

For most of his adult life Stevie has made his living as the town's handyman, shoveling snow in winter, mowing lawns in the summer, tilling gardens in the spring, raking leaves in the fall. During all seasons he digs graves for the Cemetery Association, hauls away garbage the trash contractor won't accept, paints an occasional house, cleans out an occasional garage. He would like to have a girlfriend, but he is not anybody's idea of an eligible bachelor, even by local standards.

"I don't see where it would hurt to ask," Stevie continues. "I'd even work in Packing, I don't care."

Harvey crosses to the police scanner and turns it down. "How can you even hear the TV with this thing blaring all the time?"

RANDALL SILVIS

"Harvey, please," Lacy says. "If you don't mind."

"I can't even hear myself think."

"Well, how am I supposed to hear if there's a fire or a car wreck or something?"

"You'll hear the siren, same as everybody else in town."

"But I need to get there with my camera *before* everybody else in town. So if you don't mind . . ."

To placate her, Harvey pretends to turn the volume up. He returns to flop on the chair by the window. Lacy gets up and crosses to the scanner and turns it to its original volume.

Though nearly forty, Lacy is small and still as lithe as a gymnast. Stevie has to deliberately avoid looking at her ass when she stands up. Later, when he is back home at his trailer, he will think about her ass and probably about Jennilee's, too, which is even better. He knows that afterward he will feel guilty and lonely, but he is seldom able to control his thoughts once they begin.

Harvey stares at the TV. Nicolas Cage is standing at the top of a high building, the wings of his trench coat flaring as he peers down at the street far below. *Jump*, Harvey thinks. *Go ahead and jump, you idiot.*

Lacy says, "So where's Jennilee tonight?"

Harvey squints hard and stares at the television.

Stevie says, "I guess that's another story he doesn't want to have to tell twice."

Will enters his apartment carrying a pizza and a six-pack and a handful of napkins. He deposits them all on the coffee table and sits beside his wife. They open beers and steal glances at Harvey.

Lacy says, "Have some pizza, Harvey."

Harvey remains motionless.

After a while Will says, "Is this the movie where Nicolas Cage is an angel?"

And Harvey says, "So are you going to lend me that .357 or not?"

"Tell me how that would be in either of our best interests."

Stevie grins and asks, "Who are you going to shoot?"

Harvey says nothing.

Will says, "I only know of one person who can make him grind his teeth like that."

Stevie keeps grinning. "Kenny got your goat again, brother?"

Jennilee's brother Kenny used to be Harvey's best friend in high school and every bit as carefree and wild as Harvey had been until, at the age of twenty, Kenny decided to sell his half of the modified Chevy to Harvey and to quit painting houses for a living, thereby dissolving what Harvey had thought of as their partnership. Six years later, Harvey was still churning up dust clouds on the local track and still scraping paint, but Kenny with his brand-new master's degree was hired as the assistant principal at the junior-senior high school from which they had all graduated. By the time he was thirty he was the principal, and eight years later he was made the superintendent of schools.

It was Kenny who had talked his sister Jennilee, by then a third-grade teacher, into going out on a date with Harvey, who, from skinned knees to sausage truck driver, had been reduced to a shivering puppy whenever in the presence of Kenny's little sister. And against what Harvey thought of as all the laws of probability, she then went out with him a second, a third, and a fourth time, went out with him so many times that he finally asked her to marry him, and when she said yes he had to get away from her as quickly as possible so she would not see him quivering again, this time from the utter wonderment and thrilling mystery of life.

Initially Kenny had been slated to be Harvey's best man, but one day not long before the event Harvey asked Will to be his best man instead.

Now Harvey sits forward in Will's easy chair. "You think I'm kidding here? I am not freakin' kidding. I am without a doubt going to blow that, that . . ."

And Lacy tells him, "You can say asshole. If it's Kenny you're talking about, feel free to say it."

"I am going to blow that asshole to kingdom come."

Will turns to his wife. "Since when don't you like Kenny Fulton?"

"He's all right. But he's an asshole all the same."

To Harvey, Will says, "Have some pizza, why don't you?"

Harvey stands. "Fine. All I've got are deer rifles and shotguns at home, but don't you worry about it a bit, little brother. Don't worry about me at all. Just because I'm your older brother and by all the laws of the universe you should cut me some slack here, fine, who gives a shit? I'll strangle him with my bare hands if I have to!"

With that Harvey strides to the door, yanks it open, strides out, and slams the door shut. His footsteps pound down the stairway.

Lacy and Stevie look at Will and wait.

Will wipes his mouth on a paper napkin, drops it crumpled onto the coffee table, and follows Harvey.

A while later, during a Visa commercial, Stevie asks, "You got any of those little hot peppers left you had last time I was here?"

"In the refrigerator. Side shelf."

And she tries not to wonder about this life she has married into, these brothers and the secrets they share. She wonders instead how many car accidents and other tragedies she will have to photograph before she can afford an air conditioner.

Downstairs, Harvey stands behind the bar, staring down into the beer cooler but otherwise not moving. He can feel his insides quivering, but he thinks that if he stands motionless he can keep his hands from shaking.

Will comes up behind him, picks a glass off the rack, and draws himself a draft and takes a long swallow. He glances around the bar. Howard sits primly at the end of the bar, but the golfers have departed, leaving several bills beneath an empty glass on their table.

And Harvey says, still staring into the beer cooler, into the cold deep bottom, "I feel like I'm going under, Will."

Will is startled by the intimacy of this confession, its unexpected nakedness.

As is Harvey, who adds with a soft laugh, feeling a fool, "Whatever the hell that means."

Will doesn't want the unexpected intimacy of the moment to slip away. He says, "What do you say we get ourselves a little air."

Will touches Harvey's arm, then turns away and goes into the kitchen and outside through the rear door. He stands there in the middle of the alleyway, breathing the dusky air. He used to love this kind of sultry evening and wonders when the heat started bothering him so much, wonders when it became such a chore just to take another breath, the way the atmosphere pulses with heat like a boiler about to blow. He used to love these summer evenings because they smelled like baseball. All through Little League and Pony League and American Legion ball, that was how every summer night smelled to him. The soft leather of his glove. The cool dirt of the infield. From his position six feet off third base he would watch between batters as the moths flung themselves at the powerful sodium lights, and their passion mirrored what he felt inside himself but never showed, an exuberance aching to burst free.

These days the town's Little League program cannot field nine players and has been forced to merge with a team fifteen miles away. The Pony League and American Legion divisions have disbanded. Scrub grass grows on the local infield now. People in passing cars toss bottles at the backstop.

Will stands there in his alleyway and tries to see some stars in the narrow space between the buildings and thinks again about how nice it would be to have a house with a yard and a real piece of the sky overhead. He wonders again, as he has been doing more and more lately, each time he looks at Molly and thinks how tall she's getting, how quickly she is growing up, he wonders again if maybe he should sell the bar and go back to running a dragline. He could work weekdays in West Virginia and come home on weekends. He likes having the bar and having nobody to answer to, but even with Lacy working as a photographer for the local paper they can barely keep their heads above water.

Then the door pops open behind him and he remembers why he is standing in the alleyway. He doesn't turn around. The door thuds shut. Then Will asks, not loud, "So what's this all about?'

Harvey comes forward to stand beside his brother. "You wouldn't understand."

Will waits and says nothing.

Harvey lets half a minute pass. "You remember that Indian Jennilee's father used to ride?"

"Sure. The one you and him restored."

"For two years we worked on it. Turned it into something beautiful again. Then he had that stroke."

"That bike must be, what—thirty, forty years old by now?"

"It's a nineteen fifty-nine. Sweeping fenders front and back, studded leather seat . . ."

Will knows to wait now, knows to allow his brother to warm to the subject.

"I'm the one scrounged the one fender plus the leather for the seat. I'm the one sanded everything down and laid the five coats of paint on it."

"I remember," Will says.

"And when they put him in the nursing home, he promised that bike to me. Said he'd put it in his will. Said it would be mine the day he died."

"Who knew he'd live another dozen years or so?"

"Actually, I wish the old guy had lived forever. The bike was always safe in storage, always kept covered up except when I went to look at it. I knew where it was."

"But now Kenny won't let you have it?"

"Turns out it wasn't in the will after all. So Kenny's saying, how is he supposed to know whether his dad promised it to me or not?"

"Like that's something you would lie about."

"Exactly."

"What's Jennilee have to say about all this?"

"According to her, it's up to her mother. And what Pauline says is that since Kenny's the oldest child and the only son and all . . ."

"That's bullshit," Will says.

Harvey grunts, an animal sound rich with contempt.

"He never even drove that Chevy you two used to own, did he?"

"Never drove it, never worked on it. All Kenny wanted was to brag about how he owned half of it."

"So maybe he'll sell that bike to you."

"Oh, he'll sell it, all right. Didn't you see the ad in the paper?"

"I don't read the classifieds unless there's something I need."

"Ad says six thousand, five hundred. Right there in black and white. So okay, that's a fair price, and I go on over, checkbook in hand, trying to be civilized about the whole thing."

Will wonders what it would be like to have that much money in his checking account. "But the bike's already sold?"

"Hell no. Because now he says he wants twelve thousand for it. Said he did some research, found out it's worth a lot more than he thought. Twelve thousand freaking dollars for a bike I practically built myself!"

"You think he raised the price just to keep you from getting it?"

"He doesn't care whether I have the bike or not. He just wants to screw me one way or the other. Anybody else shows up, offers him sixty-two, sixty-three hundred for it, you think he's not going to take it? Little pasty-faced weasel. No way I'm going to let this one pass."

This one, Will hears. Will studies the tension in his brother's face, the hard line of his jaw. "So what is it about you two, anyway? He was supposed to be best man at your wedding, for chrissakes."

Harvey raises his finger in the air, is about to speak, make an important point, but then he backs off, shakes his head, bites back his words.

"Okay, so he's a prick," Will says. "Fine. But you're not going to kill him over a motorcycle."

"What'd I tell you already? This thing with the bike is just the last in a long line of things."

"Like what, for instance?"

"Like none of your business, okay?"

"Fine. Whatever. That still doesn't mean I'm going to help you murder him for it."

"Then *don't*," Harvey says. "Go on back upstairs to your freaking little sauna and eat your pizza and watch your TV. I don't need your help or anybody else's."

The men stand side by side but do not look at each other. Will can feel the night simmering. He can smell the stale compressed heat in the long narrow box of the alleyway. Finally he says, "How about if we steal the bike?"

"And do what with it? I couldn't ride it anywhere. Besides, he'll just turn it in on his insurance. Probably end up with twenty thousand dollars, for all I know."

"So we keep thinking until we come up with something. Something equal to what he's done to you."

"You have no idea what he's done to me."

"I'm still listening, though." He waits half a minute. Harvey says nothing more.

"Fine," Will says. "But I'll tell you what. I don't like him much either. Never did."

Harvey cuts a sideways look at his brother.

"So if you want to teach him a little lesson about fairness and such, then okay, I'm with you all the way. Mainly because I don't think you have the brains to pull it off on your own without getting caught."

"You never liked him either?"

"What's to like? Back when you two were in school together, you're this big football star, right? And what's he? He's in the band! Plays the piccolo or some such thing."

"Freakin' flute."

"Same difference. *You're* the one set the All-Conference rushing record. And who gets elected class president? Who gets voted

Homecoming King? I was only in ninth grade, but, I don't know, that really pissed me off for some reason. What I could never figure out was why you even wanted him as a friend."

A thought occurs to Harvey then, as perfect as a blow to his chest, that Will has been harboring a jealousy of Kenny all these years, quiet Will, so soft-spoken and patient—a resentment because Will had wanted to be Harvey's best friend back then, but of course was not; he was the younger brother, a nuisance to be tormented or ignored. And Harvey is suddenly ashamed of his youth, all those wasted years. But how to encapsulate his regret in an apology? He can't.

Harvey says, his voice huskier now, "Jennilee thinks he's like the perfect man or something."

"Yeah, well, she's his sister. That's just loyalty talking."

Harvey nods, his jaw tight.

Will says, "What's he make as the superintendent of schools—fifty, sixty thousand?"

"Probably more like eighty."

"I used to watch him when you two were painting houses together. You were the one did all the hard work, all the scraping and patching. What did he ever do?"

"Slapped on a little paint and collected the check."

"Then why in God's name was he your friend?"

Harvey has no idea how to justify the choices he made a quarter century ago. He had admired Kenny's easy way with women, that was one thing. He admired his nonchalance, his nice clothes. But mostly it was the women. Even in high school, Kenny had bragged that he was getting laid on a regular basis, and Harvey had to admit that it was probably true. There was something about Kenny that girls seemed to like. He was a smooth talker, generous with compliments. And he had been generous with Harvey, too, had made him feel, almost, like a member of the family.

But in recent years the very things Harvey had admired about his brother-in-law had begun to irritate him. Things that had once seemed like virtues in Kenny began to feel, to Harvey, like mere sheen. Like high-gloss paint over a wall full of termites.

Will and Harvey stand there in the gathering dark. It pleases Harvey that his brother has gotten angry now, too. He doesn't know why Will's anger should please him, except that it is such a rare thing. He says, "So what are we going to do about him?"

"Give me a day or so," Will says. "I'll think of something."

"This better not be a trick of some kind just to get me to cool off."

"No, I want to do this," Will says, and even in the stink and gloom of the alley, Harvey thinks he detects a sinister turn to his brother's smile. "Seriously. I could use a little fun in my life."

When Harvey returns home that evening, after he unlaces his work boots just inside the back door, Jennilee comes toward him through the kitchen, smiling. She is wearing tight blue jeans and a white silk shirt—still, in his opinion, the prettiest woman in town, still slender and naturally blond and as graceful as a breeze. He can see her bra through the sheer blouse, and something catches in his chest at the sight of her.

"Hi, baby," she says, and then tells him that she is going across town to the ten-room Victorian Kenny has lived in all his life. It bothers Harvey that his wife always says she is "having dinner over home" instead of "over at Mom's."

He says, "How about staying here for a change and having dinner with me?"

"I had dinner with you last night, didn't I?"

"Most people, you know, when they get to be adults, they're happy not to have to be spending four or five nights a week with their mother and brother."

"You see your brothers practically every day, don't you?" She asks this with a smile, sweetly. She leans close to him, her hand on his waist. He feels the warmth of her hand through his shirt. Even after seven years of marriage, her touch still dizzies him.

She says, "You know, when we lost Daddy last month, the thing I regretted most was not spending enough time with him. And now Mom's getting up there, too, and—"

"She's barely seventy years old."

"How old was Daddy? Seventy-six. And how old were your parents? It can happen at any moment, just like that."

He takes a deep breath to steady his voice, doesn't want to sound whiny. "My point, Jennilee—"

She snuggles against him. "I know what your point is, sweetie, and I agree with you. Now you take that casserole out of the oven in about ten minutes, okay? And enjoy a nice quiet dinner by yourself. I'll be home about eight-thirty or so and we can make some popcorn and watch TV together."

He knows that the way she holds him now, both hands rubbing up and down his back, one knee between his legs, he knows it is a ploy she uses, a way to defuse him because she does not like confrontation, does not like voices raised in anger, and she especially does not like to be circumvented in any of her choices. He knows all this, yet he cannot resist the smell of her, the vagueness of apricot in her hair, still as blond as a teenager's, still cornsilk-soft. And he cannot resist either the subtlety of Obsession in the nape of her neck, the heat of her breasts pressed against him. He breathes her in and feels his arms closing around her, hands pulling at the tail of her blouse and then sliding underneath, fingers finding the cool smooth wonder of her waist.

"Baby, I'm going to be late," she says, but as he leans down to lay his mouth against the side of her throat she tilts her head back and exposes her neck to him. Gratitude swells in his chest, but he cannot ignore the swift surge of fear that washes through him, too, a heat racing up the sides of his face and into his temples, this fear for the loss of her, this only woman he has ever needed, as essential to him as air, a compulsion as inexplicable as death.

His mouth is on hers then and his hands fumbling with the snap of her jeans, fingers so thick with dumb desire that she has to take over finally, guiding him into the living room and onto the sofa. And this is the thing that keeps him from crying out in the anguish of his desire, that she has never told him no, never pushed him away with a damning look or excuse, has never once denied him. This is what he clings to, how he gauges the truth of her love.

But it is always a temporary affirmation, and afterward, as always, he is left to deal with his fear and gratitude alone, as weak-legged and hollow as ever while Jennilee tucks her blouse in and makes her exit through the kitchen, her face as bright and cheerful as ever, her body as graceful as a breeze, untouched.

As she heads for the door he calls out to her, "Tell your brother for me that what goes around comes around."

A pause; he can picture the way she cocks her head now, smiles in confusion. "Excuse me?"

"Just tell him," he says.

Now he envisions the way she rolls her eyes before answering. "If you say so."

Then she slips away and leaves him standing there in the living room hollowed out and weak and alone.

Harvey watches television with the casserole dish on his lap, bleeding its heat into his skin. He keeps the volume low on the TV, wishes there were other sounds to hear, something flesh and blood and real. He wishes they would have children, that an accident would occur. He had himself tested a couple of years ago without telling Jennilee he was going to, then was surprised by her reaction when he told her that everything had checked out okay with him. "Why would you do such a thing?" she had demanded, then immediately turned and stormed into the bedroom and locked the door. Later she explained that she wasn't really angry with him. "It's just that it means it must be me," she said.

A few months later he found the birth control pills. He had called in sick that day, a Tuesday, nausea and a pulsing headache. By noon the sickness passed, and, thinking it would please her, he had seared a sirloin tip roast and put it in the oven to slow-bake through the afternoon. Then he washed two loads of laundry, everything in the hamper. Dried and folded all the clothes and put them away in their drawers. And that was when he found the disk of tiny pills, wrapped inside a camisole too delicate to be crushed beneath the cotton pajamas he was putting away. A disk meant to hold thirty pink pills, twelve spaces empty.

He was in bed when she came home at three-thirty.

"Still feeling bad?" she asked, and brought him a glass of ginger ale, and took his temperature, and looked sincerely pained by his discomfort.

She's a good person, he had told himself. *Just doesn't want to be a mother.*

He never mentioned the pills.

And now sometimes he watches TV alone and wishes the house did not feel so empty. He wishes he could awake some morning and stumble over toys scattered underfoot, a tricycle in the yard. He knows that when he and Jennilee are older, her deceit might grate on him and make him like some of the older men in town, silent brooders, never smiling. Or maybe he will gravitate back to the bottle and his earlier ways, drinking his way to self-destruction, having conceded at last that love was not his salvation but his undoing.

"You mind if I turn this thing off?" Will asks after he has come into the bedroom. Some kind of music is emanating from the little TV atop the dresser, a repetitious bass thump that he feels against the back of his tired eyes.

Lacy peers over the paperback she holds open on her chest, a Ludlum thriller. "I didn't even know it was on."

He stands before the TV for a few moments, remote in hand. Two black men in baggy clothes are striding vehemently back and forth across a stage, jabbing their hands at the air, chanting a mostly indecipherable rhyme. "MTV?" he says.

"Molly was watching it."

He turns at the neck, cocks an eyebrow.

"She was in bed by ten, don't worry. So you can just quit looking at me like that."

And with her smile he feels some of the heaviness lift away, feels the weariness lighten just a bit, as if her smile, like the fan in the corner, is blowing the day's chaff off his skin. He comes to the bed and sits on his side, removes his shoes, pulls off his socks and then his shirt. Stands again to unbuckle his belt. Hopefully he asks, "You want maybe I should lock the door?"

"Well," she says, and lays the book flat on her stomach, "I've been staying awake in hopes that Mel Gibson might show up, but he's usually here by eleven if he's coming. So I guess it's your lucky night, big boy."

He lets his trousers slide to the floor. "You want me to get a shower first?"

"How much beer did you spill on yourself tonight?"

"Not a drop, surprisingly. But I fried several baskets of wings."

"So lock the door, chickie boy, and get yourself on down here."

She is wearing the short pajamas and sleeveless top he likes, the powder-blue set he gave her for Christmas last year, and when he touches her he is as grateful as he was the first time so many years ago. No woman has ever smelled and tasted as good to him as Lacy does, and he knows he will never need any more than this, never want another woman.

Afterward, he feels that he has fallen from a great height. He has landed softly and without injury, but the feeling of having fallen is there nonetheless. She lies curled against him, her head on his chest, her knees nudging his.

"We're still pretty good together, aren't we?" he asks.

"I think it's better than it ever was."

He runs a hand up and down her spine, feels the ridges beneath his fingers, the lovely fragile stem beneath her skin, this flower in his hands.

"I mean more than just the sex, though," he tells her. "I mean everything. We work pretty good together, don't we?"

"Mmmm," she says. "Fourteen years and going strong."

He winces at the mention of fourteen years, a tightening at the back of his skull. "I wish I could do better for you and Molly, though. I wish the bar did better."

"It will pick up again," she says.

But he does not believe it. He is not certain when he stopped believing it, but he believes it no longer. *People drink when times are good,* the previous owner had told him, *and when times are bad they drink even more!* But the previous owner had failed to mention that nearly all those people would soon do their drinking somewhere else.

"Anyway," Lacy tells him, "we're getting by okay."

"After fourteen years, I'd like to be doing more for us than just getting by."

"For instance?"

And he says, "Portugal."

She laughs softly and rubs his chest. "Not me, baby. No hablo Portuguese."

But he remembers the way she looked that night when they had eaten spaghetti in front of the big-screen TV downstairs. His rule is that Molly cannot watch TV during dinner unless it is an educational program, so they found a travel series on PBS. In this show, the host, a lanky New Englander with a mop of blond hair, was visiting the Iberian Peninsula. Molly nearly swooned at the sight of the white beaches.

"Wouldn't it be awesome if we could go there?" she asked. "Mommy, wouldn't you like to go there?"

"Mmm," Lacy had said, and then, "It would be awfully expensive, I'll bet."

Will had felt a heaviness in his chest that night, and now, in bed with the woman he adores, as he inhales the scent of her hair and absorbs the heat of her skin, the heaviness comes back to him.

It is still there long after she has fallen asleep. After a while he rises and pulls on his boxers. He sits by the open window looking out through the screen. He sits there a long time, wondering what he can do to make things better. The night is too warm and smells of the street, of road oil and dirt, of other people in transit.

We can't steal the bike, he thinks after a while. *We can't beat Kenny up. We don't want to do anything that might give Kenny's mother a heart attack. Or anything that Jennilee will divorce Harvey over. I have to be clever about this,* he thinks. *This is my role in things. I am not bold or fearless, but I can think things through. I'm nobody's genius, but I can figure this out.*

He turns away from the window to look at his wife asleep. She lies facing him, left hand flat beneath her cheek. She is still naked, and he can feel himself wanting her again, the touch of her flesh against his. And this desire somehow conjoins with his desire to help Harvey and his own desire to ease the pressure that has been squeezing at the base of his scalp all day. Maybe he can be bold, after all, if that is what the situation calls for. Maybe, after all, there exists in him a seed of fearlessness and its potential for change.

It is not yet 7 A.M. when Will pulls his car up to the loading dock beside a Jimmy Dean Sausage delivery truck. Harvey, using a dolly, is loading boxes of refrigerated sausage into the rear of the truck. Will shuts off the engine and leans his head out the open window.

Harvey asks, "What are you doing out of bed so early?"

"Didn't get much sleep last night."

Harvey comes to the edge of the loading dock. "I hope it was because of Lacy and not that pizza you had."

Will spots a couple of men several yards behind Harvey in the cave of the warehouse, one running a forklift and the other scanning boxes with his hand scanner. The forklift driver is wearing a set of headphones, and the other man is working beneath the softly whirring blades of two warehouse fans.

And Will asks in a voice barely loud enough for his brother to hear, "You still set on doing this thing?"

"Which thing you talking about?"

"You know which thing."

Harvey looks off into the distance for a moment, his body very still, as if he might be watching a bird soaring off, watching something beautiful fly away from him. "I don't know," he finally says. "I might've cooled off a little." But the longer he gazes into the distance and the longer he stands there with the smell of the delivery truck in his nostrils, the coolness of the refrigerated boxes spreading a numbness to his hands, the more the old tension comes back to him. "Even so . . . yeah. Yeah. I guess I still think something needs to be done."

"You guess or you're sure?" Will asks.

"What'd I just say?"

"Because this is no little thing we're contemplating here."

"So you came up with a plan?"

"The only thing that concerns me is that it might be a little too severe."

"Naw, severe is okay. Severe is good."

With that, Harvey jumps down off the loading dock. He bends close to Will's window, hand to the door. "So what is it we're doing?"

"You want rid of him, right? You want him out of your life?"

"I'd say that's pretty much dead-on, yeah."

"He might take the motorcycle with him when he goes. Might sell it to somebody else, I really don't know."

"Screw the motorcycle."

"Good. Because this isn't about the motorcycle anymore."

"It never was."

Will nods. "It might be good then if I was to, you know, get some of the specifics about what this really is about."

Harvey says without inflection, "You don't need any specifics."

Will studies his brother for a moment. Then, "So okay then. How's tonight work for you?"

"It just so happens I'm free tonight."

"Can you meet me behind the bar at eleven without Jennilee knowing?"

"Eleven o'clock at night? I'll be in bed by then! Jeezus, Will, I have to get up at five-thirty, you know."

"Sorry. I guess I overestimated your resolve in this matter."

"Hey, my resolve is set in concrete. It's just that . . . can't we do this a little earlier?"

"Sure we can. You want to go get some breakfast and *then* break into Kenny's office? That would be, what—right around nine? Maybe we should take Kenny a coffee while we're at it. I can't guarantee we'll be all that effective with him watching us, but hey, at least you'll be awake for it."

"That's what we're going to do? Break into his office?"

"You wanted a plan, I came up with a plan."

"I hope there's a little more to it than that."

Will blows out a breath. "You going to meet us or not?"

"Us? Who the hell is us?"

"Stevie's in on it, too."

"Ah, jeezus. Now I know we'll get caught."

"I had to use him to get something we need, and he wouldn't agree to do it unless he could come along."

"Jeezus. We're all going to end up in jail."

"You know, this is the way it's always been with us, hasn't it? You get some wild hair up your ass and come running to me about it, I lie awake all night trying to figure out how to help you out with it, and next day you're like, 'Oh, I guess it's not so bad after all.'"

"Did I say that?"

"I don't know; did you? Truth is, I don't think you even know what you're saying half the time."

"I can still beat the shit out of you."

"Still? You never could. Not since I was sixteen, anyway."

Harvey tries without success to suppress a smile. He remembers well the time Will first took a swing at him, how after all those years of torment from his big brother, all those knuckle-thumps and punches on the arm, Will, instead of running away this time, threw a short, unexpected punch that bloodied Harvey's lip, then stood there waiting for the rest of the fight, stood his ground like a man, ready to take another beating if necessary. Harvey should have told him then that he was proud of his little brother, glad to see that the boy's balls had finally dropped. But he hadn't. He had sneered, as if the blow stung no worse than a mosquito bite. And then had walked away wordless, still seeing stars.

"Eleven o'clock tonight?" Harvey says.

"Wear dark clothes. And by the way, if you're so much as three minutes late, don't ever come to me again with one of your problems."

"What makes you so eager all of a sudden?"

"Because if I do say so myself, this is a beautiful plan. I'll derive a great deal of personal satisfaction from sitting back and watching all the pieces fall into place."

"And what's the end result going to be?"

"That wild hair up your ass is going to be extricated once and for all."

"Oh yeah? Extricated, huh?"

"And I don't mean just shaved either. I mean plucked. Pulled out by the roots."

"That sounds like it ought to hurt, but I'm getting the feeling I might actually enjoy the experience."

"I expect you will, big brother."

Ten hours later Harvey ladles a plateful of pot roast out of the pressure cooker but doesn't really want any of it. He has had no appetite for a good while now, can't remember the last time he paid enough attention to a meal to actually enjoy it.

Before lifting the lid off the pressure cooker he barely glances at the note Jennilee left on his plate, *Taking Mom to the mall. See you around 9. Love you.* Now he sits in his chair in the living room, faces the TV, the plate balanced on his knees. He stares at his reflection for a while in the blackened screen.

Jennilee coming into the kitchen wakes Harvey out of a dream of hunting, a dream in which he has gotten separated from his father and brothers in the oak woods. He is awakened by a click that, in his dream, is the snapping of a twig, something crashing toward him from behind. He awakes with a start, looks around, momentarily disoriented. Then he sees the kitchen light on, hears Jennilee tearing off a strip of cellophane to stretch over the leftover pot roast, sliding the bowl into the refrigerator. He closes his eyes again before she comes into the living room; he doesn't want to talk just yet, wants the smell of the woods a while longer.

Jennilee stands there looking down at him. Before she goes upstairs she lays an afghan across him, a knitted blanket of a dozen bright colors, one of many her mother made for them. It is an act of tenderness that almost brings his eyes open, almost causes him to look up at her and smile, except that he thinks she smells different now, the odors of food from another house, wine on her breath, and a vague, fleeting fragrance he can identify only as neither his nor her own.

Upstairs, she showers and brushes her teeth, changes into the satiny panties and matching teddy she likes, turns on the ceiling fan, climbs into bed, turns on the TV. He follows her through the sounds she makes, envisions her careful movements, always so feminine and precise. He feels something like hunger in his belly, but maybe it is the nausea again, that strange and hollow hunger.

At ten-forty he mounts the stairs as quietly as he can, wincing with each creaking step. He peeks around the doorjamb, sees her asleep, curled on her side, her back to the flickering images on the screen. The ceiling fan makes a barely audible thumping sound as it spins. By the time he turns away from her he has goose bumps on his arms.

Downstairs he leaves a note on the kitchen table: *Went over to Will's for a beer or two. Love you.* He knows she will not call to check up on him. She never questions his whereabouts.

Harvey walks at a pace he recognizes as too slow to get him to the bar on time. The stifling darkness weighs him down, pulses in the ache of his bones. Here and there a window dully glows with the pale light from a flickering screen. He thinks to himself that when he was a boy, on a night like this the streets would be full of people. Kids chasing fireflies or playing kick the can. Adults scraping back and forth on their porch swings and gliders. Old folks rocking. These days everybody stays inside breathing air blown out of a box while they stare at another box until narcotized enough to sleep.

He ducks into the alley half expecting to find it deserted. They aren't really going to do this thing anyway. They aren't really going to hurt anybody. But then he sees the two silhouettes, odd shapes of gray against the darker gray of the dumpster. Will has unscrewed the 200-watt bulb over the bar's side door, but Harvey can see well enough to distinguish the silhouettes as two men on lawn chairs, and that is when he thinks, *We are really going to do it. Breaking and entering and who knows what else.* And he pushes his sudden heave of disappointment away.

Will and Stevie sit side by side in front of the dumpster. Between them is a duffel bag with a Steelers logo on the side.

"You're ten minutes late," Stevie says, his voice too loud to Harvey's ears, startling in the darkness.

Harvey asks, "What's in the bag?"

Will shines a small flashlight on the duffel bag as Stevie zippers it open and lays out the contents on the pavement. Two cans of neon orange spray paint, a long-handled screwdriver, a loop of new nylon rope still in its plastic bag, three pairs of brown cotton work gloves, five magazines. Stevie spreads the magazines out in a fan and Will plays the beam over them long enough for Harvey to see the glossy photo of a half-naked child on each cover.

Then Will flicks off the flashlight. Stevie repacks the bag. "Let's get in the truck," Will says.

A minute later they crowd into the front seat, Will in the middle with the duffel bag on his lap. Nobody speaks as Stevie starts the engine and heads toward the school at the southern end of town. Then Harvey asks, "Child pornography?"

Stevie snickers. "I had to drive almost fifty miles to get those. Clear to that adult bookstore out by the truck stop on exit forty-one. I was so nervous I thought I was going to piss my pants before I could get back outside."

Harvey looks at Will's face, relaxed and smiling.

Harvey asks, "Who's watching the bar for you?"

"Giffy," Will says, naming one of the regulars, a retired steelworker. "There's nobody in tonight except him and that cousin of his from Butler, the one they call Eight-Ball. I told them I wasn't feeling well and had to get some air for a while. Told them they could draw a couple of free pitchers if they promised not to disturb me."

"What about Lacy?"

"Sleeping the sleep of the innocent."

Harvey nods. "Jennilee, too." His mouth tastes chalky; his throat is tight.

The plan, as Will explains it, is "so simple it's brilliant." They will gain entry through one of the skylights over the cafeteria, then lower themselves the twenty feet by sliding down the rope. They will decorate the walls with sophomoric graffiti and plant the magazines in Kenny's desk. Later, when Harvey is safely at home and Will is behind his bar, Stevie will place an anonymous call to the police, reporting suspicious activity and lights at the school. Will will make certain that his wife does not sleep through the report on the scanner. During the subsequent investigation by the police and Lacy's relentless photo-taking, somebody will be sure to spot the magazines. Within twenty-four hours everyone in town will know about Kenny's secret stash of magazines, the danger he poses to their children. Rumors will fly like scattershot on the first day of turkey season. No wonder Kenny has never married. No wonder he still lives with his mother. The school board will have no option but to hold an inquiry. Kenny will be run out of town on a rail—if he isn't drawn and quartered beforehand.

The plan might be a simple one, but Harvey's head is spinning. "How do we get back out of the school?"

"Same way we got in," Will says.

Harvey shakes his head. "I know for a fact that Stevie can't climb twenty feet *up* a rope."

"Speak for yourself, fat-ass."

"Okay, me, too. I doubt like hell I can do it."

"Then we'll find some other way out," Will says. "We'll open a window. They open from the inside, you know. Every classroom's got them."

"What about janitors?"

Stevie tells him, "Last summer when I helped them tar and gravel the roof, everybody went home by six, didn't show up again until six the next morning. The place is empty for twelve hours."

"You sure we can get in through a skylight?"

"We replaced all the flashing for the roof job, had to take the skylights off to do it. All it takes is a Phillips screwdriver."

"What about security cameras?"

"Only place not covered is the rear wall of the boys' locker room. Cause there aren't any windows there."

"And how are we supposed to climb that wall?" Harvey asks.

Stevie flashes him a grin. "Can't you hear the ladder rattling in the bed?"

Harvey can think of nothing more to say. He wishes he could.

"Satisfied?" Will asks.

Harvey winds down the window and leans toward the rush of air. He says, "I'm not sure I remember the meaning of the word."

*

Will is the first man down the rope, sliding into the coolness, the cafeteria a cavern. At the bottom he stands motionless, catching his breath. He can see reasonably well in the large room, one long wall lined with tall windows overlooking the practice field where, for three years as a boy, he ran wind sprints every August until he thought his lungs would explode.

The familiar smell is unmistakable, Meatloaf Thursday, and for a moment he hears the clamor of a hundred hungry kids all jabbering at once, the scrape of chairs, clack of plastic trays, clink of forks attacking plates.

"Hey!" Harvey whispers from above.

Will aims his flashlight at the heavens, flashes an all-clear.

Harvey comes down an inch at a time, grunting. He loses his grip while still five feet above the tile floor, drops with another grunt and the smack of his tennis shoes. The duffel bag thuds against the floor.

"For chrissakes," Will says.

Harvey blows on his hands. "I forgot to put my gloves on. I got a rope burn."

Stevie surprises both of them by coming down quickly, sliding in full control with one leg wrapped around the rope. Harvey asks him, "When did you get so agile?"

"You should see me on the climbing wall at the Y."

"What the hell are you doing at the YMCA?"

"Tae bo classes every Tuesday night. Lots of tits and asses in spandex."

"Any chance we can get on with this?" Will asks. He picks up the duffel bag and heads for the cafeteria exit. Out the wide doorway and into the hall, turn right past the trophy case, up the four steps, administrative offices on the left, faculty lounge, boys' and girls' restrooms on the right. The hallways are dark but navigable. His eyes have adjusted to the dimness; his memory is flooded with details.

The door to Kenny's office is locked. The glass panel in the door is opaque, rippled and thick. Will says, "We're going to have to pry the hinges off."

But Harvey points to their brother at work four feet away, leaning close to the door that opens into the front office. Stevie has stuck a small suction cup to the clear glass and is now dragging a glass cutter around it in a slow circle.

"He's just one surprise after another," Will whispers.

Stevie smiles but says nothing. Finally he pockets the glass cutter, taps his knuckle around the circle he has cut, wiggles the suction cup until the circle of glass snaps free. Then he inches a gloved hand through the circle, feels for the door lock on the other side, gives it a twist. He swings the door open wide and says to Harvey, "*Now* will you ask around for me over at Jimmy Dean?"

And Harvey says, "I guess maybe I will."

Just inside the front office he sets the duffel bag on the floor, zips it open, reaches inside for the spray paint. He hands one can to Will, extends the other toward Stevie.

"Gimme the magazines," Stevie says. "I'm the one drove to Ohio to buy them, I'm the one should get to plant them."

Harvey considers this for a few moments, then thinks, *What the hell,* and places the stack of magazines in his brother's hands. "Not that it matters," he says, "but why do you really want to go in there?"

Stevie grins. "That was Big-Ass Bole's desk before it was Kenny's, and I've been drinking water and saving up for this all day." Harvey remembers Conrad Bole, too, the pear-shaped guidance counselor who told each of the brothers in turn to forget about college, don't even consider it. He had recommended the army for Harvey, a two-year business school for Will. And he had recommended that Stevie, then in his junior year and a gifted portrait artist, a boy who had covered his bedroom walls with pen-and-ink likenesses of movie stars and famous singers but was too shy to show his work to anyone outside the family, Conrad Bole had recommended that Stevie drop out of school and fill the school's new vacancy for a janitor.

"Have fun," Harvey tells him. He and Will watch as Stevie crosses behind the front desk and makes his way toward the door in the rear of the room. There Stevie pauses, puts a hand on the doorknob, gives it a slow turn. The latch clicks. He swings the door open, turns back to his brothers, gives them a thumbs-up, and swaggers into Kenny's office.

"Piece of cake," Will says.

With their cans of paint he and Harvey scrawl neon orange epithets in three-foot letters on the corridor walls. Will writes *Death To Teachers!* and *School Sucks!* Harvey writes *Fulton sucks dick!* Both men giggle as they wield the cans in looping flourishes. Will paints in an evenhanded script, Harvey in thick, angry letters.

Harvey has finished his first composition and is contemplating his second, trying to envision *Fulton is a pervert!* emblazoned across the tile floor, when he hears Stevie's hoarse whisper. "Hey, Harve! Harvey! You might want to come have a look at this!"

Harvey looks over his shoulder and sees Stevie leaning out the door to Kenny's office. Will asks, "What's wrong?"

And Stevie says, "You're not gonna believe this."

Will is closest to Kenny's office and disappears inside. By the time Harvey crosses the threshold, Will is already coming toward him, hands outstretched to stop Harvey's progress, nearly shouting over his shoulder at Stevie, "Get that shit off there!"

But Stevie, standing behind Kenny's desk, unsure of what to do, looks from the glowing computer monitor to Harvey, and Harvey knows in an instant that he cannot let Will keep him out, and he shoves his brother hard, pushes past him, all but lunges toward the desk.

"I was just going through the drawers," Stevie tells him, his words spilling out in a nervous torrent of self-acquittal, "when I came across one that was locked, and I figured if it was locked there must be something good in there, so I jimmied it open and I noticed this CD stuck clear in the back and I was just curious, you know? I swear I had no idea what was on it till I booted it up."

Harvey grips the back of Kenny's leather chair. All the air has gone out of his lungs. He is aware of nothing Stevie tells him, aware of no natural sounds whatsoever. The air is dead but for a buzzing growing louder and louder in his ears, burrowing deeper, a drill inside his brain.

Tiled across the monitor are the photo files Stevie found on the CD, pictures he opened one by one and arranged neatly, working in a kind of stunned amazement until horror set in, four photos on top and four underneath, all of Harvey's wife, Jennilee, gorgeous but appalling.

It is Will's hand on Harvey's shoulder that starts the fulmination in Harvey's brain. Harvey jerks away and shoves the chair with such force that Kenny's heavy desk is jarred several inches across the thick carpet. The monitor wobbles on its pedestal but doesn't fall, so Harvey seizes it in both hands and rips it into the air, only to have the cable jerk it out of his hands again. It falls onto the edge of the desk, then capsizes to the floor, the glass and plastic housing shattering. The screen crackles and goes black.

Then Harvey seizes the desk itself and, driving hard, he shoves it across the floor, slides it crashing into a wall. Will grabs him by the arm, but again Harvey jerks away, lunges for the door, arms swinging blindly at everything in his way.

Will turns to Stevie now, who has retreated against a wall, eyes wide. "You get that CD," Will tells him, "and everything we brought with us. And I mean *everything!* And then you get the hell out of here."

Stevie nods in response, but Will doesn't see it, he is already in pursuit of his brother.

A shattering of glass—a trash can hurled into the trophy case. Trophies heaved one by one against the cement-block wall. This time Will does not merely take hold of his brother's arm or lay a hand upon his shoulder. This time Will runs at Harvey and tackles him around the waist, drives him well away from the broken glass and ringing metal, slams him against a wall.

"Listen to me!" Will shouts, his face two inches from his brother's. "We have to get out of here, you understand? First we get out, and *then* we kill the son of a bitch!"

Now Harvey faces him, eyes flooded with furious tears. "She told me she got rid of those."

At this Will draws back an inch, puzzled, unsure of what he has heard. Harvey shoves him aside and turns down the hallway, strides furiously toward a door marked EMERGENCY EXIT ONLY.

Will races after him, shouts "No! Come this way!" But Harvey continues on, and when he is close to the exit he kicks the lever bar running across the middle of it and the door pops open and the fire alarm shrieks. Will catches his brother on the run two steps outside the door, grips Harvey's arm just above the elbow, and pulls him along despite Harvey's wriggling to free himself.

But Will cannot let go, cannot surrender his brother to rage. "Run, damn it!" he shouts while the alarm shrieks and echoes down the empty hallways. "Goddammit, Harvey . . . Run!"

They cut across the practice field and through the yard behind an abandoned house. Stevie's pickup is parked on the unlighted street in front of this house, a street lined with small homes in disrepair. They lean against the tailgate, Harvey bent forward toward the bed of the truck, Will watching in the opposite direction. After a few moments Will says, "Listen," and they hold their breaths. In the distance a soft clanking noise, as rhythmic as footsteps. "Go ahead and get in the truck," Will says. "I'll be right back." And he disappears into the darkness.

Will meets Stevie coming across the practice field, the extension ladder hung over one shoulder and clanking with each step. Will snatches the duffel bag from his brother's hand. "I got everything but the rope," Stevie tells him.

"Forget the rope."

"Harvey didn't have his gloves on when he came down it."

"They can't get fingerprints off a freaking rope," Will says. "I'm pretty sure they can't. How could they?"

On the other side of the field, the alarm whines inside the school. Will calculates that the police won't arrive for another three or four minutes. Only one deputy is on duty this late at night, either Ronnie Walters, all two hundred pounds of him and as lugubrious as a black bear in January, or his polar opposite, skinny Chris Landers, the one folks call Barney Fife because he is always patting his pockets, checking for his keys, a nervous talker always fiddling with his tie. In either case the deputy at this hour will be watching TV at the fire station, maybe playing euchre with a couple of volunteers who prefer to spend their nights away from home. Too far from the school to actually hear the siren, they won't be alerted to the break-in until called by the county dispatcher.

They're probably getting the call right now, Will thinks as he and Stevie slide the extension ladder onto the truck bed. "We'll be fine," Will says aloud, and Stevie answers as he heads for the driver's door, "We will if we get the hell out of here."

Four minutes later, Stevie slows to make the turn into the alley beside Will's bar, but Will tells him, "Don't. Just pull over and let us out."

Stevie pulls close to the curb, keeps his foot on the brake. Will slides out and holds the door wide for Harvey, who without a word heads into the alley. "You sure you got everything?" Will asks his younger brother, and Stevie tells him again, "Everything but the rope."

"I'll call you sometime tomorrow," Will says, closes the door as softly as he can, and turns away.

The moment the truck disappears around the corner Will can hear Harvey retching at the end of the alley. Harvey is on his knees beside the dumpster, his face to the wall. Will stands over him, a hand on his brother's back. He can feel the rigidity of Harvey's spine, the way his shoulder blades quiver. Will has never before felt so helpless. Every breath is redolent with dumpster stink.

Harvey climbs to his feet finally, shaking, and allows himself to be steadied by his brother's hand. Will says, "We better get back inside."

Harvey wipes his mouth and nods.

"Wait here by the door. I'll check things out first."

Will walks softly through the kitchen, peeks out behind the bar. Giffy and Eight-Ball are seated at a table facing the big-screen TV, watching a boxing match on ESPN, two Hispanic featherweights slamming away at each other. A pitcher of beer, nearly empty, sits in the middle of the table, accompanied by a couple of bags of potato chips.

Will tiptoes back to the door and ushers Harvey inside. Harvey sneaks around to the front of the bar, slides onto a stool while Will silently lifts two bottles of Schlitz from the cooler, twists off the caps, and hands a bottle to his brother. They settle into position as if they have been there all night.

Overhead, footsteps hurry back and forth. Will knows that Lacy has been awakened from her sleep either by the police scanner or by a telephone call. Now she is throwing on a pair of jeans and a shirt, making sure she has fresh batteries for her digital camera, sitting on the bed to tie her shoelaces. It isn't long before Will hears the quick patter of her footsteps on the back steps, then coming through the kitchen. When she appears on the threshold to the bar, Will asks, "Where's the fire tonight?"

She digs around in a cooler for the coldest bottle of Coke. "Break-in over at the high school."

"Kids," Will says, and shakes his head. "They bitch about having to be there, and then what do they do but break back in over summer vacation."

Harvey stares at the bottle in his hand.

"Molly still asleep?" Will asks.

"She was thirty seconds ago." Lacy gives him a peck on the cheek. "I shouldn't be long."

"Take a lot of pictures," Will says.

"I always do."

"And hey."

She turns at the door. He points to the front of her blouse, sleeveless yellow cotton with a rounded collar. She looks down, sees that it is buttoned incorrectly, one side of the shirt higher than the other.

"Geez," she mutters as she yanks open the door, unbuttoning on the run.

Now Will notices that Giffy is looking his way. Will says, "Anything you fellas need back there?"

"Where the hell did you two come from?"

"Been here quite a while, Giff. Not that you two would've noticed, drinking up all my profits the way you've been doing."

Giffy grins. "These two little Cuban guys are pretty good. They're pounding the shit out of each other."

"We've been watching," Will tells him. "My money's on the one in red trunks."

At that moment the boxer in red trunks, Morales, having driven his opponent into a corner, delivers a mad flurry of punches to the midsection, then caps it with an unexpected hook to the head. The referee shoves the two boxers apart and gets in between them, pushing Morales back. His opponent collapses against the ropes just as the bell signals the end of round seven.

"I don't think I'm going to take that bet," Giffy says.

Twenty minutes later, Will and Harvey are alone inside the bar. Will thinks of Molly asleep upstairs, dreaming sweet dreams. Dreaming of bright possibilities. He wishes he could hand them to her on a platter, pave her path with the softest of carpets, remove every thorn from every rose she will ever pluck. He feels very tired suddenly with the knowledge that he can do none of that for her, can never shield her from disappointments or failure, can offer her nothing more than his own helpless love.

He gazes down at Harvey then, only forty-three years old. He looks ancient sitting there. He looks beaten.

"What can I get for you?" Will asks.

"We should have taken that CD."

"I'm pretty sure Stevie grabbed it."

"You think he did?"

"I'm pretty sure of it."

"Christ, I hope so."

Will leans back against the cash register, the hard metal edge across his spine. The beer tastes bitter this late at night, it sours in his stomach. He thinks he can hear a police siren across town, but he isn't certain, it might be nothing more than the residue of the school's alarm still ringing in his brain. He thinks about locking the front door but knows that nobody will be coming in anyway. He thinks of several things he might say to his brother, but he doesn't say any of them because what good would they do, clumsy phrases, useless; there is no magic in words.

It is Harvey who breaks the silence. "The two of us were over at the Ramada one night," he says. He picks at the label on his beer bottle, tears off tiny pieces and leaves them lying on the bar. He speaks haltingly, in no hurry to hear this or to be heard.

"This was just a month or so after we'd gotten engaged. We were dancing, drinking, having fun. And then this band-geek friend of Kenny's, he comes over and keeps trying to drag Jennilee out on the dance floor. He's so shitfaced he can barely stand up. She sees I'm getting kind of hot about it so she excuses herself and goes off to the ladies' room. But the guy still won't leave. Suddenly I'm his best buddy in the whole damn world and he's telling me how she's got the nicest body he's ever laid eyes on, all that kind of crap. I'm just about ready to deck the guy when he up and asks me if Kenny's still got those nude photos of her he had in college."

"Jeezus," Will says.

"I just went cold."

"So . . . what happened then?"

"Soon as Jennilee came back, I dragged her outside. We sat in the car and . . ." He tears the last of his label free. Scratches a fingernail over the rough smear of glue.

"At first she denied it," he says. "Claimed she didn't know what the hell I was talking about. So I threatened to haul that geek in the bar outside there with us and beat the truth out of him. Funny, but she didn't seem to mind that idea. So then I said, 'No, no, on second thought I think there's somebody else who needs it even more.' So I started the engine and peeled out of the parking lot. I must've laid rubber for fifty yards down the road, I was so pissed."

"The somebody else meaning Kenny."

"She made it sound like it was all so innocent, you know? Like something brothers and sisters do all the time. Just fooling around, she called it. She'd let him take pictures and maybe touch her once in a while, but she swore up and down that it never went any further than that." He looks at his bottle as if he is considering taking a drink, then changes his mind, too weary to raise it to his lips.

"So I drove her over to Kenny's and told her either she went in and got those pictures or I did. And if it was me, I was more than likely to turn her into an only child."

Will waits for the rest.

"She used the cigarette lighter from the car and burned them right there along the curb. Then she used her bare hand to sweep the ashes down into the sewer drain."

And you probably thought that was touching, didn't you? Will thinks. *Jennilee's beautiful, perfect hand sweeping away the ashes. You poor helpless son of a bitch.*

Will says nothing for a while. Then, "So now what?"

"Now?" Harvey asks, and looks up finally, his eyes as fierce as embers. "Now I kill him whether she wants me to or not. And this time *nobody* is going to stop me."

"Hell, brother," Will tells him. "I'm not going to stop you. I'm going to load the revolver and drive the getaway car."

Harvey smiles, though there is not a trace of happiness in his expression. He holds out a hand to Will. Will takes it, grips it hard.

"But first we wait," Will says.

Harvey jerks his hand away. "Wait? Wait for what?"

We wait for you to cool down, Will thinks. He says, "News gets out about those magazines in Kenny's drawer, a lot of people around here are going to want his hide."

"Yeah? So?"

"So in the meantime, you don't say a word about any of this to Jennilee. We can't say a word to anybody. You think you can do that?"

"The same goes for you and Stevie, you know."

"It goes for all of us. What we have to do is just stand back and let the shit fly on its own. Hell, we might wait a year before we do anything. Because by then, at the least Kenny will have lost his job and be living somewhere else. Us, we're just going on with our lives same as always. Until that one night, a long time from now, when we pay Kenny a long overdue visit."

Harvey nurses his beer, turns the bottle slowly in his hands. The glass is warm now, sticky against his skin.

Will wishes his brother would say something more, offer his hand again, some affirmation. Instead, Harvey sets his bottle down. He slides his stool away from the bar. He stands.

Will asks him, "Where you going?"

"I'm not feeling so hot. I think I'll call it a night."

"Have a ginger ale. It'll settle your stomach."

"I guess not."

"At least stay until Lacy gets back. We can quiz her on how things went."

But Harvey is already headed for the door. "I'll talk to you tomorrow," he says.

Out on the street, halfway through town, Harvey hears a dog barking somewhere. A dog on a chain, he thinks. Poor bastard, what a life that must be, even for a dog. Chained up and howling at distant sounds, wanting to chase after them, snap his tether, revert to the dog he should have been, a hunter, meat-eater, not some neutered pseudo-dog grateful for an occasional pat on the head and a bowl of dry kibble.

This heat, he thinks, *is something strange. It's like a steam bath out here.* Every breath is a heavy one, a soggy lump of air.

Yet he feels chilled at his core. Every now and then a shiver wracks through him, a quick icy rattle up and down his spine. His body aches with the hot, heavy drag of the heat, but he can't stop the chills from rattling through him.

He approaches the high school from the long front drive, walks toward the white illumination of the lights in the windows, the lobby lit up like a jack-o'-lantern, a big brick Halloween pumpkin on a steamy August night. He counts four vehicles lined up around the circular drive. A patrol car, Lacy's Subaru, Kenny's Sebring, and a red Jeep Wrangler. *Must be the janitor's,* he thinks.

He cuts across the circle of grass in front of the school, drags a hand over the flagpole. The metal is cold, flaked with rust. No flag flapping in the breeze, not the slightest breath of wind. He pauses there beside the flagpole and looks at the front entrance, can almost hear the sounds the kids make piling out of the buses every morning, the yips and laughs and moans like the ones he used to make.

If I had any kids, he wonders, *would they be happy here? Would they be popular and smart?*

I was never smart, he tells himself. *I got passing grades, but I was never very smart.*

From twenty yards away he can see through the window of Kenny's office, can see Lacy with her back to him in there, bent toward something with her camera in hand. Kenny is there beside her, standing in profile, watching. Half a minute later, Deputy Walters comes into the room, stands close to Kenny and tells him something, finger pointing toward the hall.

Harvey watches it all as if it is a television show with the sound turned off. They are just characters in a show, nothing more. Superintendent Fulton, good-looking and well dressed even at midnight, khakis and a red polo shirt, every hair in place. Lacy the photographer, the girl next door, cute as Doris Day. And Deputy Walters, not the sharpest tool in the shed but wholly likable, self-deprecating, constantly trying to lose a few pounds but never able to resist just one more Big Mac, one more order of fries.

The show leaves Harvey cold and he tires of watching it. No drama, no comedy. He is not involved in any of it but feels as distant from it as a chained dog must feel when it howls at the moon. He turns his back to the school and starts down the long drive, past the darkened homes of people he knows, the lives he has no involvement in, the secrets they hide.

He has been standing at the corner for maybe fifteen minutes, maybe more, when the lawn directly across the street is lit up by a car's headlights. The car comes up behind him, slows, stops. Lacy leans toward the open passenger window and asks, "You lost?"

Harvey turns to look at her. He smiles. Wonders if she can see his coldness inside, if she can feel it radiating off his flesh, the chill off refrigerated meat. "Just thought I'd walk over before heading home, see what all the fuss is about."

"Some kids broke in and trashed the place. Spray-painted the walls, tore up Kenny's office pretty good."

Harvey makes a sound that is supposed to be a laugh. "Maybe Kenny did it himself. You know how he loves to redecorate."

Lacy slips the gearshift into park, then slides the whole way across the seat. "You still pissed at him?" she asks. "I mean, earlier, you were mad enough to kill him, you said."

"Yeah, well, you know how I get. Lucky for me, Will talked me out of it. Even so . . . I can't honestly say I'm sorry for any trouble that comes Kenny's way."

She nods. "I can see why a person wouldn't like him."

"Oh yeah? You mean you're somehow able to resist his legendary charm?"

"He gives me the creeps," she says. "He's one of those touchy-feely guys, you know? Always has to have his hand on you during a conversation. Ten minutes with him and I feel like I've been licked all over with a long, wet tongue."

Harvey smiles, pleased with her analogy. "So," he asks, "you find anything interesting?"

"On the kids, you mean? No, nothing. I think Ronnie Walters was kind of hoping they had autographed their graffiti, but no such luck."

Harvey wonders how deeply he should probe, whether any of it matters anyway.

"Apparently we're not the only ones Kenny rubs the wrong way," she tells him.

"How's that?"

"Those kids planted a stack of porno magazines in Kenny's desk. Kiddie porn."

"Seriously?"

"Whoever they are, those kids must really have it out for him."

"I guess so." Harvey stands there looking in at Lacy. He feels so much affection for her, his brother's wife. He wishes he could climb in beside her and sit with her and tell her everything. Wishes he had had the good sense to marry a woman like Lacy, wishes he could fall asleep every night with a woman like Lacy in his arms. Knows it would change everything. Knows he would be a different man.

"So who's to say those aren't really Kenny's magazines?" he asks. "What I mean is, how do you know for sure the kids put them there?"

"It was just too obvious, is all. They even left the drawer hanging open so we'd be able to see inside. They just weren't very smart about it. I mean, if they were, they never would have broken in in the first place, am I right?"

"I've never known you to be wrong," he tells her. He would like to throw up again, would welcome the relief, but he knows he is too empty for that now, there is nothing left inside.

"You get some pictures of them, too?" he asks, trying to sound offhanded about it. "The magazines, I mean."

"And give the kids what they want? Naw, Ronnie confiscated them. Said there might be some way to track them down, find out who put them there."

Harvey nods, a vague smile on his lips, a twist of gathering pain.

"So you want a ride home or what?" Lacy asks.

"Thanks anyway," he tells her, and pulls back from the window. "I had a couple beers with Will and now I feel half sick to my stomach. I'm going to try to walk it off."

"It's a good night for walking, I guess. Better than for sleeping, anyway."

"That's what I figure," he says.

When she pulls away he feels like crying, though he isn't sure why. Something about the way the red taillights look as they shrink smaller and smaller. Something about the vast darkness ahead.

Will sits alone in the darkened bar with the doors locked and the television off. He is ashamed of his stupidity and ashamed that he has involved Stevie and Harvey in it. Ashamed of wanting something that could never be his. He would settle now for having things the way they used to be, back when his mother and father were still alive. Back in the innocent times. The first day of buck season, for example, between Thanksgiving and Christmas, one of the holiest of days.

Because hunting had never been about violence, not as far as Will was concerned. It had been about the tenderness of the woods and of walking tenderly through them with his brothers and father, the way the sun rose on naked trees limned with ice or hoary with frost, of black branches looking diamond-encrusted, the sunlight as soft as candlelight, the woods as hushed as a murmured prayer. And it had been about that almost sacred moment of coming upon a magnificent animal in the heart of those woods bathed in shafted sunlight and shadow, the breathless stillness of seeing one another in that sudden sanctified moment, hunter and hunted, the two connected by the invisible thread of the bullet about to fly.

Nor had he ever felt violence in the ritual of gutting and skin-ning, nor later around the camp stove with their bellies full, mouths pleasantly numbed by the whiskey they sipped. All this had never seemed violent to him but an ancestral ceremony that strengthened and cleansed him for the other part of his life, the tedium and labor.

But to Will all that seems a long time ago now. The woods are smaller now, and there are more hunters in them. Even deep in the woods, eighteen-wheelers rumbling along the highway can be heard. The stillness and the tenderness are gone now, Will thinks. The world is not a tender place.

Harvey has to pound on the door of his brother's trailer for three solid minutes before Stevie finally appears behind a curtained win-dow, peeking out. Then the door comes open and Stevie whispers, "Jeezus. I thought you were the police."

Harvey pushes past him and goes inside. The place looks fairly clean for a change, not the way it usually looks, as if a couple of suitcases and a refrigerator had exploded. Harvey goes straight to the computer on the kitchen table, says before he gets there, "I want that CD you have."

"It's in here," Stevie tells him, and opens the hallway closet, bends down, reaches inside one of his work boots. He takes the disk in its jewel case to Harvey, who is seated at the kitchen table now, facing Stevie's computer, a six-year-old IBM he bought at a yard sale for $75.

Harvey sits there staring at the jewel case for half a minute. Then he hands it back to his brother. "Plug this thing in for me."

"Ahh, I don't know if I oughta be looking at those again—"

"Who asked you to look at them in the first place? Just plug it in and get it started for me."

Stevie inserts the disk and opens the untitled folder. Icons for fourteen consecutively numbered files appear. Stevie explains how to open each of the files separately, how to line them up like play-ing cards across the screen.

Then he turns toward the living room before Harvey can open the first file, and he stands there at the window, looking out into the darkness. Harvey knows that this modesty is a farce, that Stevie has certainly looked at each of the photos already, has probably made a secret copy of the CD for himself. Harvey knows all this, but he doesn't care. He is very nearly beyond all caring now, except for one last thing.

Harvey opens a half-dozen files in a row, studies each one carefully. He tells himself that he is cold to them, he doesn't care anymore. He gazes more intently at one photo in particular, leans closer to the screen. He asks, "Is there any way to make this picture bigger?"

Stevie wants to turn away from the window but doesn't. "You mean the whole thing?"

"The whole thing, parts of it, I don't care. I just need it bigger."

"There's a little icon up in the toolbar, up along the top of the screen, looks like a magnifying glass. You see it?"

"Okay. Now what?"

"Click on that once. Now go down to the picture and click on it."

Harvey clicks on Jennilee's hand. He clicks a second time, makes the image larger still. Finally he can see her wedding band in the enlargement, not just a golden glow on her finger anymore, not a trick of the light.

Calmly, too calmly, he asks, "How do I turn this thing off?"

"Just click on the little *X* in the corner of each picture."

Harvey closes each picture. His hands are off the mouse now, palms flat on his knees. He knows that if he lets his eyes close now, as they want to, he could drift away on the emptiness he feels, undulate down into the center of it like a leaf falling from a high branch, a leaf yellow and dead, a wasted thing.

Stevie comes over to the computer and ejects the disk. Quietly he places it in the jewel case and quietly closes the lid. Harvey looks up at him and holds out his hand.

Harvey comes quietly into his bedroom. It is at once familiar and foreign to him, as if he has been away a very long time. The room seems smaller than he remembers it, and parts of it are ugly now. Jennilee has fallen asleep with the reading light on, a magazine face-down on the bedspread, the television on with the volume turned low. A part of him wonders what magazine it is, what she might have chosen to divert her thoughts at a time like this. On the back cover is an advertisement for Absolut vodka. He thinks about coming forward off the threshold and turning the magazine over, but he does not move.

Jennilee sleeps on her side, her knees drawn up. She is wearing only panties and a matching teddy, eggshell white. The ceiling fan turns. He can feel the slightest of breezes across his face. He can smell the refrigerated air from the vents in the walls.

She awakes with a start, though he has made not a sound. Her head jerks up off the pillow, legs straighten. For a moment she lies there blinking at the wall. Then she turns her head slightly, sees him there in the doorway. She says nothing. She tries out a smile.

Harvey tells her, "There was a break-in at the school tonight."

She tries to make her voice sound sleepy, though she is wide awake. "I know, Kenny called me. A bunch of kids, apparently."

"He sure didn't waste any time letting you know."

She isn't sure how to respond to this, decides that the best answer is none at all. She reaches for the sheet, draws a corner of it over her thighs.

He says, "If you're cold, why do you have the fan and air conditioning on?"

She rubs a hand over the goose bumps on her arm. "I'm just keyed up, is all. Kenny was all worked up when he called and, I don't know . . ."

"Like brother, like sister," Harvey says, and he immediately regrets it, regrets that the emptiness he had felt is slipping away with those words, regrets that silence as he now understands it is impossible, the silence of not thinking or feeling, of not doing or being.

Jennilee lays a hand on the empty side of the bed. "You could come join me and help me get my mind off things. We could just lie here and talk a while. Remember when we used to do that?"

"I don't remember when you ever had the time to. Not with me, anyway." The emptiness has left him quickly, rushed out of him like blood from a gaping wound.

"Come on," she says, a supplicant now, seductively pleading. "Come get me warm."

He puts a hand to the wall switch and shuts off the ceiling fan. Looks at her a last time before turning away.

She calls to him. "You want me to come down and watch TV with you a while?"

He squeezes his eyes shut, goes down the stairs with eyes closed, wanting blindness but shutting out nothing, all images clear inside his head as his fingers slide down the polished rail.

*

Harvey clings to the shadows as he walks close to the side of Kenny's house. He peers into one window after another, all rooms dark. He wonders which of the rooms belongs to Kenny, which to Kenny's mother. He acknowledges a kind of affection for Kenny's mother, Pauline, though he hasn't spoken to her for several months now, not since the homecoming game last fall when he and Jennilee sat with her in the bleachers. He has always liked Pauline, thought her very attractive when he was a boy, though she was always on the plump side and even more so now. He remembers all the late nights when he and Kenny had stumbled in, trying without success to conceal their drunkenness, and she would come padding into the kitchen in robe and slippers, chide them for their behavior even as she was pouring out a glass of wine for herself, and soon she would have a skillet full of eggs and sausages ready, a mountain of toast. On the other hand, he remembers, too, the disappointment on Pauline's face when he and Jennilee turned away from the minister at the front of the church, turned to face friends and family for the first time as husband and wife. Pauline's frown was fleeting, yes, a small pout of her lips. But Harvey had noticed it. He never resented her for it, though. He understood her disappointment. Understood that she wanted and deserved someone better for her daughter, her perfect flower of a child.

Eventually Harvey crosses to the rear of the house, and there he sees a soft light glowing at ground level, bends low and peers through the small window and into the basement game room. Kenny is sitting on the edge of the brown leather sofa, a drink in hand, the television on. With his free hand Kenny is bouncing a small blue ball, a racquetball, bouncing it up and down on the parquet tile floor. Too anxious to sit still. Haunted by possibilities. He takes a drink and then bounces the ball four or five times in a row, a few seconds between each bounce. Then another drink. Meanwhile he stares at the television.

Harvey lets himself into the house using the key from Jennilee's purse. The key doesn't work on the front door, but it works on the back. He enters into the pantry. Then three paces to the kitchen. Every creaking step makes him wince. He spots the knife block atop the refrigerator, is stopped by the sight of it, nine blades within easy reach. He thinks about wrapping his fingers around one of those black handles. It would be easy, just like a hunting knife. Though not the same at all.

Then Kenny's voice calls up through the open basement door. "I thought you were asleep already! You want me to get you something?"

Kenny waits for an answer, hears nothing. He takes another sip from his drink, half a glass of scotch and a few ice cubes that have nearly melted, but still the scotch burns pleasantly going down, single malt, the good stuff, he only drinks the good stuff.

He calls out again. "You looking for a Valium or what, Mom?"

A moment later Harvey comes down the last step and appears around the corner. Kenny sucks in a sudden breath at the sight of him, jerks back so abruptly that some of his drink splashes onto his slacks.

Harvey says, "Looks like maybe you're the one could use the Valium."

"Harvey, geez, I thought you were . . ."

Harvey approaches him slowly. "You thought I was what—your friend? Is that what you thought?"

Kenny's smile is pale and thin. Even as he sits there smiling, he is casting about with his eyes, looking for something with which to defend himself. Harvey has the only exit blocked and Harvey is a strong man, a man who has used his muscles all his life, not like Kenny, who, though he has managed to keep his weight down, is soft inside and out, has always been soft, always needed some-body else to take the first risk, always needed to feed off somebody else's boldness and daring, a weak man on his own—this he knows about himself.

Harvey has the only exit blocked, and the billiard table to Ken-ny's right is too far away, the rack of cues on the farthest wall. To Kenny's left, just a yard away, is the fireplace with its andirons and tools, the poker and the shovel and the fireplace brush, none ever used, never dirtied by ashes because the logs in the fireplace are made of ceramic, they glow but never burn. And the mantel is lined with Kenny's and Jennilee's trophies, hers for tennis, his for debate and State Band. He needs to work his way over there, he thinks. Needs to get something in his hands.

Kenny lets the rubber ball drop. It bounces three times, rolls across the floor. He holds up his empty hand, palm out, a gesture of surrender as he slowly rises to his feet. "If this were the middle of the day, Harvey, I wouldn't mind you coming into my house without knocking. But seeing as how it's, what, nearly twenty minutes after one in the morning—"

"Stand still," Harvey tells him.

Kenny forces a smile. "I'm not going anywhere."

"I saw that same smile on Jennilee not long ago." And with that Harvey reaches toward his back pocket.

Kenny doesn't wait to see what kind of weapon Harvey will produce, revolver or knife. He knows Harvey's anger well, has in fact been waiting for it all these years, has somehow known it would come to this. Kenny doesn't wait but lunges in a ducking sidestep toward the fireplace, tossing his drink at Harvey so that he can seize the set of fireplace tools in both hands, can pivot and swing them in a heaving arc at Harvey's face. Kenny holds on to only the gold-handled shovel, letting everything else fly.

Harvey spins away, covers his face. The tools sail past him to bang against the wall, but the heavy metal base of the holder catches him in the chest, a sharp corner stabbing in hard, knocking him breathless. The thing he had been holding in his hand, the weapon he had reached for earlier, now falls clattering to the floor. A plastic jewel case with a disk inside. The jewel case pops open, the lid breaks off.

A part of Kenny recognizes the object on the floor, but he is already in motion and cannot stop himself, cannot freeze the movement of the shovel in his hand, cannot stop its momentum. The flat side of the shovel slams against the side of Harvey's head.

Harvey staggers and goes down on one knee, everything black and filled with streaking white sparks. With one arm twisted over his head he waits for another blow, but it does not come. He hears Kenny's huffing breath, turns his head just enough to look at him, sees him standing there with the little shovel raised like a baseball bat, Kenny poised like a boy ready to step out of the batter's box, afraid of the speeding pitch, too timid to swing.

And in that moment when Harvey turns his dazed eyes on Kenny, in that moment when the clouds in Harvey's eyes seem suddenly to ignite, that moment when his face goes scarlet with rage, in that moment Kenny suddenly understands the error of his fear and puts his arms in motion again.

But Harvey dives in under the swing and drives forward, plunges forward with all his might. Together he and Kenny go back over the arm of the leather sofa, twisting as they fall. With Harvey beneath him, Kenny attempts to lift himself high enough that he can take another swing with the shovel, but Harvey seizes him by the wrist, yanks the shovel free, and, holding it close to the blade, slams it against the back of Kenny's skull.

Kenny falls away from him, falls onto his hands and knees and crawls toward the doorway. But Harvey stands over him now and brings the shovel down again. Long after Kenny's arms have collapsed beneath him and his body is still, Harvey continues to swing. Until finally the blade breaks off and Harvey is left holding only the handle itself, gold-plated and shining wet with blood, slippery in his hands.

Harvey stands over him and does not understand what has happened here. The room is suffocatingly warm and his lungs burn with every breath. His pulse is a hammer inside his head and his heart hammers at his chest. In the distance he hears the television playing, a late-night talk show, canned laughter and a strain of music.

Harvey drops to his knees beside Kenny and he thinks he hears a woman screaming in the distance, thinks he hears a dog barking. He thinks he would like to turn that God-awful television off once and for all, would like to put his fist through the screen. He thinks about Will and wishes Will were here to explain all of this to him, wishes he had the strength to find a telephone and to dial the numbers.

Even when he looks up and sees Kenny's mother coming toward him, sees at once the horror in her eyes and the small dog yipping behind her, cowering at her heels, even as he sees her stoop to pick up the fireplace poker, he is moving away from all this, he is walking away in his own mind, walking down the street in front of Will's place, heading for the front door, going inside to have a beer with his brother.

And everything else that happens is the work of somebody else, a man he does not know. Harvey watches it all as if from across the street, as if watching a television screen through a shop window. While now and then a pleasant scent drifts by. The smell of the bakery across the street from Will's place, of doughnuts and fresh bread. He is able to enjoy the fragrance in a detached kind of way, the way a man who doesn't eat might enjoy it, with longing and regret, man who has never tasted sweetness because he has no mouth, no tongue, no stomach for this life.

And when Harvey leaves Kenny's house a quarter of an hour later, the woman is no longer screaming and the dog has stopped barking. He has turned the television off. A bone is broken just below his left wrist where he raised it to block the poker that the woman was swinging at his face, and the flesh is swollen and pulsing, the splintered bone is pulsing, too. Otherwise, as he walks back through town, he is as still inside as the night itself, and the only thought he will permit himself is that he wishes Will's place were still open, he could really use a cold one now.

He requires no lights in order to see his dark rooms clearly; the details are emblazoned on his mind. The kitchen with its painted cupboards, the noisy icemaker in the refrigerator. The living room with the rose-colored sofa Jennilee begged him to let her buy, nearly $2,000, he does not regret the expense anymore, regrets nothing. His recliner facing the television set, the gun cabinet against the rear wall, all those seasons of hunting deer and turkey with his father and brothers, and then just his brothers. Even as he eases himself onto his recliner he can recall the scent of autumn leaves kicked up beneath his boots, can recall the fragrance of pine woods in those minutes before dawn when the fog is lifting and the air is chill. It all comes back to him now, all the happy moments unfettered by desire, because he knows it is all he has left now, and that it is all slipping away from him this night, it is nearly out of reach already.

He is not startled when the light flares on overhead. There is an inevitability to revelation, too. Just as there is to Jennilee's sharp intake of breath at the sight of him. He can only imagine how he must look to her, as if he has dipped his head in blood, his torn shirt splattered with it and sticking to his chest. He smiles to tell her it's not as bad as it looks. The pain is there but far away.

"My God!" she says, and comes as near as the television set, no closer. "What happened to you?"

He lifts up the compact disk he has been holding, shows it to her. Then, with a tired flick of his wrist, he sails it toward her feet. She stares down at it, a perfect roundness, chromium-bright, smeared with bloody fingerprints. Tears slide down her cheeks.

She shakes her head, wanting to push away the inevitable, deny the obvious.

Her voice is hoarse and weak. He is surprised by its plaintiveness. "Did you hurt him?" she wants to know. "Harvey, please, please. Please tell me you didn't hurt him."

He has no desire to move, to say anything. But he knows she will keep talking if he does not speak. And so he tells her, "He isn't hurt anymore."

Her response is an explosion, too loud, he feels it deep inside his head. "What did you do to him?" she screams. *What did you do?*"

His voice in comparison is as placid as sleep. "What would any man do?"

Her knees buckle, she drops to her knees, she clings to the side of the television cabinet. Her sobs are wails as sharp as glass.

Only now does it dawn on him that she is still wearing only her panties and teddy, that she looks so inelegant there, naked knees spread apart. The soles of her feet are dirty.

She sobs, hyperventilating, forehead against the cabinet, until a thought occurs to her, and she climbs to her feet, drags herself up, and then crosses to the telephone on the end table beside the sofa, punches in the seven numbers, listens to the repetitious ring.

He can hear the ringing too, hollow and distant. How long is she going to stand there listening?

"There's nobody to answer it," he tells her. He is about to say, *Not even the dog,* but she responds with a prolonged scream of "Nooo!" and flings herself at him, pulling the phone off the end table. She swings the receiver at him again and again, screaming all the while. He sits with arms wrapped around his head but does nothing else to defend himself, only feels the distant blows and the distant pain and thinks, as if he is watching from far away, *You're just like your mother.*

She stops screaming finally, is too breathless to continue, and leans away from him, moaning, a kind of whimpering sound he has never before heard.

He lifts his eyes to hers, can scarcely recognize her now. His voice is whisper-soft. "Tell me the truth, Jennilee. It was never just the pictures, was it?"

She is as quick as a snake, lunges forward and spits in his face, three times before his hand comes up and slaps her hard, dropping her to the floor, where she curls into a fetal position and again begins to sob. He had not known he was going to slap her, never intended to do so.

Ten or fifteen seconds pass, neither knows how long. Harvey has his eyes closed now, has settled back in his chair. Jennilee climbs to her feet slowly, and with cautious glances to see if he is watching, she makes her way to the gun cabinet. She expects him to jump up and stop her as she feels for the key atop the cabinet, but he never stirs. Eventually she finds the key, inserts it in the lock, pulls open the door.

She moves more quickly now, in a hurry before he looks her way. She pulls a shotgun off the wooden rack, reaches into a box of shells, knocks the box over, fumbles for a shell, tries to break the shotgun open so as to insert the shell the way Harvey taught her the one time he took her turkey hunting, the time she thought it might be fun that year they were married, except it wasn't fun, it was boring, and after an hour he drove her home and she never accepted his invitation again.

But this shotgun will not break open the way the other one did and she turns it in her hands, wild with fear because Harvey has opened his eyes and is watching her now, he is staring at her reflection on the TV's black screen.

And now he is rising from his chair, pushing himself up and coming toward her, moving as if under water, thick and warm and heavy.

When he is a step away, she turns the shotgun around and, holding it by the barrel, swings the heavy stock at his head, but he catches it easily and with one pull wrenches the shotgun from her hands.

He reaches toward the spilled shells and picks up three. Slides one into the magazine, and then a second. "This is a twelve-gauge Winchester," he tells her. Snaps open the breech and slides a third shell directly into the barrel. "It loads like this." He pushes a tiny lever and the breech door snaps shut.

He holds the shotgun in both hands now, looks at her as she shrinks away from him. "The safety is off," he tells her, and hands the weapon to her. For a moment she does not comprehend. Then she reaches out, jerks the shotgun from his hands. He returns to his chair and eases himself down.

He would like to close his eyes now, but he has one more thing to say. And soon she crosses to stand in front of him. She holds the shotgun's stock tight against her shoulder, the way he taught her. He does not look at her but at her reflection on the television screen, Jennilee in miniature, shrunken by the truth.

"It's nice," he says, and she says, "What is?"

"That I don't want you anymore." He looks up at her and smiles. She thinks the gunshot is the loudest sound she has ever heard.

And after a while she lays the shotgun across the arms of his chair. She goes to the kitchen, trembling; the entire house is trembling, a frozen place, so cold. And soon she returns, dragging a kitchen chair, which she pulls in front of his. She sits facing him with her bare feet straddling his legs, their knees touching. She leans forward and picks up the shotgun, ejects the empty shell, rams another one home. Then she wedges the shotgun's stock into Harvey's crotch, rests the barrel between her breasts, holds it there with her left hand. Now she leans toward Harvey, bends toward him as the barrel pushes hard against her chest and her right hand reaches out, hand and fingers stretching. Finally she finds the trigger, that scimitar moon of metal. And this time she hears no sound at all.

A week, two weeks, sixteen days later, or so Will has been told. Long enough that life has resumed much of its routine. But soon enough that even routine seems unreal. It is a morning in September, the streets are quiet, the rumbling school buses have completed their routes. Will has kissed Molly and Lacy and has watched them go and now he is standing in the bar's open doorway, a broom in hand. He can smell the bakery across the street, a sweetness in the air, leaden in his stomach.

He has swept out the two wide rooms of his bar, and now he doesn't know what to do with himself. All the glasses are washed and all the shelves are stocked. The bar will not open for business for another hour and a half, and Will can think of nothing left to do until that time. So he stands there in the open doorway with a broom in his hand. He thinks about sweeping the sidewalk in front of his bar. It is an exercise in futility, he knows. But sometimes that is all a man is given.

He has been sweeping for ten minutes or so when he hears the low growl of a motorcycle, sees it coming toward him down the street. He does not recognize Deputy Landers until the man is just a block away; he looks too tall for the machine, all elbows and knees. A few seconds later the deputy pulls to the curb in front of Will, he shuts off the motorcycle, he takes the key from the ignition. He climbs off finally, nods to himself, crosses to Will, holds out the key.

"Sheriff thought it would be safer here with you than in Kenny's garage. Somebody broke a window out of the house last night. Kids, probably."

Will stares at the key.

"I know it's only been a couple of weeks, but . . . sheriff asked me to remind you that you need to hire somebody to get your brother's place cleaned up. And he says he hopes you don't mind, but you oughta take care of Kenny's place, too. The way the sheriff figures it, you're going to end up with both places more than likely. Jennilee being the beneficiary, and her married to your brother and all. It's all fairly convoluted from what I hear, but the lawyers will straighten it out, I wouldn't worry if I was you. You're going to end up with Kenny's place, too, when it's all said and done, just you wait and see. One house for you and one for Stevie, that's the way I figure it. Get him out of that trailer of his finally. I'll bet he won't be complaining about that."

The deputy continues on like this for a while, none of it registering with Will except as a kind of buzzing drone, a drill in his ear. *This is the deputy who never shuts up,* he tells himself. *The other one . . . who's the other one? What's his name? It's Ronnie Walters,* he reminds himself, though he has known both men all their lives. Ronnie Walters. A man as close-mouthed as God himself.

Finally Deputy Landers starts to walk away. But as he does so he crosses once more to the motorcycle, runs his hand over the gas tank, trails his hand over the leather seat. "Somebody sure did a great job of restoring this beauty," he says. "Still rides good, too. Be sure and let me know if you decide to sell it."

Will isn't aware of when the deputy stops talking and moves away. His next awareness of the deputy is when Will looks up and sees him walking briskly toward the center of town, already maybe fifty feet away, as if time has moved in a fragmented leap, lurching over moments irretrievable.

This is what it's like, Will tells himself, *when everything is broken.*

He feels the key in one hand and the broom handle in the other. He doesn't know what to do with either one of them. He should go inside, maybe. Except that he doesn't want to go inside. He doesn't want to go or be anywhere.

He looks at the motorcycle parked at the curb, its chrome and painted surfaces waxed and buffed to a glassy sheen, and reflected on the side of the shiny gas tank is the image of an odd-looking man looking back at Will, a man reduced to the size of a bird, his body bent to fit the curve of the tank, warped and shrunken and compacted by the weight of his own weariness, a weariness that glitters in his eyes like splinters of chrome, eyes that are asking for something, forgiveness maybe, redemption, or maybe just begging for an answer now and then, each man pleading to the other but neither having anything to offer, nothing but a key clutched invisibly in the fist, and in the other hand a broom good for cleaning nothing for very long, man and broom alike no bigger than a toothpick in the face of life's storm.

And because Will does not want to think of all that, because as long as he has a daughter or wife or brother he cannot allow himself to be crushed by what he knows, cannot grant himself the gift of oblivion, he lifts his eyes to the horizon and thinks of autumn coming and of what it will be like in the woods this year. He thinks maybe he will not hunt anymore, because nothing will ever be the same. The fine powdered snow on the dry leaves will not be the same, and neither will the wind through bare branches or the shafted sunlight or the sharp crackling of ice-encrusted limbs. But Molly is old enough to go into the woods this year, and he does not want to disappoint her. Stevie will be looking forward to it, too. So maybe even though nothing will be the same, Will should take them hunting after all. But no, nothing will ever be the same. Nothing ever is.

And with this thought Will pauses for a moment in his sweeping. Only then does he realize that without even knowing when he started again, he has swept thirty feet of the sidewalk clean. The motorcycle key is still in his hand, pressed against the broom handle now and biting into his palm, leaving an impression on his skin. But it is Harvey's key, and Will grips it tightly as he resumes his sweeping. The bristles make a rhythmic sound as they scrape the concrete, *chhhhh, chhhhh, chhhhh, chhhhh*. And before long he is thinking of Portugal again, that fantasy impossibly serene. Maybe Molly will get there someday. Maybe now she can.

As for me, he tells himself, you weren't made for traveling, you weren't made for big ideas. You were made for sweeping. For frying wings and making daiquiris. For opening bottles of beer. For keeping a room clean and relatively quiet and as dim as an old cathedral. For maintaining the coward's refuge from a sun-bruised sky.

PATRICIA SMITH

When They Are Done with Us

FROM *Staten Island Noir*

Port Richmond

MAURY'S EYES WERE crazy wide, staring right into the camera, just like they were on yesterday's show and the show before that. His hand rested on the shoulder of some blubbering white girl, Keisha or Kiara something, her hair all hard-curled and greased up into those stiff-sprayed rings, smeared black circling her eyes, greening gold Nefertitis swinging from her ears, more faux preciousness twinkling from her left nostril. Seems like K or K's baby daddy could be any one of the fidgeting young black men and—surprise!—she kinda didn't know which one.

The contestants were all sloe-eyed, corkscrew braids, double negative, mad for no reason except that they had been identified on national television as fools who didn't give a damn where their dicks went.

It was time, once again, for the paternity test and Maury's dramatic slicing open of that manila envelope. For some reason, the prospect of finally knowing whose seed had taken hold reduced Kiara or Keisha to unbridled bawling and a snorting of snot.

Jo had the show on more for background than anything, but she stopped for a closer look at the little nasty who'd opened her legs and been done in. It amazed her how anybody, let alone a white girl, could look at any one of those sad sacks and feel bad enough about herself to fuck him. "I ain't never been, or ain't never gonna be, that damned horny," she said out loud, just as

Tyrell, sloe-eyed and corkscrewed, was revealed to be the father of the squirming little bastard in question.

"I'm gon' take care of my 'sponsibility," he monotoned, a semiearnest declaration which was greeted by wild hooting and hand-clapping from Maury's drama-drunk studio audience. Even after receiving the sudden blessing of papahood, Tyrell avoided looking at or touching the mother of his child. Kiara or Keisha stood, shivering in a whorish skirt and halter top, in dire need of at least an orchestrated hug. She continued to keen.

I cannot watch this shit, Jo thought, just after thinking, *Where did she find an actual halter top in 2010?* Although she made a move to punch the television off, she didn't do it. Instead she lowered the volume so the string of skewed urban vignettes could still distract her from what she really needed to be doing. Maybe the next segment would feature some tooth-challenged redneck hurling a chair across the stage upon discovering, after a week or so of sweaty carnal acrobatics, that the he he thought was a she was really a he fervently embracing his she-ness.

Jo revisited her mental to-do. Last night's crusted dishes, still "soaking." A mountain of undies and towels, waiting to be lugged to the Bright Star laundromat, where the guy who guarded the dollar changers — to make damned sure that no "nonlaunderers" used them — never missed an opportunity to converse with her tits. Oh, and she'd skipped breakfast again. After her last tangle with an oil-slick omelet at the New Dinette, a succession of Dunkin's dry toasted things, and her own ambitious attempts to get healthy and choke down oatmeal, the idea of a morning meal had lost its appeal. By 3 P.M. she'd be trolling Port Richmond Avenue, inhaling a loaded slice or two at Denino's or resigning herself to the New's lunch menu and one of their huge, dizzying burgers.

There wasn't much in the fridge — various leftover pastas curling in Tupperware and cold cuts she could practically hear expiring. Ravenous, she spotted the pack of Luckies on the edge of the dinette table, and her whole mouth tingled with crave. Although the pack was half empty, she didn't remember buying it. *Just one,* she thought. Just one, and maybe a little drinkie to follow. Instead she closed her eyes and took a deep breath, shutting it out, and did what Katie had told her to do. She said the word *poem* out loud.

That's it, she thought, scrambling for her wire-bound notebook and new pen. *I'm going to write me a poem.* From the flickering Panasonic, Maury asked, "When did you first suspect that Aurelio was sleeping with your mother?"

Poetry was Jo's new medicine. During her last trip to the university hospital's emergency room, her vague complaint that she had been "sleeping too long and smoking too much and maybe drinking a little harder and my kid is driving me crazy" earned her a useless nicotine patch and the advice of Katie McMahon, a perky community counselor, who suggested she put little bits of her life into lines. Rhyme or not, no matter. About anything she wanted it to be about. "If you call it a poem, then it is," Katie had said.

Surprisingly, the little scrawlings helped. She'd written more than a few choice lines about Al, the ex-cop who showed up with his monthly hard-on to pound her into the mattress with something he called love. She wasted whole pages on Charlie, who'd inhabited her womb for nine months and now had no patience for her "stupid fuckin' rules." He dropped by occasionally to pilfer weed money from her wallet, gobble the contents of the refrigerator, or sleep off an encounter with too many shots of Jäger. On good days—or when she needed to remember that there had actually *been* good days—she wrote all pretty about a moment when she was full of light, strolling over the Bayonne Bridge like she was walking on water. From up there the island magically shed its dingy and became more than gossip, stench, and regret. The key to happiness on Staten Island, she decided, was to get as close as you could to the sky and make the assholes as small as possible.

Flipping to a fresh page in the notebook, she clicked the top of her pen and licked the point the way she'd seen real writers do before they—

A key rattled in the lock and the front door was flung open with such force that it banged into the wall, knocking more mint-green chips from the plaster. Jo felt her heart go large and stone.

"Hey, what the hell is up, Jo?"

He refused to call her Mom. Or Mother. Sixteen years old, six feet, two inches of swaggering explosive. Her son.

"It's hot as shit out there. What's in this place to eat?"

"I think there's some ham in the—"

"The same ham as last time? That shit's old. Ain't nuthin' cooked in this bitch?"

Jo steeled herself. "Charlie, I told you not to come in here—"

"Cursing? Hungry? And you gon' do *what*?"

Jo knew the answer. Nothing. She had never not been terrified of her son. Charlie had ripped her open at birth, glared at her as he bit her breast to demand milk, pinched and pummeled his kindergarten classmates, set fire to wastebaskets in school restrooms, been suspended from sixth grade for showing up plastered on a vile mix of Kool-Aid and vodka, and greeted all attempts to control and educate with a raised middle finger. He strutted and primped in Day-Glo Jordans, a too-big Yankees cap twisted sideways on his head, pants two sizes too wrong pulled down so far the waistband backed his ass. He adopted the lyric swagger of black boys, taking on their nuance and rhythms while hissing about "niggers" in the circle of his crew. While Jo watched in horror, Charlie grew as wide and high as a wall. He arced over her when she dared make mama noises, and huffed in her face with dead breath, which stank of cheap tobacco.

His eyes looked like someone had died behind them.

She wasn't sure what he did during the day. It wasn't school. She'd gotten letters and phone calls from Port Richmond High attesting to his continued absence. "He's a dropout," she finally blurted to one well-meaning guidance counselor, before hanging up the phone.

There were even rumors that Charlie had managed to father a child. Sometimes, when she closed her eyes, Jo could see him snarling, fully erect, a gum-cracking girl laid wide and waiting. His lovemaking would be thrust and spit. When she thought of a child built of Charlie and air, a thick shudder ripped through her.

"Did you hear me? Food! I'm fuckin' hungry! I swear, Jo, don't make me have to—"

She sprang from her chair and bolted for the kitchen with no idea what she would do once she got there.

He'd only hit her once.

One clouded August night, a week after Charlie turned sixteen, Jo saw him on the street just after finishing her part-time job at Bloomy Rose, a florist in Midland Beach. She'd worked late that night, helping with a huge order for the funeral of a local politician. As she wound her way toward her bus stop, a fierce rain needled her cheeks. Assuming the rain had driven everyone inside, she was surprised to see a dark human huddle on Father Capodanno Boulevard just before Midland Avenue, and even more surprised to see her son at its edges.

But there he was, hanging on yet another corner with Bennie Mahoney, a no-gooder from New Dorp, and two other boys she didn't know. Their backs were hunched against the downpour, and she saw the orange flare of cigarettes. She wanted and didn't want to know what they were up to.

The sign on the nearest building on Midland read Q.S.I.N.Y., and she could hear the guttural thump of dance music from inside. The letters made no sense to her until she realized where she'd seen them before. The island's first openly gay club had launched on the Fourth of July weekend to much fanfare and trepidation. Staten Island wasn't known for its tolerance, and there were worries that the patrons of the club would become targets for ham-handed haters.

The letters stood for Queer Staten Island New York.

Jo felt an ominous drop in her belly.

Charlie's views on all things gay were well known and frequently bellowed. While Jo admitted a cringe when she thought about man-on-man, and a starkly uncomfortable curiosity when she considered girl-on-girl, Charlie's florid vocabulary was peppered with references to "fuckin' fags," "cocklickers," and "turd burglars." Jo remembered a bespectacled whisperer from their block who had packed up and hightailed it off the island with his family after being on the receiving end of a vicious beatdown. He never identified his attackers, but Jo remembered how he would practically shrivel when he passed Charlie on the street.

The Charlie who now, for no good reason, was in the middle of a meeting outside a gay dance club. Afraid of what he might be planning, and before she thought about the consequences of doing so, Jo shouted his name.

The group stopped its conspiratorial grumbling. All eyes snapped to her, standing across the street from them, the wind crimping her cheap umbrella, her cotton blouse plastered to her breasts and darkening with rain.

Her son's eyes bored holes into her. He did not move.

Bennie punched Charlie's shoulder hard and laughed. "Hey, it's your fuckin' *mommy*." The two other boys joined in the merriment. But Charles Liam Mulroy, his steel-gray eyes locked to his mother's, did not speak. Jo couldn't bring herself to utter his name again.

They stood that way, three of the young men snickering, one son motionless and burning, one drenched mother craving the world of ten minutes ago. Finally Jo spotted the approaching bus spewing puddles. She scurried to the stop and boarded, never looking back.

Late that night, she woke from a fitful sleep to an angry wall in her room, a wall dripping rain and hissing through its teeth. After two deep glasses of screw-top wine, gulped to calm her nerves, Jo hadn't heard Charlie come in.

"Don't you ever fuckin' do that again. You wanna be somebody's mother, get your ass a dog. Don't you ever admit you even fuckin' know me. Not in front of my crew. You see me, you don't say shit. You lucky I didn't lay your bitch ass flat right there on the street."

She didn't realize she was holding her breath until her head began to pound. Charlie was panting, fists clenched, backlit and glowing in the moonwash. She was just beginning to think how oddly beautiful the image was when it grabbed a fistful of pink pajama top, pulled her up from the pillow, and then knocked her back down with a slap that rattled her teeth.

"Don't. You. *Ever.* Fuckin'. Embarrass. Me. Again."

He dropped his body down on the side of the bed, waiting for Jo to meet his eyes. She couldn't. She lay with her head flattened to the left, the way it had fallen after the slap. She felt his hard gaze. After a wet intake of breath, he slowly lifted the pajama top and clamped her bare right breast with a huge, calloused hand. Jo silently willed her spirit out of the room. Charlie squeezed rough, then pinched the tip of her nipple so hard she whimpered.

He laughed. "This some sick shit. Wow. Man. You done got my cock hard in this bitch."

He popped up and strutted out of the bedroom, leaving behind the dead green smell of bad weather.

They never talked about it. She never called anyone, never thought about reporting him, never even mentioned it to Al, the ex-cop. From that day on, she never acknowledged him in public, no matter what he was doing, who he was with, where he was. And she stopped remembering the thick smear of blood she'd seen on his skinned knuckles that night. She stopped wondering whose it was.

"I am fuckin' starvin' up in this bitch!" Charlie screamed again.

Jo clawed through cabinets and the fridge, searching for something, anything, that wasn't the same old ham. In the front room, Maury had probably morphed into another screechfest. She wanted to be back in that room, opening her notebook, finding that empty page, picking up her pen . . .

"Ooooohhhhh, godDAMN! What is *this* shit?"

Jo bolted for the living room and swallowed hard at the sight of Charlie holding the purple notebook, starkly focused on a particular page.

"Give that to me," she said, as calmly as she could manage. "That's mine."

"Oh, hell no. I'm seeing *my* name, so this shit is *my* business. I already read the one about you gettin' naked and fuckin' that cop. Mama's a muthafuckin' freak."

His eyes scanned the page, and she saw it all take turns in his face—confusion, anger, embarrassment, confusion, realization, anger again. She wondered what poem he'd found. She wondered what she'd pay for writing it.

Charlie started reading, his voice all exaggerated white:

Charlie is not a son, not a boy, not a man
He is the way a day turns toward a storm
He is a star that screams before disappearing
He is night without a bottom
I can't wake up from him, can't give
him back, can't even give him away,
can't think of anyone who would even want
that kind of exploding. I can't even say his
name without my heart stopping. I wish I
could remember giving him a home
in my body. I wonder if it would just
be easier to stop stop stop loving him
as easy as it was to stop loving me

Hearing the poem out loud, Jo couldn't help noticing that she was using the word *even* too much. Concentrating on that kept her from focusing on the ominous silence that followed Charlie's booming of the word *me*.

The silence was broken by a laughter Jo had never heard before. Charlie threw back his head and opened so wide she could see the collapsed gray teeth at the back of his mouth. He laughed so hard he sputtered, and when he could manage it, he spat out snippets of her poem. *"Not a son! Give him back! Give him away! Home in your body! Stop, stop, stop!"* He laughed until there were tears in his eyes. *"Stop!"*

Still snorting, he pushed past her into the kitchen, waving the notebook over his head. He slapped it flat on a burner of the gas stove and held Jo at arm's length while he turned the knob up as far as it would go. Flames leaped up around the notebook and burrowed toward its heart. The smoke alarm started thin, warbled, then blared. Above the din, Charlie laughed maniacally.

As Jo's poetry flared and sizzled, all those words she had scraped directly from the surface of her skin, Charlie turned the water on full blast in the kitchen sink, where last night's dinner dishes were still soaking. With a pair of metal salad tongs, he lifted the blazing notebook and tossed it under the running water. Jo could swear she heard it moan.

"You are such a sensitive bitch," a suddenly solemn Charlie hissed. *"Getting in touch with your feeeeeeelings.* Grow some fuckin' balls."

Jo fell to her knees on the tile and felt the day collapse around her. Before she could scream, she heard the front door squeal on its hinges and bang shut, so hard the smoke alarm hiccupped and died. And the laughter stopped.

No, it didn't.

That night Jo woke to the sound of shouts and sirens outside her bedroom window. That wasn't unusual for Port Richmond, but there was something jagged about it this time. For a moment she was disoriented. She had fallen asleep in her clothes, so tangled in her bed sheets that she couldn't move right away. She smelled liquor somewhere—on her pillow? in her hair?—and remembered swilling Jack Daniel's after Charlie stormed out, hoping to drop the curtain on one bitch of a day. She felt bleary. Her eyes opened behind a cloud. She peered at her alarm clock. Four-fifteen A.M.

Jo imagined that an acrid whisper of smoke was the dying breath of her poetry, still floating in the kitchen sink. Until now she hadn't realized how important the pages had become to her, and

PATRICIA SMITH

nothing in the notebook could be salvaged. The heavy thought of beginning again made her head drop to the pillow, to the left, the way it had when her son slapped her. She wanted sleep to pull her under again. But the street noise grew louder and more insistent, the stench more disturbing than the island's usual garbage-tinged funk.

Jo freed her legs from the sheets and lumbered to her window. Number 302, directly across Nicholas, was burning. Had burned. The two windows on the top floor were soft-sputtering black and orange. Her mouth hung open, torn between awe and panic. She'd slept through a damned fire? Had there been people inside? Were they okay? Why couldn't she picture the people who lived there? Were they black or white? After all, they were right across the street. She must have seen them hundreds of times. Were there kids?

Where was Charlie?

The weight of the question sickened her. Was she concerned about the safety of her son, or worried that he could somehow be responsible for the blaze?

Jo pulled on her old CSI sweats and a T-shirt, slipped into her sneakers without tying the laces, and ran outside, careful to lock the door behind her.

Nicholas was clogged with fire trucks, firefighters, and people spilling excitedly from two-flats. Jo's eyes darted wildly, searching the crowd for Charlie's sneer, his chopped reddish hair. She wanted to cover her ears against the *Oh my God, oh Jesus, Dios mío* babble of panic. All those upturned faces, the shouting, the questions, that bladed smell.

And the screeching woman, suddenly flailing, throwing her body against a knot of people determined to hold her back. Grim-faced firemen hauling four body bags out of the still-smoking building. More screaming.

Jo squeezed her eyes shut then, and she saw them clearly, the people who lived on the second floor. A smiling black woman holding the hands of a toddler and a little girl. An older girl. A teenage boy trailing behind, lugging those light-blue plastic bags from the Port Richmond market. She saw them stop to climb the stairs at 302 Nicholas.

But the screeching was not that woman.

*

The screeching woman was the mother of the woman who died, the grandmother of the four children who died.

Jo found that out during breakfast at the New Dinette. Exhausted and shell-shocked, her clothes smelling vaguely of smoke, she gnawed a slice of bacon and slurped peppered eggs while listening to tragedy's hum. No one could talk about anything but. She half expected to hear her son's name.

The woman Jo had seen behind her closed eyes was dead. So were the two boys, the two girls. They had all died, but it wasn't the fire that killed them.

"That boy killed his brother and his sisters and his mama," Marla, a waitress, said to everyone who would listen, and to a few people who wouldn't. "Slit they throats, set that fire, then killed hisself."

Jo hovered over days of congealing breakfasts at the New long enough to hear different versions of the same story, which meant it must be true. Or most of it. Melonie, seven, her throat sliced open, dead. Brittney, ten, throat slit, dead. The mother, Leisa, her throat not slit, smoke exploding her chest. The little one, Jermaine, still whole and unbloodied, clung to a chance but lost his fight at Richmond University Hospital. The fire had loved him so hard that when he first reached the emergency room, no one was sure if he was a girl or a boy.

Then there was C.J., manchild at fourteen, collapsed in a river of blood, an old-fashioned straight razor under his body. His own throat slit. The whisper was that he had a history of setting small fires. His charred note nearby: *am sorry.*

Jo couldn't grasp the mathematics of it, the impossibility of killing your family, then sliding a blade across your own throat. She had seen that boy. She had seen him laughing, bouncing his little brother on his shoulders. She had seen him watching his sisters ride their bikes, barking like a big brother when they veered too close to the street. She had . . .

Charlie setting fires in the boys' room.

Charlie burning the words that wondered what he was.

But C.J. wasn't Charlie. Thank God. Her son hadn't gone that far, hadn't burned that house down, hadn't killed anyone.

Then her next thought, before she could stop it: *But if he had, someone would come for him. Someone would take him away.*

*

Charlie and Bennie, smelling like men, sat on the couch half watching the Red Sox beat the Yankees. The two of them overwhelmed the room. Their flopping arms and spread-eagle. Their vile mouths, open and chewing. Their uproarious stink.

Jo's son was on full blast: "Man, you hear about that crazy nigger killed his mother? And his sisters? With a razor, *then* burned them up. Nigga got some balls though. Cut his *own* throat, too. Gotta give him credit for going out tough like that. Musta not liked his mama. Bitch musta been ridin' his fuckin' nerves. He took her *out*."

Bennie snorted as Charlie pointedly met his mother's eyes and grinned. He raised a dirty glass of something clear.

Whenever he was home now, which was less and less, Jo folded herself into the smallest corner of the place, stitched her lips shut, and learned to nod. She fried huge slabs of fatty meat, mashed mounds of potatoes, and became a regular at Mexico Supermarket. (She couldn't shop at the Port Richmond store anymore because of the light-blue bags.) She crammed her basket with honey buns, jalapeño chips, taquitos, powdered doughnuts, Red Bull, ice cream, cigarettes, pork rinds, and moon pies, then slathered everything with butter and served it up to her ravenous ass of a son.

She wouldn't give him time or room to want for anything. She didn't want him to realize that she'd already served her purpose. She wouldn't give him reason to open her throat, burn her down.

All Charlie did was eat, sleep off highs, and grow taller and wider. His pores leaked poison and stained the walls. Jo cooked and nodded, answered promptly to "Hey, bitch," and hid her new notebook, a smaller one, behind a row of vases on a high shelf in her room. When she was sure that Charlie was out, she wrote poems to her new dead friend Leisa, who had a son who killed her.

> When they are done with us
> When they are done with us
> When there is no longer a road
> From our blood to theirs
> All we do is remind them
> of need
> And it is us who taught them
> never to need
> anything
> Suddenly there is no river deep enough
> for us

No fire blue enough to strain for our bone
No love
at all

Jo tried not to imagine what Charlie would do if he found this notebook, if he saw how she held whole conversations with a woman she did not know. She had lived for years just across the street. Jo wished she had spoken to her past the occasional nod, wished she hadn't assumed they'd have nothing in common because the woman was black and Jo was white.

No. Not *the woman*. Leisa.

They could have shopped together at the market, waddling home laden with light-blue plastic bags filled with cans of tuna, spongy white bread, brown fruit. And when the moment was right, Jo could have taken Leisa's hand and said, gently, *Describe your son's eyes*.

They could have saved each other.

One morning Jo copied a poem she'd worked on the whole day before, trying to make it perfect.

Leisa, it is hard to admit
the poison that burned through our bodies
and became them
Hard to recite this crooked alphabet
Hard to know we can no longer
circle them with our arms
and contain their whole lives
Their horrible secret is how they
burst like flowers from our bodies
They damn us for remembering
They damn us for wanting
to sing
that story

It still wasn't perfect, but there was something Jo felt she needed to do.

She pulled the page carefully from the notebook, folded it four times, and wrote *Leisa* in her best flowing cursive. Then she crossed the street to the makeshift altar, a raggedy explosion of blooms and mildewing stuffed animals in front of 302 Richmond's scarred shell. There had been people milling around the altar every day, but now there was no one. She studied it for a minute, then tucked the poem beneath a bug-eyed duck. She whispered a run-on sentence that may have been prayer.

Then she walked down to the bodega to pick up coffee and copies of the *Advance* and the *Post*. Reading both the Staten Island and NYC papers was her entertainment, akin to watching *Maury* and *Springer* in the mornings. Wallowing in the grime and drama, she was reminded that she lived both in and close to a cesspool.

The place was packed with people, which was unusual for the hour. There was that tragic hum again, that sad tangle of different languages in stages of disbelief. Jo wondered if something had happened during the night.

At the newspaper rack, she read the headline and the first graph of the *Post*'s front-page story before she even picked it up.

IT WAS MOM IN STATEN ISLAND MASSACRE HORROR
The mother did it. The horrific murder-suicide that ended in an arson on Staten Island was committed by the deranged mom, who slit three of her kids' throats before she killed herself and her baby in the blaze, law enforcement sources said yesterday.

Autopsies showed that C.J., Melonie, and Brittney had pills in their stomachs. They were dead before the fire. They hadn't just lined up and waited to be killed. They'd been drugged first.

And the note: they'd found Leisa's diary and compared the handwriting. *She* had written *am sorry*. *She* had left the note close to her son's body, which was like putting a smoking gun in his hand.

Jo felt a needle traveling in her blood. She picked up the paper and left, without talking to anyone, without paying. She didn't remember her walk back home, but when she looked up, she was there. And so was Al, the ex-cop, hovering around her door, grinning like a Cheshire and, as always, leading with his zipper.

"Hey, Jo-bean," he hissed. "Been thinkin' about you like craaaazzy. Came by as soon as I got a break." His chapped lips brushed the side of her face, then his tongue touched. Jo thought maybe the heat of another body would burn away the rest of the day. Wordlessly, she let him in. Then, as soon as the door was closed, she blurted her usual fears, the fears a man was supposed to take care of. The fears were Charlie, Charlie, Charlie.

"You know, that kid needs a father to keep his ass in line." That was always Al the ex-cop's first suggestion, although he never hinted at who that father might be. "You want, I'll have some of the guys pick him up, scare the shit out of him."

Al seemed to have forgotten again that he was an *ex*-cop for a reason. Al seemed to have forgotten that once, sick with drink and aimlessly speeding in his cruiser, he'd scraped a sizable stretch of concrete barrier along the entry ramp from 440 to 278, stopped, and was promptly hit from behind by a grandmother in a Subaru station wagon. Two squad cars showed up to sort through the mess. They secured the silence of the terrified granny, scrubbed the scene clear of Al's airplane miniatures, and concocted a cover-up tale that would move a hardened judge to tears.

But later, when Al was oh-so-vaguely pressed on the details, he caved and admitted . . . well, everything. Swilling in his cruiser. Shooting sparks as he hugged the barrier. Getting rammed from behind. And being helped by his pals in blue. Babbling, he even named the pals.

Of course, he was fired. Even cooled his heels in the slammer for a bit.

So none of "the guys" he spoke of so lovingly would be inclined to do any favors for good ol' Al. Jo didn't bother reminding him about the circumstances of his ex-ness. He liked playing cop, so she let him.

He even fucked like one. Like he was alone. Everything he said to Jo — *at* Jo — was addressed to Al, the ex-cop: "Oh, you're hitting that pussy today, boy." "She's gonna remember this." "She's gon' be calling your name for days."

Jo had hoped that a body against hers would blur the day, dim the smell of fire. But not this body.

When he left, her room smelled like his deluded monologue, his miserable spurt. The newspaper sat on the bedside table. *The mother did it.* Leisa had killed herself and her children. *Tell me why,* Jo tried to beg her dead friend. But what came out was *Tell me how.*

Maybe the smiling C.J. she'd seen playing with his siblings and lugging home groceries was just another kind of Charlie, one who'd learned to paint his snarling face with light. Maybe Leisa was crazy, out of her mind, her head crammed with the kind of wounding Jo was beginning to know.

Jo started to cry. She wept from bone, from memory, from loss.

She wept for Leisa, for C.J., for the stranger who'd escaped her body and named her *Bitch*. She wept from lack of love, unleashed wracking sobs that hung wet in the air. She wept for the shadows that were Staten Island, the prison she lived in. She wept past the pushing open of her bedroom door, the brash boy who suddenly stood there.

"Fuck you cryin' for?"

Jo's head drooped as Charlie filled the door, swaying, smelling like he'd drunk something with blades. "It smells like ass in here," he slurred. "Like your ass mixed with somebody else's ass." He laughed then. "Was the dick that good? It made you cry? Hell, if it wasn't nasty sick, I'd hit that. Make you call *my* name. Give you some shit to cry about."

He lumbered off. Jo heard him fall into bed in the other bedroom, still laughing, snorting. Soon he would rock the house with snotty snores. He would sleep deep into the night as poison spilled from his pores. He would wake up hungry, snarling, looking to be fed *up in this bitch*.

She pulled the notebook down from its hiding place, found her pen, and wrote another poem for Leisa, the mother, the murderer.

> Where did it seep into you,
> the ghost of the only answer?
> How did you pull it in,
> breathe it in, own it?
> How did you find the teeth
> you needed to take back your
> own body, to build a revolution
> in darkness? And how brave
> of you
>
> to take all of them
> with you

There was more she wanted to say, but Jo was afraid that writing more would lead her to a road she couldn't travel. *Not the why, but the how.* She craved Leisa's strength (the how), not her weakness (the why).

She went to the kitchen and pulled down a note Charlie had written and taped to the fridge months ago: *DAMN GO BY SOME*

FOOD. Already she could hear his drunken snoring. She took the note back to her room, sat down, and began her work.

Going back and forth between her son's scrawled note and a page in her notebook, she worked for hours to get it right. The fat *O.* The swirl of the *S.* The strangely elegant *Y.* She felt Leisa gently guiding her hand as she traced the letters, traced the letters, mirrored the letters.

Down the hall, Charlie sang razors. But in Jo's room, he was writing an apology for what he was about to do. He was saying, *I'm sorry,* finishing with that strangely elegant *Y.*

This time the dead boy would sign his name.

BEN STROUD

The Don's Cinnamon

FROM *Antioch Review*

WHEN BURKE RETURNED to his rooms from his morning visit to the sea baths, Fernandita, his maid, was shaking the bugs out of his mosquito net. He lived in cramped quarters, on the second floor of an old mansion between the wharves and the post office. The mansion's ground floor was given over to a molasses warehouse, and its top floors had been cut into apartments. Burke occupied one of these, an old bedchamber in the back of the building that was partitioned into three rooms and looked over the harbor. One room served as his bedroom, its neighbor as his small study and parlor, and the third room, barely a closet, was Fernandita's.

"Your food is on the desk," Fernandita said, giving the net one more vigorous shake before sweeping the loosed mosquitoes and other insects onto a scrap of newspaper. A skinny, toothless, yellow-skinned woman past middle age, Fernandita was Burke's only companion in the city.

Inspecting his breakfast, Burke picked a green beetle from his eggs and tossed it into the grate, where Fernandita had lit a small flame, then he sat and ate as he read again the letter he'd received from Don Hernán Vargas y Lombilla. *My business is most delicate,* Don Hernán had written, giving no further clue to the nature of his problem. Burke hoped for a challenge, and let his mind wander once more, imagining all the possible conundrums the don might present him.

He was at the start of his life, twenty-two, a free gentleman of color who had left his home in the lower Brazos not a year before. His mother had been a slave, his father a Texas sugar planter, and Burke had come to Havana after his father died, freeing him, thinking that here he might make use of his Spanish and his knowledge of the sugar business. But his various inquiries at those trading houses open to negroes met only with vague promises of later openings, and within four months he was down to his last pennies. It was then he'd read an account of a mystery baffling the city: a nun in the Convent of Santa Clarita had been poisoned, yet she seemed to have no enemies and the walls of the convent were most secure. Puzzling over the story and the details of the nun's life, Burke had soon figured out how it must have been done. The dentist who visited the convent had mixed her toothpowder with arsenic. Burke wrote the captain-general with the solution, and the dentist, taken by the police, confessed to the crime. Unknown to the nun, she had been named in the will of a wealthy coffee grower, an uncle, and were she to die the legacy was to pass to a distant cousin—the man who'd bribed the dentist.

At a loss for income and facing mounting debts, Burke had seen then how he might support himself. What's more, he found he enjoyed the work. After the small fame he earned from the Case of the Poisoned Toothpowder came another, and soon he began to be approached at least once a week by *habañeros* burdened with seemingly insoluble problems. He took any case offered him, stringing together enough money to pay his creditors while slowly, steadily establishing his reputation.

After he finished his breakfast, Burke was fetched by one of the don's *volantas*. It was driven by a negro postilion and fitted out with soft leather seats, a Turkish rug, and, lodged in a teak case, a brass lorgnette for observing passengers in other carriages. As he rode, Burke tried the lorgnette but, feeling foolish, soon put it away, sitting for the rest of the trip with his hands in his lap. Within twenty-five minutes he was delivered to a sprawling estate near the top of the Jesús del Monte. The postilion stopped at the front door, and Burke alighted and was immediately led by another negro down a marble-floored hallway, into a courtyard with a tinkling fountain encircled by orange trees, and then into the don's office, where gilt-framed ancestors stared down from the walls and old account ledgers filled the bookshelves. For fifteen minutes Burke sat alone. Then, at ten precisely, the don strode into the room. Burke had worn his dark coat, white waistcoat, and white drill trousers, the uniform Havana fashion demanded of its gentlemen, but Don Hernán, a stout man with gray, slicked hair and a waxed imperial, was in his silk dressing gown. He snapped at the liveried slave, who then stepped forward and presented two plates piled with eggs and sausages of the plump red variety they'd lately begun selling in the markets.

"No, thank you, I'm quite full," Burke said, refusing his plate with an apologetic smile. The don snapped again at the slave, and the slave transferred Burke's servings to the don's plate.

Don Hernán did not speak as he ate, and Burke remained silent. He watched as the don cut each sausage into three pieces and shoved the pieces into his mouth, grease dribbling into his imperial. Now that he was here, Burke was nervous about the meeting. One of the island's wealthiest sugar planters, Don Hernán held more sway in Havana than any other creole and could, with a single whisper, ruin Burke's career before it had even begun. A man in his sixties who looked younger than his years—he was childless and a carouser—he was known to be fickle and demanding. Whatever the don's request, Burke couldn't afford to fail him.

When the don finished eating, he shoved the plate away, dabbed at his lips, then lit a cigar. Once he had the cigar going, he eased back in his chair. "A month ago," he said, "the manager of my Santo Cristo estate sent up a load of fruit along with two slaves to work in the house. The next day the mules, still bearing the fruit, were found grazing in a field off the Infanta highway, three miles outside the city. The two slaves were gone without a trace."

The don paused. Burke waited, uncertain if he was supposed to speak.

"That was a month ago. A week ago I lost my treasure, my Marcita." The don fumbled in the pocket of his gown and pulled out a gilt-framed daguerreotype and passed it to Burke. "My cinnamon," the don said. "She is most precious to me."

Burke examined the photograph. A *mulata* in a muslin dress, her hair curled and tied with ribbons, stared out from the photographer's painted landscape—a wooded hill, a distant temple. Her face was soft-featured, her eyes heavy-lidded, her mouth drawn into a coquette's half-smile. Her skin, from the picture's tint, indeed seemed a bronze, cinnamon hue. Burke gave the picture back to the don, who returned it to his pocket.

"I'm not the only one with losses. It has been the talk of the

Planters' Club for weeks. Don Sancho is missing four slaves, Don Nicasio is missing five. And these just from the city. It seems to be the season of runaways." He took a puff of his cigar, let out the smoke. "I have put her description in the papers with the offer of a reward, and I've had two of the city's best slave hunters watching for her. All to nothing. So now I try you." He put his hand on his desk and leaned forward. "I want you to find Marcita. It is hard, without my cinnamon here to comb my hair and soothe me." In that moment, the man seemed truly distraught.

As the don had spoken, Burke had felt an unease ripple through him. So far he had avoided any cases that touched on slaves. He was no slave hunter, and he couldn't abide the thought of such cruel work. But there was his livelihood to consider. Don Hernán could ruin him. And so he clenched all feeling from his heart and said, "I am at your service."

Marcita, Burke learned, had disappeared in the Calle O'Reilly while marketing in the company of two slave boys, Domingo and Miércoles. They were out on an errand, so he arranged to have the boys meet him in the city at five. Then, before leaving the don's villa, he made an inspection of Marcita's quarters. She lived in a small room near the kitchens. One wall was decorated with an advertisement for an Italian soprano who had appeared on the stage two years before, and another with a collection of Honradez cigarette labels from a series depicting the progress of a *pollo*, a fop, from prince of the ball to beggar. Another series of labels, these for a Villargas brand, lay on her bedside table. They showed each of the islands of the Antilles as ladies, Cuba regal and bedecked with pearls and tobacco leaves, sprinkling sugar onto a globe, Santo Domingo a weeping negress with torn skirts. In a plain earthen jar Burke found a bundle of feathers and dried leaves, of the kind you could buy from the guinea women in the night markets for good luck, and beneath a loose tile he discovered a burlap sack filled with coins. He paused over this last item before he left, wondering what might have compelled Marcita to forget the sack when she ran—perhaps it meant she had fled on impulse.

Burke didn't return to the Calle del Sol, where the old mansion his rooms were in stood, until past one. The midday heat had already blanketed the city, and after a light lunch he isolated himself in his bedroom and rested. At three he woke to the call of a water vendor in the street below. The city was not yet stirring—the water vendor's cry was the only noise that came from outside—and he moved to his study and remained there while the heat lifted. He tried to compose a letter to Don Hernán, regretting that he could not finish the case and begging the don that it would not cost him his esteem, but he could not find the right words. No matter the phrasing, the don would be disappointed and insulted. Besides, Burke had already given part of his fee to Fernandita to pay off the butcher. He had no choice now, and when his clock struck four forty-five he rose and left his rooms and went out the courtyard gate to keep his appointment with the don's two slave boys.

The sky was high and blue, and with the worst of the day's heat finally past, the city had spilled once more into the streets. Gentlemen in broad-brimmed straw hats walked together speaking of business, Capuchins delivered alms, a company of soldiers marched in seersucker uniforms, a lottery ticket seller cried out that his numbers were blessed. Burke had to pass through this throng as he crossed the Plaza de Armas, skirting Ferdinand VII on his pedestal, then going along the university walls and into the Calle O'Reilly. There he found the street, as usual, blocked with *volantas*. Pale ladies shaded by umbrellas sat in the carriages while shopkeepers came out of their shops to present them with their wares. Burke picked his way around them and after a block found the two boys waiting for him by the sweet shop. They were dressed in the don's blue livery and engrossed in a game of punching each other in the arm. Burke introduced himself, then took them aside from the bustle and asked them to show him where Marcita had disappeared.

Miércoles, who was the older of the two boys, pointed toward a row of shops past the Calle Habana intersection. "She tole us to get some oysters, so we were loadin' up the baskets, and when we done, she was gone."

Domingo, the smaller and darker-skinned of the two, nodded.

"And you saw nothing?"

Miércoles said he'd been watching the road while he held his basket and hadn't seen her come back past. He thought she'd gone farther up the street.

Burke put his hands on the boys' shoulders and walked them

closer to the shops. The first shop off the Calle Habana intersection was the oyster stall, and next was the narrow stall of the Gallitos brand's tobacco shop, and after that a bookseller's. A corpulent, red-bearded fellow was dressing the Gallitos window with rolls of cigarettes. The prices were absurdly high, even for Havana standards, and the shop looked empty. Next door the bookseller was doing a brisk business selling copies of *David Copperfield*. He sat beside his crate and handed copies up to passing *volontas,* catching the coins in his palm, all without looking up from the newspaper in his lap. Burke asked what the boys had done after Marcita disappeared, and Miércoles told him that they waited a half-hour, then returned to the don's villa on the horse trolley.

"And you didn't worry?"

"Not on Tuesdays," Domingo said.

Miércoles glared at Domingo, and Domingo clapped his hand over his lips.

"What happened on Tuesdays?" Burke asked.

Domingo kept his hand over his mouth, and Miércoles looked at his feet.

"I'd hate to have to tell Don Hernán you were uncooperative," Burke said.

The boys needed little time to think this over. Miércoles nodded to Domingo, and Domingo said, "That's when she met her man."

"Her man?" Burke asked.

"But last time she didn't give us any money," Miércoles added.

"What money?"

"She always gave us money to keep quiet," Miércoles said.

Burke had the boys lead him to the lover's rooms. They took him up the block to the Calle Compostcla, turned right and past the Church of Santa Catalina, then walked north two blocks, then turned again, toward the city walls. They stopped finally before a dingy, mud-daubed building in the Calle Villegas. Burke asked which room was the lover's, and the boys pointed toward a window on the top floor, the one farthest to the right. Leaving the boys in the street, Burke walked into the courtyard, up the stairs and onto the interior veranda, found the lover's door, and knocked. There was no answer. Beside the door someone had tacked a piece of paperboard that read *Enrique López, Merchant*—a grand title, Burke thought, for one who lived in one of the poorest buildings in the city. He waited and knocked again. Still no answer. Burke wasn't sure what to do—this was his first case of this kind—and at last he took his card, wrote Marcita's name on it, and slid it under the door. Then he came out and walked the boys back to the sweet shop, where he bought them sugar sticks and sent them on their way.

The case, it seemed, was already shut—Marcita had absconded with her lover. That was an explanation he could give Don Hernán. Tomorrow morning he could send him the man's name. Surely that would be enough—he couldn't see himself tracking the two further, clamping Marcita in irons.

He sat in a café and drank a *horchata*. As he sipped the cool drink and watched the street, he remembered what his mother had last told him. Burke had been brought up in the plantation house by his father, taught to read the books in the library, and allowed to range freely over his father's land with his own gun to shoot birds in the marshes. There was no white wife—Burke's father had been a bachelor—and so Burke's mother was allowed to come spend evenings with him every month or so. "You sure make me proud," she'd told him that last time, pulling on the sleeves of his little velvet coat. He was eleven. "And you're gonna keep making me proud. You're gonna grow up and do good and be good to people." She'd died two weeks later, when fever spread up the bayous.

When he'd stumbled on detective work, he'd thought again of his mother's words. It was all he'd wanted, to do good, and here was his chance—he eased troubled minds, rooted out wrongs.

Later, hours past supper, Burke lay down to sleep and found he couldn't. A thought had come to him and refused to leave. Sending the lover's name to the don—would it be any different from putting the irons on Marcita himself?

The next morning Fernandita brought him coffee and a buttered roll and set them on his desk. As he ate the roll, he watched the tangle of masts outside his window and considered whether he could write the letter. Then he heard a shout below. He was so lost in thought that it came twice again before he caught it. "Murder!"

Burke leaned his head out the window and looked down. It was a beggar in a tattered hat, looking to sell his news to the street.

Burke whistled and the man looked up. "What murder?" Burke asked.

"Toss me a roll and a *real* and I'll tell you."

Burke did so, and the man told how some soldiers had been drinking in a field outside of town when they found a slave's body.

"Where?" Burke asked.

"Between the Paseo de Tacón and the railroad."

"Man or woman?"

The beggar shrugged.

Burke crossed the study to the door, and once in the street he hailed a carriage, a hack with a negro driver. It was a stretch, but it gave him an excuse to delay writing to the don. "Take me to the Paseo de Tacón," Burke said, and the driver began weaving out of the city, moving his carriage skillfully through the crowds.

Twenty minutes later they came to a field scattered with soldiers. An army lieutenant and two government clerks stood at the back of the field, beside a grove of bushes, smoking, and behind them an orderly tended a coffee urn. When Burke got out of the hack, he made for them. As he approached, one of the clerks, a short man with gray sideburns and the flat, bland face of a sheep, stepped forward.

"You have no business here," he said.

"I might," Burke answered, and offered the man his card. "I'm in the employ of Don Hernán Vargas y Lombillo."

The man broke into a grin and thumped the card with his forefinger. "I know of you," he said. "You solved the case of the false pirates for Braganza. My name is Galván. You are most welcome."

"Thank you. I only want to see the body."

"Ah, that is a problem," Galván said, looking across the field, where soldiers and policemen in brown holland uniforms were beating the grass with sticks. "We haven't yet found the body. All we have is the head."

"Only the head," Burke said, then asked, "May I look?"

"Of course." Galván spread his arm. "It's just over there." He pointed to the grove. "Forgive me if I don't join you. I've had my fill."

Burke thanked the man, then went over to the grove, parted

the branches, and saw the head. His heart sank. The head belonged to a dark-skinned man with a scar running from his forehead to his cheek. He'd not admitted it to himself, but he'd hoped
to find Marcita here and so be free of his burden. He thought
to leave, but then decided to take a closer look. As he knelt and
examined the head, all the noises behind him—the lieutenant's
guffaw, the policemen's and soldiers' complaints, the *sush* of their
sticks against the grass—fell away. The head lay face up, the skin
ragged with gore along the neck where it had been severed. But
no blood had drained onto the soil—a fact Burke found curious.
The head must have been severed at some other place. He looked
at the eyes, felt a chill when their gaze seemed to catch him, and
wondered why the body was not here as well. He stood and went
over to Galván.

"What's near here?" he asked.

"Only the railroad tracks, the woods, the field, and those factories."

Burke looked around the area. The tracks divided the field
from the woods, and the factories—three of them, a nail factory,
a cigarette factory, a snuff mill—stood on the field's western end.
Any evidence of the killer's path had been destroyed by the soldiers beating through the field with their sticks.

He had no business with the murder, but he found himself
interested. "Would you mind sending me word once the body is
found?"

"It'd be a pleasure," Galván answered.

When Burke returned to his rooms, he found a note under his
door. Fernandita was out, marketing for his supper, and the note
was from Marcita's lover. He'd come by, hoping to speak.

After leaving his card at the lover's room, Burke had both worried and hoped that the man would flee, if he hadn't already, that
he would take Marcita from her hiding place and disappear. But
instead the lover comes to seek him out? Burke stuffed the note in
his pocket and turned around, going back out into the courtyard
and through the streets toward the man's dismal building.

When Burke arrived and knocked on the lover's door, the man
answered and beckoned him inside. He was a mulatto, at least two
shades lighter than Burke and twenty years his senior. His cheeks
and nose were covered with freckles, and he had a high, wide

brow. The flesh beneath his eyes was puffed, the eyes themselves red.

"Please, sit," the lover said, clearing stacks of handbills from a chair. Burke did so and looked about the cramped room. Its walls were stained a pale yellow, and aside from another chair, the only other piece of furniture was a couch whose crimson velvet had been worn to bare pink patches. He was about to ask the lover about Marcita when the man, unable to contain himself, shot out, "Tell me where she is. I beg you. Tell me what you know. Tell me anything."

Burke, alarmed, straightened in his chair. "I was hoping," he said, "you'd be able to do that for me."

"But I thought she'd sent you!" Enrique said, then pleaded, "Why torture me with your note?"

"I'm trying to find her," Burke said.

Enrique was silent a moment. Then something seemed to catch. "Why?" he asked. A nervousness entered his voice. "Who hired you? Was it Don Hernán?"

"I'm under his employ, but he didn't—"

"He knows?" At that he went to the window. A gauzy sheet hung there, luffing in the wind. "Oh, no no no."

"I can assure you Don Hernán knows nothing," Burke said, "and I can further assure you that he will learn nothing. You are safe. I'm charged only to find Marcita. That I will do, and nothing else."

Enrique pulled back the curtain and looked out. Then he stepped back toward Burke. "I love her," he said. "When she is free, we're going to move to Santo Domingo, away from the don, away from this island. I've been saving money to help her. See?" He offered Burke a handbill. It was for a brand of tinned butter. "I sell this, for my living, for her. I was waiting for her last Tuesday. We were going to have an hour. But then she didn't show. I worried. I thought the don had found out. Then I saw the notices the don put in the paper, and I thought maybe she had run."

Burke's mind began to leap with what Enrique had told him. "You were waiting for her on Tuesday?" he asked.

"Yes, yes," Enrique said.

"Where, exactly?"

"At the corner of O'Reilly and Compostela."

"And you kept a hard watch for her?"

"I always do."

Burke rose. "Thank you," he said. Then, without another word, he went to the door.

"Is that all?" Enrique asked, still standing by the window and staring after Burke.

"It is enough."

Burke walked directly to the Calle O'Reilly. There, halfway between the Habana and Compostela intersections, he planted himself in the center of the street. He looked eastward, toward the intersection where Miércoles and Domingo had waited, O'Reilly and Habana. Then he pivoted and looked westward, toward the intersection where Enrique had kept a sharp lookout, O'Reilly and Compostela. Between these two lookouts, one at either entrance to the block, Marcita had vanished.

On the left side of the street were the oyster shop, the bookseller's, and the tobacco shop he'd seen before, and farther on a linen shop and a silversmith's. On the right stood a tea shop, a music shop, a large shop selling glassware, and a perfumery. There was nothing strange about the block. The shops were all elegant, glass-fronted establishments that catered to the city's gentry. They had preposterous names like the Empress Eugénie (the perfumery) and the Bower of Arachne (the linen shop) written in gold letters above their doors. Burke walked up and down before them, observing everything around him, looking again and again into the same glazed shop fronts and at the crowds moving past, the gentlemen, the vendors, the slaves. He even knelt and examined the street itself, paved in smoothed cobblestones. But after two hours' investigation, Burke had found nothing. Returned to the Calle del Sol, he sat at his desk to think, and when Fernandita brought in his supper, he refused the plate of red sausages and rice with a distracted wave of his hand.

"As you wish," Fernandita said. In a moment, though, she had returned. "I almost forgot," she said. "A boy brought this." She handed Burke a message. It was from Galván, and he'd written only three words: *Body not found.*

Later that night, once full darkness had fallen, Burke dressed in trousers and a shirt made of old sailcloth and left his rooms to walk through the city. It was all he could think to do. He hoped that,

passing among slaves, visiting their night haunts, he might hear
rumors—of Marcita, of the murdered slave, of the others the don
mentioned had gone missing. He went to the abandoned lots and
shadowy groves where slaves were known to gather for their dances
and their guinea magic, but each one he found deserted. The only
slave he saw that night he stumbled on by chance—a fresh *bozal*
standing outside a tavern, far from any of the slaves' usual places.
He seemed agitated—he was staring in through the tavern's window at white men eating and drinking, gnashing his lips.

Burke approached him. "What's the matter?" he asked.

The slave turned to him. Tribal scars ridged his forehead and
shoulders. His front teeth were filed into points, and his breath
stank of *aguardiente.* "I lost my little Anto," he said.

Just then the tavernkeeper came out and waved a stained rag at
the two of them. "Bah!" he said. "Go on! Get moving!" He snapped
the rag at the slave and then at Burke, who, as he leaped back,
bumped into a creole passing by. Without breaking stride, the man
struck him with his gold-tipped cane, then continued on down the
street, paying him no more attention. Burke recognized the fellow
—Maroto? Sánchez?—had even shaken his hand at a salon where
he'd been invited to play cards and share stories about his cases.
He wanted to shout, but by the time he'd overcome his shock at
being struck, the creole was gone, disappeared into the night. He
turned to find the slave with the pointed teeth, but he was gone,
too.

After an hour's more wandering, Burke returned to his rooms,
lit a lamp, and sat at his desk. The slaves were frightened of something—he could see that in their emptied gathering places and
in the eyes of the *bozal.* But what was the connection to Marcita's
disappearance? He thought of the head found outside the city,
and of the street where Marcita disappeared. He could sense a tie
between them, but try as he might, his brain failed to take hold of
it. Outside, the *sereno* called the second hour of morning. Burke
took a cigarette from the canister on his desk—Fernandita had
just restocked them with the don's money—and struck a match.
As he brought the light to the cigarette tip, he stopped, letting the
match burn down and singe his fingers. The labels in Marcita's
room—the shop in the Calle O'Reilly with the too-high prices—
the cigarette factory next to the field where the slave was found.
He recalled now that its owner, Pedroso y Compañia, had gone

bankrupt two months before. Theirs was the Gallitos brand, theirs the shop where Marcita must have disappeared.

"Fernandita!" he shouted. "Fernandita!"

After the fourth shout she emerged from her closet, cursing and blinking.

"Go to the captain-general's palace. He'll be up, playing cards. Give him this message." As Burke spoke, he quickly scrawled a letter telling the captain-general he was acting in the affairs of Don Hernán and asking him to send troops to the Pedroso y Compañia factory without delay.

"Why? What's happening?" Fernandita looked about the room, as if someone else might be there.

"I'm not sure yet," Burke said, the unlit cigarette still in his mouth. He shoved the letter in Fernandita's hands. "But I'm going to find out."

At that he left his rooms and ran through the dark streets until he found an idle *volanta* waiting near the cathedral. Dropping a handful of *reales* into the postilion's palm, Burke yelled for him to drive to the Calle de la Soledad, outside the city. "Race the devil!" he shouted. Then he threw himself into the *volanta*'s seat and the man took off.

They came past the field where the head had been found, then to an empty lane just off the paseo—the Calle de la Soledad. The *volanta* pulled to a stop, and Burke got out, telling the driver to wait. The white macadam glowed in the light of the moon, and the air carried the scent of meat cooked over a fire. A night bird called from a far line of trees, but otherwise everything was still. Just up the lane stood the three factories Burke had seen earlier that day when he'd come to inquire about the murder. The snuff mill lay dormant, and Burke stepped quickly, carefully past its low, silent hulk. Just beyond it was the yard of the cigarette factory. He halted. The factory's yard was untended, overgrown with weeds and littered here and there with bottles, but light shone through the cracks in its shuttered windows, and once he stilled his own breathing, Burke could hear the murmur of men talking.

He knew he should wait for the captain-general's soldiers, but he couldn't hold himself back. What were these men up to? Might Marcita still be alive, trapped inside? He crept to one of the windows and edged open a shutter and looked. In the factory's single hall, where women once worked rolling cigarettes, a black-skinned body hung from a hook. It was being stripped by one man while two others worked at one of the old rolling tables, turning a grinder. The grinder jammed and one of the men working it kicked at the table while the other shouted. The man stripping the body, cutting meat from the legs, just whistled. Burke recognized him as the corpulent, red-haired tobacconist from the Gallitos shop.

It took Burke a moment to understand, and once he did he felt his reason trickle away. He couldn't turn away—the ghastly sight held him. Instead, without noticing, he leaned forward. His hand was still on the shutter, and it creaked. At that all three men looked up from their work. Burke let go of the shutter and it creaked again, and now they saw him. Burke tried to move—tried to run —but his legs felt suddenly weak. A lightness was washing forward from the back of his skull. The men at the grinder snatched knives from the table, and the one stripping the body picked up an ax. Burke watched, paralyzed. He could hear the cannibals' footsteps —they were out of the factory now, on the grass, closing. At last Burke beat back the lightness, pulled his feet from the morass, and ran. Just as he made it to the *volanta,* he heard the trumpets of the captain-general's troops. The men chasing him turned, but two cavalrymen appeared in the street and ran them down. Burke, wishing to see nothing more, ordered the *volanta's* driver to take him home.

"In the sausage!" Don Hernán repeated, his face green. He was sitting in Burke's bedchamber, slumped in a cane chair. "Oh, my poor cinnamon! To think I—" He stopped. It seemed for the moment he could not bring himself to mention the sausage again.

Burke lay on his cot. When he'd returned to his rooms, he'd felt the lightness return, a sickness overtaking him, and he'd not been able to stand or sit. Now, morning having come, he was explaining his findings to the don. Fernandita stood by the door folding and refolding a cleaned sheet as she listened.

"The shop was a ruse. That's why the price on the cigarettes was so high, to keep people away. Marcita must have wandered in, looking for new labels for her collection, and that's when they took her."

What he'd seen through the window of the cigarette factory flashed again before Burke's eyes.

"All of Havana eating slave flesh!" the don said. "Horrible."
When the don first arrived, his skin was tinged green. But already
he seemed to be recovering a little. "What I can't understand is
why. I've thought over the numbers. There couldn't have been
much money in it, not nearly as much as the slaves were worth in
the field."

"For that," Burke said, "I'm afraid I'll never have an answer."

Once the don had left, Burke called to Fernandita to help him
to the window. She held him by the arm, and he pushed aside
the curtain and looked out. The sun shone brightly on the harbor
ships, ignorant of all that had just passed.

In the moment of his discovery, along with horror, along with
disgust, Burke had felt relief. In the end, he had been working to
save slaves, not trap them. But in the light of the morning his relief
had begun to crumble.

"I took this case before I knew the slaves were in danger," he
said now. "I didn't like it, I fashioned excuses, but I was willing to
hunt Marcita for pay."

Below him a bell was tinkling—a procession of priests taking
the viaticum to a dying man. He turned back from the window.
Fernandita, grown uncomfortable, smiled uncertainly up at him.

"Oh, I think I shall never loose these villains from my mind,"
he said, and, shaking free of Fernandita's hand, he stepped back
toward his cot. In taking this case, had he become the equal of the
men he caught, had he stepped irrevocably away from the goodness he'd not long ago imagined his? This he wondered as he sat.
To these questions, too, he worried he'd never have an answer.

Bullet Number Two

FROM *Tin House*

HAWLEY HADN'T BEEN in the desert since his mother died. That was four years ago. The hospital had tracked him down with the news and he'd taken the bus all the way from Cheyenne to Phoenix. They made him identify her body in the morgue. The place was dank and cold compared to the heat outside and smelled of chemicals and bleach. He stood underneath the fluorescent lights and they rolled his mother out of a drawer in the wall.

She'd been dead for more than two weeks. Her face had sunken in and most of her teeth were gone, but she still had that square chin and those long, delicate fingers, the ones he remembered running through his hair in the dark when he was a kid. He buried her alone in a cemetery near the hospital. Then he took the bus back to Cheyenne.

Now Hawley had a car of his own, an old Ford Flareside, and he opened up the engine on the highway, the windows rolled down and the blazing hot air channeling through, the sand blowing against his skin and the red cliffs of Arizona stretching into the distance. Behind his seat were a twenty-gauge Remington shotgun, a 9mm Beretta, a Sig Sauer pistol, a crossbow tire iron, his father's rifle from the war, and $7,000.

He'd gotten a postcard from his old partner, McGee, who was working in Colorado at an Indian casino. McGee had dreams of buying a boat and sailing it down the East Coast, but he had a bad habit of burning through his money fast. Now he had an angle for ripping off the casino, and he'd asked Hawley if he wanted in.

It was night by the time Hawley crossed into the Four Corners.

He'd taken Route 191 to 160, and for more than an hour his was the only car for miles. When he looked in the rearview it was nothing but blackness, and when he looked out the windshield it was nothing but blackness and he could see only to the end of his own headlights beaming into the dark. An hour later he was in the middle of a dust storm, tumbleweeds flashing past like ghosts, sometimes hitting the grate or getting caught under the body of the truck. The wind swept down in gusts, shimmying the Ford left and right. It was late and his eyes were already bleary and now he had to struggle with the steering wheel to keep his tires on the highway.

After a long while of this he saw a light ahead, a motel standing all by itself at the crossroads. He pulled into the parking lot and went into the office to get a room. The guy at the desk was a Navajo Indian. He was wearing a red bowling shirt with a white collar and a pair of pins embroidered over the heart. Behind the desk was a small back room, and Hawley saw another Navajo and a freckled guy at a table playing cards. It was close quarters and they looked like they'd been going all night, empty bottles of beer lined up on the floor and ashtrays full.

"You're big blind," the man with the freckles called out.

"Just take it from my stack," said the Navajo in the bowling shirt. "Want to join us?" he asked Hawley.

The other two men leaned forward in their chairs. The Navajo gave Hawley the once-over and returned to his beer. But the one with the freckles kept staring. He had hair the color of motor oil and marks that blossomed across his face and neck like a rash. There was something about those freckles that made Hawley's stomach ache.

"What's the game?"

"Hold 'em."

Hawley was tempted. He hadn't held cards in nearly a week. He watched as the man with the freckles reached over, grabbed some chips from the Navajo's pile, and threw them in the center of the table. The sleeves on the freckled man's sweatshirt were pushed up and his forearms were covered with homemade tattoos, the kind done in prison. One was a poorly drawn figure of Christ on a cross; the other was the number 187, the section of the California penal code for murder. The ink was still blue. The edges had not faded.

The Navajo slid a key across the counter.

"Thanks," said Hawley, "but it's late. I'll pass."

He made his way back to the truck, holding his shirt over his face to keep the sand out of his eyes, then drove around to the back of the building and pulled into the parking spot with his room number spray-painted on the asphalt. He climbed the stairs to the landing, carrying his bag full of guns and clothes and the money, which he'd been keeping in a jar of black licorice. The bills were stuffed at the bottom of the jar and the thin strips of candy were layered on top, like a pile of shoelaces. He hated licorice and he figured most people didn't like it either.

The motel room smelled like corn chips and cigarettes, and there was a hole punched through one of the walls. On the bed-side table was a clock, the digital kind with glowing numbers. He stretched out on the bed and closed his eyes for a few minutes, and when he opened them he noticed the clock hadn't changed —the numbers were stuck on 4:16. His own watch had stopped outside Flagstaff, and he had no idea what time it was. He un-zipped the side pouch of the bag and took out his Beretta and set it on the bedside table. Then he put the bag with the rest of the guns in the closet.

When Hawley was a boy, he had trouble keeping his hands still while he was shooting. His mother taught him to set a quarter on the barrel, but it would fall off, again and again. *Take a breath,* she told him, *take a breath and let half of it out.* She'd said it so often that he nearly always breathed this way, even when he didn't have a gun in his hands. He took in what he could and he held half of it back, and that's how he kept himself steady, day to day, year to year, every time he squeezed the trigger.

Hawley went into the bathroom and turned on the light. He had a bad case of trucker's tan—his left side all burned from keeping his arm out the window. He turned on the shower and stepped into the cold water and washed the sand out of his hair. When he finished, he wrapped a towel around himself and then he got back into his jeans. He'd just turned on the TV when he heard a knock on the door.

It was a girl, maybe twenty years old. She was rail-thin and nearly as tall as Hawley. She had a black eye, and her blond hair was pulled back tight in a bun. Seven or eight piercings lined the sides of her ears, tiny hoops looped one after the other and a purple feather dangling from the top like some kind of fishing tackle.

"I'm locked out," she said.

Hawley kept his hand on the door frame. "Can't the front desk let you in?"

"No one's there," she said, "and I saw your light on."

Hawley wondered if she was a hooker. Then he saw that she was carrying a baby. It was about six months old, and she had it in a sling with her coat zipped up around it.

"Wait," Hawley said. He closed the door on her and took the licorice jar out of the duffel bag. He made sure the lid was screwed tight, then put it in the toilet tank. He grabbed the Beretta and slid the chamber to see that it was loaded and tucked it into the back of his jeans and pulled his shirt over it. Then he opened the door again. "I'll go check with you," he said.

They went through the storm to the front side of the building. The girl walked backward against the wind, holding up the collar of her coat to protect the baby. The door to the motel office was locked and the lights were out. Hawley put his hand to the glass and peered in. It was too dark to see anything.

"I told you," the girl said.

Hawley banged on the door. He considered busting the lock. The baby started fussing, and the girl bounced up and down on her toes. Then another big gust of wind came and they both got sand thrown in their faces and the baby started to cry.

"Let's go back," said Hawley. He put the girl behind him this time and held his arms out so he'd get most of the sand and not her and the baby. When they reached his room, he let them in.

"Those guys will probably be back in a minute or two," he said.

The girl unzipped her coat. Her eye was only a few days old, still bloodshot, with a streak of black along the nose. "Is it okay if I change him?" she asked.

"Go ahead," said Hawley.

She took the baby out of the sling and put him on the bed. He was dressed in pajamas printed with elephants. There were snaps along the insides of the legs, and the girl pulled them open and undid the diaper and then she grabbed both of the baby's legs with one hand and lifted his bottom in the air and slid the diaper out. The baby stopped crying as soon as she did this.

"How long you been here?" Hawley asked.

"About a week," the girl said. "Only ones in the place, besides that guy from Kansas." She opened her purse and took out a fresh diaper and put it under the baby. Then she took out a tube of white cream and rubbed some between the baby's legs and across his behind before she closed the diaper and snapped the pajamas up. The baby stared at her face from the bed and kept waving his arms back and forth and opening and closing his fists, reaching for her the whole time.

The girl rolled the dirty diaper and used the plastic tabs to close it. "Where's your trash?"

Hawley looked around the room. "Maybe in the bathroom. Here." He reached out and she gave the dirty diaper to him and he carried it across the room. It was warm and heavy against his fingers, like a living thing. He put the diaper in the trash can and washed his hands. When he came back, the girl was sitting on the bed and she had a bottle of vodka on the table.

"You want a drink?" she asked.

Hawley always wanted a drink. "Sure."

"I don't have any glasses."

Hawley went back into the bathroom and got the plastic-covered cups by the sink. He handed her one, and they ripped open the little bags and slid their cups out. She poured a finger for each of them. "Cheers," she said.

Usually Hawley drank only whiskey or beer. In his mind, vodka was the drink alcoholics drank, because you couldn't smell it on them. It was what his mother used to drink. He remembered the bottles. He'd even saved one for a while, after she'd left, until his father found it and threw it out. This vodka was cheap stuff, and it burned Hawley's throat on the way down. The girl swigged hers fast and poured another.

"What's your name?" Hawley asked.

"Amy," she said.

"That's a pretty name," he said.

She looked at him strangely, the black eye like a shadow splitting her face in two. Hawley didn't want her to think he was hitting on her, so he moved farther away, toward the door, and leaned against the wall there. She was still sitting on the bed. The baby had fallen asleep beside her, his cheek to the side and his arms over his head like he was in a holdup.

"Did those hurt?" Hawley asked, pointing at her ears.

Her fingers floated to the hoops, caressed the purple feather. "The ones up top did," she said. "But now I don't even think about

it. I get a piercing whenever something important happens, something I want to remember." Amy poured a third drink for herself.
She threw it back like a shot and sighed. "Is that the right time?"

The clock on the bedside table still read 4:16 A.M. Outside, the
sandstorm had turned the sky so dark and yellow that it could have
been two or even five. Hawley took another sip of his vodka. "Probably not."

"I'm so tired," Amy said. She closed her eyes and rubbed them.

"I'll go see if they're back," said Hawley. He put his drink on
the table, unlocked the door, and stepped onto the landing. He
jogged down the stairs and around the building, thinking about
the holes in Amy's ears. He wondered if she'd ever want to forget
those things that had happened to her. Remove the hoops and let
the skin close back over itself.

He tried the office door again. It was still locked. He beat on
it, but nobody came. He checked for cars. There were two parked
in front, a pickup with an Arizona license plate and a brown van
from Kansas, but they were both empty. He walked back toward his
room, fighting the wind. His Ford was right where he'd left it. A
few spots down, there was a blue hatchback with a big dent in the
passenger's side. Through the window he could see piles of clothes
and a few taped-up boxes and a baby seat in the back. He stood in
the parking lot and looked up at his room. All the other windows
were dark.

Amy was stretched out next to the baby when he opened the
door. He could tell from the way her shoulders moved that she was
asleep. He closed the door gently, went into the bathroom, and
checked the toilet tank. The licorice jar was still there. He threw
some water on his face, and then he walked over to the closet and
pushed the bag of guns in deeper. He moved to the other side of
the bed and took the Beretta from the back of his pants and put it
in the drawer of the table, next to the Bible. Then he slipped off
his shoes and sat down on the bed.

The scent of cigarettes still hovered in the corners of the motel
room, but all the bed smelled of now was baby powder and apples.
Hawley leaned back against the headboard. He could barely keep
his eyes open, but he didn't feel right lying down with them. The
baby made little sighing noises and sucked on air, its mouth moving like it was going at a bottle. The bruised side of Amy's face
was against the bedspread, and without the black eye showing she

looked even younger. She'd taken her hair out of the bun and it was fanned across the pillow. Hawley listened to the girl and the baby breathing. Then he reached over and turned out the light.

When he woke it was still dark and Amy was kissing him. Hawley didn't know where he was at first, and then he saw her face leaning over him in the red glow of the motel clock. She was soft and warm pressed up against him. Hawley was afraid that touching her would end it, so he didn't move. She was kissing him slowly and carefully, and when he couldn't help himself anymore, his hands went to her waist and she pulled away. After a few moments, she slid forward again and kept her mouth just out of reach, hovering over his, their faces close and their breath going into each other.

Her hair fell down and brushed his lips, and there were the apples—the smell was coming from her hair. He wound his fingers through to her scalp and pulled. His knuckles brushed the hoops in her ear, all that cold metal going through her skin. She tugged at his shirt and he threw it off and she ran her teeth along his shoulder. And then they got hold of each other's belts and tried to unlatch them in the dark. She got his done first and threw it to the ground, then pushed his fumbling fingers away, stood up next to the bed, slid her jeans down her long legs and stepped out of them, her bare skin shining in the clock light.

Hawley caught her around the hips and buried his face in her neck, and together they fell onto the carpet. He pushed her knees open, and she made a sound like it was hurting her. Hawley tried to see her face, but she only wrapped herself tighter around him, and their bodies spun and he cracked his head on the bed frame. And that's when he heard the gunshots. Two quick pops in a row and then silence.

The girl was still panting and shaking beneath him. Hawley covered her mouth with his hand. They waited like that in the dark on the floor of the motel room. And then there was another blast, and the baby woke up and started crying.

Hawley scrambled to the table and pulled open the drawer and took out the Beretta. He went to the window and peeked through the curtains. He couldn't see anything but the two cars. He turned back, and Amy was still lying on the floor, staring up at the ceiling.

"Shut him up," Hawley said.

The girl climbed onto the bed. She pulled the baby to her chest and started rocking. Hawley found his jeans in the dark and hurried over to the closet. He grabbed some clips and his father's rifle and went back to the window. The baby was still crying. Every scream screwed Hawley's nerves tighter. The girl was standing now, searching through her bag. She found a bottle, but her hands were shaking and she dropped it twice, and then she got back on the bed and stuffed the nipple into the baby's mouth and the baby was quiet.

Hawley took a deep breath. He told the girl to keep the light off. Then he told her to take the baby and go into the bathroom and lock the door. She cleared her throat a few times as if she was going to say something, but she didn't. He listened to her gather the kid and her clothes and then he heard the door to the bathroom click. His eyes never left the parking lot. He could still sense the clock behind him, the stagnant numbers like heat, illuminating the side of his face in the gloom.

A few minutes later the brown van, the one from Kansas, eased around the side of the building. It circled the lot and slowed by Hawley's car, then stopped right before it came to Amy's. A man got out of the driver's side, holding a handgun. It was the man with the freckles. He was wearing the red bowling shirt the Navajo'd had on earlier. His arms were bare and his prison tattoos wound past his elbows. He checked the license on Hawley's truck and peered in the windows of Amy's hatchback. Then he looked up at the line of rooms.

They'd both seen him—Hawley and the girl. If he'd only stolen some money, Hawley figured he'd get in his car and leave. But if he'd killed the Navajos, he'd probably come after them. The man went back to the van. He took out a box of bullets, opened the chamber on his revolver, and reloaded. Then he wiped his hands on the red bowling shirt, picked up the gun where he'd set it on the driver's seat, flipped the safety, and started up the stairs.

Amy's hatchback and Hawley's truck were both parked in spots marked with their room numbers. Hawley waited to see which door would get tried first. The freckled man reached the landing, then made his way along the row of doors. He took out a set of master keys, fit one into the lock of Amy's room, and slipped inside. As soon as he did, Hawley stepped out onto the landing. He leveled the rifle, and immediately the wind swept up and started pushing against the barrel.

Hawley knew how to read his surroundings, to compensate for

drag while lining his sights. When the leaves changed direction, the wind was seven miles per hour. If branches began to bend, it was closer to nine. But there were no trees here to tell how fast the storm was blowing, not even a plastic bag caught in a fence—only the sand that had crossed the open desert and was now circling the motel, pelting the windows with dust.

Start with your feet, his mother had told him. *Your heels are already on the ground. Build from there when you lose your way.* Hawley eased his weight back. He shook the tension from his calves and loosened his knees. He turned at the waist. He braced his elbow against his ribs and felt the gun steady. Then he pressed his cheek gently to the stock of the barrel and dragged it down behind the rear sight.

Hawley took in a full breath. He let half of it out.

The man with the freckles stepped from Amy's room, not even careful. Hawley could have shot him in the head, but he went for the shoulder. The man cried out and staggered, then lurched for the stairs, but before he made it halfway down, he turned and fired off all the rounds he'd been holding. Hawley stepped back too slowly and felt a burn through his right side, and suddenly his arm couldn't support the rifle anymore. It was falling and it fell and he watched it fall and then he was scrambling for the Beretta. He staggered over to the balustrade with the handgun. There was blood —it was streaming out over the walkway, and Hawley's head was spinning. He grabbed the railing and watched the man struggling into the van below, the red shirt billowing sideways like a cape in the wind. Thirty miles an hour, Hawley decided. Then he raised the gun and took the shot.

Hawley's legs went weak and he slumped to the ground. He was having trouble breathing—it was as if there was a sponge at the back of his throat. He crawled across the landing on his knees. The concrete was cold and hard and unforgiving. He called Amy's name and pushed open the door. When she came out of the bathroom, she was fully dressed, like when he first met her, her hair pulled back tight in a bun once more and the baby in the sling and zipped up in her jacket.

"We got to leave," he managed. But he couldn't get up from the floor.

Amy grabbed towels from the bathroom and wet them and pressed them to his side. Then she took some diapers and opened them and put them under the towels, taping the plastic tabs to his skin. Hawley told her to get the bag with the guns and to fetch the rifle he'd dropped, and then he told her to open the toilet tank and get the jar of licorice out and put it in the bag, too. She did all he asked, and when she came back and kneeled beside him, her face held that same strange look from earlier, when he'd told her that her name was pretty.

He barely remembered coming down the stairs. Amy threw some towels across the rear seat, then maneuvered him into the back of her car. She put the bag in the trunk. She opened the other door and took the baby out of the sling and strapped him in next to Hawley. The van was still running, the windshield sprayed with blood, the man with the freckles half in, half out of the driver's seat.

Amy got into the front of the hatchback and slammed the door. She gripped the steering wheel and kept her eyes on the rearview mirror. "Do you think the manager's dead?"

"We should check," said Hawley.

They drove around to the front of the building. Amy got out, and this time the office door was unlocked. Hawley and the baby stayed in the car, the kid watching the spot his mother had disappeared into, kicking his tiny feet and drooling. Hawley pressed the diapers against his ribs and drifted in and out. When Amy came back, she froze for a moment, holding on to the handle of the car, looking like she was going to be sick, and Hawley knew he'd been right and the other men were dead, and he wished he'd listened to his guts when he checked in and saw those freckles. He could have been miles away by now or even drinking beers with McGee and not dying in the back seat of some girl's car.

Amy fumbled with her seat belt. She put the car in reverse, backed out of the parking spot, then pulled onto the highway. "There's a doctor on the reservation," she said, "about ten miles down."

The seat cushion beneath Hawley was wet with blood. There was blood on the seat belt, blood on the floor. "He'll report it."

"Not if you pay him," Amy said.

And that's when Hawley knew she'd opened the jar.

He tried to say something about this, but it came out slurred. He focused on the little boy strapped in the carrier next to him and tried to stay awake. The elephant pajamas had blood on them, and the baby was staring at the back of Amy's head and his arms were grabbing for his mother as if she was the only thing that mattered in the world.

The sun seemed to be coming up, the sky a multitude of pinks and oranges, and Hawley wondered again what time it was. The bullet was turning now, spinning its hardness into a dark place and taking him with it. He touched the diapers taped along the side of his stomach. They smelled of talcum powder and were heavy and warm and felt alive in his hands, just like the baby's diaper had when he'd carried it into the bathroom and put it in the trash.

"We're nearly there," Amy said. Then she said, "I'll go back and get your car for you."

Hawley hoped she would. He hoped that when he woke up and stumbled out of the doctor's house into the blazing desert heat, she'd be there with the baby and the money and it wouldn't just be his truck covered with dust on the side of the road, the keys in the ignition. That he wouldn't have to check the trunk for the guns, and that there'd be at least a grand left for him in the licorice jar. She owed him that, at least, he thought. She owed him something.

Hawley pressed his face against the back window. He eyed the side mirror, the highway as it stretched behind them. A black line reflecting through the desert morning. A single, lonely path. Then the car went over a bump, and there was a flash of fur and feathers. Roadkill—something already dead. A rabbit and an eagle, he thought. A coyote and a vulture. In the seat beside him the baby moaned and whimpered. His tiny mouth opened. He began to cry.

"He's hungry again," said Amy, but they couldn't stop, so she started singing. "Twinkle, Twinkle" and "Hush-a-bye, Baby." Hawley closed his eyes and listened. Her voice was off-key, but she was trying.

"You're a good mother," Hawley said, or at least he thought he did, and then the bullet pulled him the rest of the way into the dark.

MAURINE DALLAS WATKINS

Bound

FROM *Strand Magazine*

YES, MR. HEDGES, *I'm deaf but I can read your lips and understand perfectly: anything I say may be used against me, and I'm making this statement voluntary and of my own free will. And I'll write down exactly what happened last night, and how. But I wish you wouldn't read over my shoulder like that — I'll hand you each page when I'm done.*

Miss Thyrza took me to raise when I was thirteen.

"I don't want a boy that's too bright," she said. "None of these young smart alecks for mine. In fact, I'd rather have him more on the dumb side."

"We've got one here that's all on the dumb side," said the matron. "Ha, ha." She was always a great one for jokes that way. "Fetch Ernie, girls."

I was less than a rod away, reading every word they said, but I waited for the girls to fetch me, for if Mrs. Simpson had ever learned I could read lips like that, it would have been much harder for me to find out her plans and pass them on to the boys.

Miss Thyrza and me eyed each other, and I wasn't any more pleased than she was. That was seven years ago and she was in her middle thirties, but she looked to me like an old woman: partly her blue-gobbler nose and long yellow neck with its folds of fat going round and round, and partly that "ancestral" look, as I learned later when I studied her family photograph album on Sunday afternoons. People who resemble their folks too close always look old before their time, as if they've inherited their age along with the features.

"Of course, if you want a boy for company, Ernie can't gab none," said the matron brightly, laying an affectionate arm around my shoulders and giving me a pinch that meant I should close my mouth. It's a bad habit I have, letting my mouth hang open.

"Not for company," Miss Thyrza answered shortly. "But with Pa's death it leaves just me and the hired hand, Amos McGill. And you know how tongues wag—a woman alone that way and a man."

Then she turned and her black eyes burned me through. "Humph, is he healthy? Is he strong? Has he had all the children's diseases? For I can't spend my time nursing boys through the measles—I've got a hundred and sixty acres to tend!" And she ran her fingers over my teeth—just like I was a horse—to be sure there'd be no dental work till she'd had me a few years.

"How's his appetite? Will he eat me out of house and home? Can he work? Is he willing? Milk? Look after chickens? Hogs? Chop wood? Any bad habits? Does he lie? Steal? Smoke? Chew? No goings-on like that, mind you." She paused for breath, then finished: "And what schooling has he had? I aim to board a teacher this winter, and he can pick up some there if he's eager."

The matron wrote on the slate, which I wore around my neck: "Ernie, wouldn't you like to go with this nice, kind lady and have a nice, good home?"

And I wrote back, "Yes, ma'am."

But Miss Thyrza wasn't one to leap before looking, so she said she'd take me on trial from Friday till Monday.

When I explained to the boys how it was, they all went without apples for dinner and gave me half their biscuits that night to put in with my bundle of clothes, so that I could eat them between meals and be sort of delicate at the table. For our experience at the Home had taught us, unless you were a little girl with golden hair and blue eyes, the best way to make a good impression when tried out was to go easy on the victuals, do chores without being told, and keep from underfoot.

Yes, sir, I know what you want, Mr. Hedges, and I'm getting to it. But first I've got to make you see how things were, so you'll understand all that led up to last night.

Well, the next Monday Miss Thyrza signed up the papers, not adopting me, you know, but binding herself to give me room and board, clothes, and medical attention, in turn for which I was to "help reasonably" around the place.

And many's the time I wished I was back at the Home.

It wasn't the work: up at four for milking and feeding, and filling the woodbox; breakfast by lamplight; then to the fields for what-ever was to be done, or working around the barn or henhouses, fixing fences, clearing out timber, blasting and digging stumps; and at night rounding up the stock and doing evening chores be-fore supper and bed.

And it wasn't the food, though Miss Thyrza had a way of cook-ing up great batches ahead: biscuit and salt pork for the week, stacks of buckwheat cakes in crocks from morning to morning, and green-grape pies by the half dozen.

And Miss Thyrza wasn't mean to me. She didn't have time to be.

But the lonesomeness of it, that's what I hated. Of course I'd never had anyone to talk to, but the boys at the Home always let me watch them play and kind of help along carrying water, chalk-ing off bases, keeping scores, and things like that. I used to nearly die in the evening when Miss Thyrza would sit sewing carpet rags and Amos, who was over forty and had false teeth, would nod in his chair an hour or so before bed. I would get so homesick for something young that I'd chase the calves around the barnyard for company till I don't wonder folks thought I was simple.

Yes, Mr. Hedges, I'm getting on. I just want you to see what it meant to me when Jasper Thorley came to board.

If I had just one word to describe Jasper Thorley, it would be *kind.* Kind to everything and everybody. He's the first teacher Oak Ridge ever had who didn't have to lick the daylights out of the older boys just to prove he could. Jasper would just smile and get their minds off on something else, or maybe laugh with them if the trick was really good. He seemed to feel they were all there to learn something, him along with the scholars. Why, once he took a whole afternoon to let Pete Marsden talk about trapping, and then Jasper showed them how to make a new kind that caught but didn't hurt the rabbits.

And it came out at the trial how he and Amos had almost come to blows over the mare Amos used for plowing when he shouldn't. And he walked all the way to Tabor to find homes for Priscilla's kittens, the ones Miss Thyrza had told him to drown. Why, Mr. Hedges, that cat didn't even have a name till Jasper came; it was just the cat to rid the barn of mice, but he made her a personality.

And as for me —

It wasn't only that he was always patient and ready to explain, while most folks cut it short rather than bother with a slate and squeaky pencil, but he acted like he was glad, that it meant something to him, too, that he was learning from me. And he used to tell me how Edison said it was a blessing to be deaf as it let him concentrate on his work, and that Beethoven, who was a famous musician, couldn't hear a note. And he said nature always made it up to people like me by increasing their other faculties, that I could "feel" things other people couldn't—like the corn shooting up on hot nights, or a rain coming on miles away, or bees getting ready to swarm.

And he gave me books.

It's hard for you to understand what that meant to me, Mr. Hedges, for you believe the world is the way it seems here at Tabor and are content. But life isn't like this. There are places where it's bright and exciting, gay like a song, where people are noble and great and kind. Whatever comes to me, I'll be happier for knowing there are people like that, someplace, wherever it may be, though I'll never see them myself.

They were books from the school library, and he'd slip them, careless-like, into my room at night with a candle (for Miss Thyrza would miss the oil from the lamp), and there I would sit, propped up in bed, with the quilt tucked around like a shawl, and my fingers stiff and blue, so cold that my breath was smoke, while the green-plastered ceiling dripped sweat and the frost traced pictures on the windowpanes—and ride with d'Artagnan and fight with Ivanhoe and dream of Lorna Doone.

But Dickens was the one I loved best. Oliver Twist and Little Dorrit—I know them, and they would know me better than any of you in Tabor ever could. David Copperfield and Sidney Carton—"It is a far, far better thing that I do, than I have ever done . . ."

Yes, Mr. Hedges, I was only resting a minute. My fingers were cramped. This is the longest, and hardest, writing I've ever done. And I've hardly started. But I know what you and the district attorney want and I'll be to it soon. "We'll be here all day if that dummy keeps on at this rate," you are saying. Have you forgotten I can read lips, Mr. Hedges, or don't you care? There's all the time in the world. (I never noticed before how Mr. Morgan bites off his words: "Let him tell it his own way. Give him rope enough . . .")

I never knew why Jasper married Miss Thyrza, but I'm sure it wasn't for money like you folks thought.

And I don't believe Jasper knew either. Maybe he felt sorry for her, or maybe she told him there had been gossip. All I ever knew was what she said to Amos at breakfast one morning: "Me and Jasper was married Saturday"—they always went to town on Saturday to take the eggs to market—"and you and Ernie can start plowing the crik field today. Everything will be just as usual."

And it was, except that she started wearing wrappers to breakfast. Amos and I still called her Miss Thyrza, and every now and then Jasper would catch himself doing the same. That's the way he felt toward her, too, I think; ten years' difference between them seemed even more, for he was young for twenty-five.

As for her, she never loved him, leastways not what I mean by love. But she liked to feel he was hers, that all the girls and women could flutter around him at church socials and school suppers but she owned him.

Like she used to stand on a hilltop in the wind, and her nostrils would quiver and her jaw set tight, because as far as she could see the land was hers and all the crops on it, and the grain in the barns and the silo of fodder, horses, cows, hogs, and chickens—everything that breathed belonged to Thyrza Rudd!

She took me because I could be "bound," and marriage was her way of binding Jasper.

That's why she was willing to take Effie, when her father skipped out to no one knew where and her mother died and it looked as if she would have to go on the county, since she didn't have money enough to get back to some second cousins in Tennessee and she was too old for the Home—seventeen.

"Bring her here for a couple of days," she told Jasper, and he did: an ugly, scrawny little thing, with peaked face, leaf-brown hair, and dull eyes, red from crying, who trembled all the time and jumped when anyone spoke to her. Miss Thyrza liked that, and when she saw how the girl took hold, what a cook she was, how quick and quiet, how grateful and beholden for any kindness, like a stray half-starved dog, she gave her a little room under the eaves and let her stay on to do for us all.

You've seen spring beauties, all wilted and drooped, come back to life when you put them in water? Well, that's the way it was with Effie for the next two years.

Yes, sir, like spring beauties, sturdy but with a delicate grace. Her face and throat still white but stained now and then with a wildflower pink, her hair still brown but with glints of gold, and her eyes a deep blue, quiet and steady, except when she was talking to Jasper over her books (he'd helped her go on with her schooling outside), and then they'd turn black with excitement and glisten like stars.

For Jasper helped her, lifted her up, as he did us all, and with him she had wings.

Then suddenly Amos stopped teasing her. He'd always done things to annoy, such as tracking up the floor when it was fresh scrubbed, upsetting her kindling, eating slow to hold her back with her work. But now he began to pay her compliments and bring her store candy from town and make excuses to follow her about her work and brush against her. And once, when she was carrying a crock of milk from the springhouse, he slipped up in back and kissed her cheek. She wheeled around and threw the milk, crock and all, straight in his face, then ran to the house, crying, to scrub her cheek with lye soap. Miss Thyrza scolded her terrible for her carelessness, and she took it, afraid to tell the truth. But from then on she hated Amos and drew back whenever he came near, shivering like he was some animal she feared. And that's the way things were up to the trial.

Yes, Mr. Hedges, I know you know all about the trial and you needn't swear at me either. But what you know was like the wrong side of a carpet; the pattern's the same as on the right, but the colors are all turned about. That's the way it was with what really happened and what came out in court.

It was Saturday night, you remember, and Jasper and Miss Thyrza had gone to town in the afternoon as usual and stayed for the band concert. Amos was out in the yard smoking (Miss Thyrza wouldn't allow it in the house), Effie had gone to her room, and I was reading in bed. I remember it was *Heart of Midlothian*. It must have been pretty late, anyway after nine, when I felt a sudden shaking of the rafters and walls, and an instant later there was the smell of smoke. *A lamp's overturned,* I thought, and rushed to the door.

There, across the hall, on the threshold of her room, stood Effie, in her nightdress, hair flying, hand clutched to her heart, and eyes wide and staring in horror. And by her side, with one arm around her shoulders and the other holding a gun, was Jasper.

And Amos lay dead at their feet. That was the thud I had felt.

I know that's not the story you got at the trial, but there's nothing you can do about it. I looked that up last night in the eighth-grade history book: the Constitution says no man shall be twice in jeopardy of life and limb for the same offense; and Jasper's been tried once for killing Amos McGill. Else I shouldn't be telling you now. And there wasn't any perjury either—but I'll come to that later.

I don't know how long we stood there, the three of us, for you can't judge time in a moment like that.

Then the front door opened and closed, the stairs quivered and trembled, and Miss Thyrza stood on the landing. She didn't see Amos's body, nor me, just the two in each other's arms, for Jasper had dropped the gun and was trying to hush Effie's sobs.

And you could tell from her face all that was in her mind.

If it hadn't been so awful, it would have been funny. In fact, it was kind of funny anyway—at least I wanted to laugh or scream, do anything to break up the hideous thoughts that were racing through her brain.

At last she found her tongue. I'm not sure of the words, for they poured out so fast; you've heard of tongue-lashings—this was one.

"So this is why you pretended to go to Hebron and left the Birches to bring me home! No wonder you wanted to get an early start! No wonder you didn't want me to go with you! I can see now why you were so anxious! And this hussy—" She started on Effie. "That's what comes of taking in trash! How long has it been going on? How many times have you two—"

Jasper cut in to explain. His face was turned so I couldn't tell what he said, but as I learned afterward, Amos had watched Effie from the yard and when he saw her lamp go out had sneaked up the stairs to her room. Her screams had roused Jasper, who'd been home an hour or so, he'd grabbed his gun, which was always kept handy for chicken thieves, and it had gone off in the struggle.

For the first time Miss Thyrza noticed the dead man, but even that didn't stop her.

"What's it to you where Amos was going or what happened? Why should you care? Tell me that! Answer me! Tell me!"

Tears were streaming down her face, her eyes were hawk-bright, and her fingers clasped her throat as if she was choking while she waited for him to speak. In spite of all that has happened, looking back, even now, I'm sorry for her then, for she was stripped of her pride and vanity and saw things as they were: that she was old and yellow and wrinkled and Jasper had never loved her, that no one had ever loved her or ever would.

His answer was quick and stern: "She's a young girl we've taken in our home and it's our place to protect her."

Her color flowed back at that. "You'll swear there's been nothing between you?"

"Yes, I'll swear it, but I'm ashamed of you for asking, Thyrza. I'm ashamed of you and for you."

She believed him. It was so clearly true—you could have told by Effie's innocent eyes as well as Jasper's words.

He went on: "But whatever you think, there's no time for it now. There's a man that's dead—and I've got to give myself up."

Effie gave a little moan and caught his arm. Miss Thyrza's fear came back. "What'll you tell them?"

"The truth," said he.

"And what'll they say?" Thyrza replied. "I believe you, Jasper, but they won't. You know they won't. And they'll say you've been carrying on with the hired girl under my very eyes. And they'll say—" She broke off, and the awfulest fear a human can know came into her eyes—the fear of laughter. An old wife made a laughingstock by a young husband who'd married her for her money—that was in her eyes.

Effie hadn't even heard her words, so busy was she thinking of him. "But they can't do anything to you, can they, Mr. Thorley?"

"Of course they'll do something to him! Send him to prison for life or hang him!" She was glad to turn on the girl again. "And it's your fault. If it hadn't been for you, none of this would have happened!"

"Let me go with you," Effie begged, clutching Jasper's arm, "and tell them it was my fault, that you had to do it!"

"To save you? That's no defense!" Thyrza cut in savage-like. "Why should he kill a man for you? He's got no call to protect you —you're nothing to him! There's no law says he's got a right to kill anyone for you." She turned slowly to Jasper, and you could see the plan a-borning in her eyes. "But if it was for me—if you'd done it for your wife, Jasper. If it was my bedroom Amos had come to . . ."

For an hour we rehearsed the story we would tell—they wrote it down for me, word for word.

Then we acted it out, for Miss Thyrza said she didn't want any

perjury on her soul; whatever she said on the witness stand must
be the truth. Even carrying Amos to their room, with Thyrza alone,
and Jasper coming up the stairs and finding him there, even the
second shot to call Effie and rouse me from my book. And at midnight Jasper rode into town and gave himself up for shooting and
killing Amos McGill, with a plea of the unwritten law. But Miss
Thyrza needn't have worried about the perjury, for as wife she
couldn't testify, and the only one who lied was Mr. Nichols, the
lawyer, and that doesn't count. It may in heaven but not in law,
for he's not sworn to tell the truth like witnesses. Why is that? Why
doesn't it count when a lawyer lies? Why don't they make them
swear to tell the truth like other people?

The Birches earnestly swore how they'd brought Miss Thyrza
home at half after nine that night, as Jasper had gone on to Hebron to see a man about some hogs. Then Mr. Nichols insinuated
how when Jasper reached the crik he'd found the spring freshets
had washed out the bridge and so had come home sooner than
his wife expected. And what was to show his mare had lost a shoe
and he'd never been near the crik but had reached home a good
half-hour before Miss Thyrza?

And Effie, standing out from everyone else in the courtroom
—do you remember how she looked, Mr. Hedges, as if there was
a light shining over her, and through her, and from her!—described the scene she saw when the shot was fired.

Then I wrote down my answers, and also told how, back when
she took me to raise, Miss Thyrza had told the matron it was to
keep tongues quiet about her and Amos; and that when she was
in the garden, he was in the garden, when she was in the barn,
he was in the barn, and when he was in the orchard, she went
traipsing after. And it was true—she was trying to egg him on
with his work, but they never asked me why. Why do they make
you swear to tell the whole truth, Mr. Hedges, then snap you off
the minute the lawyer's got the answer he wants and never ask
you why?

Jasper didn't take the stand at all, just sat with his head in his
hands, meeting no one's eyes.

But Miss Thyrza held hers high, for though she couldn't testify,
there was nothing to keep her from nodding yes to all the lawyer
said so the jury could see her do it and think that's what she'd

like to say. With her eyes all bright and shiny, her hair curled and cheeks painted (the lawyer had said she must look kind of fast to bear out his story while he told what a dangerous woman she was, how irresistible and appealing), she looked real handsome, just like all the papers said.

Altogether it was a great week for her, for it's not every woman that's left on the carpet for forty years who lives to hear herself called a Cleopatra with all the neighbors standing around to hear —women she'd gone to school with, men who'd called her an old maid, all standing around now, gawking and wondering.

"Well, what any man can see in her!" That was the womenfolk's verdict.

But the men all kind of snickered and looked wise and said they couldn't exactly explain but there was "something," they'd always felt it, a certain "something."

Then the newspapermen from the city tried to analyze the strange lure that had set Amos and Jasper to battling for her charms. Some said it was her hawk-black eyes that held them spellbound, others said her throaty voice, others the line of her jaw and the Mona Lisa smile, cold and enigmatic; and they called her the Iron Woman Who Lures Men to Destruction, and ran her picture alongside of Circe, Madame de Pompadour, and Ninon de Lenclos, who had lovers at the age of ninety, which was very encouraging as Miss Thyrza was still well under fifty.

But once the verdict was in, it was like a pin in a balloon or a Fourth of July tableau when you take away the red and blue lights.

The reporters and picturemen vanished back to the city; the lawyers, who'd got their pay in advance, melted away. Only the townsfolk were left, and Jezebel was the one she made them think of. Even the jury that had said "not guilty" because of the unwritten law skulked off as if they thought he'd protected a home, all right, like any real man should, but it wasn't the kind they'd care to set foot in. So it was that no one grabbed his hand to wish him luck when at last he walked out of the courthouse, free; and alone he followed Miss Thyrza down the narrow, dark stairs, through the empty hall, and across the square to the hitching rings, where the surrey stood waiting.

They were in back, I climbed in front with Effie, and we started the long drive back to the farm to pick up life again.

I'll never forget that cold winter sunshine and the sundogs that came up just as we turned in the lane.

The house, on the hilltop, looked dark and lonely and evil —like a house where a murder had been, like a house where love could not live, where decency would be strangled. The tree branches twisted and writhed in the wind like black snakes over the roof; and the windows, shot with the last yellow light from over the hill, gleamed like a nest of copperheads I'd found in the woods one day.

And it's here my statement really starts.

Yes, thank you. I would relish a little coffee if it don't put you out too much, for being up all night this way and walking to town on an empty stomach has left me kind of weak—besides what happened, and I'm getting to that pretty soon.

Fear of being the butt of the town's jokes had started Miss Thyrza on what looked like a noble sacrifice, and vanity had buoyed her up during the giddy, gaudy whirl of the trial. But now it was over, a darker, uglier feeling raised its head.

"Effie, get supper on. And Jasper, you can help Ernie with the chores when you've laid a fire. For we've got no hand now, and there won't be none." Jasper stood white and silent as she went on. "And Effie here can take her turn when she's through with the work in the kitchen—there'll be fewer to do for now and she'll have more time. You've cost me enough, you two, in shame and money; I've bought you both ways and now you can start paying me. Get to work!"

Over and over in the days that followed she'd remind them how it was her money that had paid the lawyers, even bringing out bills to prove all it had cost her, how it was her stock and crops had suffered from neglect at harvest time.

And when folks passing by would stop and stare at the house, she'd say bitterly, "See, I'm a scarlet woman. That's what I've made of myself to save you from the gallows."

Again and again she'd fling at them what they owed her: "If it wasn't for me, you wouldn't have any life, or her any reputation. They're mine, both of them—I've bought them."

And every night at prayers she'd remind them of their sins, which only the blood of the Lamb could cleanse, while she begged God to save their souls from eternal fire. Through it all Effie was scared and ashamed, like a child that knows it's done wrong and is being rightly punished. But Jasper was steady and serene — untouched.

And that nearly drove Miss Thyrza wild: to think she'd bought him and he still belonged to himself, that he had the power to lift himself up and beyond anything she could say or do. He was never defiant, always gentle with her as if humoring a sick person, but quiet and smiling as if his mind was on other things. I don't think he even realized how she was reaching out, like something with feelers and claws to suck its prey down into the mud.

But her chance came that spring.

The work wasn't so hard that winter, but when spring came, with all the plowing and planting and farrows besides the regular work, there were days when the three of us worked, with our tongues hanging out, from four in the morning till nine at night and still weren't through. And on top of it all she decided to clear out the timber along the crik and dredge out the gravel pit (the road commissioners had made her an offer) — Effie and Jasper shoveling and me to haul.

I had just started off with a load of the gravel and was halfway up the hill when the singletree broke, and I went back to get Jasper's help. I'll always remember them like that, standing there on the bank of the crik, half hidden by the new green of the willows that dipped here and there in the water, a turtle peeping up through the mud, and the sunshine everywhere warm and lazy — and she looking up at him with that winging, soaring look in her eyes that were blind to everything in the world but him. And he was saying only her name over and over and over. And you knew from that look, whether ever a word was said, that come what may, the bond between them was for all the days of their life.

I stole away, thinking how she, Miss Thyrza, I mean, had really brought it about. The way she had hurled at them always, "You two — you two — you two." Seeking all the time to make them hers, she had only bound them together in a suffering that had turned to love.

That night after supper they told her and asked that she let Effie go; fifty dollars would take her back to her mother's people, or else to the city, where she could find work. But she couldn't stay on there with Jasper, her loving him and knowing that he loved her — it wouldn't be right.

Miss Thyrza refused. Effie had caused her the loss of Amos Mc-

Gill, the best hand she ever had, and she had no mind to go out hunting another. If she was so particular about doing right, that was it: to stay and, so far as she could, fill his place.

Of the love between Effie and Jasper, she said not a word. But from then on she tortured him through the girl. Effie was afraid of the dark, so Miss Thyrza'd make excuses to send her with only a candle that threw ghastly shadows into the dry cellar, where we kept the potatoes and turnips, apples and squash. She was afraid of rats, so Miss Thyrza would make her set the bit-steel trap in the corn crib (Priscilla had died with her last batch of kittens) and hold it, full of slick, fat rats, in the watering trough till they were drowned, or else pick up the bodies when they'd eaten the poison she scattered around. She couldn't stand the sun, so all summer long Miss Thyrza kept her working in the fields and Jasper inside at easy jobs; then she could watch him suffer when Effie came in sick and dizzy from overheat. And once, when she gave way and fainted, Miss Thyrza wouldn't even let him go near her, but she brought her around, all the time smiling, a smile that was meaner somehow than her harshest words had ever been. Jasper broke under this. At last she had found a way to reach him! And the more haggard he grew, the happier and brighter she was—like she was feeding, really eating and feeding, on his suffering. It was horrible to watch, for she seemed to be circling and circling about them, like a buzzard, waiting, waiting.

Yes, I know I'm going slow, but I'm tired. I'm terrible tired. It's two nights now.

For they came to her again night before last and all night they pleaded and begged: that she should let them go away together, that Jasper would send what money he could earn and she could divorce him.

"No," she said. "You can't drive me to a thing like that. I've been a good woman all my life—you have sinned, but you can't force me to."

Then let Effie go—Effie would have to go, they said.

And she flung in his teeth all the words he had said that night of the murder: "'A young girl we've taken in our home and our duty to protect her!' Fine way you've got of protecting! I took her sin on me once, but this time she shall know disgrace."

"Then we'll both go away," Jasper said slowly. "We've put it up to you fair."

"I'll have the law on you first! I'll tell them the truth about the trial. Effie perjured herself and they'll send her to prison, and as for you—"

"I wish they had hanged me," he said. "I wish to God that they had!" And all Effie asked was that Jasper be forgiven; she wouldn't mind prison herself, only—

"You needn't worry about that," Miss Thyrza said, still smiling, "for I'll bring the child up like mine."

Morning came and she sent them about their work, Jasper to town with a load of hogs and Effie to clean out the henhouse and rid it of rats, while she went upstairs to sleep. Effie gave me a snack for noon (I was husking in the bottom field), and all day I figured and wondered. Had Miss Thyrza known from the very first, had she planned it all, had she meant this should happen—the final link for her chain?

I came to supper and found her there at the table alone, and I took the rope I had brought from the barn and wound it round her, with a cloth tied around her throat and head—and you'll find her like that, bound and dead.

I waited all night, but Jasper and Effie didn't come. They have gone as they told her they would, and I am glad. There's no need to bring them back—they know nothing about it all. This is my statement, voluntary and of my own free will.

I don't know what Miss Thyrza ate that night, Mr. Hedges. Why do you ask me that? What she ate had nothing to do with it! I don't care what the doctor and coroner say—tell Mr. Morgan not to believe them! She died, like I told you, from being bound! Poisoned? The autopsy shows poison? With the stuff they give rats! And Effie and Jasper have confessed—oh no! Why didn't they wait! Give me back my statement! You said it would be used against me, not them. I'm as guilty as they are: I wanted her dead but didn't know how. And they did.

Contributors' Notes
Other Distinguished Mystery Stories
of 2012

Contributors' Notes

Tom Barlow is the author of the story collection *Welcome to the Goat Rodeo*. Other stories of his have appeared in anthologies, including *Best New Writing 2011*, and magazines and journals, including *Redivider, Temenos, Apalachee Review, Hobart, Needle*, the *William and Mary Review*, and the *Hiss Quarterly*. He is a graduate of the Clarion Writer's Workshop for fantasy and science fiction. He has also written about personal finance for websites, including *Forbes.com, DailyFinance.com*, and *Dealnews.com*. He writes because conversation involves a lot of give-and-take, and he's always thought of himself as more of a giver.

▪ "Smothered and Covered" started, not surprisingly, with a visit to one of my favorite restaurants, Waffle House. At the time I was working a pressured job, which caused me often to be awake in the middle of the night. Knowing that I wouldn't fall back to sleep, I would occasionally head over to the Waffle House and dawdle over a 4 A.M. breakfast. Looking at the other clientele, I realized that WH is one of the few places where those who desperately need to get out of the house in the middle of the night can nurse their demons for the price of a cup of coffee.

Knowing that one of those people was destined to become my main character, I searched for a conflict that could account for his malaise. I'd been thinking about the awful preponderance of fatal car accidents caused by drunk drivers and the guilt that must, or at least should, haunt those who survive, especially if the fatality is a loved one. How could he carry on with such a burden? How could a marriage survive?

That darkness led me to a noir style and voice, which seemed to capture a sense of inevitability. After agonizing for weeks over a proper ending, I spent one day trimming the fat from the story (for me, a crucial step in the process), only to discover that I already had an ending that worked well. I just hadn't recognized it as such. Older, wiser, and a devotee of Lunesta,

I now trawl for characters during the daylight hours, usually at coffee-houses. I'm not sure, however, that the pickings are quite as rich.

Michael Connelly is a crime-beat reporter turned novelist. He has written twenty-five novels in twenty years, most of which center on the pursuits of Detective Harry Bosch of the Los Angeles Police Department. He also has written several novels about Bosch's half-brother Mickey Haller, a criminal defense attorney, thus pursuing an exploration of crime and justice from both sides of the aisle, so to speak. Connelly is married and the father of a teenage daughter. He lives in Florida but spends a lot of his time in Los Angeles, the city he writes about.

▪ The subject of the *Vengeance* anthology naturally lent itself to ex-plorations of the fine line between punishment and retribution. When people take matters into their own hands, is it always vengeance, or can there be justice? It's a theme I have played with before, and I was happy to be asked to contribute to the collection edited by Lee Child. When I was a reporter I wrote about a major gold fraud in which hun-dreds of people lost their savings in a gold-buying scheme. There were many threats against the perpetrators' lives and I started with that, thinking, What if a victim made good on the threat or hired someone to make good on the threat? Would it be justice or vengeance? I re-member these guys had really been callous in the extent they went to rip people off. They would crawl under their desks while on the phone with a customer and say they had just entered the gold vault to pick out their gold bars. The slight echo made under the desk sounded like they could actually be in a vault, and it helped them sell the fraud. Of course, there was no gold. They were just taking people's money. So that was the starting point of this story, and of course I wanted to bring Harry Bosch into it. It had been quite a while since I had writ-ten about Harry in the short form. It is always fun to do that.

O'Neil De Noux's crime fiction has garnered several awards: the Shamus for best short story, the Derringer for best novelette, and the 2011 Police Book of the Year. His recurring characters include New Orleans Police detectives Dino LaStanza (1980s), Jacques Dugas (1890s), and John Raven Beau (twenty-first century) as well as private eye Lucien Caye (1940s). In 2013, De Noux was elected vice president of the Private Eye Writers of America. He also writes in other genres, including historical fiction, fan-tasy, horror, western, science fiction, and erotica.

▪ Writing about New Orleans AK (After Katrina) is difficult, as the city changes just about every day. Some areas have come back faster than oth-ers; some will never return, buildings still gutted, slabs where houses once stood, restaurants torn from the piling. The only constant is the crime rate, which returned with a vengeance. This inspired me to write a story about a citizenry that acts as if its police department is an occupying army. New Orleans has always been the hardest city in America to police. It's a city of great promise and great disappointment, where the good times roll and crime is always around the corner. The New Orleans Police Department is understaffed, underpaid, undertrained, and held up to standards few humans can achieve. And most of the time the men and women in blue feel alone.

The *New York Times* bestselling, award-winning author **Eileen Dreyer** has published thirty-eight novels and ten short stories in multiple genres, ranging from historical romance to medical-forensic thrillers. Living in St. Louis with her husband and children, she has turned in the nurse's whites she wore during a career in trauma medicine and made writing, travel, and St. Louis Cardinals baseball her full-time hobbies. She has animals but refuses to submit them to the glare of the spotlight.

 ▪ I was invited to submit a short story for the *Crime Square Anthology,* in which all the crimes took place in Times Square. Each story was set in a different decade. When asked which decade I wanted, there was no question. I picked the 1940s because immediately I saw in my head that iconic photo of the sailor kissing the nurse on VJ Day. It has always really spoken to me. There had to be a story there somewhere.

I studied the photo. I researched it and found that Alfred Eisenstadt, who took the photo, had followed the sailor down the length of Times Square as he kissed every woman he passed. Then I learned that there was more than one photo and in each different people are seen in the background. What of *those* people? What is going on that day that we're missing because we're watching the performance put on by an exuberant sailor? My story is about two of those other persons, another sailor and the wife who has waited for him to come home. It's about not assuming that you know what you see.

David Edgerley Gates lives in Santa Fe, New Mexico, and many of his stories take place in the West—period pieces like the Placido Geist bounty hunter stories, and others more contemporary, dealing with the meth plague in Indian country, say, or the border war, drugs and human traffic moving north, guns and money going south, and the corrosive influence of the Mexican cartels. "The Devil to Pay," although it's set in present-day New York, nods in passing to the long reach of cartel money and the increased Latino gang presence in the American prison system.

Gates is a past Shamus and Edgar Award nominee. His stories appear regularly in *Alfred Hitchcock's Mystery Magazine* and *Ellery Queen's Mystery Magazine.* His website is www.davidedgerleygates.com.

▪ Tommy Meadows is small-time, a pilot fish swimming in an ocean of larger predators. He's not as ruthless as some, but neither is he that nice a person. I think the character's influenced, to some degree, by the guys Donald Westlake used to write about, grifters and also-rans, who never quite make it into the heavy or the big score. And Tommy is more of a catalyst than a major player. He just finds himself in the wrong place at the right time. The ending of this story is one of my few ventures into what might be called metafiction. The fairy tale Tommy tells his gramma is, of course, the story you've just read.

Although best known for his true crime books, notably the Edgar-nominated *Six Against the Rock*, about Alcatraz, and *Zebra*, also nominated, which examined the infamous San Francisco murders of the early 1970s, **Clark Howard** has developed a great following for his short stories, five of which have been nominated for Edgar Allan Poe Awards; one, "Horn Man," was picked as the best of the year for 1980. He has also won the Derringer Award and in 2009 was voted the Golden Derringer for Lifetime Achievement in the mystery genre. Other nominations have been for Shamus and Spur Awards, and five times he was named as the favorite for the Ellery Queen Readers Award by that popular magazine.

Andre Kocsis lives in the West Chilcotin, a remote area of British Columbia, Canada. His work has been published in the *Dalhousie Review,* the *New Orphic Review, Skyline Magazine, The Oak,* and *Couloir Magazine* as well as a number of online publications. Currently he's working on the fifth and, he fervently hopes, final draft of a novel entitled *Canyon Marathon.*

▪ It has been my lifelong ambition to use the name Sierra for a protagonist. However, this was not the sole impetus for "Crossing." Marijuana is a $6 billion industry in British Columbia, with an estimated 95 percent of this cash crop destined for the United States. A news story about the capture of some smugglers started me thinking that the mountains along the Canada-U.S. border could provide an interesting way to move drugs. I felt, however, that it was prudent to try out this idea in fiction rather than in real life.

The southeast of British Columbia, where the Rocky Mountains cross the border, has a history of serving as a haven for dissidents. The Doukhobors, a pacifist religious sect with strong antigovernment beliefs, escaped persecution in Russia with the aid of Leo Tolstoy and settled here in the early 1900s. As well, a community of polygamous Mormons have made this area their home since 1946. And during the Vietnam War many American youths escaped the draft by settling here. They've had a noticeable impact on the culture of the region.

During the late sixties, I was a Canadian student in Berkeley and observed an American social fabric rent by the war. Ever since, I have been fascinated by characters like Sierra, who had to decide between risking their lives in a war with which they disagreed and leaving their homes, their families, and the country they loved. No doubt many have never resolved internal conflicts that reflect the larger drama that was played out on the national stage during the Vietnam War.

The wilderness has always drawn me, and mountainous terrain has a special fascination. There's an inherent drama in the harsh conditions, with the abruptly changing weather, which tends toward the extreme. It's an environment that tests the spirit, and many of my short stories take place with this backdrop. Consequently, skiing in the backcountry has become a passion that I indulge at every opportunity. In this context, I have met a number of mountain guides, and without exception, they have been fascinating, if often flawed, characters.

Sierra strives to escape the complications, the frustrations, the ambiguities of civilization. In the wilderness, decisions are without ambiguity because they are about survival. Ironically, his desire to escape is what traps Sierra in a situation in which he must again make a choice, a choice that he thought he had made once and for all in his youth.

Kevin Leahy's stories have appeared in the *Briar Cliff Review, Slice Magazine,* and *Opium Magazine.* He lives in Chicago with his wife and son and is working on a novel.

• Years ago I read a statistic that stuck with me: there are now more prisoners than farmers in the United States. I found myself thinking about what that might mean, so I started writing about a farm community that became a prison town. The seed of the story was the sentence "No one recalls who built the prison." While that exact phrase didn't make it into the final version, the sense of anonymity and communal amnesia behind it helped me find a way into the story. It sounds orderly and analytical when I explain it like that. But the truth is, it was trial and error the whole way, and I didn't get anywhere until I put my own fears on the page—of being jobless, having a sick child, losing my son.

I'd like to acknowledge a debt to Tracy Huling for her excellent paper "Building a Prison Economy in Rural America," which was invaluable in my research. When I reread my story now, I also hear the influence of fiction I read and loved in the years before I wrote it—Chris Bachelder's *U.S.!,* Kevin Brockmeier's "The Year of Silence," and especially Faulkner's "A Rose for Emily." Whatever defects my story has are mine, and whatever resonance it has, the echoes of those earlier pieces helped me find it.

Nick Mamatas is the author of several novels in the fantasy and horror genres, including the Lovecraftian Beat road novel *Move Under Ground* and the crime fantasy *Bullettime*. His shift to crime fiction will be nearly complete with the publication of the mostly noir *Love Is the Law* in late 2013. His short fiction has been published in *Asimov's Science Fiction, Weird Tales,* and the *New Haven Review* and in anthologies, including *West Coast Crime Wave, Psychos,* and *Lovecraft Unbound*. Nick's fiction and editorial work have been nominated for the Bram Stoker Award five times, and also for the Hugo, World Fantasy, and Shirley Jackson Awards.

▪ My influences have always been broad—science fiction, "cult" fiction of all types, including the Beats, horror, and crime. I'm also a Long Island boy, and years ago was sent out to Northport, where Jack Kerouac had made his home, to cover a marathon reading of *Big Sur* for an online magazine. I had found Akashic Books through my interest in punk/cult stuff and eagerly read the volumes of its fill-in-the-blank Noir Series as they came out. When Akashic announced *Long Island Noir,* I queried editor Kaylie Jones with a story idea about my hometown, Port Jefferson, but another writer had already called dibs on the location. I immediately thought back to Kerouac and my trip to Northport and quickly suggested an idea about that town. Kerouac isn't the only thing Northport is famous for; the "acid king" Ricky Kasso's murder of Gary Lauwers ranks high as well, especially for any 1980s LI kid who had long hair and liked horror and fantasy. (Guilty.) Obviously I had to combine the two and add other bits and pieces of Long Island: fears of breast cancer clusters, Mobbed-up waste management firms, and the tourism industry. In proper Beat fashion, the story came out in a mad rush. Luckily, Jones was there with her red pen to make it more comprehensible. I've grown to like writing crime fiction. I think I'll stick around.

Emily St. John Mandel is from the west coast of British Columbia, Canada. Her most recent novel is *The Lola Quartet;* her previous novels are *Last Night in Montreal* and *The Singer's Gun*. She is a staff writer for *The Millions,* and her essays and short fiction have appeared in numerous anthologies. She is married and lives in Brooklyn; her website is www.emilymandel.com.

▪ My second novel, *The Singer's Gun,* involved a man who finds himself drawn unwillingly into a criminal transaction, and an associate of his ends up getting shot. Although the associate, David, was a relatively minor character in the book, I found myself thinking of him a great deal. He was a young widower who'd been drifting across Europe, trying to avoid the ghost of his wife, and at the moment of death I had him see her again.

Murder your darlings, writers are told, but sometimes those darlings refuse to stay dead. I cut most of David's backstory from *The Singer's Gun* because it slowed the pace of the book at exactly the point where I needed the narrative to pick up speed. In the final version of the book, not only is David's backstory mostly gone, but his death takes place off-stage. But that deleted backstory stayed with me in the ensuing years, and eventually I developed it into "Drifter." I remained fascinated by the idea of a brokenhearted traveler trying to disappear, running from the memory of a lost beloved but at the same time secretly longing to see that person again.

Leaving home is a formative experience in anyone's life, and when I left home, I did so in a somewhat extreme fashion — I moved alone from rural British Columbia to downtown Toronto (a distance of some three thousand miles) when I was eighteen years old — and it was like flying into an entirely different life. I've been thinking ever since about the power and joy and hazard of relocation and travel, the way we can reinvent or lose ourselves through movement over the landscape. "Drifter" is about one of the very darkest possibilities of travel, which is to say, traveling in an effort to erase yourself.

Dennis McFadden lives and writes in an old farmhouse called Mountjoy on Bliss Road, just up Peaceable Street from Harmony Corners. His stories have appeared in dozens of publications, including *Alfred Hitchcock's Mystery Magazine, New England Review,* the *Missouri Review,* the *Massachusetts Review, Crazyhorse, Fiction, PRISM international,* and the *South Carolina Review.* A story from his 2010 collection, *Hart's Grove,* was selected for inclusion in *The Best American Mystery Stories 2011.*

- Okay, I admit it, I love Lafferty best. I've written a hundred stories, made up a hundred heroes, but Lafferty's my favorite by far. I spoil him half to death. I treat him better than his brothers and sisters. I indulge him more (five stories of his own and counting), let him have his own way more, let him get away with bloody murder. I just don't have it in me to scold him, to try to keep him in line. Who could blame me? He makes my writing life a hell of a lot easier than any of the others (most of whom, ungrateful bastards, don't even try). All I have to do is imagine an inkling of something a little bit Laffertyesque, and wham, bam, here we go, Lafferty off to the races, barreling gangways here and there, this way and that, rambling on and on in that pseudo-rogue-brogue of his. I pretty much just sit back and listen, along for the ride. What can I say? I love this guy.

Micah Nathan is a bestselling author, short story writer, and essayist. He has written several novels, some ignored, most well received. He received his MFA from Boston University, where he was awarded the 2010 Saul Bellow Prize for fiction.

- "Quarry" was one of those rare pieces that emerged fully formed. An isolated farmhouse, a body in the woods, two children left alone with a murderous thief — if I couldn't make that scenario work, I have no business writing.

Joyce Carol Oates is the author of a number of novels of mystery and suspense, including most recently *The Accursed, Daddy Love,* and *Mudwoman,* as well as collections of stories, including *Give Me Your Heart, The Corn Maiden and Other Nightmares,* and *Black Dahlia & White Rose.* She is a member of the American Academy of Arts and Letters and was the 2011 recipient of the President's Medal in the Humanities. "So Near Any Time Always" will be included in *Evil Eye: Four Tales of Love Gone Wrong.*

▪ Stories about stalkers always fascinate me. Years ago, a man whom I'd known in Detroit, who had tried to exploit me as a means of advancing his literary career, set out to stalk me—but through the mail, not literally. Thank God, this was an era long before the Internet—what devastation he might have wrought in the twenty-first century, under aliases, attacking "Joyce Carol Oates," who would have been helpless to combat a many-pronged online attack.

As it was, the Detroit stalker sent hundreds of letters to me and to others, bitterly denigrating me, over a period of ten to twelve years. He managed to publish, in a small literary magazine, a story with the ominous title "How I Murdered Joyce Carol Oates." (No, I didn't read the story!) His threats were clever, elliptical, and taunting—the kind of vague threat that wasn't clear enough to be actionable, even if I'd wanted to appeal to the police.

"So Near Any Time Always" is about a teenage stalker and his naively complicit victim. It has two distinct origins: the first, a blurred memory of adolescent yearning, misunderstanding, anxiety, and unease; the second, a more adult perception of the terrible harm people can inflict upon others, in their failure to take responsibility for, even to acknowledge, a potentially dangerous family member.

Fundamentally, the story is about a young girl's wish to believe that she is "special"—that a boy could be attracted to her, and feel emotion for her, on her own terms. So badly the narrator wants to believe, she overlooks clues in the boy's bizarre behavior that would alert most of us to the possibility of danger. Foolish as the girl is, she is after all *young*—she is inexperienced, naive, intelligent, but not skeptical like her sister.

It's the unconscionable behavior of the boy's parents that generates the story: their pretense that their son, who killed his young sister years before, was "cured" and "harmless"—and would not harm anyone ever again. This moral blindness is outrageous—yet a commonplace—as families protect relatives who are a danger to others and themselves.

Of course, the great irony of the story is that the girl will never forget her "first love"—though the boy was insanely fixated on her as a reincarnation of his (murdered) sister. Never will she be pursued again in such an impassioned way. It is the girl who recalls the boy—the stalker—in darkly romantic terms; always she will remember him—"So Near Any Time Always."

Nancy Pickard is the winner of Agatha, Anthony, Macavity, Shamus, and Barry Awards for her novels and short stories. She is a four-time Edgar Award finalist. Her novel *The Virgin of Small Plains* was the Kansas book of the year in 2007. Her most recent novel, *The Scent of Rain and Lightning,* was a finalist for the Great Plains Fiction Award in 2011. Her next novel, set in Kansas, will be published in 2014.

▪ "Light Bulb" is based more on my own life than any other story I've ever written. I was the child who walked home alone from church school and was frightened by a man who tried to lure me into a church. I am the woman who had an epiphany many years later that shocked me with the realization that although he had failed to molest me, he had surely also tried with other children and had probably succeeded with some of them. Like my protagonist, I visited the police to report him, knowing he could still be alive, he might be a grandfather, he could still be doing damage. In real life, I never found a way to stop him, so I invented one.

A full-time professional writer since 1969, **Bill Pronzini** has published seventy-seven novels, including five in collaboration with his wife, mystery novelist Marcia Muller, and thirty-seven in his iconic "Nameless Detective" series. He is also the author of four hundred short stories, articles, essays, and book reviews and four nonfiction books, and he has edited or coedited numerous anthologies. His work has been translated into eighteen languages and published in nearly thirty countries.

In 2008 he was named a Mystery Writers of America Grand Master, the organization's highest award. He has received three Shamus Awards, two for best novel; the Lifetime Achievement Award (presented in 1987) from the Private Eye Writers of America; and six nominations for the Mystery Writers of America's Edgar Allan Poe Award. His suspense novel *Snowbound* was the recipient of the Grand Prix de la Litterature Policière as the best crime novel published in France in 1988. Two other suspense novels, *A Wasteland of Strangers* and *The Crimes of Jordan Wise,* were nominated for the Hammett Prize for best crime novels of 1997 and 2006, respectively, by the International Crime Writers Association.

▪ John Quincannon and Sabina Carpenter are characters I created for the novel *Quincannon* (1985). In that book they were not as yet a detective team. Sabina was then employed as an operative for the Denver office of the Pinkerton Detective Agency (her character is loosely based on Kate Warne, the first female PI, who worked for Allan Pinkerton in his Baltimore agency during and after the Civil War); Quincannon was a field agent attached to the San Francisco branch of the U.S. Secret Service. They joined forces to open their San Francisco–based detective agency shortly after the events described in *Quincannon* and have since appeared in more than a score of short stories, including one, "The Chatelaine Bag"

(2010), that my wife, Marcia Muller, and I wrote together on a whim. The story turned out so well that we decided to do a series of collaborative novels featuring the duo, with Marcia writing the scenes told from Sabina's point of view and me writing those from Quincannon's. The first of these, *The Bughouse Affair,* was published in 2012; the second, *The Spook Lights Affair,* is due out in December of this year. "Gunpowder Alley" is the most recent Carpenter and Quincannon short story, and the last to be published under my solo byline.

Winner of the Drue Heinz Literature Prize for his first book, a collection of literary short stories, **Randall Silvis** is also the author of eleven critically acclaimed novels in various genres and a book of narrative nonfiction about the exploration of Labrador. He has written feature and cover stories for the Discovery Channel magazines, has won two NEA literature fellowships plus several national playwriting and screenwriting competitions, and is a published poet, an unpublished songwriter, an unreliable blogger, and a primary source of profanity on his local golf courses.

▪ I can't remember the genesis of "The Indian" or, for that matter, the genesis of most of my other work. This is probably because I typically work on three or four projects simultaneously. And by "work on" I don't mean that I write them simultaneously, but that while I am writing one I have a few others knocking around in my head and clamoring for attention. (See reference to Uncle Dave, below, for suspicious parallels.) Sometimes one of them will clamor so loudly that I have to stop writing, grab a different notebook, and write something else for the rest of the morning. I hate it when that happens. But I love it, too. Better to have too many ideas than to have too few. Or, worse yet, none at all.

What I do remember about "The Indian" is that it used to be longer. So did my hair. I cut most of it back in the '90s, I think, when it started falling out on top faster than it was growing on the sides. I just didn't want to end up looking like my Uncle Dave, who covered his naked dome with aluminum foil and also made foil plugs for his ears. The foil plugs stuck out like stubby antennas through his scraggly hair. Now that I know about the government's projects Bluebird and MKUltra, I wish I had taken Uncle Dave more seriously. He'd start talking about the crazy messages being beamed into his brain and I'd say, "Okay, yep, you mind if Cindy and me go out for a little ride?" Cindy was my second cousin, a few years younger than me but something of a sexual prodigy. Of the two of them, I miss her more.

(Side note: No matter how strong the urge, no matter how enticing the temptation, no matter how freaking nostalgic you get for your sweet young lover from the good old days, DO NOT search for current photos of that lover on Facebook. Ewwwwww!)

Anyway, "The Indian" used to run to nearly 30,000 words. Janet Hutchings told me she would publish it if I cut it to under 20,000, which I could probably do just by taking out the f-words. I spent a few more of those words cursing silently, then started cutting.

I had intended to use this space to say something about how much I love to write novellas and why don't more places publish them, something about how "The Indian" is an elegy to small-town life, something about what an idiot my former dean of liberal arts is, and, finally, to direct a few hundred expletives at the pompous Magoos who continue to insist that genre fiction cannot be literary . . . but it looks like I've already used up my miserly ration of page space. F**k!

Patricia Smith is the author of six books of poetry, including *Blood Dazzler,* a finalist for the National Book Award, and her latest, *Shoulda Been Jimi Savannah.* Her work has appeared in *Poetry,* the *Paris Review, TriQuarterly, Tin House,* and both *Best American Poetry* and *Best American Essays.* She was the editor of *Staten Island Noir,* in which "When They Are Done with Us" appears; the story won the Robert L. Fish Award from the Mystery Writers of America for the best debut story of the year. She is a 2012 fellow at both the MacDowell Colony and Yaddo, a two-time Pushcart Prize winner, and a four-time individual champion of the National Poetry Slam, the most successful poet in the competition's history. A professor at the College of Staten Island and in the MFA program at Sierra Nevada College, Patricia is married to Edgar Award winner Bruce DeSilva, author of the Mulligan crime novels.

- "When They Are Done with Us" has at its center a true Staten Island story that dominated the news for days. After a fire, the bodies of a mother and her four children were discovered. The throats of the mother and three of her children were slit, and near her thirteen-year-old son's body was a razor and a note with the scrawled words *am sorry.* The assumption was that he had killed his family and then committed suicide by sliding a blade across his own throat. People were horrified; hastily penned editorials screeched about young black boys and their frightening dysfunctions. Later it was discovered that it was the mother who had written the note and effectively framed her son for the killings.

As a writer with a fierce curiosity about all the ways the world goes awry, I couldn't push the story from my head. When I decided to write a piece for *Staten Island Noir,* I saw my chance to process the horror.

It happened in Port Richmond, a diverse but divided community, so this was initially a story about race: Jo, a white woman uncertain of her rooting, never quite sure how to respond or relate to her black and Latino neighbors, wrestles with feelings of disconnect and guilt when the tragedy occurs directly across the street from where she lives.

But once her teenage son, Charlie, walked in and opened his mouth, I immediately saw another direction for the story. He started as a bit player, a chalk outline, but he urged me to step back and see just how poisonous he could be. He allowed me to develop a tension created by those dueling levels of familiar violence and to make Jo's options, her space in this world, smaller and smaller, until her horrible choice was inevitable. Charlie created the reason for the necessary bond between Jo and Leisa, the woman who'd murdered her children and killed herself.

Since I primarily identify as a poet and this was the first short story I've ever written, I chose poetry as Jo's lifeline, her one shot at sanity and salvation. Having poetry be a part of the story linked the two genres and kept those voices ("Whatta ya think you're doin'? You don't know how to write a short story!") at bay.

Ben Stroud is the author of the story collection *Byzantium.* His short stories have appeared in *Harper's Magazine, One Story, Electric Literature,* the *Boston Review,* and the anthology *New Stories from the South 2010.* He lives in Ohio and teaches at the University of Toledo.

▪ I drafted this story over a cold January weekend in Michigan in 2007. While researching another story, I came across a rumor in a history of Havana about vagabonds who came to the city and started selling "French sausage" in the market—sausage that was eventually discovered to be made of slaves who'd been kidnapped and murdered. Whether this truly happened, I don't know, but the rumor stuck with me for a few months (it was too good, too rich with thematic and dramatic possibility), until that cold weekend. I wanted to get as far from Michigan as possible and so decided it was time to write about Havana. I started with the rumor about the sausage and built the story out from there. How would the truth be discovered? I'd need a detective. Who would be the ideal detective? Someone who could pass through the different racial worlds of nineteenth-century Cuba. This is how I came up with the character of Burke, who appears in another of my stories as well. That he is an American rather than a Cuban is a result of my own ignorance. I didn't know enough about Cuba to pull off inhabiting a Cuban, so I made him a newcomer to the city. He would mirror me, also a newcomer.

In writing the story, I ended up doing far more research than reading that initial history. I even tracked down a tourist's map from the 1850s with fold-out views of the city (this I found in the University of Michigan Library's Special Collections). The story became a novella. Then it became the first section of a novel. And then, after five years, it became a story again. I didn't plan it that way—it was a blind search all the way through —but it took that long process of growing and cutting away and leaving the story aside and coming back to it for it to finally become what it needed to be.

Hannah Tinti's story collection, *Animal Crackers,* has sold in sixteen countries and was a runner-up for the PEN/Hemingway Award. Her best-selling novel, *The Good Thief,* is a *New York Times* Notable Book of the Year, recipient of the American Library Association's Alex Award, winner of the Center for Fiction's First Novel Prize, and winner of the Quality Paperback Book Club's New Voices Award. Hannah is also cofounder and editor-in-chief of *One Story* magazine and received the PEN/Nora Magid Award for excellence in magazine editing. Recently she joined the Public Radio program *Selected Shorts* as its literary commentator.

▪ I based "Bullet Number Two" on an experience I had while driving through the Four Corners. I got caught in a dust storm, just as Hawley does in the story, and had to pull over at a strange motel run by Navajos. There wasn't a shootout, but my room did have a hole punched through the wall. The storm was wild, and the sand and the colors and the light of the desert in the morning stayed with me. I'm grateful to *Tin House* for taking a chance and running this story, and to *Best American Mystery Stories* for giving it a second life.

Maurine Dallas Watkins (1896–1969) wrote the 1926 play *Chicago,* on which the musical is based. Winner of six Tonys and a Best Picture Oscar for the 2002 film, Watkins based her Broadway-bound play on the newspaper articles that she wrote as a young crime reporter for the *Chicago Tribune* while covering the sensationalist murder trials that rocked 1920s Chicago. Her tongue-in-cheek features on the "beautiful murderesses" turned media darlings were the inspiration for *Chicago*'s Roxie Hart and Velma Kelly. Watkins wrote several other plays, including the long-lost *Revelry,* about the scandal-ridden White House of President Warren G. Harding, and the acidly cynical farce *So Help Me God!,* which received its first production in 2009, eighty years after its creation. She wrote or contributed to several films, including two Best Picture nominees, *Libeled Lady* and *Up the River,* as well as such screwball comedies as *Professional Sweethearts, No Man of Her Own,* and *I Love You Again.*

Other Distinguished Mystery Stories of 2012

FRIEND, TIMOTHY
Dog Night. *Needle*, Fall/Winter

HALL, PARNELL
Times Square Shuffle. *Crime Square*, ed. Robert J. Randisi (Vantage Point)
HELLER, GABRIEL
Fugitive. *Inkwell Journal*, Spring
HOFFMAN, ALICE
Conjure. *Shadow Show*, ed. Sam Weller and Mort Castle (William Morrow)

LAW, JANICE
The General. *Vengeance*, ed. Lee Child (Mulholland)

MACLEAN, MIKE
Just Like Maria. *Thuglit*, no. 2
MAKSIK, ALEXANDER
Snake River Gorge. *Tin House*, vol. 13, no. 4
MORAN, TERRIE FARLEY
Jake Says Hello. *Alfred Hitchcock's Mystery Magazine*, December

OAK, B. B.
Death from a Bad Heart. *Blood Moon: Best New England Crime Stories* (Level Best)

PENNCAVAGE, MICHAEL
Mistakes. *Staten Island Noir*, ed. Patricia Smith (Akashic)
PHELAN, TWIST
The Fourteenth Juror. *Vengeance*, ed. Lee Child (Mulholland)
PRUFER, KEVIN
Cat in a Box. *Kansas City Noir*, ed. Steve Paul (Akashic)

SHANNON, JAMES
Shame the Devil. *Ellery Queen's Mystery Magazine*, July
SHEEHY, HUGH
Meat and Mouth. *Kenyon Review*, Summer
STEVENS, B. K.
Thea's First Husband. *Alfred Hitchcock's Mystery Magazine*, June

VAN DEN BERG, LAURA
Opa-Locka. *Southern Review*, Summer

WARTHMAN, DAN
Pansy Place. *Alfred Hitchcock's Mystery Magazine*, January/February
WHITE, DAVID
Runaway. *Lost Children Protectors*, ed. Thomas Pluck (CreateSpace)